SURPRISE DEFENSE

The NVA commander looked at his watch and smiled. Everything was right on schedule. The artillery was firing and giving his sappers cover to move the last critical few meters toward the American base with their satchel charges.

The North Vietnamese raised his binoculars to his eyes just in time to see the hand grenades explode. He dropped his glasses in shock as his elite sapper team was cut to fish bait by the hundred or so hidden grenades going off simultaneously in the barbed wire and along the berm.

But it was too late to call off the assault—even though he now knew he was facing a new kind of American officer who wasn't making old mistakes. . . .

THE SOLDIER'S MEDAL

MAJOR DONALD E. ZLOTNIK (Ret.) served in Vietnam as a Green Beret with MACV-SOG, on two A-teams, and as a paratrooper with the 173rd Airborne Brigade. He earned the Soldier's Medal for Heroism, the Bronze Star for Valor, and the Purple Heart for wounds received in combat. He served after the war as an adviser in West Virginia and as a liaison officer to an Air Force fighter wing and flew as a rear-seater in F4 Phantom jets.

FIELDS OF HONOR #4

✪✪✪✪✪✪✪✪✪✪✪✪✪✪✪✪✪✪✪✪✪✪✪

THE SOLDIER'S MEDAL

Donald E. Zlotnik
Major (Ret.), U.S. Army Special Forces

A SIGNET BOOK

SIGNET
Published by the Penguin Group
Penguin Books USA Inc., 375 Hudson Street,
New York, New York 10014, U.S.A.
Penguin Books Ltd, 27 Wrights Lane,
London W8 5TZ, England
Penguin Books Australia Ltd, Ringwood,
Victoria, Australia
Penguin Books Canada Ltd, 10 Alcorn Avenue,
Toronto, Ontario, Canada M4V 3B2
Penguin Books (N.Z.) Ltd, 182–190 Wairau Road,
Auckland 10, New Zealand

Penguin Books Ltd, Registered Offices:
Harmondsworth, Middlesex, England

First published by Signet, an imprint of New American Library,
a division of Penguin Books USA Inc.

First Printing, August, 1991
10 9 8 7 6 5 4 3 2 1

REGISTERED TRADEMARK—MARCA REGISTRADA

PRINTED IN THE UNITED STATES OF AMERICA

PUBLISHER'S NOTE
This is a work of fiction. Names, characters, places, and incidents either
are the product of the author's imagination or are used fictitiously,
and any resemblance to actual persons, living or dead, events, or locales
is entirely coincidental.

ARMY REGULATION (AR) 672-5-1
Section II, Criteria

2-14. Soldier's Medal

The Soldier's Medal is awarded to any person of the Armed Forces of the United States or of a friendly foreign nation who, while serving in any capacity with the Army of the United States, distinguishes himself/herself by heroism not involving actual conflict with an enemy. The same degree of heroism is required as for the award of the Distinguished Flying Cross. The performance must have involved personal hazard or danger and the voluntary risk of life under conditions not involving conflict with an armed enemy. Awards will not be made solely on the basis of having saved a life.

(extract from the regulation)

CHAPTER ONE

✪✪✪✪✪✪✪✪✪✪✪✪✪✪

BLOODY SPAGHETTI

She had started to feed on the sweating Vietcong's blood the night before and would not have required finding another donor if the man in his delirium hadn't brushed her off his arm before she had finished filling her stomach with the protein she required to complete her breeding cycle. The warm night breeze had carried her away from the village out over the open sand dunes to a man-made enclosure where she found refuge from the wind under the lid of an empty C-ration can.

The fighting bunker faced Highway 1 in the distance. It was one of the most coveted bunkers surrounding the artillery fire support base because it faced the South China Sea and a cool breeze often blew through the firing ports. The soldier pulling guard duty on the roof of the bunker checked his watch then turned around toward the base camp to see if his replacement was coming up from the mess tent where they were beginning to serve lunch. He felt his stomach growl and flexed his jaws; his replacement wasn't due to arrive for another fifteen minutes. The guard stood up on the sandbags and stretched in the hot sun. He bent over and picked up his M-16 by its canvas carrying strap and climbed down from the bunker. The guards were allowed to sit inside when it became too hot up on the roof. He looked back again toward the headquarters area of the base to make sure that nobody was coming and disappeared inside of the bunker. Three of the two-by-four and plywood bunk beds had sleeping gear on them, but the occupants had gone over to the mess hall to eat. He took a seat on one of the empty beds and bit his lower lip.

"Fuck it!" The soldier reached down in the side pocket of his jungle fatigues and removed an ornate ivory pipe. He glanced back at the entrance before removing a black, plastic film case from the rear ammunition pouch on his web gear. He used his thumb to pop open the gray lid and checked inside the container before tapping the remainder of his marijuana into his well-used pipe.

"Startin' early, aren't you?" The voice came from behind the guard.

"Fuck!" The man on guard duty nearly dropped his pipe on the dirt floor of the bunker. "Damn you, Pilgrim! I should shoot your fucking white ass for sneaking up on me like that!"

"I didn't *sneak* up on you, Jenkins. If you didn't stay stoned on that shit all of the time, your hearing might improve." The young soldier spoke with a southern drawl. "I hear that smoking that shit makes it so your cock doesn't get hard . . . is that true?"

"What in the fuck do you southern boys know about hard cocks?" Jenkins lit his pipe and inhaled deeply before speaking again in a deep raspy voice as he exhaled. "You . . . Georgia boys . . . don't know . . . *how* to fuck . . ."

"You must be a stud." Pilgrim laid his rifle against the sandbag wall of the bunker and rested his arms on the sandbags that lined the firing port facing the barbed wire.

She felt the heat coming through the sun-warmed lid of the can and decided that she would find a cooler place to spend the day. The instant she was airborne she located the scent of a large warm-blooded creature and flew up-current until she reached the dark firing port of the bunker. She hesitated for only a second and flew in past the barrel of the M60 machine gun.

Pilgrim swatted at the mosquito as she buzzed past his head.

She dodged the irritating smoke and landed softly on Jenkins's cheek.

"Check out the highway." Pilgrim pointed to the thin dust cloud moving rapidly along the sand blown asphalt strip in the distance.

Jenkins struggled to his feet. The marijuana was slowing his motor movement. "Who in the fuck would drive the highway before the engineers clear it for mines?" Jenkins reached for the binoculars hanging from a support post in the bunker and held them up to his eyes. Everything was out of focus. "Here, motherfucker! Look and see who's coming!" Jenkins handed the binos to Pilgrim.

"I told you that shit fucks you up. I don't know how you guys can pull guard duty stoned all of the time." Pilgrim adjusted the setting to zero. He had perfect vision and was proud of it.

"You just watch out for your own ass on this fire-support base and I'll take care of mine."

Pilgrim held the binos up under his eyes until he located the fast-moving vehicle on the highway and then lifted the glasses up over his eyes. He could see his buddy from Tennessee behind the wheel and a strange officer riding shotgun in the jeep with a strange short barreled M16 laying across his lap. Pilgrim moved the binoculars slightly and saw the duffel bag on the rear seat. "It's Dotson returning from Quang Tri with our new battery commander."

"Fuck me!" Jenkins shook his head. "Is it another white motherfucker?"

"Does it make a difference?"

"Us black troops would like to have a brother every once in a while."

"He looks like he might be Mexican."

"Damn! That's worse than a honkie officer!" Jenkins tried snatching the binos out of Pilgrim's hands but missed. "Fucking Mexicans make you work your ass off!"

Pilgrim handed the binos to Jenkins. "Don't black officers make you work?"

Jenkins caught the tone in Pilgrim's voice and lowered the glasses down so that he could see the white soldier's eyes. "Don't go fucking with the black folk . . . whiteboy! Alls I'm saying is that black officers are *fair*."

Pilgrim answered the threat with a smile. "There's a mosquito on your cheek."

Jenkins kept glaring at Pilgrim and reached up with one hand and crushed the blood-gorged female anopheles mosquito with his fingers and smeared his own blood out over his cheek. "Fuck!"

"Here . . ." Pilgrim handed Jenkins a couple pieces of C-ration toilet paper that someone had left on the firing port sill after using it to clean the lens of his binoculars.

Jenkins took the offered white paper and wiped the blood off his cheek. It was too late to stop the sporozoites. The anopheles mosquito had ejected the *falciparum* malaria parasites into his body with her saliva and they were ready to complete their life cycle living in his red blood cells.

The jeep driver pulled off the side of the oiled, packed sand road and waited fifteen minutes until the last M48A5 General Patton tank pulled out of the only entrance to the fire-support base.

"What were the tanks doing in there?" The captain spoke to the driver through the olive-drab triangular bandage that he normally wore around his neck to absorb his sweat, but had pulled up bandit-style to filter out the dust the tanks created.

"Brigade usually sends a platoon of tanks from the 1st of the 77th Armor Battalion or a platoon of M113s from one of the infantry battalions to help secure the base at night." The jeep driver looked over at the captain and continued feeling him out. "The battery is the only thing here at Hai Lang, except for an occasional engineer unit that gets caught on the highway and spends the night with us."

"Interesting . . . so the men in the battery have to pull their own guard duty on the perimeter?"

"Yes, sir . . ." The soldier was impressed by how fast the new captain had noticed the biggest bitch of the troops. It was extremely difficult to work on the 155mm howitzers all day and through half of the night and then have to pull a four-hour tour of guard duty in the bunkers. It was so difficult that it was rare that two guards were awake around the perimeter by two in the morning, and that included the armor or infantrymen who considered the Hai Lang duty as a break and a chance to get some sleep. "That has been a sore spot with most of the men."

The captain looked over at the rusty and poorly laid barbed wire surrounding the fire base. He could see at least three wide gaps in the wire from where he was sitting. "It looks like there are a few more problems here than guard duty."

The driver gave the captain a quick glance out of the corner of his eye as if to say that the new captain didn't know half of what was going on. He shifted gears and released the clutch slowly as soon as the dust had settled enough so that he could see to drive. The guard inside of the first bunker next to the entrance waved at the driver and smiled at the new captain.

"Who's he? He seems like a friendly enough soldier." The captain kept his eyes on the packed sand road as the driver turned right on the inner-perimeter tank trail.

"He's on gun number three . . . my old gun." The jeep driver slowed the vehicle down to a slow crawl. "Where do you want to be dropped off at, sir? The orderly room or the mess hall?" He nodded to the line of soldiers waiting to enter the mess tent complex. "They're serving lunch now."

"Drop me off at the orderly room. I want to meet the first sergeant and executive officer first." He turned slightly on his seat so that he could reach back and grab his duffel bag.

"I'll put that in your hootch for you, sir."

"Thanks . . . Dotson . . . right?"

"Yes, sir." The driver was pleased that the captain had remembered his name.

"Why don't you get something to eat and take a shower before picking me up again after chow? . . . I want to take a drive around the fire base and maybe tour the outside of the perimeter if we have time." He could see that the man was filthy from all the dust on the road.

"I'll get something to eat, sir, but I don't think there's any water for showers . . ." Dotson looked away from the captain out over the firing battery, "except for your shower."

"What do you mean by that?"

Dotson kept his eyes averted so that the captain wouldn't see the hate. "Our old battery commander had his own shower set up by his hootch and it's always full of water."

"Where is it?"

Dotson pointed to the engineer constructed shower that had been built next to the orderly room where the battery commander and the first sergeant shared rooms in the back of the plywood and tin building. There were only two of the base-area type hootches on the fire base; one was used for administration and the other one intended for the mess hall, but the troops ate under a GP large tent. The mess sergeant had sectioned off almost half of the building for sleeping quarters for the cooks and the old battery commander had done the same thing to the orderly room.

"I tell you what, Dotson. You go take a shower in *my* shower and if anyone asks you what you're doing tell them that I'm giving you my share of the water." The captain smiled and winked at the soldier.

"I appreciate it, sir. Normally, when I'm back at Camp Red Devil, I can sneak in a shower, but . . ."

The captain understood what the soldier was going

to say. He wasn't supposed to have left the brigade base area until later in the afternoon and had asked to leave earlier to get out to his new command. "Showers are that big of a deal out here?"

Dotson rolled his eyes. "Shit, sir, if you only knew . . ."

"I've got time . . . tell me . . ."

Dotson looked over the captain's shoulder and saw the first sergeant walking toward them. "I think the first sergeant wants to talk to you, sir."

"Then tell me later . . . all right, Dotson?"

The soldier nodded his head and looked down at the steering wheel. He wished that he would have kept his mouth shut.

"Captain Arrowood?" The first sergeant saluted the captain.

"Yes, First Sergeant."

"Welcome to Hai Lang . . . LZ Sandy as we call it and for good reason!"

"I can see that you don't have any problem filling sandbags out here."

The first sergeant started laughing. "I didn't think of it *that* way."

"Think *positive*, First Sergeant . . . always think positive." Arrowood looked over at the line of troops waiting to get into the mess hall. "That's a long line."

"He's just started feeding, sir." The first sergeant was referring to his friend, the mess sergeant.

"A war is going on." Arrowood looked directly at the senior NCO. "The men should be a little more dispersed."

"You ain't going to come on with that basic training bullshit . . . are you, sir?" The first sergeant rolled his eyes. "The troops won't put up with that kind of crap right off the bat, Captain."

"How long have you been in-country, First Sergeant?" Arrowood continued staring at the NCO.

"*Nine* months, sir." The NCO smiled his short-timer's grin.

"I've been in Vietnam for five years, First Sergeant." Arrowood's expression didn't change. "We should be able to work something out so that all of the men don't leave the guns at the same time . . . can't we?"

The first sergeant nodded. He didn't trust his voice to answer. The personnel sergeant back at Camp Red Devil had told him the captain had just been assigned to the brigade and he had assumed that he was just arriving in Vietnam on his first tour.

The battery executive officer sat at the small, dark green folding field table and waited for the fire-direction-center officer to join him before he started eating the spaghetti on the paper plate in front of him.

"He's arrived. He's over in front of the orderly room talking to the first sergeant." The second lieutenant took a seat across from the executive officer.

"Shit, I should go meet him."

"Don't rush it, Terry. The first sergeant will probably bring him over. You know Top hasn't missed a meal since he's been here."

Lieutenant Zimmerman smiled. "You're right there, Dick." The executive officer looked up from his food when he heard one of the soldier's yelling from one of the picnic-style tables the enlisted men used under the hot tent.

"Motherfuckers!" A tall, skinny black soldier stood up and threw the packet of plastic silverware down on the wooden tabletop.

The FDC officer glanced over at Zimmerman. "It's Talbot." The fear in his voice wasn't masked. Talbot had been assigned to Bravo Battery from the battalion ammunition section, where he had been a trouble-maker. The battalion executive officer had personally assigned him to LZ Sandy because the base was the most isolated place in the brigade's area of operations.

"The white motherfuckers took the fork out of my packet!" Talbot screamed over at the mess sergeant who was standing behind the serving line.

"Come on and get another packet. It's probably

a manufacturer's error." The mess sergeant held up another clear plastic package that contained a knife, fork, and spoon along with a napkin and tiny packets of salt and pepper. The packets had been designed for the airlines, but the Army had incorporated them into their field system for Vietnam.

"Fuck you! You bring it over here!" Talbot screamed across the tables.

The mess sergeant shrugged his shoulders and dropped the packet back down in its box. "Fine, eat your spaghetti with your fucking spoon for all I care."

Talbot's face turned into a mask of pure hate and he stepped back away from the table.

"I'd better go handle this before it gets out of control." Lieutenant Zimmerman cut across the tent so that he would intersect Talbot before he reached the mess sergeant.

The FDC officer watched from his seat. He was terrified of the black soldier, who had been threatening the officers and NCOs ever since he arrived. A tear-gas grenade had been thrown into the fire-direction center the week before, right after he had jumped on Talbot for sleeping in his bunker when the rest of the ammunition section was unloading ammo from the battalion five ton trucks. Lieutenant Fields knew the tear-gas grenade was only a *warning*.

"What's the problem, Private Talbot?" Zimmerman stepped out in front of the soldier.

"That motherfucker took my fork!" Talbot pointed over the lieutenant's shoulder at the mess sergeant.

"I doubt that, Talbot."

"You calling me a *liar*, Lieutenant!"

"No . . . I'm just saying that I doubt the sergeant would intentionally remove a plastic fork from *your* packet, even if he knew which one you were going to take from the hundreds of packets in that box."

"You *are* calling me a liar!" Talbot took the paper plate of spaghetti he was holding in his hand and pushed it in the officer's face.

The mess tent became totally quiet. All of the soldiers watched to see what the lieutenant was going to do.

Talbot left the mess tent and hurried outside before he stopped in the narrow street and turned around. "You motherfucking honkies think you can push us black people around whenever you feel like it!"

Lieutenant Zimmerman stepped out of the tent wiping the spaghetti off his uniform. The sauce and long pieces of the pasta were stuck in his hair. If it wasn't for the look on his face, the incident would have been funny. "Talbot, go over to the orderly room, right now!"

"Fuck you, Lieutenant!"

A small group of blacks had gathered outside of the mess tent, but Talbot could see that Jenkins was with them and knew they would not support him if he was wrong. He faced the lieutenant and decided to play it out. He knew that what he had done had been witnessed by thirty of the men in the battery and there was no way he could claim that he had been provoked. "What did you call me!"

"I didn't call you anything, soldier. Now move it!" Zimmerman wasn't about to back off now, especially when half the battery was watching.

"You just called me a *nigger*!" Talbot screamed the hated word out.

"Stop your shit, Private Talbot, and start moving your worthless ass over to the orderly room or I'll have it dragged there!"

"You can't call me a *nigger* and get away with it!" Talbot ran toward the bunker hootch he shared with three other soldiers.

He paused and screamed back at the battery executive officer. "You're *dead*, motherfucker! Dead white meat!" He disappeared into the dark entranceway.

Zimmerman felt the sweat breaking out on his forehead. He felt for his pistol and remembered that he had left it hanging on the aiming circle because it had been so hot outside. Fear started creeping into the pit of his stomach and mixed with the heat, he felt like throwing up. Zimmerman said a silent prayer that he wouldn't throw up in front of the men.

"We have a problem here, Lieutenant?"

Zimmerman turned and saw the new captain standing next to him. The first sergeant had gone inside of the mess tent to talk with the mess sergeant. A great sense of relief flooded through the young officer. This was his first real confrontation with a soldier who had totally refused to respect his rank. He had dealt with mouthy drunks before, but never like Talbot. "A little, sir."

"I'm Captain Arrowood . . . your new battery commander." Luke held out his hand for the lieutenant to shake.

"Terry Zimmerman, sir. I'm your executive officer and he's your FDC officer . . ." Zimmerman nodded over at his friend, ". . . Dick Fields."

Captain Arrowood smiled and nodded his head. "I'll have a chance to talk to you a little later . . . right now I had better handle this little problem before it gets out of hand."

"Sir . . . Talbot is a really fucked-up case. I think he's tripping out on drugs." Zimmerman reached up and grabbed the captain's arm. "He's going to get a gun."

Arrowood's eyebrows shot up. "Really?"

"He'll use it, sir." Lieutenant Fields spoke up from where he was standing near a wall of sandbags. Talbot scared the shit out of Fields and he wasn't afraid to admit it.

Captain Arrowood saw a buck sergeant standing behind his self-propelled howitzer holding an M-60 machine gun that he had just finished cleaning. "Sergeant . . . does that weapon work?"

"Yes, sir . . . I just put it back together again."

"Load it and crawl up on that bunker . . ." Arrowood pointed to a personnel bunker that had been built next to the M109 howitzer. Each of the gun sections had built a protective sandbag wall around their tracked howitzers in a rectangular U-shape with one end open so that the vehicle could be backed out and placed on the perimeter in the event of a ground attack or if they needed to run it for a couple of miles. At each side of the open end of the horseshoe was a personnel bunker and, across from it, a ready bunker for ammunition and powder charges.

"Yes, sir!" The buck sergeant ran over to an ammo can and removed a belt of linked bullets.

"If that soldier fires *one* shot at anyone in this battery . . . I want you to blow his ass away." Arrowood started walking down the sand road toward the bunker where Talbot had disappeared into a few minutes earlier.

"Do you want me to *kill* him, sir?"

"That's a machine gun you've got up there. If you're a good enough shot, just shoot the gun out of his hands . . . but I don't want to give him a chance to shoot a *second* round at anyone. If he just shoots up in the air to scare me, hold off shooting . . . Do you understand?"

"Yes, sir!" The buck sergeant loaded the machine gun and took up a low-profile position behind the weapon.

Captain Arrowood walked alone down the road. The rest of the battery stayed back where they could find some cover.

Talbot stepped out of his bunker holding his M-16. "Who in the fuck are you!"

"Captain Arrowood . . . your new battery commander."

"Another white motherfucker!"

"I would ease up on the language if I were you, soldier."

"Well, lookie here!" Talbot's face contorted into a maze of hate. "*I've* got the gun, honkie!"

"I just arrived here and don't know what's going on inside of the fire-support base. If you have a legitimate bitch, I'll listen to you . . . but first put that weapon down!"

Talbot curled his upper lip and pointed the weapon at the captain.

Arrowood heard the first crack of the M-16 after a dozen rounds had traveled past him. Two bullets smashed into the sandbags of the bunker the buck sergeant was on and three of the high velocity rounds impacted in the sand at his feet. The rest of the magazine escaped in the air around him. Arrowood's thoughts flashed to his wife and children in the States. He knew that he was going to die in the next couple of seconds. The look in Talbot's eyes was that of a demon about to feed.

A stream of tracer rounds appeared over Arrowood's right shoulder and tore a hole in Talbot's chest the size of a pie plate. The soldier's expression briefly turned into surprise before he tumbled down to his knees. Then he fell forward and his openmouthed face thudded against the windblown sand.

Captain Arrowood felt his heart pounding against his chest. He had underestimated the problem and had nearly been killed. His thoughts didn't dwell on what *could* have happened to him, but went to the men of the battery. Something was very wrong at LZ Sandy.

He used the toe of his boot to roll Talbot's body over on its back and could see the small particles of sand sticking against the man's eyeballs. There was no way Talbot could be faking. Slowly, Arrowood turned around after he had gained his composure and looked at the faces of his men. "Lieutenant Zimmerman . . . have a detail put him in a body bag and call in a report to battalion . . . I'm quite sure they're going to want to come out here." Arrowood started walking back toward the orderly room. "First Sergeant! Come on, we've got to check the battery perimeter before dark."

Dotson looked over at his buddy. "Christ, Pilgrim! Did you see that!"

"Fah-u-ck yes!"

"Unbelievable!"

"I would say that a mean motherfucking captain has just taken control of this firing battery!"

Dotson spoke in an I-told-you-so voice. "He didn't talk all that much driving back here from Camp Red Devil, but I told you that he seemed *weird*, not like any artillery officer I've ever met."

Captain Arrowood stopped walking when he reached the bunker where the buck sergeant was sitting up on the roof, still holding the M-60. He looked up at the NCO. "Thanks, I like men who follow *orders*."

"Th . . . thanks, sir." The sergeant was visibly shaken over what he had done, but not so shaken that he didn't catch what the captain had said. The officer had taken him off the hook by making that statement in front of the whole battery.

The first sergeant stepped out of the hootch and looked down the oiled road in the direction the gunfire had come from and saw Captain Arrowood walking toward him followed by Dotson and Pilgrim who were keeping their distance.

"First Sergeant, I want you to assemble as many of the men as you can so that I can talk to them."

"What about the fire missions and prep fires for this afternoon?"

"They have first priority, but I want to talk to as many of the men as I can as soon as possible. Private Talbot has been killed, and I want to nip any rumors in the bud."

"Talbot?" The first sergeant's face turned white. "Who killed him?"

"I did."

"*You* shot one of our own men?" The first sergeant looked at the captain as if the officer had gone crazy. "Do you know who Talbot is?"

"Was." Arrowood looked back at the men standing around the mess tent talking in small groups. He saw a group of black soldiers walking up the inner fire base road from the ammunition section and all of them were carrying their weapons. "It looks like you won't have to call a formation, First Sergeant."

"Sir, this can be very serious." The first sergeant used the back of his hand to wipe the sweat off his upper lip. "We've been having some racial problems and Private Talbot was the leader of the black faction."

"Why wasn't I briefed on that problem back at battalion when I was in-processing?"

"We've tried to keep a lid on it in the battery. Your predecessor didn't want the battalion commander finding out about it."

"Well, First Sergeant . . . let's go earn our pay." Arrowood started walking back toward the mess hall facility and reached the tent at the same time the black group did.

Jenkins and the black soldiers who had been eating lunch at the same table as Talbot under the mess tent joined the group. Jenkins went over to a solid built, but short black soldier who was wearing a red bandana around his head and whispered in the man's ear. Arrowood could see the man's eyes flashing around the area as Jenkins briefed him over what had gone on.

Captain Arrowood went straight over to the black caucus and addressed the black soldier, who was obviously the leader of the group. He didn't waste any time with introductions. "I've been told that there are some racial problems going on in this unit. I'm your new battery commander and personally I don't play *any* racial crap. I see only the color *green*." Arrowood kept his eyes locked with the black soldier's. "Talbot was shot and killed on *my* orders. He threatened me with a weapon and opened fire in a hostile manner."

The leader blinked slowly. He had known that Talbot was tripping out on LSD-25 and warned him not to leave the bunker. Talbot had ignored his warning and left to go eat the noon meal.

Arrowood casually scanned the assembled black faces and saw that, behind most of the hate masks they were wearing, most of them were scared. "I want all of you to go back to your section chiefs and if you have any complaints about the way you have been treated in this battery, I want your section leaders to present a list to me. I give you my word that I will make any adjustments necessary to prove to you that I don't play racial favorites."

The black leader slipped the carrying strap of his M-16 over his shoulder and held out his hand. "I'm Sergeant Cole, sir. Your ammunition section chief."

All of the blacks were bareback because they had been working inside of the hot ammunition and powder tents unloading the pallets of 155mm artillery rounds and metal powder canisters. It was against battalion policy for the men to work bareback around the ammunition and the guns, but the men had ignored the regulation because of the heat.

"Talk to your men and get back with me this afternoon or later this evening . . ." Captain Arrowood smiled, ". . . I'm not going anywhere."

The first sergeant watched from a distance and shook his head when he heard the captain's last statement. He would bet a lot of money that the new captain would be relieved before dark over the shooting incident.

The lieutenant colonel sat with his back to the wall and looked out of the Plexiglas window of the air-conditioned officer's dining area of the battalion mess hall. He could see half of Camp Red Devil from his seat and had a perfect view of the main entrance of the brigade headquarters. The 1st Brigade from the 5th Mechanized Infantry Division stationed at Fort Carson, Colorado, was the last major Army unit to be shipped to Vietnam. The brigade was headquartered outside of Quang Tri in the northernmost Corps area that ended at the DMZ.

One of the KPs entered the officers mess carrying two tin plates of food. He placed one of the plates in front of the battalion commander and another plate in front of the battalion executive officer who was sitting across the table from the lieutenant colonel.

"Thank you, soldier."

The KP just nodded at the officer and left the air-conditioned room.

"Do you think we should send the battalion-maintenance warrant officer out to LZ Sandy to inspect the vehicles for Captain Arrowood?" Major Montgomery unwrapped his silverware and laid the white napkin down on his lap.

"When?"

"I was thinking this afternoon." The major tested the mashed potatoes by taking a small bite.

"No . . . he won't be back in time for our bridge game and you know he's my partner!" The lieutenant colonel grinned. "You're trying to pull a sneaky trick, aren't you!"

"No, sir . . . I heard rumors that our ROTC friend who commanded Bravo Battery before Arrowood arrived let things get a little out of hand." The major looked up when the door to the room opened. "I just want to make sure that everything is going all right."

A nervous-looking captain approached the battalion commander's table. "Colonel Jeffers, sir."

The battalion commander ignored the captain. "No! Let's see what this Captain Arrowood can do on his own before we go jumping in to bail his ass out! Personally, I'm getting sick and tired of these damn *instant* officers. They run them through a six-month Officer Candidate School and pin gold bars on their collars and then a *year* later they make them *first* lieutenants and another year later . . . captains!" The battalion commander continued ignoring the captain and spoke to his executive officer over his plate of mashed potatoes and rare fried steak. "Do you know how long I had to wait to make captain? *Three* years, and I am a graduate of West Point!"

The major smiled. He, too, was a graduate of Hudson High and knew that if he could make it through his tour of duty in Vietnam that he had a fantastic staff job waiting for him back at the Pentagon. He hadn't wanted to even come to Vietnam for his first tour, but the general who was his mentor insisted that he serve at least one year in combat. "You know what's going to happen as soon as this war ends . . ." He looked up at the waiting captain and decided to continue what he was about to say, ". . . we'll have a reduction in force and all of those OCS types will be put back into civilian life."

"Thank God for that!" Jeffers looked over at the captain. The tone in his voice changed to sarcasm. "Now what do *you* want?"

"Sir, there's a problem out at Bravo Battery." The captain's voice broke.

"For Christ sakes, Kreps! I made you the battalion S-3 so that you could *solve* problems!" Jeffers glared up at the captain at the same time he lifted a piece of steak to his mouth. "What's the damn problem and I hope it's not going to ruin my lunch!"

The captain swallowed and looked over at a tableful of captains on the other side of the room.

"Well, damn it! You interrupted us . . . now tell me why!" Jeffers glanced over at the major and gave him a look as if to say that he had made a mistake by putting the captain in a major's job.

"Sir, the executive officer radioed in a message from Bravo . . . there's been a shooting out there and a black soldier has been killed."

"VC?" The battalion commander's eyes lit up. He would love to see the infantry battalion commanders during the evening briefing at brigade if he could brief the colonel on a ground attack against one of his batteries. LZ Sandy was the only fire-support base in I Corps that was commanded by an artillery unit.

"No, sir . . . Captain Arrowood had one of his NCOs shoot one of the black soldiers . . ." The captain's voice faded away.

The officers' dining room became quiet. The captains that had been eavesdropping on the conversation all turned their heads to look at the battalion S-3.

"What in the hell did you say!" Jeffers screamed the words out around his mouthful of meat.

"Something happened out there where a Private Talbot threw a plate of spaghetti at the XO and then went to get his M-16 to kill him, and Captain Arrowood ordered one of the NCOs to get a machine gun and shoot Talbot . . ."

The battalion executive officer looked over at the table of captains. The battalion service battery commander was there, and their eyes locked. Both of the officers knew all about Private Talbot and that was why the major had shipped the black militant out to Bravo Battery. Talbot had sworn that he would frag the service battery commander and then he had threatened to kill the major.

"Oh, shit!" Jeffers threw his fork down on his plate. "I knew that goddamned son of a bitch was going to cause us trouble the fucking minute he walked into my office!"

"Sir . . ." Major Montgomery tried calming the battalion commander down.

"Damn it, Montgomery, we should have sent that damn captain back to those Special Forces people!" Tears of frustration coated the lieutenant colonel's eyes and that made him even madder. "I want his ass out of there! Now! Today!"

"I agree with you sir, but let's get a complete report before we do anything hasty." The major was doing what he did best under pressure; he plotted to protect *his* position.

"You're right, Montgomery." Jeffers gained control of his emotions almost instantly. "Captain Kreps, you take one of your operations staff and fly out there as soon as possible and get me a full report."

"Aren't you coming, sir?" Kreps looked shocked.

"That's what I have you for, damn it!"

Major Montgomery smiled at the S-3 officer and then spoke to the lieutenant colonel. "He might have a good idea there, sir. I don't think the brigade commander will like it if you don't personally go out to the battery and head the investigation."

"I hate that goddamn place!" Jeffers threw his napkin down on his plate and stood up. "This *has* ruined my whole lunch!"

CHAPTER TWO

✪✪✪✪✪✪✪✪✪✪✪✪✪✪

WOULD YOU BELIEVE . . . ?

The first helicopter to arrive at the isolated fire-support base carried the brigade provost marshal, Major Tony Redmond, and a heavyset criminal investigations agent who was wearing a gray polyester leisure suit. Lieutenant Zimmerman had described the incident between Talbot and the mess sergeant in the mess hall and had shown the investigators where Talbot had shoved the plate of spaghetti in his face. Captain Luke Arrowood walked the military police major through the sequence of events that led to the soldier's death.

Redmond listened as Captain Arrowood calmly described the M-16 rounds landing at his feet and the bullets whizzing over his head. The troops stopped working and watched the officers whenever they paused along the route from the mess hall to the personnel bunker Talbot had lived in. They were sure that the new battery commander would be relieved of his command and arrested before the day was over. What the soldier's didn't know was that the black provost marshal knew more about racial unrest in the brigade than they did. Talbot had belonged to a secret militant organization in the brigade that was advocating fragging officers and NCOs who were hard on black soldiers. Talbot's name had appeared on a number of confidential reports and was well known to the military police.

The MP major looked over at the CID agent, who

27

looked out of place in his Saigon-tailored leisure suit. "It looks like a solid case of self-defense to me . . . what do you think?"

The chubby agent shrugged his shoulders and flipped through his notepad. "We should have an autopsy done to check for drug usage."

"I agree." The military police officer knew from working on other cases with the agent that the man was prone to playing games with the people who were being investigated. It gave the man some sort of pleasure to lord it over combat troops. As far as Redmond was concerned, the captain had done a good job, and the fact that he ordered a sergeant to back him up with a machine gun was a wise decision under the circumstances. Weapons and hand grenades were readily available to the troops on isolated fire-support bases and a soldier tripping out on drugs and in the possession of a weapon was extremely dangerous. The major didn't wait for the agent to finish playing his mind games with the artillery officers. "The way that I see it right now, you've done a fine job, Captain Arrowood . . . and so have you, Lieutenant Zimmerman, and even though I'm sorry a soldier was killed, I feel that there was too much potential for a real disaster here, if he hadn't been stopped."

The agent stuck out his lower lip and started pouting. Redmond had stolen all of his thunder. "I'll compile everything and gather the eyewitness statements, but as things stand *right now*, I agree with the major that there is no reason to arrest you or your lieutenant and take you back to Quang Tri." The agent made the point that the case was still very much open and by referring to Quang Tri and not the brigade's base camp at Red Devil, he was trying to tell the officers that he influenced a much larger area than the provost marshal, who only represented a brigade-sized unit.

"Thanks, sir. I appreciate your trust." Arrowood spoke to the black military police major and ignored the CID agent. "If you will excuse me, I have to go and inspect my perimeter before it gets dark. This is my first day at LZ Sandy."

"Your *first* day out here?" The major smiled and shook his head. "Well, I don't think you're going to have much time to check your defenses now . . ." He nodded up in the sky at the helicopter approaching the base.

"It looks like the battalion commander's chopper, sir." Zimmerman volunteered the information.

The provost marshal had landed his helicopter outside of the main entrance to the base so that it wouldn't create a huge cloud of sand and dust but still be protected by the guards in the perimeter bunkers. The battalion commander was having his pilot land his chopper next to the battery orderly room, and a huge cloud of blowing sand and dust covered the howitzers and the men working on them. Lieutenant Zimmerman reached up to hold the brim of his floppy fatigue hat and leaned forward in the prop blast as the chopper landed. Arrowood and the brigade provost marshal turned their backs until the pilot had turned off the engine. The CID agent had disappeared into a nearby bunker to escape the stinging sand.

Lieutenant Colonel Jeffers stepped down from the open door onto the hot sand. The battalion executive officer, Major Montgomery, exited the opposite door along with Captain Kreps. The top three officers from the battalion were all together on the LZ. Arrowood wondered who was running the battalion fire-direction center.

Jeffers unbuckled his pistol belt and fixed his fatigue jacket as he approached Arrowood and the brigade investigators. The look on his face was a pathetic attempt at neutrality. Captain Arrowood reported to the senior officer and waited at the position of attention for the battalion commander to give the command for him to be at ease. Major Montgomery used the opportunity to try and analyze the captain. He had tried having Arrowood assigned to a different unit, but the Special Forces qualified officer's basic branch in the Army was artillery, and there was only one artillery battalion in the brigade. Montgomery had been trying to keep the Bravo Battery commander's slot open until he could recruit a West Point officer for the command. There were only six West Pointers in the battalion and both he and Jeffers wanted to increase the number, especially in the command-and-control slots. West Pointers did not get assigned to Vietnam as second lieutenants, so all of the forward observers in the battalion were either ROTC or OCS graduates. When he had seen that Captain Arrowood had received a direct battlefield commission into the artillery, he was shocked that the young captain was going to be given a command of a self-propelled 155mm battery with only twelve weeks of training in the artillery during a rushed course at Fort Sill. In fact, Arrowood had spent only twelve weeks and a couple of days out of Vietnam in the past five years.

Lieutenant Colonel Jeffers made an exaggerated sigh and puckered his lips before speaking. "Well . . . Captain Arrowood, what do you have to say for yourself? . . . I'll listen to your side of the story before I take action." Jeffers had already made up his mind on his course of action.

"If you would like to come with me, sir, I'll show you the area and walk you through what happened." Arrowood caught the look in the battalion commander's eyes.

"I am an intelligent human being, and if you're capable of *verbally* explaining what occurred, I am capable of understanding it." Jeffers looked over at his executive officer and smirked.

The provost marshal glanced over at the new battery commander and decided that he would stick around until Jeffers had been briefed on the incident. He had sat through hundreds of brigade briefings in which Jeffers had participated, and even back at Fort Carson, Colorado, before the 1st Brigade of the 5th Division had deployed for Vietnam, Jeffers had been a perverse fool. Redmond tilted his head down so that a shadow from the front edge of his helmet fell over his eyes. He changed his gaze over to the field artillery battalion's executive officer. Major Montgomery was the one who required watching between the two of them. Jeffers normally spoke what was on his mind, and even though he usually spouted forth unrealistic garbage, he let you know what he was thinking. Montgomery was just the opposite, he always smiled, said one thing and meant another.

Captain Kreps tried moving the conversation into the shade. "Sir, would you like to go over to the orderly room?"

"Why don't you go and inspect the fire-direction center while we're here, and let Monty and me handle the *murder* case."

The provost marshal had guessed right, and was glad that he had decided to stay for a while on the fire-support base.

Captain Arrowood briefed the senior officer in a matter-of-fact tone of voice and didn't let the lieutenant colonel's comment in reference to the man's death disturb his chain of thought. He was glad that the battalion commander had taken his time getting out to the fire-support base and that the provost marshal had completed his preliminary investigation. Jeffers interrupted Arrowood at least a dozen times during the briefing, telling him to skip over many of the details.

"So *that's* your story, is it?" Jeffers smiled without showing his teeth.

"As best as I could explain it in such a short period of time, sir." Arrowood glanced over at Montgomery and saw in the man's eyes that he didn't have an ally. He looked over at the provost marshal and Redmond winked.

"Captain Arrowood . . ." The lieutenant colonel's voice sounded like his patience had been tested to its maximum extent, ". . . we do not *kill* our own soldiers." He raised his eyebrows. "Under *no* circumstances do we order one soldier to murder another! That is not a lawful order, *Mister* Arrowood!"

The provost marshal anticipated what the lieutenant colonel was going to say next and interrupted him. "Sir . . ."

Jeffers removed his eyes from Arrowood and glared at the black major. "Wait until I'm finished talking!"

"Sir . . . this might be important and save you a lot of *embarrassment.*"

The last word the provost marshal had said struck home with Jeffers. "Make it short!"

The black major's upper lip quivered but he maintained control of his emotions. "Yes, sir. Very short. My initial investigation has *cleared* Captain Arrowood and all of the other participants in the shooting of Private Talbot of any wrongdoing. In fact, at the risk of making this briefing longer than I would like to, I will add that my report is going to reflect that he performed in a superb manner under pressure."

"You are going to do *what*!" Jeffers sneered. "I am the one who conducts investigations in this battalion and *I* am the one who makes recommendations!"

The provost marshal shrugged his shoulders. He had had enough of the lieutenant colonel's antics. "True . . . and *I* am the one who conducts *official* investigations on suspected criminal activity and make recommendations." The black major tilted his helmeted head slightly to the right and added, "You've just heard mine."

Major Montgomery knew that with the provost marshal's report, it would be very foolish to relieve Captain Arrowwood of his command. He smiled knowing that he would have other opportunities. "Please . . . *gentlemen* . . . I know all of us have been under a lot of pressure . . . let's calm down and handle this matter like the officers and gentlemen that we are."

Arrowood flashed a grin at the major. The man was smooth. "Is there anything else you would like to see while you're out here at LZ Sandy, sir?"

"No, I have to get back to the battalion . . ." Jeffers

flashed a look over at the provost marshal, telling the junior officer that he had just made his "most wanted to screw over" list.

"If you would like to stay and sleep over, Major Montgomery, we could find some room for you." Arrowood was trying to be courteous.

Lieutenant Zimmerman felt his throat tighten. The new captain didn't know that the battery had been located at LZ Sandy for over eight months and this was the *first* time that Jeffers or Montgomery had ever visited the location.

"We are in a hurry to return back to the battalion." Montgomery looked at his watch to confirm his concern.

"Let's go!" Jeffers started walking toward his helicopter.

"What about Captain Kreps, sir?" Zimmerman looked over at the FDC track located on the far side of the fire-support base.

"He can catch a ride back to Camp Red Devil in the morning with one of your supply trucks." Jeffers ignored Arrowood's salute and hurried off.

The provost marshal waited until the two artillery officers were on board their aircraft before commenting. "You've got a real problem there, Captain Arrowood."

"I know . . . worse than I thought."

"Watch the major." The provost marshal saw the CID agent approaching from the bunker he had escaped into, and stopped talking.

"Thanks for your support. I had a feeling he was about to relieve me there for a couple of minutes."

The black major smiled. "He was."

Captain Kreps looked up from the plotting chart he was checking in the battery's FDC when he heard the helicopter engine start to crank up. He dropped the plotting pin he was holding and left the bunker without saying good-bye to Lieutenant Fields or the fire-direction sergeant. The chopper had already lifted up off the sand and was banking over the Vietnamese graveyard that bordered the south side of the fire-support base.

Arrowood and the provost marshal watched Kreps struggle through the loose sand, waving his arms up at the departing chopper.

"I can't believe he left his S-3 out here." The major shook his head. "Jeffers has been an ass since the first day he joined the brigade back at Fort Carson."

"Have you been with the 1st Brigade since the States?" Arrowood watched the captain stop on the perimeter road and wave frantically up at the departing aircraft.

"Sure have . . ." The provost marshal smiled, ". . . you're probably one of the first replacements to get assigned to the brigade in Vietnam."

"Hmmm . . . I never thought of that, but it answers some of the questions I had during my in-processing briefings with the battalion commander and the executive officer." Arrowood realized that he was dealing with a clique that had been formed back at Fort Carson.

"You've got your work cut out for you, Captain Arrowood." The major held out his hand for Arrowood to shake. "You can find me in the brigade headquarters complex most of the time."

Arrowood took the man's hand and shook it. "I'll look for you."

"Well, Luke, it looks like your S-3 officer is about to ask me for a ride back to Camp Red Devil."

"Why are they so damn afraid to spend the night out here?"

"It's not the Vietcong they fear." A ray of light caught the crystal of his watch as he looked at the time, and it made him blink. "There's a lot of cut-throat going on back at the main base camp, and they're all afraid to leave the camp for very long." Redmond smiled and a soft sound left his throat. "Politics, my young friend, politics. If you don't watch your ass, they'll have it for a snack."

"I'm more concerned over the war." Luke looked over at the approaching captain.

"Did Colonel Jeffers leave?" Kreps was out of breath.

"Yes . . . a couple of minutes ago."

A look of total despair covered the captain's face. He was sure the battalion commander had left him on purpose.

"He said that you can catch a supply truck back to Camp Red Devil in the morning." Arrowood passed on the message the lieutenant colonel had left.

"That's impossible! I've got to be back at the battalion FDC to personally clear every fire mission!" Panic filled the young captain's voice.

"I think that I've got enough room on my chopper for you." Redmond beckoned for the CID agent to join them. He looked at Captain Arrowood and added, "I'll have my official report ready in the morning and your copy should reach you no later than the day after tomorrow. I'll personally send you a copy."

"Thanks, sir." Luke shook the provost marshal's hand again.

"You watch your rear!" Redmond started walking toward the entrance of the base.

"For sure!"

Captain Kreps was holding his steel helmet in his hand and wiping the sweat off his forehead using the back of the same hand. He still couldn't believe that the battalion commander had just gone off and left him. "Was the colonel angry when he left?"

"I wouldn't say that he was very happy over what I had to tell him." Major Redmond winked at Arrowood.

Lieutenant Zimmerman waited until the sound of the chopper was gone before approaching his new battery commander. "Sir, would you like a tour of the base before it gets dark?"

Luke was in deep thought and simply nodded his head in the affirmative. He had run across some real characters during his five years in Vietnam, but the clique he was now colliding with at the speed of light was almost unbelievable. Zimmerman led the way along the packed sand perimeter road. They left the main gate and walked along the western row of bunkers. There wasn't much along that stretch of the base camp except for five perimeter bunkers and one gun section. The northwest corner of the camp was where the battery ammunition section was along with two GP large tents that housed the pallets of 155mm shells and the powder canisters.

"There's a big gap in that bunker line." Arrowood pointed to the hundred yard space.

"A tank or one of the infantry 113s, usually goes there during the night, sir."

"What happens if the brigade doesn't send us a platoon of tanks or infantry?"

"We move a .50-caliber machine gun there for the night, sir."

Arrowood pointed over at the tents. "We're storing ammunition and powder so close together under *tents*?"

"Yes, sir. I've called back to battalion at least a dozen times asking for materials to build bunkers, but they always say the brigade's short of engineer materials for bunkers."

"Well?"

Zimmerman glanced sheepishly at the new captain. "They're using the materials for Camp Red Devil. If we requisition building materials, first the brigade will take their cut and then the battalion will take what they want, and we usually end up with little or nothing."

"I know how to cure that shit." Arrowood kept the solution to himself. "Watch what happens." He removed a small hardcover notebook and wrote something on one of the pages as they walked around the perimeter.

Lieutenant Zimmerman briefed Arrowood on where everything was located inside of the fire-support base as they slowly circled around the inner perimeter road. Arrowood paused in front of the mess hall tent and looked down the track trail cutting through the center of the base to where Talbot's body had laid only a couple of hours earlier.

"That's about it, sir, except for the mess hall and headquarters complex." Zimmerman pointed to the buildings and tents that lined the oil-coated road along the south side of the fire-support base. "If you'll excuse me, I have to check the lay of the guns before we start our nightly H&I fires."

"Sure . . . go ahead." Luke could see that the cooks were watching them through the screen windows of the small hootch. "Thanks for the tour."

"The first sergeant had Dotson put your gear in the old battery commander's hootch." Zimmerman hesitated and then added, "You should know that it was the battery aid station, but our old commander decided that he wanted to be closer to the orderly room after the last monsoon season."

Luke heard the sarcasm in the lieutenant's voice. "Thanks for the advice." He watched the young officer's eyes when he asked the next question. "I gather my predecessor wasn't very well liked? . . ."

"You've gathered your information correctly, sir. He was an alcoholic . . . along with half of the NCOs in the battery." Zimmerman turned and nodded at the small plywood and tin building located at the far end of the oiled portion of the perimeter road. "They usually met in the supply sergeant's hootch and played cards most of the night. We'd see the captain for the first time around noon."

"That answers a lot of questions for me concerning the perimeter defense and basic fields discipline."

"We've got our problems, sir . . ." Zimmerman left the question open.

"Well, with your help and Lieutenant Fields's expertise in the FDC, I think we can turn this battery around."

"We have one more officer assigned to the battery, sir, but we rarely see him. He's assigned to A Company, 1st of the 11th Infantry as a forward observer."

"When you finish with the guns, meet me in the mess hall for coffee."

"I don't think I'll be done for a couple of hours, sir." Zimmerman felt the first cool breeze of the evening coming in off the South China Sea and turned slightly so that the moving air could cool off his face.

"That's fine . . . I'll be around."

"The mess hall closes after supper, sir."

Lieutenant Zimmerman left to check the guns, and Luke took his time walking around the row of hootches that made up the battery headquarters section. He noticed that there was a garbage pit directly behind the mess hall and next to it was a four-seat latrine. Luke changed his course and entered the mess hall through the rear door.

"Can I help you, sir?"

"Are you the mess sergeant?"

"Yes, sir."

Luke looked around the screened in tin and plywood hootch and noticed that the two-by-four window-sills were covered with dead flies. "Are they dying from the food?" He pointed at the dead insects.

The staff sergeant shrugged his shoulders. "We spray the area with DDT every once in a while when they get bad, sir." He grinned showing his rotting front teeth. "Vietnam is full of flies, sir."

"You spray DDT inside of the mess hall?"

"Every once in a while, sir."

"Do many of the men in the battery suffer from diarrhea?" Luke watched the cook's reactions as he talked to the mess sergeant.

"Sir! I run a clean mess hall . . . we do the best that we can out here in this fucking hole!"

"I don't doubt that at all, Sergeant . . . but I wonder why the latrine is so close to the mess hall and why you're operating an open garbage pit less than fifty feet from where you prepare the food and the troops eat . . . under an open tent."

The mess sergeant glared at the new officer. "My cooks have to shit too, sir!"

"I want that shitter moved at least to the other side of the orderly room and that garbage dump closed down." Luke returned the sergeant's glare. "I don't want anything that draws flies within fifty feet of the mess hall."

"Your going to have my cooks carrying empty cans back and forth all damn day long!"

"While you're at it . . . have one of your men buy some Vietnamese flypaper down in one of the cities and use that to kill the flies that get near the food."

"Vietnamese flypaper isn't *issued* in the American supply system, *sir*."

Arrowood reached into his pocket and removed a small bundle of Vietnamese piasters. "Here, this should cover it." He handed the mess sergeant a couple thousand P-notes.

"I don't think that's my job, sir."

"You've got a choice, Sergeant. Start running this mess hall so that it *supports* the troops in this battery *or* I'll have your ass humping ammunition for the guns." Luke didn't leave any room for doubt. Everyone in the mess hall sensed that he would do it. "I expect that mess back behind this hootch to be cleaned up by noon tomorrow."

The mess sergeant watched Luke walk slowly past the garbage pit and shitter. He mumbled under his breath. "Motherfucking officer!"

Luke made a quick check of the bunkers behind the orderly room and crawled up on top of the bunker in the far southwest corner of the fire-support base to survey the area. He figured the perimeter surrounding the base area was at least a mile and a half; a lot of area to secure for a single firing battery when you considered that at least half of the men had to stay on the six guns during a ground attack. He didn't understand how the battalion commander could allow one of his batteries to have been placed in such an isolated location without proper protection. He had seen the battalion's version of the brigade's area of operation and had realized that in order to adequately cover the area with artillery fires, a fire-support base was required in that sector. That wasn't the problem; protecting the base was.

The sound of tanks approaching the base camp turned Luke around on the bunker. He could see four M48 tanks escorting a couple of deuce-and-a-halfs and a jeep followed by two Caterpillar D6 bulldozers riding on the backs of trailer trucks. Luke watched as the armor platoon pulled up in the large open area in the southwest corner of the base and parked, followed by the trucks and the jeep. He had wondered what the large open area was used for and his question was answered; it was a transit motor park.

Luke located the armor platoon leader and walked over to his tank. "Are you our security for tonight?"

"Yes, sir. Do you want us to use the usual spots on the perimeter?"

"Sure . . . for tonight so that I can see how it's done."

"You the new commander out here?"

"Yes." Luke nodded at the other vehicles. "Who are they?"

"A Seabee unit working on the highway. They got caught working late and couldn't make it back to Quang Tri for the night, so their lieutenant asked us to escort them in here for the night." The armor lieutenant smiled. "They're really a nice bunch of guys."

Luke grinned. He had an idea that just might work. "Thanks, Lieutenant." He started walking over to where the Seabee lieutenant was supervising the parking of his platoon's vehicles for the night. He could see that the Seabees were covered with dust and filth from working with their heavy equipment all day. "Hello, Lieutenant . . . I'm Captain Arrowood."

"Hello . . ." The Navy officer nodded a greeting and returned his attention back to his men.

"I hear that you're working on this section of Highway 1 for the next couple of days."

"More like a couple of weeks . . ." The Navy officer paused and then added, "sir." He was going to

address the Army officer as captain, but that was a
sore spot with the Navy. A captain in the Navy was
the same rank as an Army colonel and a Navy lieutenant was equal to an Army captain. He was a lieutenant
JG; *junior grade* and equal to an Army first
lieutenant.

"You have to drive back and forth to Quang Tri
every day?" Luke felt out the Navy officer.

"Yes, sir, we lose a lot of time doing that, but I
guess that's the only way we can get the job done."

"Maybe we can work a deal."

The Seabee officer stopped watching his men and
turned his attention to what the captain was saying.
"How's that, sir?"

"Well, I think I could arrange some decent quarters
for your platoon, feed them breakfast and supper, and
have some decent shower water ready for them when
they finish working for the day . . ." Luke grinned a
devilish smile.

"And what would you require in return?"

"The way that I figure it, Lieutenant, you lose a
good six hours a day of daylight traveling back and
forth from Quang Tri to your work location . . .
right?"

The lieutenant nodded cautiously, not wanting to
commit his men to something he couldn't back up.

"Do your men have to pull perimeter guard duty
when they get back there at night?"

The lieutenant nodded again that they did.

"As you can see . . ." Luke swept his hand out over
the fire-support base's perimeter, ". . . I need a berm
built and a few garbage dumps closed out . . . that
sort of thing. Maybe a little work done on my inner-
perimeter road. In return, for a couple of hours worth
of dozing after you return in the evening . . . your
men will not have to pull guard and, like I said before,
food, shelter and showers will be provided by my
battery."

The lieutenant smiled. The Army captain was offer-
ing him a very fair deal. "Let's shake on that." He

looked over at the setting sun and added, "We can get in a couple of hours tonight before it gets dark . . . where do you want us to start?"

"I need a ten-foot-high berm built around the whole fire-support base. You're the engineer . . . advise me."

The Seabee lieutenant smiled. "I like your style, Captain. Consider the job done."

Luke started walking away toward his orderly room when the Seabee called out. "Save some chow for twenty-two men!"

Luke gave the lieutenant the thumbs-up sign and continued walking. Twenty-two additional men inside of the fire-support base would make things a little safer. Even though they wouldn't be used for guard duty, they could always be used for a ready reaction force in the event of a ground attack. Luke skirted around the back of his large shower tower and started to step up on the wooden pallets that had been laid down for a sidewalk that ran from the showers around the orderly room to the first sergeant and his sleeping quarters.

"Afternoon, sir."

Arrowood paused and looked over at the young soldier who had driven him to LZ Sandy from Quang Tri earlier that day. "How are you doing, Dotson?"

"I took you up on your offer to use your showers." The soldier wrapped an olive-drab towel around his waist and stepped out of the shower stall. The showers had been built with a waist-high wall around them to afford a little privacy but at the same time save lumber. The shower's construction was simple: Four four-by-fours supported a platform that normally had one fifty-five-gallon drum on it with a shower head welded underneath it. The drum was filled with water from the top and allowed to warm up during the day. Gravity operated the actual shower, and the person taking the shower stood on a couple of pallets, allowing the used water to soak up in the sand. It was a primitive operation, but very effective.

"Anytime . . . you work for the first sergeant, right?"

"Yes, sir . . . so does Pilgrim."

"Tell Pilgrim that he can use the shower, too . . . if he likes." Luke noticed that the soldier glanced over at the orderly room. "I'll pass it on to the first sergeant that I gave my permission."

Dotson smiled. "Thanks."

Arrowood started walking away just as Dotson reached up to tighten the handle on the shower head that was dripping a little. The towel around his waist fell down on the pallet as he stretched. Luke gasped. "What in the . . . hell!" He couldn't help staring at the soldier's groin area.

Dotson bent over and quickly replaced the towel back around his waist.

"Soldier!" Luke was angry. "Have you seen a doctor?"

"No, sir . . . our medic is giving me a salve for it. He says it's only a minor bacteria infection that's caused from the heat."

"Minor!" Luke's anger boiled out. "Soldier, you have a *major* infection! Man! That has to hurt."

Dotson nodded his head. "A little, but there are guys out on the guns who have it a lot worse. It usually gets better if we can shower every day, but lately there hasn't been any water."

"Why?"

"The water truck is dead-lined and can't go to Quang Tri or it'll get written up by the brigade MPs."

"Are you telling me that battalion won't *deliver* water to us until we can get our truck fixed?"

"Yes, sir."

"Is this the only shower on this base that has water left?"

"Yes, sir . . . maybe the supply and mess hall have some left, but I know the showers on the guns and ammunition section are empty and have been for almost a week."

Captain Arrowood felt anger for the first time that

day. He could tolerate petty politics, but not to the extent that the troops had to suffer from severe groin infections and the lack of adequate medical attention.

The screen door slammed shut behind him as Captain Arrowood strode down the narrow hallway of the orderly room hootch. The first sergeant dropped his feet down off the edge of his desk and used his hand to signal for the supply sergeant to leave the office.

"How did it go, sir?" His voice was neutral. He had heard that the battalion commander had left the fire-support base without relieving the new captain.

"How did what go, First Sergeant? How did the Talbot Incident go? Or how did my tour of the perimeter bunkers go? Or how did my conversation with Specialist Dotson go?"

"What about Dotson?" The first sergeant sat up in his chair.

"Have you seen Dotson's groin?"

"I don't normally go around looking at soldiers' cocks, sir."

Arrowood flashed the first sergeant a look that warned him he was messing with something that would fire his ass up. "Do *you* know that most of the men in this battery are suffering from a bacterial groin infection?"

"Come on, sir! A little rash isn't going to stop a soldier from doing his job." The first sergeant rolled his eyes.

"A *little* rash!" Luke pointed at the supply sergeant who was trying to slip out of the office area. "*You!* Go find Dotson and bring him back here, now!"

"Sir, I know you've had a trying day. The Talbot Incident would shake anybody up, but I think that you should calm him down a little bit before you make an ass out of yourself in front of the troops." The first sergeant smiled. "Go have a couple of stiff belts and you'll feel better."

Luke's eyes darkened. "Is it true the men on the guns haven't had any water to shower with for over a week?"

The first sergeant stuck his lower lip out and nodded his head. "Yes, it's been about a week since *any* of us have had a water delivery. The mess sergeant is down to one five hundred gallon trailer."

"How many trailers does the mess hall have?"

"Three . . . one issued and two scrounged."

"There's water in the shower by our hootch."

"Your predecessor was pretty clear about that, sir. He liked taking two showers a day; once in the morning and once before going to bed. He said that he slept better when he was clean." The first sergeant smiled. "Speaking of showers, sir, I noticed that you let Dotson use yours. I don't recommend you repeating that again or you'll have every soldier in the battery wanting to use it."

"Every soldier in this battery *will* use it, if that's the only shower with water in it!" Arrowood pointed at the first sergeant and was about to speak when Dotson entered the hootch. "Come over here, soldier, and drop your pants."

"Drop my pants, sir?" Dotson's face turned red.

"Yes! In front of the first sergeant . . ." Arrowood ground his teeth, ". . . that's an order, soldier!"

Dotson hesitated and then unbuttoned his fly. He glanced over at the screen door and slowly lowered his pants. He was wearing a pair of boxer shorts.

"The shorts, too!"

Dotson obeyed. The first sergeant stared for a couple of seconds at the oozing and bleeding scrotum. The infection had spread from the warm area between the soldier's legs up above the line of his pubic hair leaving open sores.

"That is a minor fucking rash?" Arrowood slammed his fist down on the first sergeant's desk. "Pull your pants back up, Dotson. Thank you. You can go now." Luke waited until the soldier had left the orderly room before continuing. "He says that his *rash* isn't all that bad because he's seen *worse* cases down on the guns." Luke's voice lowered to a growl. "What in the fuck is going on out here, First Sergeant?"

The senior NCO shrugged his shoulders. "War is hell, sir."

Luke ignored the sarcastic remark. "Right now, I want you to go and tell the section sergeants that *all* of the showers are open on this fire-support base for the troops to use and tomorrow, First Sergeant, you are personally responsible for finding *clean*, chemically treated water for the troops to use and that includes water for the showers."

"Sir, *nobody* gets quartermaster water for the showers."

"You find the water, if you have to, find the chemicals to treat it with and I want all of the showers filled and spare water standing by before noon tomorrow. There will be enough water for the troops to shower *twice* a day until this bacterial epidemic is over."

"Sir, I think that you're being unreasonable . . ."

Luke cut the first sergeant off. "No! I'm not fucking unreasonable . . . there will be water for the troops, even if you have to pump it yourself out of a Vietnamese well!"

"I think that I'm going to have to see the battalion sergeant major, sir."

"Why?"

"I can't work for an officer who talks to me this way, especially in front of the troops and curses me."

"I've hurt your feelings, First Sergeant?"

"Yes you have, sir."

"Well, listen to what I have to say next . . . From now on, all of the battery NCOs and officers will shower and eat *after* the soldiers."

"You've just cut your throat, sir. You can't run this battery without the support of the NCOs!"

"That's true . . . but you left out one thing . . . without the support of the *good* NCOs!" Luke pointed to the door. "Now get your ass moving, First Sergeant, and do what I've told you—and my policy starts right now! The NCOs and officers will eat supper after the troops have been served."

· The first sergeant hesitated and then left the orderly

room without stopping to take his helmet or pistol with him.

Captain Arrowood went over to the door with the sign above it that said: BATTERY COMMANDER, and opened it. A soft blast of air-conditioned air came out of the small office to great him. The walls had been boarded up with plywood to keep out the light and the heat. A small portable air conditioner hummed quietly in the dark office. Luke shook his head and slammed the door shut again. He left the building and started walking out to the nearest perimeter bunker. The sound of a bulldozer stopped him halfway, and he stood there for a couple of minutes watching the Seabees building the berm around the fire-support base before finding himself a seat on top of the fighting bunker, where he watched the sun set in the western sky.

CHAPTER THREE

✪✪✪✪✪✪✪✪✪✪✪✪✪✪✪✪

SCROUNGING

The sea breeze picked up when the sun slipped behind the tree line, drying the layer of sweat that coated Luke's whole body. He kept shaking his head as he sat on top of the bunker, thinking about the mess he had gotten into by taking the assignment with the artillery battalion. The letter he had received from the artillery branch back in Washington, D.C., was straight to the point; he had to get his ass assigned to an artillery unit or his name would head the list when the reduction in force came after the war. The gunshot wounds he had received during his last assignment with the 5th Special Forces Group were the perfect excuse for him to go to a line unit. The wounds were clean and had only punched through the muscles in his legs, but he still needed a couple of months to rebuild his strength again before trying to hump through the jungles.

Arrowood's thoughts returned to the current problems facing him. He knew that he couldn't rely on any real help from the artillery battalion or the staff at the brigade headquarters, maybe with the exception of Major Redmond. Within the battery, it looked like the officers were reliable and the sergeant on the howitzer near the mess hall seemed like a good man. Luke's forehead wrinkled. The ammunition section chief, Staff Sergeant Cole was questionable. He seemed like he was a professional soldier, but was trapped between two factions and was siding with his own race. The junior enlisted men seemed to have taken the brunt of the poor leadership and were suffering for it. There wasn't any doubt in Arrowood's mind that the battalion commander was using Bravo Battery as a dumping ground for the whole battalion. He frowned and wondered if that was why he had been assigned to the battery.

"Evening, sur!"

Captain Arrowood looked down from the bunker and saw the soldier approaching. He nodded.

"Thanks for letting me use your shower. Dotson said that you gave permission."

"You must be Pilgrim." Luke stood and looked out over the barbed wire. "At least you've got an excellent field of fire from here."

"Yes, sur. When the moon comes out, it's like daylight when it reflects off the white sand." Pilgrim climbed up on the roof of the bunker. "I've got first shift out here tonight."

"It's good meeting you, Pilgrim. I've got to get over to the FDC and make some calls back to the battalion." Luke started getting down from the bunker and was stopped by Pilgrim's voice.

"What you did was right, sur." Pilgrim didn't look at the officer. "Talbot even had the NCOs scared of him and was pushing so much dope in this battery that I don't think we've conducted a fire mission since we've been here where half the guns weren't operated by men under the influence of *something*, dope or booze." Pilgrim's voice lowered. He knew that sounds traveled far over sand at night. "Maybe I shouldn't be telling you this, but the men are really impressed with you already, even the blacks. We're all sick of the racial bullshit and the dope. We want to get back to the States alive!"

"You can bet your ass that I'll give it my best shot!" All the doubt in Luke's mind over the assignment disappeared. "You can pass the word around that everybody's slate has been wiped clean. I'll judge each man on how he performs from today on."

"I think the men will like to hear that." Pilgrim placed a piece of cardboard down on the sandbags to sit on because they were still very hot from being in the sun all day. "These new nylon sandbags suck!"

"You can tell that they've been designed by someone who's never been in *combat*." Luke agreed with the soldier's comment. "The cloth ones don't reflect light at night and they don't hold the heat like the nylon ones do."

"I hear the NCOs are bitching because you've let us use your shower." Pilgrim smiled. "They've been treating the headquarters showers like their own private property since we've been out here."

"There are a few more things that need to be changed before we can really start kicking ass as a battery and I plan on starting with the leadership." Luke nodded and started walking away from the bunker toward the FDC that was located at the far corner of the fire base.

Pilgrim watched the officer disappear behind one of the gun bunkers. Dotson had been right; the new captain was worth protecting. All of the enlisted men knew that some of the NCOs were already planning on getting rid of him because he was upsetting their little kingdoms, and it would be only a matter of time before he would discover their nightly poker and drinking parties and put a stop to them. Dotson had suggested that they take turns pulling guard outside of Arrowood's hootch. At first he hadn't agreed with his buddy, but now he was for the idea, Captain Arrowood was worth a few extra hours of guard duty.

It was dark when Luke reached the FDC track. The men had built a small bunker next to the lightly armored vehicle to give them a little more room, but the track could pull away from the bunker if it had to. Luke pushed the canvas flap back and entered the busy area. Lieutenant Fields was getting the data ready for a fire mission that was being called in from the field. Luke found himself a seat out of the way so that he could watch. The men plotted the mission and worked up the firing data for the guns in a few minutes. The FDC sergeant called the data down to the guns and then sat down to wait for clearance from the battalion to fire. The sergeant went over to the small coffeepot near where Arrowood was sitting and poured himself a fresh cup. He looked at the captain and smiled. "This can take awhile, sir."

"How long's awhile?"

"We've waited for over an hour, but normally we can get battalion clearance in thirty minutes."

Luke shook his head. "We are a *direct* support artillery battery and we make the infantry wait for thirty minutes to receive their initial adjustment round?"

"Sir . . ." Lieutenant Fields joined the conversation, "the battalion commander has his own policy that states either the executive officer or himself must personally clear every mission for one of the units."

"Personally?"

"Yes, sir, and that's why it takes an hour sometimes because they have to find them and wait until they go over to the battalion FDC and check the data."

Luke shook his head. "The armor and infantry units must really like that."

"They don't have very much respect for the artillery, but Colonel Jeffers doesn't really care what they want just as long as he doesn't have an incident like they did down in the 101st."

"What was that?"

Fields glanced over at the radio operator, hoping that the battalion FDC had called. The soldier shook his head, and Fields went back to briefing Luke. "One of the 105mm batteries fired short and killed three of their own infantry. The battalion commander was relieved because the battery's data hadn't been checked by battalion."

"Doesn't battalion check our data?"

"Yes, sir, but the battalion commander doesn't trust Captain Kreps."

"This is some shit, I hope you know that!" Arrowood was getting angry.

One of the young soldiers working a slide ruler glanced up at the captain and smiled. It was some shit, but the new captain was just scratching the surface.

"See if you can get me the battalion S-3 on the line. He must be in the FDC waiting for his data to be checked." Luke poured himself a cup of the thick coffee.

"Land-line or radio, sir?" The radio operator called over to the captain from where he sat behind a panel of radios and field telephones.

"Land-line." Luke walked over to the operator and took the offered direct line to the battalion FDC. A sergeant answered the telephone and Luke asked for Kreps. It was a couple of minutes before he came on the line.

"Kreps here, what do you want, Arrowood?"

"Seeing that we're waiting for this mission to get cleared, I thought that I would use the time to pass on some requests through you."

"Shoot." Kreps's voice sounded tired.

"I'd like the battalion surgeon to fly out here in the morning and be prepared to treat at least fifty men for severe bacterial infections in the groin and underarm areas." Luke took a sip from his coffee and continued: "Also, I have a severe diarrhea problem that is probably coming from poorly prepared food, so I'll need a food service representative to fly out here also and check out that area."

"We have a sick-call procedure already established to handle that, Arrowood. Check with your first sergeant and he'll brief you on how it operates."

"I already know about the sick-call truck that leaves here as soon as the road is opened in the morning and returns at night." Luke glanced back into the FDC and could tell that everyone was listening to his conversation but they were acting like they were busy. "Besides, Kreps . . . it's a tough task to ride in the back of a truck all the way to Camp Red Devil when you have a severe case of diarrhea."

"The other batteries do it and I haven't heard any complaints yet." Kreps's voice was sharp.

"Do the officers from those batteries ride trucks to sick call?"

"Don't pull any smart-assed shit with me, Arrowood! I'm tired and I'm not in the mood!"

"I need a doctor to fly out here and treat my men, and I don't need any shit from you!" Arrowood didn't hear the man behind him trying to swallow the laugh in his throat. Nobody had ever talked back to a battalion officer before.

"Well, the battalion surgeon can't be in two places at once and he has a regular morning sick call here at battalion headquarters for the rest of the battalion."

"Why don't you just pass my requests on to the battalion commander and let him decide."

"I'll do that!"

"What's the status of the fire mission?"

"We're waiting for the colonel to get over here."

"Thanks, we'll be standing by." Arrowood let the sarcasm show in his voice and shoved the telephone back into its cradle.

Lieutenant Fields kept himself busy checking firing data for the nightly H&I fires. He knew that battalion wouldn't support Captain Arrowood's request.

The radio broke squelch, and it took a couple of seconds before a voice could be heard coming over the speakers. "Red Bucket 6 . . . this is Red Dragon 6 . . . over."

Fields flashed a scared look over at the new captain. "It's the battalion commander on the radio."

"Why isn't he using the land-line?" Luke sat his coffee cup down and went over to the radios. Just before he took the handset from the radio operator, Lieutenant Fields spoke up rapidly.

"He always uses the radio when he's going to chew ass so that everybody can hear, especially the other batteries." Fields risked warning the captain. He had seen the old battery commander receive too many asschewings over the radio to let Arrowood get caught off-guard.

"This guy is a fucking basket case!" Luke couldn't believe that a commander would intentionally embarrass one of his subordinate commanders. He took the handset and answered the radio call. "Red Dragon 6, this is Red Bucket 6 . . . over."

"Dragon 6 . . . I hear that you've been harassing my S-3." He didn't give Arrowood a chance to answer and added, "There are established battalion sick-call procedures that everyone will follow, including you. I know that you were spoiled while you were serving with those undisciplined Special Forces types, but we obey orders in this unit and follow established regulations . . . do you understand me?"

Luke waited for the battalion commander to say, over and figured that he wasn't going to. "This is Bucket 6 . . . I have over half of my battery ill and feel that that warrants a special visit from the surgeon . . . over."

"Damn you! I'll decide when something is *special* in this battalion . . . not you!" Jeffers had dropped all radio procedure. "Do you understand me, damn it!"

Lieutenant Fields risked commenting. "He's drunk, sir. Don't fight him."

Luke glanced over at his second lieutenant and nodded his head. "This is Red Bucket 6 . . . roger, sir . . . over."

"You stand by in your FDC! I want you personally to handle this fire mission and by that, I mean that I want *you* to personally compute the data for the mission . . . do you understand?"

"Red Dragon 6 . . . roger that, sir . . . over."

Lieutenant Colonel Jeffers looked over at Captain Kreps and held out his hand for the fire-mission data. Kreps couldn't look at the senior officer's face. He knew that Jeffers hated OCS officers, but it was beginning to really show how much he hated officers who received a battlefield commission like Arrowood had.

Jeffers keyed the handset. "Red Bucket 6, this is

Red Dragon 6 . . . what is the deflection you have for the mission, over."

Luke hadn't had time to even walk over to the plotting chart. Lieutenant Fields handed him the data and smiled. Luke took the paper and keyed the radio. "Red Bucket 6 . . . deflection . . . 168 . . . over."

". . . and your quadrant?"

"This is Red Bucket 6 . . . quadrant zero four niner . . . over."

"Correct! You have permission to fire the mission . . . *out*!" The radio link went back to static.

Arrowood handed the handset back to the operator. "Thanks." He looked over at Fields and asked, "Do you go through this shit for every mission?"

"Sometimes it's worse, sir . . . it all depends if the colonel is winning at the bridge table and on how much he has drank." Fields busied himself with a couple of manuals.

"Unbelievable . . . truly . . . unbelievable!" Luke picked up the land-line and placed a call with the brigade operator to a unit down at Camp Eagle that was located a little south of LZ Nancy in the 101st Airborne Division's area of operations. "I'll be waiting outside when the operator gets through."

"Yes, sir." Fields watched Luke leave the FDC bunker. "I'll give the commands to the guns."

Luke leaned up against the sandbags and released the emotion that had built up inside of him by smashing his fist against the bags. He allowed the rage to show on his face in the dark. It had been extremely difficult maintaining control of his emotions inside of the bunker. Jeffers was playing with him and intentionally trying to humiliate him in front of his subordinates. Luke knew that Jeffers had told him to work up the data for the fire mission hoping that he would screw up or, worse yet, not know how to work the problem. He had only gone through a rush artillery course, designed more to familiarize an officer receiving a direct commission than teach the subject of gunnery.

The radio operator stuck his head out of the bunker. "Sir, a Sergeant Jones is on the line for you."

"Thanks." Luke paused for a second to watch the silhouettes of the gun tubes moving in the direction of the target. He glanced at his watch as he stepped into the FDC and saw that it had taken forty-six minutes to get clearance from battalion to fire. He shook his head as he picked up the land-line telephone. "Jones?"

"What in the hell does your leg ass want now!" The deep-voiced master sergeant always sounded like he was about to break out laughing. "I told you going to a leg unit was a dumb fucking move."

"How true!" Luke smiled. It felt good talking to his old jump-school buddy again. "You don't know what a fucking bad move it was!"

"What can I do for you?" Jones's voice took on a serious note.

"A couple of big ones this time, old friend."

"They always are!" Jones chuckled, "especially when you call this late at night."

"I need a doctor to come up to my fire-support base as soon as possible." Luke briefed Jones on the bacteria infection and his battalion's response to his request.

"He has got to be a sorry motherfucker!" Jones broke the lead in his pencil and cursed under his breath. "What else do you need?"

"Jones, do you remember those new fighting bunkers your engineers designed and prepackaged into kits?"

"Yep . . . we're damn proud of that design, and they're easy to assemble." Jones had been the person responsible for designing the fighting bunkers for semipermanent fire-support bases and had received a special promotion to master sergeant from General Westmoreland himself for the prepackaging idea. The sixteen-foot-long, three-firing-port bunker was being used by every unit in Vietnam. "Which size do you want? We have a sixteen footer for corner bunkers and ten by eight bunkers we use for regular base camp perimeter bunkers."

Luke thought for a second before answering. "Four of the big ones and ten regular ones."

"I thought LZ Sandy had been there for a while?" Jones knew where the base was located at next to Highway 1, north of LZ Nancy that bordered his division's AO.

"Eight months, but we need to do a lot of work around our perimeter. It's been neglected." Luke knew that he had made an understatement.

"It sounds pretty bad up there." Jones tapped his notepad against his leg. "I'll tell you what I can do. I'll fly up in the morning and take a look around and we can go from there."

"Thanks, Jones . . . I'd really appreciate it if you could." Luke felt good for the first time that day. Jones was one of the best engineers in Vietnam.

"I don't know what I can do in the doctor department on such a short notice, but I'll try."

"That's all I can ask for, thanks, and I'll see you out here in the morning." Luke hung up the land-line. It had worked out better than he had expected.

"I don't think the battalion commander is going to like it, sir." Fields knew that Jeffers would come unglued if he knew one of his battery commanders went outside of the brigade for support.

Luke looked at the nervous second lieutenant and winked. "He doesn't have to know, now does he?"

Fields glanced over at the FDC sergeant before answering. "Things have a way of getting back to battalion headquarters very fast, especially if it's hot gossip like this is."

The FDC sergeant glanced up and saw the officers looking at him. The first sergeant had already passed the word to the NCOs that he wanted something on the captain. The sergeant's face turned red.

"I sure wouldn't take it very kindly if I receive a call from Jeffers before a doctor can get out here to treat our sick troops." The threat in Luke's voice was a very real one, and the sergeant swallowed a couple of times. "And I don't think the troops would like to hear how their own NCOs screwed them out of medical treatment." Luke frowned. "I wonder how many of the NCOs have groin infections or if it's only a junior enlisted problem."

"Sir, I won't say anything. You have my word on it!" The FDC sergeant's voice nearly broke. He knew that the first sergeant was going to chew his ass when he did find out and had traced the captain's call back to the FDC.

Luke looked at each one of the men who were on duty in the FDC and received nods of agreement from each one of them.

The sound of an arriving helicopter brought Luke out of the mess tent where he had been drinking coffee with Lieutenant Zimmerman and the Seabee lieutenant. Luke could see the Screaming Eagle shoulder patch painted on the nose of the chopper and smiled. Sergeant Jones had caught an early ride. The chopper had shut down by the time Luke arrived at the helipad, and Sergeant Jones and a full colonel were standing on the shady side of the parked aircraft. It was already getting hot out and it was only a little after six in the morning.

"Thanks for coming out so quick, Sergeant Jones." Luke shook hands with his old friend after saluting the colonel.

"This is Colonel Quinn, the division surgeon for the 101st." Jones introduced the distinguished looking, white-haired medical officer who stood there holding his black leather bag.

"Captain Luke Arrowood . . . I remember you from Plei Djereng." The colonel smiled.

Luke looked puzzled. He couldn't place having ever met the senior officer before, especially during his tour with the Special Forces A-camp.

"I don't think you remember . . ."

"No, sir, I'm sorry . . ."

"You were on patrol near the Cambodian border and received a Mayday from a crashing MEDEVAC chopper."

Luke recalled the incident, but still didn't recognize the colonel.

Quinn's smile widened. "The pilot was my son."

"He was pretty torn up if I recall." Luke remembered pulling the pilot out of the chopper seconds before it exploded. The lieutenant had a severely broken leg and head wounds. He had been the only survivor from the crash and Luke's patrol had to carry him for the rest of the day until they could find a place to call in a rescue chopper.

"Yes, but he has healed well and is walking with the use of a cane."

"When the colonel heard your name, he insisted on coming out here himself." Jones winked at Luke.

"I wanted to meet you in person and thank you for saving my son's life."

Luke shrugged his shoulders. "He would have done the same for me if the situation had been reversed."

"So! What can I do for you?" Colonel Quinn changed the subject to the reason why Luke had asked for medical help. "I hear you have an epidemic of sorts out here? Something to do with severe rashes?"

"Yes, sir—and severe diarrhea. Together, they're making it very difficult for my men to work in this heat."

Quinn wiped the back of his hand over his forehead. "I can see that! Where can I set up a sick call?"

"You can use my orderly room. It'll give you a clean place and some privacy." Luke looked over at Dotson, who had pulled up next to the chopper in his jeep. "Dotson will show you where it is, sir, and he can be your first patient."

Dotson blushed when everyone looked at him.

"Sergeant Jones, are you ready to check out the perimeter?" Luke held out his hand and led the way over to where he wanted to build the first bunker. They took their time walking around the perimeter and stopped often to check out the fields of fire for the existing bunkers. Jones shook his head each time they stopped and climbed up on a bunker. Some of the fighting positions had two rows of sandbags in front of them and some had up to eight rows, but there wasn't any regularity. The construction of the bunkers had been left up to the men who had been detailed to build them.

Arrowood and Jones were halfway around the perimeter when the 101st helicopter cranked up and flew south. Jones looked at Luke and shrugged his shoulders. "The colonel must have sent it back for more medical supplies."

Luke's forehead wrinkled. "I hope it's not as bad as I think it is."

"What kind of fucking statement is that?" Jones reached up and squeezed his friend's shoulder. "This is fucking bad!" He waved his hand at the perimeter. "I don't know who designed it, or who selected the locations for the bunkers, but in almost every single case the bunkers have been built in the *worst* possible locations."

Luke watched the helicopter disappear in the cloudless sky. He could feel the sun's heat against his fatigue jacket and knew that it was going to be an especially hot day; even the breeze had decided to go somewhere else. The dust and sand cloud from the departing helicopter just hung in the air and slowly started settling back down on the ground near the orderly room. A soldier left the front of the small hootch wearing only his boots and a cutoff pair of jungle fatigue pants. He was followed closely by another man who was dressed in a similar fashion. "Something is going on back there in the orderly room."

Jones looked over to where Luke was pointing. "Colonel Quinn knows his business. You can rest assured that whatever he's doing is in the best interest of your men."

"I know that, Sarge . . . but there's a battalion policy that states that the men must remain in uniform at all times when they're outside of their sleeping bunkers." Luke shook his head as he recalled the smile on Major Montgomery's face when he had told him about the regulation. It was obvious now that the major knew how hot it was out at LZ Sandy.

"Well . . ." Jones rubbed his chin, ". . . Captain . . . if you can get the Seabees to prepare the sites for the bunkers in the next three days, I can have those bunker kits delivered by the end of the week by chopper. Have a Roman numeral I placed where you want a sixteen footer and a Roman numeral II placed on the perimeter where you'll want the standard model kit. I know the officer who commands our heavy-lift chopper company, and it shouldn't be too much of a problem to squeeze you into our schedule."

"I really appreciate your help, Jones." Luke adjusted his pistol belt. Wherever the belt or the holster had touched his fatigues, the cloth was saturated with sweat.

"I'll figure out a way to collect from you. Hell, if you stay in Vietnam much longer, you'll know every fucking person by name!" Jones pointed over to the ammunition storage tents. "Those have to go, Captain."

"What's that, Sarge?"

"Those ammo tents. You need bunkers for your powder charges and projectiles. I'd say two fifty-by-thirty footers . . ." Jones used his thumb and little finger on his right hand to judge the scale of the bunker sizes.

"That would be a bit much to ask of you," Luke grinned, "but what the hell . . . would you have that kind of material on hand at Camp Eagle?"

"Does a bear shit in the woods?" Jones hooded his eyes. "Does an owl shit through feathers? Now ask me; does Master Sergeant Jones have engineer building materials?"

"Come on, Sarge, let's get out of this heat and see what the colonel has been up to. I'm worried about my men. I saw what Specialist Dotson looked like in the showers, and if there are worse cases than his in the battery . . . shit!''

Luke and Jones used the inner-permeter road to walk around the guns and passed the battery first sergeant and a small group of NCOs who were charter members of the old battery commander's clique. Jones nodded a greeting and was answered by hate-filled glares. "It looks like those NCOs have attitude-adjustment problems, Captain.''

"I've got a feeling that this battery has been a dumping grounds for the battalion's misfits and drunks.''

"Really?'' Jones maintained his step with Luke's and glanced back at the group of malcontent noncommissioned officers. "You know I've got a friend of mine in the 101st who would love to be the first sergeant in a field artillery battery. He's half black and half Spanish-Irish and all hard-core paratrooper. That would be the only problem; getting him to come off jump status.''

"Give it a try. I could use a good top sergeant to help me square away this shit.''

"I'll ask him, but even if he agrees to come here, it'll still take some real good personnel work to insure that he's assigned to your battery. If your battalion commander is as bad as rumors say he is . . .'' Jones felt his face turning red. He had just slipped and said too much.

"Rumors?'' Luke stopped walking and grabbed his friend's arm. "Rumors?''

"Shit! If I tell you . . . you'd better not tell anyone else or I'll have my asshole relocated to under my arm by the division artillery commander.''

"What's going on, Jones?'' Luke's voice deepened. He sensed that there was more to all of this additional voluntary support than met the eye.

"Your Lieutenant Colonel Jeffers is a well-known, classic asshole in artillery circles. Our division artillery people hate him and even the division commander would like to see Jeffers get his due—and they're classmates from West Point!"

"So all of this building material and . . ." Luke looked over at the orderly room, "high-level medical help is all because of . . ."

Jones cut Arrowood off in mid-sentence. "Not the doc . . . he really wanted to come out here when your name was mentioned to thank you personally for what you had done for his son."

"Fuck! Motherfucking *politics*!" Luke slammed his right fist into his left palm.

"Luke . . ." Jones used his friend's first name, ". . . hey, buddy . . . that shooting incident has spread throughout Vietnam. You might not know it, but it has created a lot of high-level interest. Some people want to hang your ass and some want to make sure that your ass *isn't* hung." Jones started walking again. "Now you know the real reason you're going to be getting a *lot* of help from the 101st Airborne Division. You have friends there who want to help. If we can't nip this racial shit in the *bud*, it'll spread like a cancer to all of our units in Vietnam."

"Thus the offer of the first sergeant?" Luke smiled.

"Yeah . . . he's about the best that there is."

"Thanks . . ." Luke was sincere. It felt good knowing that there was still a system out there in the Army that gave a fuck. It was operating in secret, but it was still there among the career officers who were punching their tickets during the Vietnam War gathering all of the *right* assignments with just enough time spent commanding units and working on the *right* staffs; and of course, *winning* the *right* awards.

The door was closed to Luke's office when they entered the orderly room. A dozen troops were waiting to see the doctor, and there were a couple more standing next to the clerk's desk cutting the legs off their jungle fatigues. As soon as they saw Arrowood and Jones enter the building, the battery clerk spoke for the whole group. "Sir! The colonel has ordered all of us to wear cutoffs with no underwear until this rash is gone."

Luke nodded his head and waited until the door to his office opened and Sergeant Cole stepped out followed by the colonel. The black sergeant went over to Arrowood and stopped in front of him. "Thanks, sir. The men really needed to see a doctor. A lot of us were really worried about this rash in our groin areas. I'm due to go to R&R in three weeks to see my wife."

Luke nodded again and went over to where the colonel was standing in his office doorway. "Come in here a minute, Captain Arrowood." He looked at the men who were waiting in line to see him. "This will only take a minute."

Luke felt the cool air against his face from the air conditioner. "Yes, sir."

Colonel Quinn sat down on the corner of the office desk and raised his arms over his chest before speaking. "I have never in my twenty-five years of service seen such a case of medical abuse! Your men are suffering from *severe* cases of erythrasma with lesions on their scrotums that have penetrated all of the way through the skin in some cases! It is unbelievable how those men could be expected to work when they're in so much pain!"

"Sir . . . I asked for help as soon as I knew . . ."

Quinn waved his hand at Luke. "I'm not holding you to blame. In fact, you've done the right thing. I've sent my helicopter back to Camp Eagle to get a special antibiotic that is particularly good in treating erythrasma, but . . . oh God! Some of those boys are very bad off. I might have to hospitalize them."

"Whatever it takes, sir." Luke's thoughts went to Jeffers. He knew that there was going to be big trouble when his battalion commander found out that he had gone outside of the battalion for help.

"It'll probably take a few hours for the chopper to return because of the large quantities of the antibiotic, called erythromycin, that we're going to need." Quinn stood up, signaling that he wanted to get back to treating the troops. "They might have to fly to one of the field hospitals, too, because I've ordered a Wood's light that will confirm if I'm right in my diagnosis. The light will reveal a characteristic coral-red fluorescence if it is erythrasma."

"Thanks for coming out here, sir."

"Also, Captain Arrowood, they're going to need vast quantities of water. I want each infected man to shower in *treated* water twice a day with an antibacterial soap."

"Sir, that could be a real problem right now."

Quinn waved his hand at the captain. "I've already taken care of that for you. Chinooks will be arriving shortly with five-hundred-gallon collapsible drums filled with treated water. Just have all of your showers emptied and cleaned so that they can be refilled."

"Most of the showers are already empty, sir, and I think the sun has sterilized the drums. That damn sun will sterilize anything in an hour!"

The colonel smiled. "I want your men to wear shorts until we get a handle on this infection."

Luke nodded.

"Now let me get back to work!" Quinn opened the door and waved for the next man to enter as Luke left the office.

Lieutenant Fields called an in-battery cease-fire when the Chinooks arrived so that the large helicopters could drop a five-hundred-gallon collapsible drum near each one of the showers, or close enough by it so that the drum could be rolled over to where the water could be hand-pumped up into the fifty-five-gallon drums. None of the troops complained about the sand and dirt the choppers kicked up because they knew that the water was for them and there was lots of it!

CHAPTER FOUR

✪✪✪✪✪✪✪✪✪✪✪✪✪✪✪✪✪

BUILDING!

The fire-support base at Hai Lang had transformed from an open garbage pit into a well-designed fighting camp in the first three weeks of Captain Arrowood's command. The 101st Airborne Division had not only sent out the building materials for the new bunkers, but had sent an engineer platoon along with the needed supplies. Master Sergeant Jones had accompanied the Army builders, and a good-natured rivalry had developed between the Navy Seabees and the Army engineers that turned into a contest to see who could do the most work each day. The Seabees were famous throughout Vietnam for the tremendous amount of construction they did each day. The Seabee bulldozer operators had built a ten-foot-high berm around LZ Sandy, working at night after they had returned from their main job rebuilding Highway 1 during the day. It was rare at night when the artillerymen couldn't hear the sound of the heavy dozers. The whole atmosphere in the fire-support base changed from apathy to one of old-fashioned American competitiveness.

There were only a few of the artillerymen who still suffered from the erythrasma infections and they were healing rapidly from the more severe cases. Colonel Quinn had made sure that one of his division doctors went out to the fire-support base daily to check on the men. The influential officer also used his connections with the 101st staff to have mechanics and special staff personnel sent out to LZ Sandy to bring all of the vehicles off dead-line, especially the much-needed water truck. The battery medics were supplied with adequate medicine to combat heat infections and chemicals with which to treat the water for the showers so that they could pump water right out of a nearby river instead of having to go all the way to Camp Red Devil for it.

Captain Arrowood sat at the mess hall table across from the Seabee lieutenant. "I can't thank you or your men enough for what you've done for my men."

"Believe me, *Captain* . . . it was a mutually rewarding experience. My men had a chance to catch up on their sleep and they enjoyed making the Army engineers look bad . . ."

"Hold on there, Lieutenant!" Jones sat his Styrofoam cup of iced Kool-Aid down on the field table. "I can't see where you Navy types did all that much work around here! Pushing a little sand around with bulldozers ain't all that much."

The Navy officer smiled. His Seabee detachment had performed superbly and everyone knew it. They had not only built over a mile and a half of berm for the fire-support base, but they had brought in all of the extra tar and oil from their highway construction job and rebuilt the inner perimeter road from the main entrance around the southern side of the base back to the FDC where the vast majority of road traffic occurred to hold down the dust. "Well, we enjoyed our stay here, but they need us to do some work up near the DMZ."

"Thanks again." Luke stood up and shook hands with the lieutenant. He hadn't told the officer, but he had signed the paperwork for an Army Meritorious Service Medal for the lieutenant and his men that the 101st Airborne Division had promised to staff for them.

Arrowood sat back down again at the table after the Navy officer departed from the mess tent. He listened to the background noise of his men laughing and talking to each other as they ate their lunch. "I hate to see those guys leave."

Jones placed both of his hands on the edge of the table and leaned back slightly in his chair. "We're gone too in the morning."

Luke nodded his head. "I could never have pulled this off by myself . . . you know that."

Jones smiled. "What are jump buddies for if they don't help each other out every once in a while?"

"Yeah." Luke felt the beginning of tears coating his eyes and blinked rapidly to stop their progress. He looked over at the tables filled with happy artillerymen and slowly shook his head from side-to-side.

"I heard from our division personnel people that Master Sergeant Verduzco has accepted the job as your battery first sergeant, now all you have to do is get rid of that fucking trash." Jones glanced over at the table of NCOs who were from the old battery clique and who had done very little during the reconstruction of the fire-support base, besides get in the way of those men who had wanted to work.

"I'm going back to the battalion headquarters as soon as I finish eating and I've got a strong feeling the battalion commander is calling me there to *discuss* what I'm doing out here. I think that will be a good time to tell him that he can find another job for him." Luke stared directly into the eyes of the hostile NCO. "How in the hell can someone promote people like him?"

"Hey, sir, the *officer* corps has their losers, too." Jones rubbed his upper lip with his index finger to hide the smile on his face.

"I can't argue that point, Jonesy." Luke pushed himself away from the table. "Specialist Dotson is waiting to drive me back to Camp Red Devil . . . if I'm not back in the morning by the time you have to leave . . ." Luke held out his hand and shook hands firmly with Jones. *"Thanks."*

Dotson saw Captain Arrowood leaving the mess tent and started the jeep's engine. Pilgrim was riding in the back of the jeep carrying Arrowood's CAR15 submachine gun. Luke had decided he would carry a pistol while he commanded the battery as a measure of showing trust in his men. He had told them *his* job was to plan and make sure that they did their jobs and they would all go home alive. During the three-week period, all of the men had test-fired their weapons and all of the crew-served weapons had been test-fired by the men assigned to them. Over half of the machine-gun crews had not fired a machine gun since completing their advanced individual training. Luke had been livid when he had heard that from the men and had chewed the first sergeant's ass. There was no way the men could have any confidence in their weapons if they didn't know how to fire them. The first sergeant's excuse was that they were *artillerymen* and only needed to know how to fire their howitzers.

Luke nodded at the two men as he removed the large piece of cardbord off the passenger seat and stored it on the floor in the back. The cardboard kept the canvas seat from becoming too hot to sit on. "Camp Red Devil, if you please, driver." Luke tried making light of what he knew was going to be a very unpleasant trip.

The last of the Seabee vehicles was pulling out of the main gate, and Dotson was forced to wait for the small convoy to clear the opening in the berm. The Seabees had constructed the entrance so that the berms would overlap, and a very sharp turn was required at the entrance if you were coming from the direction of the mess hall and orderly room. The entrance had been designed to accommodate the large five-ton trucks from battalion that hauled in the artillery rounds. When the trucks left the main road into the camp, they had a straight shot at the overlapping entrance to the inner-perimeter road so that they could pull around into the ammunition unloading point without having to do a lot of jockeying around. During the night, one of the M-48 main battle tanks would block the entranceway behind the rolls of concertina wire. The tank made an effective gate.

Luke looked back at the bunkerline as they drove slowly past behind the Seabee vehicles. Jones had come up with an excellent idea of putting hinged plywood flaps over the firing ports in the bunkers to keep out the constantly blowing sand and dust and at the same time allow for the men to have lights in the bunkers at night. The man on guard duty would sit behind a sandbag wall on top of the bunker, which made it a perfect setup when he moved the battery personnel out of the tents they had been sleeping in out to the bunkers. At first the men resented the idea, but they had quickly accepted sleeping in the new bunkers with the built-in bunks and ammo box storage areas. They could open the firing port flaps at night and get a cool breeze blowing through the bunker, but the best factor was that they were already inside of their assigned fighting positions in the event of a ground or mortar attack. The men who were already on duty on the howitzers were protected inside of the old personnel bunkers and inside of the howitzer itself. Luke had changed the operating procedures so that if a man was off duty, he would know that he stayed inside of his fighting bunker during a ground attack. The tactic eliminated needless exposure during the critical initial assault the NVA would make where mortars and rockets were firing. Luke had also made it a policy that each man would automatically throw two M26 hand grenades into the barbed wire that surrounded the camp before they did anything else during a ground attack or when the first enemy mortar round landed inside of the fire-support base. Luke had been in Vietnam for five years and knew that when the NVA started firing their mortars that their sappers were already inside of the camp's barbed wire. The grenades would solve that problem quickly.

The small group of Vietnamese peasants continued working in their rice paddies that ran at an angle to the northwest corner of the fire base. The nearest rice paddy was a little over a hundred meters from the corner bunker with the road running through the middle of the paddy complex. The fire-support base had been tucked in between a Vietnamese cemetery and the long stretch of rice paddies occupying the low ground. The base-camp site selection was poorly done because there were Vietnamese constantly visiting the graves of their ancestors and Vietnamese working in the fields and, until the berm had been built, they could see directly into the fire-support base from outside of the camp. One of the Vietnamese pulled his wide-brimmed bamboo peasant's hat down lower over his eyes. He kept his head down as if he were watching the convoy leaving the fire-support base. He had been scouting the Hai Lang base for over a month and had been leaving the fields every day with detailed drawings of the location of the howitzers and ammunition. The Navy Seabees had built the southwestern side of the berm first and had stopped his sketchings. He had already located the positions of the perimeter bunkers and the howitzers and he had drawn to scale on his map the location of the battery orderly room and mess hall, but his sapper commander had wanted a detailed map that showed even where the American latrines were located so that his unit could train and study the whole setup before they made their attack. It had been very bad luck for them that this new captain had been assigned to the battery. The local barber had told him that the captain was very energetic and was making many improvements inside of the camp. The barber had a small shop set up just outside of the camp as close as he could get to the perimeter, so that the soldiers could walk to his barbershop for haircuts. The old battery commander had tolerated the small plywood shack so close to his wire, but the new captain had forced him to move it back to the other side of the graveyard. He still got some business from the fire-support base, but not as much as before, so he added an attraction that brought the soldiers back again. He hired a Vietnamese whore who would give the waiting G.I.'s her personal services while they waited for their haircuts. The Vietnamese spy flexed his jaws and watched the hated American captain's jeep slow down and the officer look over at him. He had wanted to move the attack date for Hai Lang forward before the berm had been completed, but his commander was very cautious and wouldn't move that fast. The attack date remained the same, even though the base was now a much more difficult target than before.

Captain Arrowood watched the group of peasants moving down the field and noticed that one of them never changed the angle of his head. The peasant hat blocked the man's face so that Luke couldn't see his eyes, but he knew the Vietnamese was looking at him. He could feel it. Luke slowly lifted his arm off his lap and waved at the staring peasant. The Vietnamese's head changed its angle slightly, and Dotson pulled the jeep away from the group of Vietnamese and followed the convoy at a distance to escape from the dust cloud billowing up behind it.

Once Dotson turned the jeep onto Highway 1, the dust problem was over and the ride became a matter of dogging in and out of the convoys that cluttered the main highway that ran north and south along the South Vietnamese coast. Arrowood relaxed against the canvas seat and watched the activity in the rice and vegetable fields that lined the highway. The Vietnamese had moved away many of their small villages close to the main road for protection from both the Vietcong and from American artillery and air strikes.

Luke noticed a woman walking next to the highway holding the hands of a boy and a girl who were almost the same ages as his children. The incident caused his thoughts to leave Vietnam and return to where he had left his family in a comfortable beach house just a little north of Malibu, California, at a place called Point Dume. The area was very expensive and way out of his price bracket, but they had lucked out and leased a house from an older couple who had decided to go back east and visit their relatives before they got too old to travel; that had been four years ago, and his family had stayed on in the beautiful beach house without a rent increase. The only condition the owners had put on them was that his wife had to maintain the extensive flower gardens surrounding the house and send snapshots of the house and grounds back east once a month. The requirement was easy to comply with because his wife loved gardening.

Arrowood's eyes regained their focus when the jeep came to a complete stop behind a long convoy of ammunition trucks that blocked the road. Luke knew that they had reached the two-lane bridge and that a convoy of tanks was probably crossing it. A couple minutes later the roar of the tank engines and the clanking from the metal tracks reached them. Luke's mind slipped back to his family. Five years was a very long time to spend in Vietnam and a lot of people thought that he was crazy, especially when they saw the pictures of his wife and kids. He had lucked out and fallen in love with a raven-haired beauty who thought that having sex was the best thing on earth. They would spend his thirty-day leaves in between tours having sex at least once a day and the five-day R&Rs he got during his Vietnam tours were spent totally devoted to lovemaking in the truest sense of the word. He could not remember a single time when they had had sex when love wasn't the dominate reason for their union. Lust had never, not even when they had first met, entered their sexual life.

"We should be there in a half hour," Pilgrim yelled above the sound of the wind from the backseat.

Luke nodded his head and returned in his mind back to his family. He had already decided that this would be his last tour of duty in Vietnam. He had promised himself that he would remain for the complete war, but no one had ever dreamed that they would be there for seven years in Vietnam. He was getting a lot of pressure from the artillery branch to return back to Fort Sill, Oklahoma, for officer training, and most of all he was missing being with his family. He had done his duty and, even though he was going to have to break his pledge, he had done more than most of his peers. Luke removed the photograph of his wife and children he had embedded between two pieces of sticky acetate and stared at their faces. He was missing them very much.

"Nice family, sir!" Pilgrim could see the color photograph over Luke's shoulder.

Luke nodded his head and kept the photograph in his hand the rest of the way to Camp Red Devil and imagined that he was driving along California's Highway 1 that paralleled the same ocean, thousands of miles away, with his wife and children in the car with him.

The smell of burning shit was the first thing to alert them that they were close to Camp Red Devil. Luke felt that that was an appropriate way to announce the base camp for the 1st Brigade of the 5th Mechanized Infantry Division. The division that was stationed at Fort Carson, Colorado, had become infamous as a refuge for officers who were trying to dodge serving in Vietnam, but still get credit for serving in a line unit. They had been surprised when the Department of the Army froze all transfers within and out of the division and designated the 1st Brigade for duty in Vietnam.

Dotson slowed the jeep down to a fast walk when they passed the brigade headquarters because of the pedestrian traffic crossing the road. Luke brushed the dust off the sleeves of his jacket and felt his stomach muscles begin to tighten as they approached the artillery battalion headquarters buildings. The plywood sides of the administration hootches were painted gray and each one of the plywood and tin huts were identified by signs with red lettering and crossed cannons as to what activity was going on inside.

"Where do you want us to wait for you, sir?" Dotson leaned up against the steering wheel.

"You guys can make a PX run if you like, but be back in front of the battalion headquarters as soon as you can. I want to leave here the second this meeting is over with."

"You got it, Captain." Pilgrim placed the butt end of the short barreled CAR-15 submachine gun against his hip pocket and pointed the barrel up in the air so that a small group of passing soldiers could see the coveted weapon. CAR-15s were new in Vietnam and it was difficult for officers to get them, let alone a specialist fourth class.

Luke got out of the jeep and smiled. "Don't *lose* that weapon, Pilgrim!"

Pilgrim blushed. "Never happen, Captain!"

Lieutenant Colonel Jeffers watched Arrowood talking to his men and could see the smiles on their faces from his seat behind the Plexiglas in the air-conditioned portion of the mess hall. He nodded with his head. "Our young captain friend has arrived.'

Major Montgomery turned slightly on his chair and looked out of the window. "They seem like a happy bunch."

"When I get through with his ass, he'll think twice about smiling again!" Jeffers slashed through the pork chop on his plate with his steak knife.

Luke sucked in a deep breath and entered the battalion headquarters. The sergeant major had seen him getting out of the jeep and was waiting for him. "The colonel's over in the officers mess waiting for you . . ."

Luke stood facing the senior NCO without moving until the non-commissioned officer became very nervous. Luke smiled and continued staring.

". . . *sir*." The sergeant major knew what he had done wrong.

"Thanks, Sergeant Major." Luke started turning to leave.

"Sir . . . I don't like the way you've been treating some of the NCOs in Bravo Battery and I only think that it's fair that I tell you that to your face." The sergeant major was regaining his courage.

"And which of the NCOs are you referring to, Sergeant Major?"

"*Who* told me isn't important, it's what you've done to them that is."

"And what have you been told that I've done?" Luke knew how to play the cat-and-mouse game as well as anyone else did. He didn't like it, but he could play the game.

"You've degraded and embarrassed a number of the senior NCOs in the battery in front of their men . . . for starters."

"It would be much easier if you would use names, Sergeant Major, so that we can get down to the specifics and find out who said what to whom."

"The first sergeant for one. He's told me that you've just about relieved him of all duties and you've ridiculed him in front of the whole battery." The sergeant major tried glaring down Arrowood and only succeeded in making himself nervous and that made him angry. "And I've been told that you brought in some engineer master sergeant from the 101st to humiliate him even further."

"I don't know when you can find any one of the NCOs you are referring to sober enough to feel humiliated." Luke turned to leave the battalion headquarters and paused halfway around to look back at the sergeant major. "We both know that the group of NCOs we are talking about have all been sent out to Bravo Battery as *punishment*. They're the worst NCOs in this battalion, and I'm not going to punish my junior enlisted men anymore by forcing them to work for that kind of NCO. I'm sending all of them back there in the morning, including the first sergeant."

"When hell freezes over, Captain!" The sergeant major's face turned red. "The battalion commander and *me* make the non-commissioned officer assignments in this battalion, Captain!"

"Well, Sergeant Major . . . get ready to see hell being air-conditioned . . . because those four NCOs are leaving my battery in the morning."

"You'll never get any replacements from me and

that includes that damn airborne first sergeant you're trying to bring in here from the 101st!"

"I'd rather be *short* NCOs, than keep trash like that in my battery . . . and as far as First Sergeant Verduzco goes, that decision will be made by the battalion commander and myself."

"Bullshit, Captain! That decision has already been made!" The sergeant major could hear the clerks typewriters in the background clicking away at a faster than normal speed.

"Thanks for the information, Sergeant Major." Luke left the frustrated senior NCO standing with his hands on his hips in the center of the office, and went over to the officers mess. He paused outside of the closed door and took a couple of deep breaths in preparation for Round Two.

Major Montgomery looked up from his plate of food and smiled when Captain Arrowood entered the room with sweat dripping off his chin. "Here . . ." He handed Luke a cloth table napkin, "dry your face."

"Thanks, sir."

Lieutenant Colonel Jeffers sat staring at Luke from across the table like a vulture waiting for its prey to die or become so weak that it could attack. He even resembled the flying creature with his hooked nose and naturally dark rings around his eyes.

"We hear that you've been doing a quite a bit of building around LZ Sandy lately . . ." Montgomery used his fork to dig into the center of his mashed potatoes and removed a forkful of the butter-drenched potatoes. He smiled and shoved the food into his mouth.

"Yes, sir. We've rebuilt a number of bunkers and put up a ten-foot berm around the fire support-base . . ."

"Who . . . in . . . the . . . hell . . . gave . . . you . . . permission!" Jeffers spaced out his words perfectly trying to act enraged.

"I didn't think that I needed *permission* to build defenses for my battery, sir."

"You smart-assed son of a bitch!" Jeffers slammed his open palm down on the table.

Luke pushed his chair back and stood up. Jeffers had gone too far. "Sir, I will not sit here and have you curse me. If you wish, we can continue this conversation in the brigade commander's office."

The air caught in Jeffers's throat. No one had ever challenged him when he was performing his tantrum act, at least none of his subordinates had, and he would never do it in front of his peers let alone superiors. He knew that Arrowood had outmaneuvered him for the moment. "Sit down . . ." He changed his attitude instantly, trying to maneuver into a better position. "You do need permission to make major construction changes at a fire-support base." Jeffers smiled a phoney friendly grin. "At least you could have kept us informed as to what you were doing out there!" He patted Luke's shoulder.

"That's why I came here today, sir. To inform you on the changes that I've made and to gain your approval on a number of personnel changes that I'm recommending . . ."

"Personnel changes?" Jeffers flashed a look over at his executive officer and then back at Luke.

"Yes, sir. I would like to replace the first sergeant with a superb NCO out of the 101st Airborne Division and return three more NCOs, who haven't been performing their duties even at the minimum levels."

"Why hasn't anyone else complained about them before?" Jeffers jammed his fork down on his tin plate.

"I have no idea, sir."

"Well, what you're asking is impossible! You will just have to live with them the best that you can." Jeffers swept his right hand across the table as a sign that the topic was closed.

"Fine, sir, then I'll just leave this paperwork with you or your executive officer and head on back to my battery before it gets dark."

Montgomery sneered and blinked his eyes slowly.

"What's wrong, Captain Arrowood . . . are you afraid to spent a night back here?"

Luke refused to be baited. "No, sir, it's just that I feel a commander should be with his men, especially during a high-threat situation."

Jeffers had been scanning the paperwork Luke had handed him and felt the color draining out of his face. "What in the hell is this!"

Luke returned his attention to the battalion commander. "Charges for court-marshals for the four NCOs listed there, sir; dereliction of duty, drunk on duty, selling supplies to the enemy . . . I think everything is in order."

"What in the hell do you think you're doing!" Jeffers left his seat. "You will not press charges against non-commissioned officers in this battalion!"

"They're all documented and statements have been signed. The charges are true and it is my *duty* to see that charges are pressed against them . . . or that they're are transferred out of the battery so that they cannot continue their criminal activities and influence my soldiers."

Montgomery realized that Arrowood had come prepared and that there was nothing that they could do for the present. "Captain Arrowood, why don't you go clean up and run any errands you might have to do while the colonel and I discuss a few things? We can continue this conversation tonight over cocktails during Happy Hour." Montgomery's voice rose a little to check Jeffers from interrupting. "You can stay in the guest officers quarters for the night and your driver will be taken care of by the sergeant major."

"Yes, sir." Luke left the two officers at the table and went out to his jeep.

"That son of a bitch! Who does he think he is coming in here like that!" Jeffers felt his heart pounding in his chest.

"Relax!" Montgomery took control. "He outmaneuvered us. I didn't think he was that damn smart, but now we know and we can make adjustments to trap him!"

Jeffers drained the glass of ice water and slammed it back down on the tablecloth. "Did you read this?" He waved the stack of charges at his executive officer. "We can't submit this to brigade!"

"He knows that!" Montgomery was watching Arrowood through the window. "Let's give him what he wants. We'll reassign those NCOs within the battalion and let him have that airborne asshole for a first sergeant . . . rope . . . we'll burn his ass!" Montgomery was making sense to the battalion commander. "Tonight we'll have a chance to observe him . . . drunk!"

Jeffers smiled. "You're right. He's a newcomer to the battalion and should be initiated as a Redleg!"

Jeffers's and Montgomery's smiles matched each other.

The look on both Pilgrim's and Dotson's faces told Luke that they had been worried about him, and he broke out into a wide smile as he approached the jeep. "We're going to spend the night here. I'll be over at the officers guest quarters or at the officers club later this evening. I think they plan on getting me a *little* drunk tonight."

"What do you want us to do?" Dotson stretched behind the steering wheel.

"You're supposed to report to the sergeant major and he'll find you a place to sleep." Luke looked at his watch. "But before you report to him, why don't you take the jeep and check out downtown Quang Tri."

"All right!" Pilgrim's face lit up.

"Just don't leave the jeep unattended. One at a time!" Luke winked at the two men.

"No problem there, sir. I have never liked that two on one shit." Dotson reached over to start the jeep.

Pilgrim slapped the back of his friend's head. "Bull-shit, you Tennessee types like all that kinky shit!"

"*Georgia* is where all of that goat-fucking shit started!" Dotson ducked the next swing.

Luke reached behind the passenger's seat and removed his rucksack that contained a change of clothes and his shaving gear. "Don't screw up and make me have to come and get you from the MP station . . . A lot of people around here would like to see that happen."

"Don't worry about us, sir. We won't let you down." Pilgrim slipped forward onto the passenger seat. "Thanks, sir."

Luke patted the fender. "See you guys in the morning. We leave here as soon as the road opens."

"Yes, sir!" Pilgrim looked over at Dotson. "Come on! Move this thing . . . my cock is already hard!"

Luke slipped his rucksack over his left shoulder and started walking toward the officers quarters. Montgomery watched him through the window. "He brought gear with him to spend the night. He had already guessed that we were going to ask him to spend the night back here." Montgomery tapped his closed lips with his index finger and slipped into a deep thought. Arrowood was going to be a very tough nut to crack.

The visiting officers quarters for the battalion were located near the sandbagged battalion FDC in the rear section of a long hootch that had been subdivided into individual rooms for the battalion's permanent cadre of officers. Luke noticed when he entered the building that the visiting officers section contained only the very bare items; a canvas folding cot and an ammo box nailed to a couple of upright two-by-fours that used to contain two main gun rounds for a tank. Luke didn't mind the Spartan furnishings because he knew that he would be spending only one night there, but he was a little upset when he had seen all of the small air conditioners sticking out of the sides of the hootch. He wondered how much of the plywood and building materials that it took to close in the rooms for the air conditioners was supposed to have been shipped out to the batteries in the field. Luke dropped his rucksack down on one of the empty bunks across from the cot that already had someone's gear on it. He went over and rotated the duffel bag until he could read the officer's name that had been stenciled on the new canvas: 2LT OSCAR INGRAM. Luke smiled, if the man's name had anything to do with what he would look like, Oscar Ingram would be a skinny man with thick glasses and would talk with a high voice.

Luke looked at his watch and decided on walking over to the brigade headquarters and visit Major Redmond, the brigade provost marshal, and follow up on the Talbot Incident. He had been briefed that the case was closed and that there wouldn't be any charges brought against him or any of the other men. The autopsy had shown that Talbot had been under the influence of three drugs at the time of the shooting.

The brigade headquarters was within easy walking distance of the artillery sector of the large base camp, and Luke took his time getting over there. He walked past a group of soldiers who were sitting on the edge of the stage that had been built across from the artillery battalion headquarters and was used for USO shows and command briefings to the troops. The area was used by all of the troops stationed at Camp Red Devil, but because the artillery had volunteered to build the stage, the area was called the Artillery Bowl. Luke wondered again just how much of the plywood and building materials in the stage was supposed to have been shipped out to his battery. He noticed that all of the soldiers on the stage were black and they were listening to heavy soul music coming from speakers that had been placed in the windows of a nearby hootch.

The soldiers stopped talking and stared at Arrowood as he walked past them as if to tell him that he was passing through some very dangerous territory and the only thing that prevented him from being attacked was the fact that the sun was still shining. They waited until Arrowood had passed out of hearing range and one of the black soldiers who had been sitting on the edge of the stage dropped down and turned around to face the rest of the group. "He's that motherfucker who killed our brother!"

"How do yu know dat!" A very large black soldier spoke up from the end of the group on the stage.

"Cause I know! He's that motherfucker! Captain Arrowood! Didn't you read his name tag?"

"He gotsta die!' The large black soldier leaned forward and rocked back and forth chanting under his breath. "He gotsta die . . . he gotsta die!"

Luke saw the sign for the provost marshal's office and entered the building from the rear. He saw Major Redmond sitting behind his desk talking to one of his lieutenants. Redmond looked up and smiled. "Luke Arrowood! Good seeing you again. What brings you to Camp Red Devil?"

Luke shook hands with the major. "The battalion commander called me back for a bunch of briefings."

"I hear that you've done wonders out at LZ Sandy."

"We've made a lot of improvements and cleaned up the place." Luke looked down at the floor. He was a little bit embarrassed because everybody in the office had stopped working and were watching.

"I'm not talking about the bunkers and stuff. I'm talking about your men."

"Yeah .. . we had some medical problems that have been taken care of . . ."

"Stop the bullshit!" Redmond cut Luke off. "I'm talking about your reassigning some of your personnel like PFC Jenkins to the fire-direction center for on-the-job training as a chart man."

Luke understood what the black major was driving at. He had assigned a number of the black soldiers out of the all-black ammunition section to jobs that were normally all white. "Well . . . Jenkins is a good man. The problem with young soldiers like him is that they don't take the *initial* battery of tests seriously when they go through the reception stations during their enlistments and then they end up in low-IQ categories for training selections." Luke avoided referring to races but Redmond knew exactly what he was talking about.

"I agree with you. Someone should tell them how important those tests are before they take them."

"They do, sir, but you know how kids are when they first come off the streets. What they should do is have a retest during basic before they make the school assignments and I think a lot of those kids would score higher."

"That's a good idea! I just might write that up and send it back to the Pentagon for staffing."

"Good luck!" Luke started laughing. He could see what that recommendation would look like after the Pentgagon staff had finished *staffing* it. The one-page idea would end up filling a boxcar. "Well, I just stopped by to say hello. I've got to get back to my battalion and clean up for Happy Hour with my leaders."

Redmond's face darkened. "Watch out, young man. Jeffers has a reputation for . . ."

Luke held up his hand to stop the major from saying anything else. "I know, sir . . ."

Soldiers from around the whole base camp were starting to assemble at the Artillery Bowl for the first movie of the evening on the outdoor screen when Luke made his return trip to the battalion. He had checked with the brigade administration personnel on his battery's awards and promotions, and had found out that most of his recommendations were still hung up in the artillery battalion headquarters. He had brought copies of all of his back paperwork with him just in case something like that had happened. There were award recommendations that were over six months old that had not been forwarded from his battery to the battalion when he had taken over command. Troops had rotated back to the States without having even been given a handshake from the unit. Luke had won over a couple of the personnel officers and NCOs, and they had promised a follow-up on the copies for awards and promotions he had left with them.

Luke was fighting his anger as he walked down the road toward his quarters. Bravo Battery hadn't received a promotion allocation in over four months, but the brigade records showed that the battalion had received hundreds of allocations that included all of the grades, except for sergeant major.

The new lieutenant was sitting on his cot smoking a cigarette when Luke entered. He stood and came to the position of attention when he saw the double bars on Luke's collar. "Evening, sir!"

"Sit down, Oscar." Luke used his hand to wave the second lieutenant back down on his cot.

"Have we met before, sir?" The new officer seemed confused.

"No . . . I read your name off your duffel bag earlier."

"Oh . . ." The skinny officer smiled and Luke could see that the lines around the man's eyes behind his thick glasses were formed from frequent smiling.

"Where have you been assigned?"

"Bravo Battery, sir . . ." Oscar's smile left his face.

"What's wrong with that?"

"I hear the battery commander out there is crazy." Oscar lit up another cigarette using the one in his hand to light the new one.

"Who told you that?" Luke smiled and unbuttoned his dirty fatigue jacket. He laid it on his cot and then opened his rucksack.

"Major Montgomery briefed me on my assignment earlier this morning. They want me to go out to LZ . . ." Oscar inhaled as he tried remembering the name of the landing zone.

"Sandy."

"Yes, sir . . . LZ Sandy." He exhaled as he spoke. "I scored fairly high in gunnery and they want me to square away the FDC out there."

"And what about Lieutenant Fields?"

"Who, sir?"

"He's the FDC officer for Bravo Battery."

"I think they're going to make him a forward observer with one of the infantry companies." Oscar felt nervous and glanced up at the captain. "Do you know him, sir?"

"You'll get to know most of the officers assigned to this battalion shortly . . ." Luke took his shaving kit with him and a towel and opened the screen door. "I'll see you at Happy Hour?"

"Yes, sir! The battalion commander has personally invited me!"

"Good . . ." Luke walked down the 155mm projectile dunnage back behind the last building to the officers showers.

Lieutenant Oscar Ingram butted his cigarette in the empty coffee can next to his cot and frowned. He didn't like it how the captain had just left the hootch in the middle of their conversation. Ingram went over to where the captain had laid his fatigue jacket and turned it over so that he could read the name tag.

"Oh shit . . ." Oscar lit up another cigarette.

Lieutenant Colonel Jeffers and Major Montgomery both looked up at the same time when Luke entered the air-conditioned officers club. Luke glanced at the faces of the assembled officers and smiled a greeting.

"You're a little late, Captain." Jeffers was already on his second martini. "Happy Hour starts at nine o'clock sharp in this battalion."

"I didn't know, sir. I had a couple of things to check on tonight because we're leaving for LZ Sandy as soon as the road has been cleared for mines by the engineers." Luke took the offered seat across from the battalion commander. "And I had to check with my executive officer."

"No problem . . . what are you drinking?" Jeffers smiled from behind the edge of his glass.

"Beer . . . is fine."

"Not tonight, Captain!" Montgomery waved his finger at Luke. "You have to be properly introduced to the rest of the battalion's officers and made a Redleg!"

The assembled officers all raised their glasses and cheered.

"You should have told me that you were going to have a special party for me, sir!"

"Don't let your ego get in your way. Lieutenant Ingram is being *honored* also." Jeffers's fangs showed for second and so did his hate for Luke. "Have you met your new FDC officer yet?"

Ingram's face turned beet red.

"Yes, I have. Thank you, Colonel. He is top-quality officer material and I'll be glad to have him."

"We're assigning Fields to the field." Jeffers giggled and added. "*Fields* to the *field* . . . I like the sound of that; Fields to the field."

"One thing, sir." Luke leaned back in his chair. It was going to be a long night. "Why is a second lieutenant replacing a first lieutenant?"

"Fields is a second lieutenant! Christ, man, don't you know your own officers?"

"Lieutenant Fields was promoted to *first* lieutenant yesterday, sir . . . according to the orders I just saw up at brigade personnel today."

"What in the hell are you doing up there!" Jeffers almost choked on his martini. "Don't you know the chain-of-command?"

"Yes, sir, I do, but I thought that applied to *people*, not staff departments."

"Don't get fucking smart with me, Captain! You will go through all of the battalion staff officers from now on for whatever you need, and that includes *medical* aid!" The martinis were beginning to talk for the colonel.

Luke could see the battalion surgeon glaring at him from across the room. The battalion medical officer had received a letter of reprimand in his files over the erythrasma epidemic in Bravo Battery after the commanding general of the 101st Airborne Division had written the brigade commander a personal note on the subject.

"Yes, sir. Excuse me while I get myself a drink." Luke felt like he could use a beer.

"We have one coming for you . . . sit down." Montgomery waved for the officer at the bar to bring the drinks over.

Luke watched and fought the smile that was trying to break out on his face. He had guessed right; they were going to try and get him very drunk and then probably set him up for an incident so that they could relieve him. The officer sat one of the potato chip cans down in front of Luke and handed the other one over to Lieutenant Ingram. "Welcome to the 4th Battalion, 5th Artillery! The fightingest artillery unit in Vietnam! Toast!"

Luke looked down into the can and saw that it had been filled to the brim with a mixture of different kinds of booze. He held the can in both hands and commented softly. "I don't know if we're all that *fightingest* if it takes us an hour to clear our fire missions."

Jeffers was about to lay into Luke but Montgomery grabbed his leg under the table and stopped him. "Drink up, Captain Arrowood!"

Luke placed the edge of the can to his lips and drank deeply. He had lowered the mixture of whiskey and booze halfway in the can before he sat the can down on the table. Even Jeffers was impressed, but the officer who had mixed the drinks was shocked. He had put a lot of soda in Lieutenant Ingram's can but in Luke's he had used only different kinds of booze.

"Good drink . . . what do you call it?" Luke looked directly into the eyes of the captain who was acting as the bartender.

"An Artillery Royal."

"I might want a second one later on." Luke looked back over at Jeffers. "Can we have the battalion S-1 check on Bravo Battery's awards and promotions, sir?"

"What's the problem?" A fat captain spoke up from the table next to the one Luke was sitting at.

"Bravo hasn't received any promotions in four months." Luke sipped again from the can.

"That's because we haven't received any promotions to give out." The captain kept glancing over at Montgomery as he spoke.

"Not true." Luke picked up the can and drained the remainder of the booze. The can held almost a fifth of liquid. "Excuse me a second, sir. I need to run over to my hootch and I'll be right back." He staggered a little when he stood up and that brought smiles to Jeffers's and Montgomery's faces.

"Sure . . . go get whatever you want to . . . just make sure you're back here in *two* minutes or I'll send someone to drag you back!" Jeffers chuckled.

"Two minutes . . . sir!" Luke left the officers club and hurried over to the row of sandbags that surrounded the closest officer's hootch. He knew that all of the officers would be at the club for Happy Hour and had stashed his supplies underneath a corner sandbag. He hurried to removed the canteen and paused only for a second before he held the green container to his mouth and drank deeply. The reaction was almost instantaneous. He threw up all over the side of the sandbags in a huge spray of booze. Luke gagged twice and threw up again. He looked back at the officers club hoping that they would give him another minute as he wiped his mouth with the towel he had hidden there after carefully removing the hunk of butter from its folds. Luke shoved the butter in his mouth and nearly gagged trying to swallow it. He wiped the grease off his face and stashed the towel back under the sandbags along with his canteen mixture of mustard and warm water.

"That took you exactly four minutes, Captain!" Jeffers threw back his head and laughed. He was on his fourth martini and was feeling very good.

"Sorry, sir. It took me a little longer than I thought it would to find these papers in the dark." Luke handed the S-1 papers that he had brought with him and had hidden in his side pocket all along. "As you can see, this battalion has had over a hundred allocations for promotion in the past four months from Brigade personnel." Luke looked directly at Major Montgomery. "Your S-1 is a liar."

"Now, let's not get too personal here, Captain Arrowood!" Montgomery slurred his words.

Luke could feel the effects from the portion of the Artillery Royal that had worked its way past his defenses. Lieutenant Ingram had tried keeping up with Luke and had finished his drink and even though it had been a lighter mixture, it had hit his small body hard. He was very drunk and fell off of his chair onto his floor.

"One down and one to go!" someone in the back of the club screamed out.

"You don't have a drink in front of you." Jeffers motioned for the bartender to fix Luke another drink.

"Make that a beer . . ." Luke waved over at the officer mixing drinks.

"No one drinks beer tonight!" Jeffers pointed at the bartender. "Mix him a *good* martini and bring me another one!"

"Does this go on every night, sir?" Luke smiled and tried acting a little drunk when he spoke to Montgomery.

"We do *relax* a little bit after duty hours . . . if that's what you mean. Don't you?"

"Duty hours are twenty-four hours a day out at LZ Sandy, sir."

"Don't pull that crap on me!" Montgomery tried standing up, but his legs refused to support him and he dropped back down in his chair. "No one can work twenty-four hours a day!"

"True, sir, but I'm *on-call* twenty-four hours a day." Luke was beginning to feel only disgust for Jeffers and Montgomery.

"Drink up!" The officer acting as the bartender sat

the jigger of martini down next to the colonel and
poured Luke a glassful over a fat olive.

"My wife sends me those olives from the States.
You can't find good ones over here, not for martinis!"
Jeffers shoved his olive into his mouth and smacked
his lips as he ate it. Luke could see that he was getting
very drunk.

The party lasted until two in the morning and Luke
had to make his trip back to the sandbags two more
times. He was feeling drunk, but could still walk and
function properly compared to the other officers who
had been drinking. Both Jeffers and Montgomery had
passed out on the table, and Jeffers was snoring
loudly. The bartender watched Luke lift Ingram up
off the floor and throw him over his shoulder. The
small lieutenant groaned but didn't struggle. Luke
paused in the doorway. "See you for breakfast?"

The bartender shook his head. "You're fucking
amazing!"

Luke felt the warm air as soon as he stepped out
of the air-conditioned building. The effect on Ingram
from the warm air and bouncing made him vomit all
down the back of Luke's uniform. "Thanks, buddy!"
Luke carried the junior officer back to their quarters
and rolled him off his shoulder down on his bunk.
"Sleep tight, kiddo . . . we travel early in the
morning."

Luke went over to the showers and removed only
his boots before stepping under the warm water. He
rinsed the vomit off his back and then slipped out of
his uniform. It had been a long day and the shower
felt good. He stayed under the showerhead until he
had used up all of the water in the tank and then dried
off. He walked naked back to the hootch in the dark
and laid the wet uniform out on the sandbags to dry
along with the towel. He could still feel the warmth
from the sunheated bags that circled the hootch six
feet off the ground and were used to protect sleeping
personnel from a surprise rocket or mortar attack.

The barrel of the M-16 poked out from behind the

corner of the sandbags of the next hootch down from where Luke was staying. The large black soldier and his buddy had been waiting all night for Luke to return to his hootch and both of them had fallen asleep. Luke had woken them up when he laid out his uniform on the sandbags, but they were both still very sleepy from the marijuana they had smoked earlier while they were waiting for Luke to return.

"Shoot the motherfucker!" The smaller black soldier hissed the words out between his clenched teeth.

The large black fumbled with the safety switch on the M-16 and mumbled a little louder than his friend. "Fuck this damn thing!"

Luke heard the man's voice and turned to see who would be up so late at night in the sleeping area. He saw the barrel of the M-16 sticking around the corner of the sandbags and part of the man's shoulder. Luke dove between the building and the sandbag wall just as the black soldier pulled the trigger, sending a full magazine of rounds into the dunnage, sidewalk, and sandbags. The space between the hootch and the sandbags was only a couple of feet wide and Luke felt the wooden edge of the building scrape against his chest and thighs and then he hit the ground and had the wind knocked out of his lungs. He struggled for his breath and crawled under the building a couple of feet at the same time. He figured that they would come looking for him and continued struggling to regain his breath.

"Let's get the motherfuck out of here!" The smaller black soldier slapped his partner's shoulder.

"I think I hit him. He fell down between the sandbags!" The large black stood up and took a step toward the visiting officer's hootch before his friend stopped him.

"Let's go! The MPs will be here soon!"

"I wants tu check tu mak'sur!"

"By you'self motherfucker! I's gone!" The smaller black soldier started running toward his hootch. The larger man hesitated and then followed him.

Luke felt the first lungful of air enter his lungs and the dizzy feeling went away. He continued crawling under the building until he reached the steps at the far end and cautiously crawled out from under the building into a circle of officers who had exited the hootch when they heard the rifle shots and were standing around in various stages of undress.

The officer who had been acting as the bartender in the club looked down and saw Luke emerge from underneath the building. "Well, look what the night has brought us . . ."

Luke staggered to his feet and tried brushing the dirt off his naked body but the blood from the deep scrape marks was acting as a glue for the dirt.

The bartender turned his flashlight on Luke and whistled. "Looks like you're going to need a medic there, Captain."

Luke nodded his head. The scrapes were starting to burn. He took the offered towel from one of the officers standing nearby and wrapped it around his waist.

"The battalion surgeon's office is the next hootch over." The bartender's voice was much more friendly than it had been in the club.

Major Redmond had been called over to the artillery battalion's surgeon's office by the brigade commander to investigate the shooting incident, and he found both Jeffers and Montgomery so drunk that neither of them could get out of bed and appear at the office. He made a point out of putting their condition in his report that would be seen not only by the brigade commander but by the Marine commanding general the brigade was attached to.

Major Redmond looked down at Luke, who was laying on a raised stretcher in the surgeon's office. The battalion medical officer was still a little bit drunk from the party, but he could function well enough to take care of Luke's scrapes.

"It looks like some of these cuts will leave scars." The surgeon wiped a cloth that had been soaked in an antiseptic over Luke's seeping wounds.

"I was afraid that something like this might happen when you visited Camp Red Devil." Redmond shook his head.

"Like what?" Luke flinched when the surgeon's antiseptic cloth went over a small piece of rock that had been caught in one of the deeper gashes.

"Talbot was a part of a larger militant movement." Redmond glanced around the room at the staring faces of the officers who had helped carry Luke to the aid station. "We have a serious problem back here and I have a feeling that this incident was just the opening shot, so to speak."

One of the officers handed Luke his spare set of jungle fatigues and boots after the surgeon had finished dressing the scrapes. He sat up on the stretcher and slipped on his trousers. "You've got your problems back here, sir, and I've got mine out at LZ Sandy." Luke looked out of the open window and saw that it was daylight. "I'm gone as soon as my men have eaten breakfast . . . that is, unless you have a reason to keep me here?"

Redmond shook his head. "I have no reason and I don't think your battalion commander or his executive officer will be up before noon."

Luke looked over at Captain Kreps. "You're the S-3 and next in command."

"No, I don't see a reason to hold you back here. Just be gone before noon."

"Rest assured on that one, Kreps!" Luke had a difficult time bending over to lace his boots, but he forced himself to the task so that there wouldn't be any reason to keep him back in the rear area.

Dotson was sitting on the hood of the jeep eating an egg-and-bacon sandwich on toast, and Pilgrim sat on the other side of the hood eating from a huge plate of scrambled eggs covered with chipped beef.

"You guys hungry or something?" Luke approached the pair from behind.

"Starved, sir!"

"Did you have a good time down at the ville?"

"I burned up a hundred thousand calories!" Pilgrim talked as he slipped off the hood and climbed on the rear seat of the jeep.

"You guys ready to go home?"

"Hell, yes!" Dotson crammed the last bite of the sandwich in his mouth and pulled himself behind the wheel.

"What did you'all do last night? Get drunk?" Luke eased himself down on the passenger's seat and groaned under his breath.

"Shit! I wish, sir! The sergeant major put us on perimeter guard!" Pilgrim looked at the remaining food on his plate and lost his appetite. He sat the paper plate down on the floor of the jeep. "Can you believe that shit, sir?"

"Sure can, soldier . . . I expected something like that." Luke looked over at the officers eating breakfast in the air-conditioned mess hall and noticed that the battalion commanders table was empty.

Dotson shifted gears and pulled away from the hootch slowly. "Say, Captain, did you hear about the shooting last night? Some fuckers tried greasing an officer."

Luke smiled. "Yeah, so I heard." He changed the subject. "Pull over by the visiting officers hootch. We have to pick up a new lieutenant."

CHAPTER FIVE

✪✪✪✪✪✪✪✪✪✪✪✪✪✪✪

NVA SAPPERS!

Lieutenant Ingram spent most of the trip back to LZ Sandy hanging over the backseat of the jeep vomiting on Highway 1. He tried focusing his eyes on a distant object, but that failed to help because he was looking backwards and everything looked like it was being sucked into the object along the sides of the road.

Luke glanced back at the new lieutenant and smiled at Pilgrim, who was trying hard not to laugh. He removed his canteen from his webgear and handed it to his unofficial bodyguard. "Pour it over his head and let him drink a little."

Ingram moaned and tried turning around on the seat when he felt the refreshing water. "Oh shit! Never again. I swear I'll never get drunk again."

Dotson couldn't contain his laugh. "Sir, I've said that a million times!"

Ingram turned around slowly and using extreme care he looked through the windshield at the road. He felt better almost instantly when his eyes focused and his alcohol-numbed senses locked in on a familiar experience: sitting in a car that was moving down a road.

"We should be arriving at LZ Sandy very soon. The cutoff is a couple of miles down the road." Arrowood nodded at the canteen. "Rinse your face off and drink a little to settle your stomach."

Ingram felt another rush of nausea and rushed to lean over the side of the jeep before he dry-heaved the remainder of the trip to the entrance of the fire-support base.

"Dotson, pull in behind the orderly room and we'll let Lieutenant Ingram sleep it off in my room." Luke didn't want the rest of the battery to see the lieutenant in the condition he was in. Luke looked back over his shoulder. "Don't throw up again until you're in my room and then use the butt can!"

"Yes, sir." Ingram tried sitting up straight on the jump seat and had to swallow hard to keep from vomiting again when Dotson made the sharp U-turn inside the main entrance to go over to the orderly room.

The two soldiers waited in the jeep for Captain Arrowood to return from putting his gear away. Neither one of them said a word but they were both ready to burst out laughing. The lieutenant had made a complete ass out of himself.

Luke hopped on the front seat of the jeep. "I need to do a little quick running around inside the base. Drive me over to the motor pool."

Luke watched the troops working on the howitzers as they drove through the center of the base over to where the motor pool was set up along the northern perimeter. The motor sergeant stopped working on the dead-lined M548 ammunition vehicle and looked over at the approaching captain.

"Something I can do for you, sir?" the NCOs voice was filled with a nervous quiver. He was a member of the old clique, but he wanted to join Arrowood's new group. He hadn't really liked getting drunk every night at the fire base, but that was what it had taken to survive with the old captain, and he was a survivor.

"Yes, I need you or one of your mechanics who can weld to do something for me today, if possible."

"We've only got this one 548 down and we should have that running again in an hour or so . . ."

"Good!" Luke opened the box that was behind the seat in the jeep and removed a large garrison-sized American flag that was still wrapped in its plastic shipping package with a slip inside that gave its federal stock number. "I want you to make me a flag pole . . . as tall as you can . . . and set it up against that bunker . . ." Luke pointed to the bunker that guarded the main entrance to the fire-support base, "and have this flag flying before supper tonight. Can you do that?"

"Consider it done, sir." The sergeant took the flag from Luke and carefully laid it down on the front seat of the M548 he was working on. "I've got some pipe and tubing left over from the mess hall project that will do just fine."

Luke looked at the surprised expressions on Dotson's and Pilgrim's faces and commented. "This is an *American* base camp. The NVA and Vietcong know that we're here, now we got to let every American driving down that highway . . ." Luke pointed over at Highway 1, ". . . that *Americans* hold this ground."

"I can handle that, sir." Dotson liked the idea. A lot of the truck drivers who had to make the run from Quang Tri south didn't even know that there was an American base at Hai Lang where they could find sanctuary if they needed it. The flag would be able to be seen from miles away against the white sand.

"I expect you and Pilgrim to make sure that it's taken down at night and put back up again at first light."

"You got it, sir." Pilgrim liked the idea of flying an American flag and hoped that it would piss the Vietcong off.

Luke saw the first sergeant walking toward the motor pool and could tell that the NCO was highly pissed off by the way the sand flew up when the man kicked his heels. He was ready for the confrontation. "You guys go check on something." Luke dismissed Dotson and Pilgrim.

"*Sir*, I would like a word with you!"

"Sure . . . now?"

"Now!"

"Come on, we can go over to the berm and talk

where we can have some privacy. That bunker back
there should be empty."

"My off-duty mechanics are sleeping in there, sir."
The motor pool sergeant nodded toward the parts
tent. "You can use that tent if you like."

"Right here is fine." The first sergeant was angry
and didn't care who heard what he was going to say.
"Sir, I think that was really chickenshit the way you
stabbed us NCOs in the back!"

"How did I do that, Sergeant?" It was obvious that
Luke didn't use the title of *first* sergeant.

"Relieving us after all of the hard work we've done
for this battery!" He swept his hand out over the fire-
support base. "Look at it!"

Dotson and Pilgrim had only gone far enough away
to obey the captain's orders, but still remained in
hearing distance. They didn't want to miss what was
going on and neither did the rest of the battery. There
were rumors floating around since the captain had left
that the first sergeant was going to kick his ass when
he returned. The old NCO clique had partied hard
the night the captain had been gone and said a lot of
things that were left best unsaid. If a photograph of
the fire-support base would have been taken at that
instant from the air, it would have shown a circle of
men moving toward the motor pool so that they could
watch the confrontation between the new captain and
the old first sergeant.

"You're taking credit for the improvements on this
fire-support base?" Luke kept his voice calm.

"You're damn right I am! I'm the first sergeant and
I'm responsible for what the men do. Everybody
knows that officers bullshit more than they produce!"
The senior NCO clenched his fists.

"Take whatever credit you think you deserve, but
I want you and your three henchmen off this fire-
support base by noon."

"What if I tell you that we're not going and we have
backing from the battalion sergeant major."

"When did you talk to him last?"

"The day *before* you went to Camp Red Devil." The sergeant was trying to show Luke that he had been way ahead of him.

"You'd better check with him again, *today*. I think he's changed his mind and you'd better hurry because it's almost noon and I'm not going to change *my* mind."

The senior NCOs upper lip trembled. "I should kick your motherfucking ass!" He hissed the words out between his teeth.

"Lose fifty pounds and you might have a chance . . ." Luke looked over the sergeant's shoulder and saw the men watching. "You can use the land-line in the FDC to make your call. I'll have the water truck waiting for you in front of the orderly room." Luke smiled and winked at the ex-first sergeant. "We might as well get something out of the trip."

"I'll see you shortly, Captain!" The sergeant went storming off toward the FDC bunker and track.

The helicopter from the 101st Airborne Division that was bringing in First Sergeant Verduzco landed just as the water truck taking the ex-first sergeant and his three henchmen was pulling out of the main gate. The timing was perfect and very symbolic to the men in the battery. Verduzco stepped out of the door of the chopper, and in ten seconds every single G.I. watching could see that they had a senior NCO *running* the battery. There was nothing missing in the top sergeant's bearing. His shoulders were at a proud angle—not cocky, just proud—and he walked over to meet Captain Arrowood leaving footprints behind him in the sand that *dared* anything to fuck with them.

"First Sergeant Verduzco, reporting for duty, sir."

Luke returned the straight-arm salute and then shook hands with his new first sergeant. "I've heard a lot of good things about you, First Sergeant. Welcome to Bravo Battery."

"You've been in Vietnam *five* years, sir?" Verduzco walked next to Luke.

"People seem to think that's something important."

"I've been here four . . ."

Luke glanced at the senior sergeant out of the corner of his eye.

". . . and for the same reason that you have. That's why I've taken this *leg* assignment."

"Thanks, I sure need your help."

"You've got it, sir."

"Come on and I'll show you around the base."

"If you don't mind, sir, I would like to meet with the NCOs first and have *them* show me their areas of responsibility."

"That's fine with me . . . I could use a couple hours sleep before it gets dark."

"Why don't you do that, sir, and I'll come and wake you up." Verduzco appreciated the captain's understanding. "What time?"

"I'll catch the midnight snack, so wake me around ten." Luke felt exhausted as soon as he thought about sleeping. He could feel the sweat saturating the gauze and bandages covering his chest, stomach, and upper thighs, and wanted to lay under a fan naked so that the scrapes could dry out and scab over.

He watched the vehicles leave and enter the main gate of the fire-support base and stopped hoeing when the helicopter flew overheard to look up at it. He had missed seeing the front of the chopper and waited until it flew back out of the base to see which unit it was from. The head of an eagle on a black background told him that the chopper was from the 101st Airborne Division again. All of the traffic recently from the American Airborne Division in the artillery base was worrying him. The American paratroopers were known as excellent fighters, and he had hoped for an easy mission for his men. The Americans made gathering intelligence much easier than it had been with the French. Painting their unit patches on their helicopters and unit identification on their vehicles made it almost too easy for him.

The NVA Sapper commander went back to hoeing in the field. He had been sent to Hai Lang at the request of the local Vietcong commander to survey the American base camp. It had been selected as one of the easier fire bases to attack in I Corps because of the poor bunker placement and barbed wire defenses, and he had agreed with the original assessment. The first week he had spent visiting the graveyard that bordered the southern perimeter of the American base had provided so much amusement for him that he would spend the evenings getting drunk and having parties with the local VC leaders, which was something he would normally never do until the mission was over, but with this assignment it was too easy. He had actually sat on a gravestone in front of a bunker that was occupied by an American guard and drawn sketches of the bunkerline with the guard watching him! He would not have ever dared doing something like that except that he had watched the guard smoking from a pipe all morning and knew that the soldier had to have been totally stoned.

The NVA captain wished that he would have attacked the Hai Lang base sooner. The new American commander had made so many improvements in the defenses of the base that it would be very difficult to penetrate the perimeter, even with his elite sapper unit of engineers. He had the best Sapper Company in I Corps, and his list of accomplishments was a long one. His company was responsible for penetrating the defenses of the huge Da Nang ammunition depot and setting off the explosion that produced results beyond his wildest dreams. The Americans had become so overconfident that they had filled the narrow roads between their bermed bunkers with thousands of pallets of powder charges for heavy artillery. His unit had been informed by the Vietcong high command in Da-Nang that the Americans had received too many shiploads of ammunition and the harbor was filled with unloading vessels and the ammunition depot was bursting at its seams. He had been given the mission to harass the American depot and slow down their resupply efforts. No one in the high command had guessed just how successful he would be. His men had easily penetrated the depot perimeter and had set only three white phosphorous satchel charges on the pallets of ammunition that were nearest to the perimeter. He had taken only a single day to reconnoiter the perimeter and select a spot to penetrate and, once inside the depot, his men had been given instructions to place the charges on the nearest pallets and leave. His Sapper Company had not taken a single casualty and the resulting fire from the charges had started a chain reaction in the ammunition storage area that burned totally out of control for three days. The explosions could be seen as far away as the mountains where his unit had withdrawn, and reminded him of the fireworks his father would set off during their annual Tet celebration when he was a child.

He continued hoeing but worked his way along the edge of the field until he reached the dirt road that cut through the center of the paddies that ran closest to the base camp's northwestern corner and the large new fighting bunker the Americans had built in a *single* day! He had been impressed with the speed with which the American engineers had assembled the pre-cut bunker kit. The Navy Seabees had bulldozed sand and the artillerymen had sandbagged almost as fast. The new design of the bunker had almost caused the abandonment of his mission, which would have been the very first time he had not completed a mission he had been assigned. It had been the first time that he had *asked* for a mission to be canceled and that had embarrassed him. The design of the new bunkers with the three firing ports would have in itself caused him to abandon the mission; the center port, housed a heavy .50-caliber machine gun, and the two slanted side ports had M-60 machine guns in them. The firepower of just one of those bunkers was tremendous by itself, but when the Americans had added a smaller foxhole-type fighting position with trenches leading to them from the main bunker so that they could fire M79 grenade launchers and cyclone fencing twenty feet in front of the bunkers to stop his RPG launchers, it had become just too much. He could see that each one of the large new bunkers had been designed to be a mini-fort and could stand alone if it had to.

One of the soldiers on the corner bunker reached down behind the sandbag wall and took something that was being handed up to him. The NVA commander paused and checked the blade of his hoe so that he could see what the American soldier was doing. The man held a small bundle of dripping clothes. Someone had handed him his washing to lay out on top of the bunker to dry, which confirmed what he had feared; they had moved from the tents and bunkers they were sleeping in inside of the perimeter out to the fighting bunkers.

He knew that he was going to take a lot of casualties as soon as it got dark. He had been ordered to attack the base camp starting at one o'clock in the morning so that it would coincide with another NVA unit that was going to attack one of the American infantry companies to the west of them. He had already been given the American radio frequency they would use for the fire mission, and he had been ordered to destroy the howitzers undercover of the adjustment rounds. What that meant was that his men had to be in position on the *inside* of the perimeter's barbed wire when the first round was fired so that they could use the noise and confusion to throw satchel charges in the six self-propelled pieces.

The mission would be difficult, but not impossible. He had each of the bunkers marked where the guards had smoked large quantities of marijuana during the last couple of nights and he was sure that they wouldn't change their habits.

First Sergeant Verduzco waited in the orderly room until all of the noncommissioned officers in the battery had assembled under the mess tent and the chief-of-firing-battery came to get him. He had been going over in his mind what he wanted to say to the assembled NCOs and had gone from a very long speech on NCO responsibility to a very short statement. He walked next to the taller chief over to the tent and entered without pausing. All of the NCOs were present; none of them wanted to miss seeing the new airborne first sergeant so many rumors were circulating around the battery about. The artillerymen were all in a mild state of *leadership shock*; they had gone from some of the worst leadership, both officer and NCO, in the Army to some of the best in a very short period of time and were having problems adjusting to it.

Three things glared out from the new first sergeant to the rest of the NCOs. First: he was wearing an immaculate set of ironed jungle fatigues with spit-shined boots. Sweat was coming through the material under his arms and around his pistol belt, but there wasn't any doubt in anyone's mind that the sergeant *always* took pride in his appearance. The second point was the man's bearing. He emitted a powerful feeling of confidence and, for the first time since they had been in Vietnam, most of the NCOs sitting under the tent felt like they had a senior NCO who was a leader. The third point had caught everyone's eye the instant he had arrived off the chopper. Verduzco was wearing a matched set of Colt long-barreled .45-caliber pistols in a custom pair of shoulder holsters that had been designed especially for the pistols and to be worn with a pistol belt. The bottom of the holsters had long leather loops with snaps that went around a pistol belt and snapped back on the holster so that the holsters rode neatly against Verduzco's sides. The handles on the pistols were made out of black walnut and were custom made to fit his hands perfectly. The pistol under his left arm had a grip designed for his right hand, and the right arm holster had a pistol grip form-fitted for his left hand.

"I can see that most of you are interested in my weapons. I'll start with them so that we can get on to more important topics." Verduzco moved slowly across the front of the NCOs, looking directly into the eyes of each one of them. "I was assigned to the Army's National Rifle and Pistol Team for five years and I have competed worldwide in thousands of matches, so the most practical weapon for me to carry is a .45-caliber pistol." He removed the right-hand pistol from its holster. "This is a hand-built weapon that fires special ammunition and is fairly accurate up to a hundred yards. If any of you would like to learn how to fire a handgun, I would be happy to teach you." Verduzco smiled. "Now on to more important things." He paused and watched the reaction on the faces of the NCOs. Most of them showed interest in what he was going to say next and he liked that. "It's simple. I'm a professional NCO and I'm proud of it. I was never asked to be an officer and I would turn the Army down if I ever was offered a direct commission. *I like being a non-commissioned officer* and I'm very *proud* to be a member of that *elite* organization." Verduzco continued reading the expressions on the faces of the NCOs as he talked, gathering much more data from them then they realized they were giving out. "And because I am what I am, I don't steal, cheat, line my own pockets at the expense of my men and I don't ask anybody to do anything that I can't or haven't done myself." Verduzco started to turn to leave the tent. "I expect you to do your jobs like you've been trained to do and I expect each and every one of you to *set* the standards for the rest of the NCOs in this battalion." Verduzco left the tent. He had been there for exactly three minutes.

The section sergeant for the third gun section sat in his seat and smiled. He had been the NCO who fired the M60 and had killed Talbot.

"What in the fuck are you grinning for, Kyles?" The battery communications sergeant wasn't sure if he should be happy or sad over the arrival of the new first sergeant. He hadn't been a member of the old clique, but the old first sergeant had left him alone to do his own thing and he liked it that way.

"I think we've finally got us a real first sergeant in this fucking battery! First a decent battery commander arrives and now a first sergeant that ain't afraid to look a man in the eyes." Sergeant Kyles was beginning to think his luck had changed. Less than a month earlier, he had been afraid to go to sleep inside of the battery perimeter and now he could take naps whenever he felt like it without having to fear waking up in a spirit world.

First Sergeant Verduzco spent the remainder of the day visiting the different areas of the battery and being briefed by the NCOs on what the problems were facing their sections. He ended the day concerned about the howitzer in the second section that was being fired with a fifty-foot lanyard because the men were afraid to get inside the cab when the weapon recoiled. The medical section had improved greatly with their support from the 101st, and the mess hall and motor pool were probably the most efficient operations in I Corps, thanks to the help they had gotten from the Screaming Eagles. Verduzco was pleased with what he had seen and knew that it was now a matter of good leadership on the part of the senior NCOs and officers to keep the morale up in the battery.

The sun dropped down behind the western berm, sending a long shadow out over the sand inside of the fire-support base. Verduzco left his hootch wearing only a pair of jungle boots and Army-issue, tan PT shorts. He tightened the metal buckle on the front of the shorts and started running inside of the base camp on the inner perimeter road that was a good mile and a half from the main entrance back to the Y in the road behind the first bunker. Verduzco started his run at a fast jog and picked up his pace once his muscles had stretched out. He knew that the battery was watching him. On his second time around the road, a person joined him back behind the ammunition section bunkers.

"Want some company, First Sergeant?"

Verduzco smiled and felt the sweat change course running down his face. "Sure . . . it's Sergeant Cole, right?"

The black ammunition section chief nodded his head and picked up the pace. "I love to run, but I felt foolish doing it by myself."

"Every night from now on. It's still a little hot out." Verduzco felt the heat coming through the soles of his boots. "We might have to have the mess sergeant hold out supper for us or run in the morning before breakfast."

Cole sucked in the hot air and replied. "Morning would be better, Top."

"Then in the morning it is!" Verduzco signaled that the talking was over by increasing the pace. The guards on the bunkers watched the two NCOs running around the road and wondered if the airborne first sergeant was going to make them run to.

Verduzco stopped in front of the orderly room after the third time around the track. "Enough! I've had my workout."

Cole smiled. "I'll just finish up running back to my section." He nodded his head. "Thanks, First Sergeant."

"For what?" Verduzco snapped his head to one side sending a volley of sweat pellets out across the dry sand.

"For coming out here. We need you a hell of a lot more than you needed us." Cole felt a little embarrassed. "We've had some racial problems in the battery and I think you can stop it."

"*Green* is the color . . . only green." Verduzco pointed his finger at Cole and winked. "Green . . . right?"

"Right!" Cole took off running at a fast clip. He couldn't believe how fast the middle-aged first sergeant was. He had been a high-school track champion and had taken pride in running all of his life, but the forty-three-year-old NCO had made him work hard to keep up.

Verduzco took his time showering. The heat was still almost unbearable coming up off the sand even though the sun had set a couple of hours earlier. He felt good about the run. It had worked all of the tension out of his muscles and had been a better relaxer than a fifth of booze. Hard exercise had always been his method of getting rid of tension. He dried off and walked barefooted with a towel around his waist back to the hootch. He paused in front of Captain Arrowood's door and knocked softly before opening it to look in. Arrowood was lying on his back with a fan blowing over his body still sleeping. The new FDC officer was snoring on a folding cot that had been set up against the far wall. Verduzco could smell the stale vomit and wrinkled his nose before letting the door close again. The captain had looked exhausted when he had met him earlier. What he wanted to talk to him about could wait until he woke up. Verduzco didn't like the idea of both of them sleeping under the same roof, and he wanted to recommend to the captain that he move out and occupy sleeping quarters at the far end of the fire-support base so that they wouldn't be together in the event of a night attack.

Arrowood looked over at the door when it closed and then closed his eyes again. The cool air coming from the fan felt good against his oozing scrape marks. He promised himself that he would sit out in the sun without a shirt on in the morning to let the sun help heal his wounds. He would end up with a number of large scars on his chest and stomach from the scrape marks, but he figured that was better than the bullet holes the soldier had intended on putting in him.

The NVA commander sat in the rice merchant's barn surrounded by his officers and NCOs. The rest of his company were hiding in safe houses throughout the village of Hai Lang waiting for their leaders to return. All of the men were dressed in tan-colored peasant suits that had been made especially for this mission by the local Vietcong women, and each of the men had been issued a large piece of the cloth that matched the color of the sand around the fire-support base.

"We will be in position to attack at exactly one o'clock so that we can destroy the American howitzers before they can fire in support of the infantry company our sister unit is going to attack. We have been told that this battery is the only one that can fire in support of that company in the field according to the American's safety charts."

"Sir, how can we be sure? They have two more batteries in their battalion of artillery that are within range."

The NVA Sapper officer smiled. "We have been monitoring the American artillery frequencies for six months now and the battalion commander who is commanding is too afraid to alter any of the rules. He's also too cautious to risk making a mistake and that is to our advantage."

"I feel a great victory for us tonight!" The NVA Sapper Company's executive officer held a tiny cup of rice wine up as a toast. "To Ho Chi Minh and the People's Republic!"

All of the NVA in the rice warehouse lifted the tiny porcelain cups to their mouths and tossed the wine down their throats. The captain was the first one to slip out of the barn into the starlit night. He moved like a shadow followed by his small command group toward the path that led out to the rice paddies. He would be with his first platoon, which was going to supply supporting mortar and recoilless rifle fire from behind the second tree line of the rice fields. The strip of rice paddies that ran at an almost north-south axis to the camp was only three hundred meters wide with sand and very low shrubs on each side. The Americans would assume that the mortars and recoilless rifles were being fired from the tree line closest to their perimeter and would concentrate all of the firepower

there instead of at the second tree line. He had assigned his second platoon to the graveyard as a diver-
sionary force but the main attack would come from
the north with his third and fourth platoons. The
Americans had bulldozed an open area two hundred
meters wide and a third of the way around the base
camp before the Seabees left. All of the small shrubs
were gone and the sandy ground had been leveled so
that grazing fire from the bunkers would be deadly.
The Americans would expect an attack through the
graveyard or even from the western rice paddies, but
they would not be prepared for a Sapper attack across
the open sand to their north, and that was the reason
for the tan uniforms and large pieces of sand-colored
cloth. His men would crawl for four hundred meters
across the open area to the barbed wire and up to
the base of the berm. Even the hated Starlight
scopes would not be able to penetrate the excellent
camouflage.

The moon was only a tiny sliver in the clear sky,
but the stars gave off enough light to make the sand
glow. On a full-moon night, the fire-support base was
lit up so brightly that it was easy to see people walking
from across the whole base. The stars by themselves
reflected enough light to walk around the base without
the use of a flashlight. That was one of the few real
benefits of being located on a fire-support base composed of an almost white sand. Verduzco left through
the back door of the hootch and walked out to the
bunkerline. He stopped to listen to the night sounds
around him before climbing the slight incline to the
rear of the bunker. The glow from a soldier's cigarette
brightened as he inhaled.

"You should hold your helmet over your face if you
have to smoke on guard duty." Verduzco looked up
over the edge of the bunker's roof at the surprised
guard.

"Sorry, First Sergeant . . . I . . . I . . ."

"If we were out in the field, I would have chewed

your ass for smoking on guard duty, but here in a semipermanent base camp, it's all right, just cover the glow with your helmet so we don't lose you to a sniper."

The soldier chuckled. "First Sergeant, the only sniper out there in that graveyard is long dead."

"Probably . . . but humor me, OK?"

"Sure, First Sergeant."

"Good." Verduzco dropped down to the base of the berm and started walking clockwise around the perimeter. He had woken Captain Arrowood, and they had decided to split the night duty of checking the perimeter by him working his way around the bunkers going clockwise and Arrowood going counterclockwise until they met.

One of the 1st of the 77th Armor Battalion's M48 main battle tanks was parked in the main entrance to the base camp and looked like a huge black bunker as Verduzco approached it from behind. One of the tank crew members sat in the commander's hatch in the turret. Verduzco climbed up on the tank from the rear and stayed close to the turret so that his silhouette blended with the tank's.

"Where's the rest of your crew?" Verduzco whispered to the shadow sticking out of the hatch.

"Sir." The man's voice was neutral. He was just making a statement.

"You the platoon leader?"

"Yes."

"Well, sir. Where's the rest of your crew?"

"Inside sleeping. We've been out on patrol for fourteen days and this is the first break that we've had."

"I understand, but this position is a rather critical one for our base camp, and we're depending on your tank holding it in the event of an attack."

"Are you new out here?"

"First day."

"*Well*, first day, First Sergeant. I've been pulling duty here at LZ Sandy for eleven months . . . eleven fucking months and this is a safer place to be stationed than Saigon!"

"You due to go home next month, sir?"

"I just told you that! Twenty-one days to be exact."

"I'd like to see that happen for you and for my men. We all want to make it back to the States alive and in one piece." Verduzco hopped down off the back of the tank onto the soft sand that cushioned his fall and walked over to the gate bunker that was still flying the American flag from the steel pole the motor sergeant and two of the track mechanics had installed against its wooden side and resandbagged. The huge garrison flag flapped in the gentle sea breeze. The American flag wasn't supposed to fly at night unless it was illuminated, but he had agreed with Arrowood that flying the flag was a morale factor for the men that was worth stretching regulations for. The sound of the nylon cloth flapping in the breeze was comforting to the senior NCO as he continued making his rounds, stopping at each one of the fighting bunkers and introducing himself to the men living there who were awake and to the guards.

The NVA commander watched the guards on the bunkers through his field glasses. He could see that someone was working his way around the bunkerline and smiled because that meant the guards would relax after the officer or NCO had left and would probably smoke some dope or fall asleep. It was working out perfectly. The second platoon had already signaled back that they were in position and the first platoon was spread out in the second tree line to the northwest of the American base waiting for orders to start the attack with a heavy mortar barrage. The third and fourth platoons had the most difficult assignment, and were still moving into position. The NVA commander looked at his watch; it was almost twelve-thirty. His Sappers had a little over a half hour to get in position inside of the barbed wire next to the bunkers before the coordinated attack would start against the fire-support base and the infantry company.

Captain Arrowood paused next to the side of the tank that was parked behind the battery FDC on the berm. The Seabees had made seven raised sites along the berm for armored vehicles. Normally, the armor or infantry platoons would come to the fire base short vehicles because one or more of them would be deadlined back in their base camps. An armor platoon was four tanks and an infantry mechanized platoon was made up of four M113s. The cavalry could be a combination of almost anything, depending on what the squadron commander had available: two ACAVs and two tanks or a combination of tanks and ACAVs. Arrowood didn't know what he was going to get for the night from the brigade until the platoon arrived. The extra sites along the berm perimeter were used for the M109 self-propelled howitzers to use in the event of an emergency and they had to fire *killer junior*. The technique was for the 155mm howitzer to fire direct fire from the berm with a very short fuze setting on the projectile so that it would explode 100 to 150 meters from the end of the gun tube, sending shrapnel down on the ground in a fan shape from about eight to ten feet. The name *killer junior* applied to light and medium artillery, 105mm and 155mm, while *killer senior* referred to the same system using eight-inch howitzers. This simple direct-fire technique for howitzers in self-defense proved more effective in many cases than the *beehive* round that had been developed for the 105mm howitzers, because the NVA could avoid the beehive darts by lying prone or crawling. Arrowood had even gone a step further and had designated two rounds of white phosphorous to be already fused and in the ready racks inside of the howitzers to be used only for killer junior.

First Sergeant Verduzco saw Arrowood leaving the corner bunker behind the FDC and joined him. "Looks good, sir, real good. I like the idea of the men living in the fighting bunkers around the perimeter."

"We had a hard time at first trying to convince them that it was for *their* best interests to live in them. The men didn't like the idea of having to walk so far to the mess hall and to the guns." Luke buttoned up his fatigue jacket. He had been walking with it open so that he could catch the breeze against his bandages.

Verduzco caught what Luke was doing. "How are you healing? I would think the heat out here would slow down the process."

"A little, itches a lot but I've seen some results." Luke pointed over at the FDC bunker. "Want a cup of coffee?"

"Now that sounds like a good idea!" Verduzco led the way inside of the bunker and was greeted by Fields. "Coffee stop, Top?"

"You guessed right."

Lieutenant Fields pointed over to the plugged in pot. "Help yourself." He returned his attention back to showing Lieutenant Ingram how he had organized the FDC. Fields had been shocked at first when Luke had told him that the battalion commander had transferred him to the field as a forward observer but, once he had accepted the idea, he liked it even though he was going to be the only first lieutenant forward observer in the brigade. He wanted to see some real action before going back to the States in five months, and serving with the infantry was about the best way to make that happen.

The FM radio broke squelch and the soft voice of a forward observer whispered over the air. "Red Bucket 14, this is Puppy Foot 14 . . . over."

Fields went over to the radio and listened as the operator answered the call. "Puppy Foot 14 . . . Red Bucket . . . over."

"This is Puppy Foot 14 . . . fire mission . . . over."

The battery FDC came alive with men running over to their plotting boards and computing equipment.

"This is Red Bucket 14 . . . send your traffic over."

Verduzco whispered to Arrowood. "Who's Puppy Foot?"

"A company from the 1st Battalion 11th Infantry,"

Fields answered for Arrowood. "They're operating to our northwest along those low mountains . . ."

The forward observer cut Fields off as they listened to the nature of his fire mission. ". . . NVA in the open . . . will adjust . . . over."

"Shit! This isn't any bullshit defensive concentration!" Fields looked over at Arrowood with a look in his eyes that asked for help.

"I'll call battalion and get clearance on the land-line. You keep the FM channel open for our FO." Luke cranked the direct line to the battalion FDC and waited for a full minute before the duty sergeant answered. "Put Captain Kreps on the line for me, please."

"He's busy, sir. He's checking the data for Puppy Foot's fire mission."

"Good, don't bother him, then. That's what I'm calling about. It's a *contact* fire mission." Luke hung up the telephone and looked over at Fields.

"We're ready to fire the first round for adjustment." Fields looked at his watch. It had taken his FDC four minutes to compute the data and send it to the guns. Sergeant Kyles was the section sergeant for the base piece and had been designated to fire the adjustment rounds.

Luke finished his coffee and threw the Styrofoam cup in the trash before going back over to the telephone and calling the battalion FDC again.

Captain Kreps answered. "Yeah!"

"Arrowood here, Kreps . . . what's the hold up?"

"We have to wait for the battalion commander or the executive officer to clear the data!" Kreps ground his teeth. "You know that, damnit!"

The radio keyed in Bravo Battery's FDC and a fear-filled voice traveled over the airwaves. "Red Bucket! When are you going to give us some artillery! They're attacking in waves!"

Luke looked at Fields. "Fire! Battalion has cleared the data."

Fields gave the command to the base piece and the

round left the tube before he could hang up the telephone.

"Puppy Foot 14 . . . Red Bucket 14 . . . base piece one round . . . over."

There was a short pause, and the forward observer came back on the air with a lot more confidence in his voice. "Drop 50 . . . fire for effect . . . over."

"Drop 50 . . . Fire for effect . . . over."

Verduzco watched the men work and could see that they were very efficient. Lieutenant Fields had done a superb job training the men. PFC Jenkins had only been with the FDC for two weeks after having been transferred from the ammunition section and already he was working his own plotting chart.

The land-line from battalion rang, and Luke went over to the telephone and pulled the wires loose. Verduzco saw what he had done and looked over at Fields and Ingram. It was obvious to all of them that Luke had not received permission from battalion to fire the mission. Fields suspected that the captain had made the decision on his own because it had been less than ten minutes from the time the FO had called for the support to battalion giving clearance and that was unheard of when the norm was thirty minutes or longer.

"Red Bucket 14 . . . Foot 14 . . . rounds on target . . . I will continue to adjust . . . left 50, drop 50 . . . battery three rounds . . . over."

"Roger 14 . . . left 50, drop 50 . . . battery three rounds . . . over." The radio operator repeated the call.

"I thought that the FDC selected how many rounds are fired." Lieutenant Ingram was recalling what he had been taught in gunnery school back at Fort Sill. "The mission order is all screwed up, too."

"The FO's a little excited. We make due with the information we have and help him out where we can. Remember . . . we're sitting back here safe in a bunker and he's getting his ass shot at." Fields smiled over at his replacement. "We *support*, not dictate to the field." He was worried that when he got out there as an FO, Ingram was going to play the game in the battalion commander's corner with his rule book.

Ingram smiled back at Fields. "You're right."

The battalion command radio broke silence and Jeffers voice filled the air waves. "Red Bucket 6 . . . this is Red Dragon 6 . . . over."

Luke waited until he heard his howitzers firing before picking up the handset. Sergeant Verduzco waved and signaled that he was going outside to check on the guns and Luke nodded his head in agreement. "Bucket 6 . . . over."

Jeffers dropped the call signs. "God damn you, Arrowood! Who in the fuck gave you permission to fire!"

Fields's face turned white. He had never heard Jeffers so angry before.

"Red Dragon 6 . . . Bucket 6 . . . Puppy Foot is in *contact* with an attacking enemy force and needs *direct support* artillery that's responsive . . . over."

There was a pause while Jeffers struggled to catch his breath. He couldn't believe that a captain would talk to him like that over the air. "You will report to my office by seven o'clock in the morning! Do you hear me!"

"Roger, sir . . ."

The first volley of NVA mortar rounds landed inside of the fire-support base, sending up huge sprays of sand. One of the 82mm mortar rounds had impacted on the backside of the FDC bunker, sending shock waves through the sandbag wall. Sergeant Verduzco was lucky that the round had landed on the side of the bunker away from him. He was outside and heard the rounds impacting, and realized instantly that they were under attack. He stuck his head back in the bunker doorway and called out in a very calm command voice. "Incoming . . . we're under attack. Anyone not needed in here . . . go to your fighting position."

Luke pushed the talk switch again. "Red Dragon 6 . . . Bucket 6 . . . we are under attack. Receiving incoming mortar and rocket rounds. I've got to defend my battery . . . out."

"What did you say?" Jeffers couldn't believe that Hai Lang was under a ground attack. "Arrowood! What in the hell did you say!"

The FDC radio operator answered the battalion commander. "Red Dragon 6 . . . Bucket 23 . . . we are under a ground attack. Bucket 6 has left this location to check the perimeter . . . over."

Jeffers threw his handset against the radio and turned around to face Major Montgomery and Captain Kreps. "What did he say?" His voice was almost a whisper. He was drunk and so was the major, but not drunk enough not to know that they were in some very serious trouble with LZ Sandy being under attack and neither one of them sober enough to go brief the brigade commander and his staff.

The NVA Sapper commander looked at his watch and smiled. Everything was right on schedule. The American artillery was firing as planned and giving his Sappers cover to move the last critical few meters to the berm and into the fire-support base with their satchel charges. He raised his binoculars to his eyes just in time to witness the hand grenades exploding along the entire berm. He dropped his glasses in shock as he watched his elite Sapper team being cut to fish bait by the hundred or so grenades going off almost at the same time in the barbed wire and along the berm.

First Sergeant Verduzco heard the machine guns go off in the bunkers facing the graveyard and started heading in that direction, when he saw the main gun fire on the tank that was positioned on the north berm. The tank commander had fired a canister round at a target in the plowed sand field. Verduzco frowned and let his instincts take over. He changed direction and headed for the northern berm holding a long-barreled .45 in each hand. A head appeared along the berm between two of the fighting bunkers and Verduzco paused to watch as the Sapper slipped over the top of the sand wall. Verduzco barely aimed and fired one round. The body slid to the bottom of the berm inside of the camp. He ran over and fired another round into the NVA Sapper's head to make sure he was dead and searched the enemy soldier until he found the satchel charge. Verduzco didn't hesitate and threw the high explosive charge back over the wall, just in case it was on a time-delay fuse. All of the years of airborne training came forward in the middle-aged first sergeant, and he moved swiftly behind the bunkers, killing the few Sappers who had made it through the hand grenades and automatic rifle fire.

Luke left the FDC bunker when he was sure that Fields had the fire mission under control and his fire-support base was under a ground attack. Dotson and Pilgrim followed closely behind him making sure that he was covered. The only thing Luke carried in his hands was a bamboo quirt that he had bought on one of his rare trips to Saigon when he had watched a polo match at one of the exclusive clubs. He started around the perimeter in a reverse order that he had arrived in at the FDC. The bunker at the corner of the fire-support base was firing long bursts from the three fire ports. A solid stream of tracers shot out of the ports in at least fifty-round bursts as the gunners swept the graveyard. Luke disappeared inside of the bunker and saw one of the mess sergeants behind the .50-caliber machine gun with his thumbs pressed down on the butterfly trigger. He lifted the quirt and hit the sergeant across his shoulders.

"When I said fire six-to-nine-round bursts and *aim* your weapon, I meant it!" Luke's voice echoed around the inside of the bunker and reached the other two M-60 gunners. One of the soliders immediately started firing the weapon in the correct manner. The other gunner still held the trigger back until he was out of ammo. Luke went over to his position and brought the whip across the back of the man's legs. "I'm going to whip your ass raw if you keep fucking up! Six-to-nine rounds and aim!"

The fear-filled eyes of the soldier looked over at Luke but didn't focus.

"Dotson! Get in here!" Luke screamed back out of the bunker door.

Dotson slipped into the bunker.

"Take over that machine gun until that soldier gets ahold of himself and then catch up to Pilgrim and me!" Luke left the bunker and could hear all three of the machine guns firing in a rhythmic pattern.

Sergeant Verduzco skirted around the back of the large ammunition and powder bunkers that bordered the inner-perimeter road on the west side of the base. He could see where mortar rounds had impacted near the sides of the bunker and on one of the roofs. The mortars had stopped firing a couple minutes earlier, telling Verduzco that the main ground attack was about to begin. He looked across the clear sandy area that separated him from the bunker line and realized that he would be exposed as he made a dash for the nearest bunker. The senior NCO decided that it would be smarter to go over to the second gun section and run from there over to the main gate bunker. His plans were changed when he saw the M48 main battle tank that was blocking the entrance to the fire-support base lift over on its side and then drop back down again on the sand in a ball of flame. Verduzco looked over at the section sergeant and pointed to the empty armor position on the west berm. "Get your track over there and start firing killer junior!"

The sergeant stared at Verduzco, trying to decide if the senior NCO was giving him a valid order. "I have to check with Lieutenant Fields. We're in the middle of a fire mission!"

"Do it and then get your howitzer over there!" Verduzco pointed with the barrel of the pistol in his right hand. "I'm going over to the main gate bunker, but I'll meet you there in five minutes!"

Sergeant Verduzco ran across the sand holding a pistol in each hand with his eyes locked on the top of the berm. He slipped behind the fighting bunker and peeked out to see if there were any survivors from the burning tank. The first rounds starting cooking off inside of the vehicle and blew the commander's hatch open. Verduzco rolled back behind the bunker and saw the Sapper setting the fuse on a satchel charge he was holding. The .45-caliber round caught the NVA soldier in his heart. Verduzco repeated the procedure of throwing the satchel charge back over the berm and the high-explosive charge detonated a second later. He looked over at the rear entrance to the bunker and saw one of the ammunition section soldiers stick his head out behind the barrel of his M-16. "Don't fire!"

Captain Arrowood saw the howitzer backing out of its firing pit and drive across the sand to cover the western wall. The Sappers had knocked out the tank blocking the entrance and a ground attack from that direction was likely. He motioned for Pilgrim to follow him and started running to where the 155mm howitzer was headed on the berm.

The NVA Sapper commander used his field glasses to watch his men climb over the berm. The hand grenades had killed or wounded over half of his men, but there were still enough of his company left to complete their mission. He had ordered the RPG-7 operators in the first platoon to destroy the tank blocking the main entrance to draw the American reserves away from the north berm.

The first 155mm rounds landed along the first tree-line and brought a smile to the NVA commander's mouth. He had guessed right. The Americans had assumed the tree line closest to their berm would be the one they would use during an attack. There was a short pause and a second volley of rounds landed a hundred meters closer to his position. The smug look on his face changed when he realized the Americans were walking the rounds toward him.

Lieutenant Fields ran his fire-direction center like a pro. He kept five of his guns firing in support of the infantry who were under attack and had given the second-gun section permission to move to the berm to fire direct fire. Ingram had been scared during the initial stage of the ground attack, but had settled down when he saw how calm Fields was, and worked as the battery's forward observer, calling in the base's defensive concentrations that were being fired by Charlie Battery to their north.

Verduzco and Arrowood met at the howitzer on the berm. Luke shook his head and glanced over at the first sergeant. "Some heavy shit, Top!"

Verduzco nodded his head in agreement. It was obvious they were fighting a well-trained NVA force and not some local Vietcong unit. "I don't think too many of them have made it over the wall."

"We had better have the guns check around their area." Luke pounded his fist against the back door of the track, and the section sergeant cautiously opened it a crack and when he saw the captain he felt a tremendous relief.

"Sir! Shit . . . I'm afraid to fire this gun direct fire from inside of the cab."

"Use a lanyard! Give me your land-line!" Luke took the field telephone from the sergeant and squatted down in the sand next to the howitzer.

Lieutenant Fields answered the ring. "FDC." His voice was so calm that Arrowood was surprised, considering the circumstances. The lieutenant should have been near panic.

"Arrowood . . . have the gun sections check the area around their pieces for Sappers."

"Roger, sir!" Fields pointed at Jenkins. "Check around the FDC for Sappers and be careful that you don't shoot any of our people by mistake."

Jenkins slipped on his helmet and grabbed his loaded M-16 off the rack. "Be right back, sir!" Fields' confidence was catching.

"Guns!" Fields yelled into the telephone. "Did you hear the captain?" Each one of the section chiefs confirmed the order.

The NVA commander knew that he only had a few

more minutes before the American gunships would arrive and make his escape almost impossible. He strained his ears listening for the satchel charges to go off inside of the base, signaling that the howitzers were destroyed. He had just received a call from his second platoon leader asking for permission to withdraw. He was suffering heavy casualties. He had denied the request because his men who had gotten inside of the base needed the diversion to complete their mission. The NVA commander had no way of knowing at that time that only seven of his men had made it over the berm and five of them had been killed before they could cross the inner-perimeter road.

PFC Jenkins stepped out into the dark and waited next to the FDC bunker until his eyes adjusted to the starlight. The sound of the weapons firing was much louder outside of the bunker, and he felt very much alone. He pushed the safety switch off his M-16 and stepped around the corner of the bunker and saw the NVA Sapper kneeling down on one knee and pulling something out of what looked like a small rucksack. Jenkins wasn't sure what he should do. He thought that he should take the soldier prisoner, but the NVA changed his mind for him when he looked up and saw Jenkins. The Sapper dropped the satchel charge and rolled his AK-47 off his shoulder in a fluid motion. Jenkins fired first, killing his first human being.

The RPG-7 round hit the top edge of the berm in front of the self-propelled howitzer and ricoheted up to hit the track. The NVA gunner made a slight adjustment and fired again, hitting the cab of the track and knocking out the direct-fire sight on the howitzer.

"Sir! We've lost our sights!" The section sergeant yelled back out of the rear door at Arrowood.

"Use Kentucky windage and fire WP at that tree line!" Luke watched Verduzco on the top of the berm.

The first sergeant slipped down from the edge of the berm and called back to Luke. "They're firing from the *second* tree line on the back side of the rice paddies!"

Luke waved above the roar of the small-arms firing and stuck his head back in the track. "Fire a round and I'll adjust it!"

The first WP round exploded in the center of the rice paddies ten feet off the ground sending a beautiful spray of the deadly white phosphorus out over the fields seeking some human flesh it could burn through.

"Up two degrees and add two-tenths of a second to the fuze!" Arrowood stuck his head through the door.

The second round landed five feet in front of the NVA Sapper commander and his small command group. The M-60 machine gunner in the corner bunker actually stopped firing and watched the beautiful white streamers of the phosphorus arch through the air and land burning on the sand. He saw a pair of Sappers start running away from the second tree line and opened fire on them.

The fighting around the perimeter stopped slowly. The NVA were either all dead or they were trying to slip away in very small groups back to the village. It took the artillerymen in the fighting bunkers a lot longer to calm down, and they would shoot at anything that moved around the perimeter. The first sergeant and Arrowood formed small teams from the soldiers inside of the perimeter to sweep the area for any hiding or wounded NVA, while Fields continued to conduct their supporting fire mission to the infantry. The NVA unit that had attacked the infantry company was trying to break contact and withdraw. The fighting had been heavy, and the infantry company had taken on the better part of an NVA battalion, killing a lot more of the enemy than tallied at first count. Units found NVA graves for weeks afterwards in the low mountains.

Luke sat in a folding lawn chair outside of the FDC bunker and surveyed his battery area. The damage wasn't as bad as it had looked the night before. The mortars had done the most damage to the base camp, destroying both of their tin and plywood hootches and the mess hall tent, along with one of the shitters. Luke tried keeping his thoughts off of what *could* have happened if the NVA had attacked the fire-support base a month earlier. They had taken five direct hits on the ammunition section's powder and projectile bunkers. Luke could see from the impact marks in the sand around the bunkers that the majority of the mortar rounds had been concentrated in that area under the assumption the powder and projectiles were still stored under tents.

"We were very fortunate, sir." Verduzco squatted down across from where Arrowood was sitting. "The armor lost one tank and crew, and we lost three men dead and five wounded. They're being MEDEVACed out soon."

"Where are they?" Luke's eyes lost their focus.

"Over by the entrance." Verduzco bit his lower lip. "It was a damn good fight, sir. We didn't do bad at all for a bunch of Redlegs."

"Have the men search the area for any hidden satchel charges that have been set for a delay explosion."

"Good idea, sir. I'll get on that right away." Verduzco stretched when he stood back up. "It's been a long night."

"Fields said that some brigade officers are on their way out here." Luke listened to the radio traffic coming from inside of the bunker. "I think something happened back in the rear because we haven't heard from Jeffers or Montgomery this morning."

Verduzco looked down at the captain. "It was too bad that our land-line went out last night right before they attacked. Those Sappers are damn good soldiers."

Luke smiled. "Thanks, Top, but I'm not going to lie. I didn't have permission to fire that mission last night."

"You did the right thing. Sometimes a soldier has to make a tough decision during a fight." Verduzco smiled back at the captain. "It looks like we're going to get a new howitzer for the Second Section. It took five RPG-7 hits!"

"We were having problems with that tube staying in battery. They were using a fifty foot lanyard . . ." Luke laid his head back and closed his eyes. The early morning sun felt good against his face. He was very glad to be alive. "I'm putting you in for a Silver Star, First Sergeant."

"Me?" Verduzco stopped in his tracks on the sand.

"I heard what you did." Luke kept his eyes closed.

"I was just protecting my ass, sir."

"Yep . . . but some people call that gallantry in action . . ." Luke opened one eye and looked at the airborne first sergeant, "I'm one of those people."

CHAPTER SIX

✪✪✪✪✪✪✪✪✪✪✪✪✪

THE VALOROUS UNIT AWARD

The artillerymen left their bunkers and looked around the fire-support base as the daylight revealed the carnage that had taken place during the night. Soldiers looked over at their buddies and hid the fear that had been there during the darkness but still wanted to emerge. Any loud noise inside of the perimeter would send men scurrying for cover.

Slowly, the men realized just how lucky they had been to catch the Sapper attack when they had, and a very strong respect grew for Captain Arrowood and First Sergeant Verduzco with each passing minute as the men discovered more and more NVA bodies. The idea of throwing two hand grenades apiece into the barbed wire had amused the artillerymen and had been the source for many jokes about the captain wanting everyone to throw their hand grenades away so he wouldn't get fragged during the night. Just the hand grenades alone accounted for thirty-eight NVA Sapper dead. Two of the northern bunkers found sapper dead within ten feet of their fighting bunkers.

Arrowood had his chief-of-battery police up the inside of the fire base while he formed two groups to go outside of the perimeter with the tanks to sweep the area and police up enemy weapons and intelligence documents. Verduzco went left out of the gate with only one of the tanks and the majority of the men to sweep through the cemetery while Luke went to the right side with two of the tanks to sweep the rice paddies and the open area out in front of the northern barbed wire. The pair of tanks moved as a team forward ahead of the men on foot and swept the first tree line with machine-gun fire.

"You have a call from Puppy Foot 6, sir." Pilgrim handed Luke the handset from the PRC-25 portable radio he was carrying on his back. He had the antenna strapped down against the side of the radio. Pilgrim had done that so that a sniper wouldn't pick him out of the group as a radio operator and they were going to be close enough to the fire-support base so that he didn't need a lot of range. The call from the infantry company commander was coming in broken, so Pilgrim released the antenna and let it stick straight up in the air. Instantly, the call came in clearer.

"Puppy Foot 6 . . . Red Bucket 6 . . . over."

"This is Foot 6. We're real busy right now, but I wanted to take a second to thank you personally for the superb artillery support that you provided last night. Us infantry guys aren't used to such a quick response from your unit . . . over."

"Bucket 6 . . . thanks. I'll pass on that information to my men . . . over."

"Foot 6 . . . I hear they threw a ground probe at your location at the same time . . . over."

"Bucket 6 . . . Affirmative . . . so far we've counted fifty-three NVA dead and we still have to check *outside* of our perimeter wire . . . over."

There was a long pause at the infantry end of the line. The company commander had been briefed by the brigade staff that LZ Sandy had received a harassing probe during the attack on his location. Fifty-three NVA dead wasn't a fucking probe, it was a serious attack. "Foot 6 . . . very impressive. I've heard that you've done wonders out there since you've taken command . . . thank God . . . over." The captain had visited the Hai Lang fire-support base a couple of months earlier and had warned his platoon leaders that when they were detailed to pull duty there that they had better stay on their toes because the base was ripe for attack.

"Bucket 6 . . . you said it friend . . . *thank God* . . . over."

"Foot 6 . . . I've got Red Diamond 6 coming in to this location shortly and you can be assured that I'll tell him how well your unit has performed . . . out."

Luke handed the handset back to a beaming Pilgrim. He smiled at the specialist. "Did you like that, soldier?"

"Yes, sir! You sure told him the way it was!" Pilgrim was proud of how well the battery had fought. Morale was as high as it would ever go in that unit, and every single man there knew that if it hadn't been for Arrowood's being assigned to Bravo Battery, most of them would be the ones dead right now and not the NVA.

Luke winked and pointed to the road that cut through the center of the rice paddies. He gave the tank commander a signal to sweep both sides of the road with machine-gun fire and advance with his men following the armored vehicle. Dotson found the NVA commander and his staff lying in a loose group behind a thick hedge. All of the NVA had died from white phosphorous burns. Dotson signaled for the captain to come to where he stood, holding his M-16 pointed at the dead NVA just in case.

"What . . ." Luke saw the dead NVA and also saw the American PRC-25 leaning up against an old rice-paddy dike. He had probably found the NVA command party, and that explained why the NVA didn't recover their dead or their weapons. The leadership had been killed and the surviving NVA Sappers had withdrawn on their own.

Luke's party joined up with the first sergeant's team at the northeastern corner of the fire base's defensive wire. The men from both groups were carrying at least one NVA weapon apiece. Luke wore the NVA commander's brown leather pistol belt and holster around his waist.

"Have you gone NVA on me, sir?" Verduzco
smiled and shook his head over his commander being
out of uniform wearing the enemy weapon.

"War trophy, First Sergeant." Luke felt good. All
of the hard work preparing the fire base for just such
an attack had paid off. He looked back to the area in
front of the north side of the base and pointed as he
spoke. "They started way back there and crawled all
the way up to the base of our berm. I cannot believe
how easily they went through our barbed wire!"

"Wire is only as good as the men guarding over it."
Verduzco wasn't a fool and knew that they still had a
major drug problem in the fire-support base. It wasn't
as bad as it had been under the old battery commander's reign, but the men still smoked dope while they
were pulling guard to make the time go by faster. The
NVA Sapper attack could be a good lesson for them.
"Look at that, sir."

Luke turned to face where the first sergeant was
pointing and saw the black thunderheads moving in.
"Hot shit! That is one hell of a storm!"

"We'd better get the men back inside before it hits.
We can police the bodies up afterwards."

"I agree, let's move it!" Luke signaled for the men
to hurry back around the perimeter. They had reached
the northwest corner when a pair of Huey command
choppers dropped down out of the sky ahead of them
and disappeared behind the berm only minutes ahead
of the monsoon storm that hit with the fury and noise
of a horny banshee. Within seconds, the men were
soaked and water ran down their legs into the tops of
their boots, draining out through the holes in the
arches. Luke wondered how any oxygen could reach
his lungs because the water was a *solid* wall in front
of him. It was as if he had fallen into the ocean. The
tank drivers couldn't see enough to keep their tanks
on the road and kept pulling off to one side. Luke
assigned a couple of his artillerymen to walk the large
vehicles to the main gate and guide them into their
positions on the perimeter. Once inside the fire-sup-

port base, Luke released his men so that they could go back to their sections and help clean up the mess.

Verduzco paused outside of the orderly room and grabbed Luke by his elbow right before he pulled open the door. "Sir, keep a cool head, if Jeffers is in there."

Luke nodded his head in agreement and set his jaw. The sound of the rain coming down on the tin roof was deafening. He saw the brigade commander and the brigade S-3 standing near the coffeepot fixing themselves a cup of coffee and Jeffers accompanied by Major Montgomery standing near the first sergeant's desk. The Huey crews had elected to weather out the storm with their aircraft. Luke could see from the expression on Jeffers's face that something was wrong, but he didn't know if he was the cause of his commander's worried look.

"Captain Arrowood!" The brigade commander looked up from his Styrofoam cup. "I hope you don't mind us helping ourselves to your coffee."

"That's fine, sir, our first sergeant always has a pot brewing for anybody who wants it." Captain Arrowood saluted the full bird colonel.

"We were on our way out to Alpha Company's location and were forced to divert to your fire base to sit out this freak storm." The colonel looked down at the pool of water at the captain's and the first sergeant's feet. "Why don't you go dry off and come back here and brief us on this probe you people had?"

"Yes, sir." Luke left with the first sergeant to go back to their rooms and change into a dry set of fatigues. He glanced over at Jeffers and nodded his head. "Sorry, I couldn't make it back to Camp Red Devil by seven this morning."

The brigade commander shot a look over at Jeffers that said that he was about to get angry all over again. He had been told that Arrowood had refused to obey orders during the light probe against his fire base and had fired artillery in an unsafe manner. The brigade commander hadn't been told that the artillery being fired was in support of Alpha Company, but had been led to believe that Arrowood was firing killer junior in an unsafe manner into a village. Jeffers had asked for Arrowood's relief of command and the bird colonel had almost gone along with it, but had decided to delay his decision until after he had visited the fire-support base and had talked to the captain. A much different picture was being painted with the coming of the morning. First, they had been in the brigade's operations center when the call had been made from Puppy Foot 6 to Red Bucket 6, the infantry company commander to Captain Arrowood. All of them heard the captain congratulate Arrowood on his superb artillery support, and they had heard the quip about how bad the artillery normally was. The brigade commander had planned on talking to the Alpha Company commander in private before coming to the fire-support base, but nature had changed his plans for him.

Luke and the first sergeant emerged almost at the same time wearing dry fatigues and dry boots.

"Thanks, sir." Luke spoke to the bird colonel. "We needed that."

"We're in no hurry. This monsoon should let up in an hour or so . . . Now about that briefing."

Luke went over to a hand-sketched map of LZ Sandy and started briefing the brigade commander on what he knew already about the attack against the base that seemed to have been coordinated with the attack against the infantry.

"Do you think the NVA actually had *planned* to hit both places at once or maybe it was just a coincidence?" The brigade commander leaned back against the chair he was sitting in.

"We're the only artillery battery that was in range to support Alpha Company, sir. I think the NVA knew that and they also knew that if they attacked LZ Sandy at the same time that we would most likely stop the mission and protect ourselves."

"I was briefed that you had a small probe against your perimeter . . ." The colonel glanced over at Jeffers. He was starting to get very angry again. Jeffers had Captain Kreps call his S-3 during the fight at LZ Sandy and tell him that the unit was being probed and there was no real threat to the base.

"Small?" Luke looked at Verduzco and then back at the brigade commander. "Probably was, sir, if you compare it to a *large* probe, whatever that would be." Luke looked back at Verduzco. "How many NVA dead did you find in the graveyard, First Sergeant?"

Jeffers cut in. "You don't think that you can get away with counting *buried* Vietnamese for a body count, do you?" The crude joke didn't even make it completely out of Jeffers's mouth before he realized that he had made a major fuck-up.

"Freshly killed *NVA*, First Sergeant." Luke had caught the look in the brigade commander's eye and rephrased the question for Jeffers's benefit. Even Montgomery was forced to look down at the floor over the stupid remark his boss had made.

"We found twenty-one dead NVA, sir."

Luke took a second to add up the numbers out loud. "We found five dead with their command party and eight more dead in the outer barbed wire, plus the fifty-three we had already counted from inside of the base and around the berm. That makes . . . eighty-seven *confirmed* freshly killed elite NVA Sappers." Luke smiled when he had said the word *elite*.

The brigade commander's jaw dropped open and he looked over at his operations officer and then shot an almost visible look of pure disgust at Jeffers. "You told me that this was a probe?"

"It seemed so at the time, sir." Jeffers's voice was slightly above a whisper. "Bravo Battery reported only a few casualties and I thought . . ."

"You thought! Damn you, Jeffers!" The brigade commander couldn't hold back his anger any longer and he stood up to face the lieutenant colonel. "This was a major NVA effort designed to overrun two . . . not one, mind you, but *two* of my units and you report it as a fucking probe!" The brigade commander rarely swore and when he did the words were heavily accented as if he were speaking in a foreign language. "This young captain had fought a major engagement with an *elite* North Vietnamese unit and has totally kicked their asses and you report it to me as a probe." The brigade commander's face turned red on his cheeks and white around his mouth. "Jeffers . . . if I find out that you were drunk again last night!" He caught himself and stopped. There were junior officers in the room and enlisted men. He looked at the first sergeant and apologized. "I'm sorry."

Verduzco almost smiled but fought valiantly to contain it. "It's all right, sir. My clerks have hearing problems sometimes."

"I think that LZ Sandy was the NVA's main target and not the infantry company." The brigade's S-3 spoke to break the tension in the room.

"I agree!" The brigade commander slammed his fist down on the first sergeant's desk and the rain stopped. He looked up at the tin roof and smiled. "Don't ask me to do that again!"

Jeffers and Montgomery were the only ones in the room who didn't find the statement funny.

"Would you like a quick tour of the fire base before you leave, sir?" Luke made the offer.

"Yes, we would."

"We can use jeeps. Dotson and Pilgrim . . ." Luke motioned for them to go and get the vehicles.

"Arrowood, you ride with my operations officer and me so we can talk." The colonel threw a glance at Jeffers that dared him to invite himself along with his party.

Jeffers and Montgomery rode alone with the first sergeant and Pilgrim in the second jeep.

Luke gave the brigade commander a quick tour of the perimeter with stops at the FDC and ammunition storage areas. They stopped for a long time at the destroyed tank and the howitzer that was on the perimeter.

The colonel placed his hands on his hips and looked

out over the fire-support base. "Unbelievable. I wouldn't have believed it without seeing it with my own eyes. A group of artillerymen kicking a well-trained NVA company's ass!"

"We're not all that bad, sir."

"I didn't mean it that way, Captain Arrowood . . . what I meant was that you aren't trained to fight like infantry."

"Speaking of fighting like infantry, sir. I would like to recommend some of my men for impact awards."

"We can handle that through the battalion, Captain!" Jeffers tried regaining control.

The brigade commander turned his head slowly so that he could stare directly into Jeffers's eyes. "I think that is a very good idea! Has it dawned on you yet, Lieutenant Colonel Jeffers, that this small, isolated field artillery battery has wracked up a higher body count than the whole brigade did last month?" The colonel's eyebrows flickered as he thought and then spoke again. "He might have it for this month too . . . unless Alpha Company has found more bodies than they've reported so far this morning! I do know one thing for sure . . . LZ Sandy has produced more NVA weapons than the whole damn brigade has since we've been here!" The colonel inhaled a deep breath. He had always wondered when one of the units would report say, a hundred NVA dead and *three* weapons captured. Arrowood's battery reported eighty-seven NVA confirmed dead and ninety-four weapons captured, including pistols.

"Sir." The chief-of-battery approached the group of officers.

"Yes, Sergeant?" Luke answered.

"Sir, the bodies are gone out in the cemetery. They must have come and gotten them during the storm. We found tire tracks leading back to Highway 1."

"That's fine, Sergeant. We've got their weapons." Luke looked over at Verduzco. "I'm glad we got out there before it started raining."

"It saves us having to bury them." The brigade

commander didn't doubt the figures Luke had reported. It made sense that the local Vietcong would have some sort of a backup force to police the battle-field. "So tell me about your recommendations for impact awards."

"Yes, sir." Luke looked out over the battery and spoke to his first sergeant. "Would you take Pilgrim and Dotson and check on the status of our perimeter wire for tonight? We can walk back to the helicopters from here."

Verduzco saluted the officers and left with the men.

"I didn't want to talk in front of him, sir, because I'd like to recommend him for a Silver Star."

"I figured it was something like that." The brigade commander smiled.

Luke briefed the senior officer on what Verduzco had done during the firefight and on all the other men that he wanted decorated for their outstanding acts of valor during the night battle. The colonel listened intently and kept glancing over at his operations offi-cer and at Jeffers, who was having a very difficult time hiding his jealousy.

"What do you think?" The colonel addressed his operations officer.

"I think the captain is right and we should impact all of the men as soon as possible for morale purposes, and I also think that we should submit Bravo Battery, 4th Battalion of the 5th Artillery for a Valorous Unit Award."

The colonel pointed his finger at his staff officer. "*That* is a very good idea!"

Major Montgomery slowly blinked his eyes. Arro-wood had completely outmaneuvered him. If Bravo Battery won the Valorous Unit Award, they would be the first unit in the 1st Brigade to have done so and it would be impossible to relieve him of his command. The difference between Jeffers and Montgomery was that the major knew when he was beat and the lieu-tenant colonel didn't and would push the issue too far.

Montgomery held out his hand to Luke. "Congratulations, you have done a superb job!"

The brigade commander had been around too long to fall for Montgomery's fake congratulations, but he respected the officer's class in making the gesture. Montgomery nudged Jeffers and the battalion commander tried smiling and shook hands with Arrowood.

"We're going to fly out to the Alpha Company site and then back to Camp Red Devil. I plan on being back here by mid-afternoon, so have the men you've recommended for awards standing by." The gray-haired officer started walking toward his helicopter.

Luke followed and saluted the senior officers as they departed.

The brigade commander looked down at the fire-support base as the chopper gained altitude and then over at Jeffers who was sitting in the jump seat across from him. "And you wanted to *relieve* him?"

Jeffers acted like he couldn't hear the colonel and cupped his ear with his hand.

Major Montgomery shook his head slowly and decided that he had better detach himself from Jeffers or he would go down with him and that wasn't what he had planned for his career goal. There had been a Montgomery every generation since Gettysburg wearing stars on his collar, and he wasn't about to break that family tradition.

CHAPTER SEVEN

✪✪✪✪✪✪✪✪✪✪✪✪✪✪✪✪✪

FIRE!

The heavy rain had cooled off the sand and had left a fresh smell in the air that the artillerymen were enjoying. Small groups of men were standing around their work sites talking about what they had done during the night battle with the elite Sapper unit. Morale within the unit was very high even though they had taken some casualties. There wasn't a man in the battery who didn't realize that it could have been much worse.

Sergeant Cole took advantage of the cool air blowing over the fire-support base behind the storm and had his men filling sandbags and fixing the damage that had been done to his two ammunition storage bunkers from the mortar rounds. One of his bunkers had taken a couple of direct hits on the roof and a number of the sandbags had been torn open and needed to be replaced along with a whole section that had been torn open along one side. The bunkers had been buried halfway up their sides with loose sand and only the top portions and the roofs were exposed and needed to be covered with sandbags.

PFC Jenkins had been visiting some of his buddies in the ammunition section and had volunteered to help them fill sandbags. He was very happy with his new job working in the fire-direction center and had told Sergeant Cole earlier that he was thinking of extending for six months in Vietnam and getting his military occupational specialty changed from ammunition handler to a job code for the FDC. Cole realized that Jenkins was the kind of young man who would proba-bly end up reenlisting and making the Army a career.

"Hey, Jenkins . . ." Cole stopped throwing the torn sandbags down off the roof, "you don't have to spend your off-duty time doing our work for us."

Jenkins looked up at the black NCO and smiled. "Ain't a big problem, Sergeant. I'd just be sleeping anyway." He felt a sharp pain behind his eyes and groaned as he looked up at the sergeant with the sun shining behind him.

"Something wrong?" Cole started jumping down from the roof.

"No . . . just the sun was in my eyes." Jenkins rubbed his forehead. He had never experienced pain like that before.

"Hold the bag open, man." One of the ammo han-dlers tried dumping a shovel of sand in the mouth of the bag Jenkins was holding and ended up spilling most of it on the ground. "Hold the damn bag open!"

The pain spread out to every nerve ending in his head all at the same time. Jenkins dropped down on one knee and then staggered back up on his feet.

"Man, are you sick or something?" The soldier holding the shovel changed his expression from anger to concern.

Jenkins lifted one of the filled sandbags up off the ground and threw it over his shoulder. He carried the green nylon sandbag over to the ammunition bunker where a portion of the wooden wall was exposed and dropped the bag in place against the rest of the stack. At the same time, he experienced a tremendous pain behind his eyes and grabbed for his forehead with both hands. If it hadn't been for the pain, he would have seen the canvas handle of the NVA satchel charge that was covered up by the sandbag he had thrown down.

Only one of the NVA Sappers had made it across the inner perimeter road and over to the two large ammunition storage bunkers. He had seen where the mortar rounds had torn the sandbags and had shoved one of his satchel charges under the top row of bags next to the wooden structural wall and had replaced a couple of sandbags to cover the charge that was made up of ten pounds of C4 plastic explosive and two white phosphorous hand grenades. The whole charge had been rigged for a twenty-four-hour delay.

Sergeant Cole jumped down from the bunker roof and grabbed Jenkins's arm. "I think you're coming down with something. Let's get over to the medics."

"Don't fuck with him, Sarge." The soldier holding the shovel patted the sand with the blade. "He's suffering from too much blow is all."

Jenkins flashed a look of pure hate at his contemporary. "I don't do that shit anymore!"

"There's your answer, man. Youse sufferin' from withdrawls!"

"Let's see the medic." Cole helped Jenkins walk over to the medic's hootch.

"I feel like I'm going to throw up." Jenkins's hands began to shake at the same time a heavy sweat broke out over his forehead.

The battery medic took one look at Jenkins and shook his head. "Malaria."

"You sure?" Cole helped tuck a blanket in around Jenkins who was lying on a stretcher.

"I'll bet a month's pay on it. He has all of the classical symptoms." The medic scratched his neck. "We'd better have a MEDEVAC called in for him."

"I'll run over to the FDC and tell the lieutenant while you get him ready." Cole started jogging toward the FDC as soon as he had left the hootch.

First Sergeant Verduzco saw Sergeant Cole running through the center of the battery and knew that something was wrong. "What's up?"

Cole didn't stop running and called out to the first sergeant as he passed him, "Jenkins had a malaria attack and we have to get him back to a hospital."

Verduzco nodded his head and went back to supervising the raking of the sand between the howitzer sections. There was an area between all of the howitzers that Arrowood had ordered be raked daily so that any footprints would show up in the sand. The troops had laughed at him *before* the Sapper attack, but now they went out of their way to make sure everything he asked for was done. The men in the Fifth Gun Section owed their lives to the raked sand. One of the section had noticed footprints along the side of the sandbags next to their gun pit only seconds after the first grenades had gone off the night before and had discovered one of the Sappers hiding next to their sandbag wall with his satchel charges ready. The chief-of-section had shot him before he could set off any of the high-explosive packages.

The helicopter circled the fire-support base one time before setting down inside of the perimeter in the area where the armored vehicles normally parked behind the orderly room. Verduzco looked over at Captain Arrowood. "It can't be the MEDEVAC. They don't make it that fast during a firefight, let alone for a routine sick-call evacuation."

"Maybe they were in the area or on their way back up north from LZ Nancy." Luke shielded his eyes with his hand but couldn't read the markings on the side of the chopper.

Dotson and Pilgrim helped the battery medic lift Jenkins up on the back of the jeep for the ride over to the chopper pad. Jenkins had become delirious and was strapped down on the stretcher.

"I wonder where he picked up malaria?" Dotson kept his eyes on Jenkins. "Can you catch that shit from his sweat?" He wiped his hands against his fatigue pants after having accidentally touched Jenkins's sweat soaked uniform.

"Are you *sure* you're from a *city* in Tennessee?" Dotson helped the medic tuck a blanket around Jenkins who had gone from a heavy sweat to chills in a matter of minutes.

"Nashville is a fucking city!" Dotson went over to the driver's seat and started the jeep.

"Well, someone should have taught you that the only way you can catch malaria is through a mosquito bite and that has to be by a mosquito that is infected with the virus."

"I wonder where he caught it, then. We haven't left the fire base except to go to Camp Red Devil and we ain't been near any jungle." Dotson jockeyed the jeep around and started to drive slowly back toward the orderly room and the waiting helicopter.

"Buzzy! You are a hopeless case, man!" Pilgrim walked alongside the slow moving jeep holding onto the stretcher. "You don't need to be in the fucking jungle to catch malaria in Vietnam." Pilgrim thought for a minute and added. "Hell, you can probably catch it while you're on guard duty at night. Shit, as soon as the sun goes down those motherfuckers come out of nowhere!"

"That ain't a MEDEVAC chopper." Dotson stopped the jeep by the back corner of the orderly room so that the sand and dust wouldn't get on Jenkins when the chopper took off again.

"Well, why don't we ask him if he can take Jenkins back to one of the evacuation hospitals if he's leaving?" The medic checked the tag on Jenkins's uniform to make sure all of the data had been filled out right.

Verduzco came around the front side of the orderly room hootch and met the occupants of the chopper. He could see the Christian cross sewn on the helmet cover of the lieutenant colonel as he approached his party. Verduzco saluted the Army chaplain. "What brings you out here, Father?" He didn't know which one of the Christian religions the chaplain represented.

"I try and make it out to the location where there's been a fight as soon as I can to hold Mass." The white-haired lieutenant colonel smiled a warm grin.

"That's kind of you, Father. I think the Catholic men would like that." Verduzco nodded at the helicopter. "Do you plan on being out here long?"

"We should be here a few hours. I need some time to set up my altar for Mass and then I like to spend some time for confessions . . ." His eyes changed color, ". . . war has a way of blackening men's souls."

Verduzco nodded his head. The chaplain knew his business. It was very smart of him to make sure he reached the soldiers as soon as he could after a fight because many of them would be suffering from the killing and needed to talk to someone besides a war buddy. "Do you think we could use your chopper to take a sick man back to the hospital while you're here?"

"Of course!" The chaplain looked around and saw the jeep with the man lying on the stretcher. "Is there anything that I can do?"

"No, Father. He has malaria."

The priest nodded his head and motioned for his assistant to sit the box down that contained his portable altar. "Where would you like me to set up?"

"How about the mess tent?"

"Excellent."

"As soon as we get Jenkins on the chopper, I'll have Dotson take you over there in the jeep."

The priest removed his helmet with his left hand and wiped his forehead with his sleeve. "It is hot out here."

"LZ Sandy is one of the few landing zones that was named right." Pilgrim smiled at the priest. "I'm a Southern Baptist, sir, but do you think I can sort of sit in on your church service today?"

"Absolutely, soldier! I don't think God will mind, but you won't be able to take communion . . . that's a Catholic ritual."

Pilgrim frowned. "Really? Us Baptists take communion and we were told that it was a Baptist ritual."

Dotson returned from helping load Jenkins in the chopper. The medic was going to ride with him back to the hospital because there wasn't a regular crew. "What'cha talking about, Tommy Lee?"

"Communion . . . is it a Catholic or a Baptist ritual?" Pilgrim saw the priest's jaw tighten.

"Christian, isn't it?"

The priest smiled. "Out of the mouths of babes . . ."

"Dotson, take the chaplain over to the mess tent and show him where to set up his things." Verduzco started walking toward the ammunition bunkers where Captain Arrowood was standing talking to Cole. "And let me know when Mass is going to start!"

"Sure thing, Top."

Luke watched as the ammunition section detail finished sandbagging the roof of the large bunker. He knew that if the attack had taken place a month earlier, the whole ammunition storage area would have gone up. The NVA had done their job when they had reconnoitered the fire-support base. The next time that he saw Sergeant Jones, he was going to kiss him for throwing in the ammunition storage bunkers along with the new fighting bunkers.

"Are they about done?" Verduzco stopped next to the captain.

"Should be soon. Who came in?"

"Chaplain—he wants to hold Mass and confession." Verduzco cupped his hands around his mouth and called up to Sergeant Cole. "A chaplain is here to hold Mass; send any of your men over to the mess tent when you're finished here that want to come."

Cole stopped stacking the sandbags and shook the sweat off his forehead. "Give us another half hour and we should be pretty much finished."

Verduzco nodded his head. "I'll hold him up."

"Is he going to have a service for our dead?" Luke had attended more than his share of the traditional helmet-and-M-16 ceremonies that the chaplains conducted in Vietnam. They would represent each dead American by sticking the bayonet from an M-16 in the ground and hang a helmet from the stock of the weapon. The symbolic gesture would usually get very emotional, especially when they used the actual helmets the dead men had worn. Photographers and war correspondents liked those kinds of scenes but the troops would rather do without the reminders.

Verduzco nodded his head. "I think so."

"No helmets and guns."

"I'll make sure he doesn't."

"Thanks. We've got to pull the battery together now and not remind them of our losses."

"Understand, sir. Are you going to come to the Mass?"

"Yes, as soon as they finish up here." Luke stepped into the dark entrance of the bunker and reached up above his head to turn on the electric lights that had been strung down the center of the bunker from the field kit designed for motor pool use. The bunker was neatly arranged. The left side was neat sections of different 155mm projectiles: high-explosive, white phosphorus, illumination, and different colored smoke rounds. The right side of the bunker had pallets of small-arms ammunition, hand grenades, flares, and fuses for the projectiles. It wasn't the perfect ammunition storage situation, but it served the combat needs of the battery. The other bunker held only powder charges for the howitzers.

Luke started leaving the bunker when Sergeant Cole entered. "Leave the lights on, sir, we're just going to do a little shuffling around a bit before church services start." Luke saw the look on the face of the black soldier who was with Cole. The man had been a close friend of Talbot's and was one of the few soldiers still in the battery who hadn't sided with Luke and Verduzco.

The chaplain's tape recorder played the entrance music that signaled the beginning of the Mass. Soldiers from all over the fire-support base started hurrying over to the mess tent. Luke could see that only the bare skeleton crews remained on the guns and perimeter with the exception of the blacks in the ammunition section who wore the skullcaps of Muslims. There were only three of them in the battery, but Luke was seeing more and more Black Muslims in the supply and rear-echelon units coming over from the States. First Sergeant Verduzco had spread the word that a church service was being conducted in the mess tent and that it would be nondenominational except for communion. All of the Christian religions were represented under the flapping canvas. The priest had changed into his vestments and stood behind the serving line that had been transformed into an altar. The sides of the tent had been rolled up, and Luke could see that all of the seats had been taken at the picnic tables and men were standing. The chaplain's idea to come out to the fire-support base had been a good one. The men needed to give thanks for being spared during the fight, and some of them needed to ask for forgiveness for taking lives during the battle.

Luke was halfway across the firing battery when the explosion sent a shock wave out over the sand.

Verduzco reacted instantly and ran out of the tent followed by half of the battery. The gold-plated chalice on the altar rocked, but didn't fall over. The chaplain placed his hand on it and felt the tremor of the explosion through it. He smiled over at his assistant, who was looking at him with huge fear-filled eyes.

Luke had reached the ammunition bunker first and saw that a whole section of the wall had been blown away and pieces of white phosphorus were burning out on the sand. He could see that the explosion had taken place *outside* of the bunker. The three Muslims from the ammunition section were the next to arrive at the scene.

"Where's Sergeant Cole?" He looked at the nearest Muslim, who nodded his head at the smoke rolling out of the bunker entrance.

Luke ran to the entrance and was met by the blast of a secondary explosion that picked him up and sent him flying backwards over the sand and dropped him down twenty feet away. He staggered back up on his feet and brushed the burning pieces of packing material off his fatigues, ignoring the pain coming from the right side of his face.

"You can't go in there, Captain . . . it's burning and gonna explode!" The tall Muslim tried stopping Luke, but he swept past him.

"Captain!" Verduzco's voice stopped Luke. "Captain! Don't go in there!"

Luke turned around in the smoking entrance and looked over at his first sergeant. The men surrounding Verduzco gasped when they saw the right side of the captain's face. It was badly burned. Luke disappeared into the smoking hole and dropped down on his hands and knees below the billowing smoke. He could see a few feet inside of the bunker as he crawled over to where he had last seen Cole and the soldier working. A hand stuck out from behind a stack of ammunition crates and Luke crawled over to it. He saw that the man was unconscious. It was Talbot's friend. Luke unbuckled his pistol belt and removed the holster so that he could extend the belt to its maximum length before looping it under the soldier's arms and around his own neck. Luke straddled the unconscious soldier on all fours and started crawling back toward the entrance. The explosion knocked Luke against the man's chest and pushed his face alongside the soldier's head. The man's hair rubbing against his burned face made Luke scream, but his voice was muffled by the explosion. Luke gasped for air and struggled back up on all fours and started crawling blindly.

Dotson was the first one to see the captain emerge thorough the bunker entrance and ran over to pull him out. The toxic smoke made him gag, but he grabbed Luke's pistol belt and pulled hard until they had cleared the bunker entrance, and then a half-dozen artillerymen helped.

Luke coughed and gasped for a couple of seconds and then grabbed his pistol belt again and started crawling back toward the bunker.

Verduzco grabbed Luke's fatigue jacket and pulled him back. "Sir, you can't go back in there! The whole damn thing is going to go up at any time."

Luke looked in the first sergeant's eyes and the senior NCO released his grip so that he could crawl back inside of the burning bunker. Luke's eyes were watering so bad that he couldn't see anything. He guided himself by instinct back to where he had found the first man and patted the sand floor until he felt Sergeant Cole's boot. Luke rigged the sergeant just like he had rigged the first man with the pistol belt and crawled back out of the bunker. He had misjudged the entrance by a foot and had run into the wall with his head. The smoke was now so thick that breathing had become almost impossible a foot above the ground. Luke was about ready to pass out when he felt the entrance support beam and made a mad dash on all fours, dragging Cole between his arms and legs.

Hands picked him up off the ground and he could feel someone lifting him up and running with him.

The chaplain's helicopter pilot banked into the wind and turned in a circle above the fire-support base and Highway 1. He was planning on flying above the secured highway back to Camp Red Devil where the medic could clear the sick soldier with the brigade medical section and have him shipped directly to a convalescent hospital in Da Nang. The explosion from the NVA satchel charge sent a spray of white streamers up into the sky from the phosphorus hand grenades. The pilot changed his course and swept back over the fire base and saw the blaze starting in the bunker. He figured that there would be some injured soldiers from the explosion and brought his chopper down again on the helipad.

First Sergeant Verduzco didn't waste any time getting Captain Arrowood and the injured soldiers over to the waiting chopper. He had the men standing nearby grab them by their clothes and carry them without stretchers to the chopper and lay them on the steel floor. Verduzco ran over to the pilot's door and yelled in through the window.

"Take them directly to the EVAC hospital in Da Nang!" He stepped back away from the helicopter and turned his back to the stinging sand that was being kicked up by the rotor blade.

"The fire is starting to catch onto the wooden beams

in the bunker, First Sergeant!" Dotson had been watching the flames leaping up the side of the bunker.

"Go crank up that 548 over there and bring it to the bunker!" Verduzco pointed at the ammunition-tracked vehicle that was parked behind the mess hall where it was being loaded up with garbage and trash. Dotson broke out into a fast run and hopped behind the steering columns of the fully tracked vehicle. He guessed that the first sergeant wanted to use the vehicle to fight the fire, and brought it around the perimeter road to the back side of the burning bunker. There had been a few more minor secondary explosions, but everyone inside of the base knew that there were over a hundred 155mm projectiles inside of the structure, and that, if they got hot enough, they would blow half the base away.

Verduzco showed Dotson where he wanted the tracked vehicle to push against the bunker, and then ran over to get some of the men throwing sand on the flames with shovels. He knew that there wasn't enough water on the fire base to put the fire out, but the storm had saturated the sandbags and the wooden frame of the bunker and the fire was having a hard time catching.

Dotson gunned the track and the steel treads gripped the sand. He stalled the vehicle and had to start it again and slowly push against the support beams. The bunker groaned and collapsed in a column of sparks. The flames were slowly being smothered by the sandbags.

Lieutenant Zimmerman had joined the fire-fighting crew and was frantically shoveling sand on any small flame that appeared. He had seen back at Fort Sill, Oklahoma, a powder pit that had caught on fire accidently, and knew just how dangerous the situation was. He had expected to be blown to pieces every time he threw a shovelful of sand on a flame.

The chaplain stood watching the fire-fighting effort still wearing his vestments. He had seen the heroic lifesaving feat by Captain Arrowood and was in shock after seeing the burns on the captain's face.

The fire was under control before Verduzco noticed the lieutenant colonel standing there. "Well, it looks like you've seen some action today, Father."

"What happened?" The chaplain made the sign of the cross and whispered a short blessing and thanks for the soldiers who fought the fire.

"It looks like something exploded *outside* of the bunker and started a fire." Verduzco pointed to the pattern of sandbags stretched out over the fire base from the north side of the bunker.

"What could it have been?" The chaplain looked puzzled. "Sabotage?"

Verduzco shook his head. "Not from our people, Father! You've heard too many stories back in Camp Red Devil. It looks like an NVA satchel charge set on a delay fuse. They do that sometimes to try and catch us off-guard. It also puts fear in the men who have to clean up after an attack." The first sergeant walked around to the side of the bunker from where the explosion had occurred and could see the spot where the charge had blown a small crater in the sand. He was sure that it had been a hidden satchel charge. "I wonder why we missed finding it?"

Pilgrim was standing next to the first sergeant holding his CAR-15 submachine gun. He wasn't taking any chances and scanned the berm constantly, expecting waves of NVA to come charging over the top any second.

"I don't think that I've seen a braver act in my life than what Captain Arrowood did to save those two men." The chaplain kept his eyes on the smoldering bunker. "We've got to recommend him for a Soldier's Medal."

"Shit, sir! He should get the Medal of Honor for that action!" Pilgrim forgot he was talking to a chaplain. "Did you see that first secondary explosion blow his ass back out of the bunker?"

The chaplain smiled and nodded his head.

"He's got guts to have gotten back up and run inside again! I mean once was enough to tell you something!"

Verduzco and Zimmerman looked at each other and Zimmerman spoke. "I think the chaplain has a point there, First Sergeant. We should write the captain up for a Soldier's Medal for heroism."

"If this would have happened last night, he probably would have gotten a Medal of Honor for it." Verduzco thought about everything that had occurred during the past forty-eight hours and agreed with the executive officer's statement.

Lieutenant Colonel Jeffers sat in his sleeping hootch with a well-used bottle of Gordon's gin held between his legs. He had discarded his glass and was drinking the water colored liquid straight from the bottle. He wasn't drunk, just very angry. Major Montgomery had reported him sick and in bed trying to sleep it off before it developed into something serious. The rest of the staff thought that he had a touch of the flu.

Jeffers looked at the wall across from his cot and talked to himself. "Why! Why did I have to get him assigned to my battalion? Why in the fuck me!" Jeffers took another sip from the bottle and set it back down between his legs and grabbed his pillow to his chest. "That son of a bitch has turned the brigade commander against me and I only have six weeks before I get another efficiency report."

The door opened to the hootch and Major Montgomery stepped inside. All of the window flaps had been dropped down and the contrast from the bright light outside to the dark shade inside made it almost impossible for the major to see. "Sir?"

Jeffers watched his roommate stagger across the floor and bump into a chair before answering. "What?"

"We have a problem."

"Can't you fucking handle it?" Jeffers shoved the pillow to one side and lifted the bottle to his mouth.

He watched the expression on Montgomery's face and then offered him the bottle.

Montgomery refused it with a sweep of his hand.

"What's wrong? Are you too good to drink with me now?" Jeffers sneered. He suspected Montgomery of changing sides, and if it were true he had already decided on burning him on his efficency report so that he would never see stars on his collar. He wouldn't write a searing report, just low enough so that Montgomery couldn't appeal it, yet bad enough so that stars would never fall on the officer's collar.

"I'd love a drink right now, but we've got problems. There's been an explosion out at Bravo Battery. We don't have all of the details yet, but Lieutenant Zimmerman has reported that their ammunition section's projectile bunker has been destroyed and three men have been MEDEVACed due to injuries; two men from the ammunition section and . . ." Montgomery watched Jeffers for a reaction to his next statement, "and Captain Arrowood."

"Arrowood?" Jeffers sat up on his cot. "Is he dead?"

"Burned." Montgomery couldn't believe it, but Jeffers was actually smiling.

"Bad?"

"We don't know yet."

"Find out for me!" Jeffers chuckled and swallowed a large mouthful of burning gin. There was a major difference between the types of burning in *his* throat and on Arrowood's face and shoulder. "I need to know!"

"Yes, sir." Montgomery pushed the door open and the sunlight filled the hootch.

Jeffers held his arm across his eyes and screamed, "Shut the door and find out for me . . . now! I want to know if Arrowood is dying!"

Montgomery let the door slam shut. He paused and looked at the plywood door and shook his head. He couldn't believe that, only a few days earlier, he was close friends with the creature inside of the hootch.

CHAPTER EIGHT

✪✪✪✪✪✪✪✪✪✪✪✪✪✪✪

BRIGADE RECON

The walk along the beach made Luke feel much better. He kept looking out over the water as if he were trying to see the coast of California in the distance. The smell of the South China Sea wasn't the same as the smell coming off the ocean at Malibu; it was the same water; some of the molecules could actually have rubbed against the rocks below the house they were renting on the ocean.

Luke reached into the waistband of the light green hospital pajamas he was wearing and removed his wife's letter. He rubbed the envelope between his thumb and forefinger for a long time before removing the single sheet of writing paper. Her letters had gone from ten pages to one.

Dear Luke,

I was thrilled to hear that you are eligible for another R&R. You mentioned two places you would like to go this time; I would like to see Sydney, Australia (we've been to Hawaii before).

The children are doing fine and they miss you; five years in Vietnam is a long time to be without a father. There was a peace rally on the beach last week and Alex started crying when they burned an effigy of an American G.I.

I'll check and see if we can fly the children half-

fare to Sydney. I know you miss them a lot, but
we have to be practical.

I'm looking forward to seeing you next week!

Love, Jodi

The letter was more of a note than a letter from a
wife to her husband who was serving in a war. Luke
tapped the open sheet of paper against his leg and
squinted as he looked out over the water. One of the
sentences stuck in his mind; *five years in Vietnam is a
long time to be without a father*. He folded the letter
and slipped it back into the envelope and walked
down to the edge of the sea. The waves lapped gently
against the sand at his feet when he squatted down and
laid the envelope on the water and watched it as the
dry paper absorbed the salt water and sunk slowly to
the bottom. A small wave rolled in and flipped open
the water-logged envelope and the single-paged letter
floated open just below the surface of the water.
Luke's eyes rested on the portion of the blurry words
that had said; five years in Vietnam is a long time to
be without a father.

"Captain Arrowood!" The voice came from the
raised deck that had been built on the back of the
convalescent ward. The DOs believed that sunshine
was as good if not better than chemicals for healing
wounds, and there had been a running battle between
the doctors of osteopathy and the medical doctors
over the value of the deck for the patients. The MDs
wanted to use the lumber to build a deck on the back
of the officers lounge overlooking the sea. There was
no official declaration as to who had won the Battle
of the Deck, except the deck was the most popular
place in the whole hospital and the patients who
used it frequently seemed to heal faster. "Captain
Arrowood!" The officer waved from the railing.

Luke waved back and started walking slowly up the
beach to where the man waited. He didn't like the
way the officer was standing; for some reason, his
body language was reflecting some kind of tension.

"Good seeing you again, sir." Luke recognized the brigade's personnel officer when he drew closer to the steps.

"I hear that you're quite the hero!" The lieutenant colonel tried smiling, but Luke could see that he was hiding something.

Luke shrugged his shoulders. "I'm glad that the burns weren't that bad and my face has healed."

The senior officer glanced at Luke's face and could see that his eyebrow was starting to grow back in and the skin on his cheek was starting to turn back to a healthy color.

"Believe it or not, the scratches I got back at the battalion headquarters have turned into some nasty-looking scars." Luke lifted his hospital shirt and showed the lieutenant colonel white streaks that ran across the front of his body.

"You seem to *attract* trou . . ." He started to say trouble and changed the word, ". . . danger."

Luke smiled without showing his teeth. He knew that the senior brigade officer hadn't flown all the way to the hospital in Da Nang just to talk about him attracting trouble. "So how are things going back at Camp Red Devil?"

"Quite good . . . quite good, in fact." The lieutenant colonel looked around for an empty chair and motioned with his hand for Luke to take a seat across from him.

"How's Lieutenant Zimmerman doing out in Bravo Battery?" Luke leaned back and crossed his legs.

"Haven't you heard?"

Luke smiled again. Here it comes. "Heard what, sir?"

"Well, you know it's been two months since you were hurt and that is a long time . . ."

"A long time for what, sir?" Luke wasn't about to let the personnel officer off the hook. He had heard that the officer was a close friend of Jeffers, but he had never seen the two of them together except for the time when he had accidentally stumbled into a private party for West Point officers that was being hosted by Jeffers in the artillery officers club.

"We can't let a first lieutenant act as a battery commander for that long, not with so many captains waiting to command a battery in Vietnam."

Luke knew.

The personnel officer continued. "Your battalion commander has given command of Bravo Battery to a new captain."

Luke struggled inside of himself not to show his true emotion. He had refused evacuation to Japan so that he wouldn't lose command of the battery.

The colonel glanced over at Luke to see what his response was to the news and saw a blank face. "The brigade commander has personally given you a new assignment . . ."

Luke could tell from the twitch in the corner of the officer's eye that the man had not liked the brigade commander's decision. "Who got command of Bravo Battery?"

"A Captain Pike . . . Class of . . ." He caught himself and stopped.

"Class of . . . what, sir?"

The personnel officer sighed. He knew that he had screwed up, but he was talking to a captain and it really didn't make a damn difference. "The class of 1966."

"A West Pointer . . ." Luke chuckled, ". . . you *didn't* give the battery to a *Citadel* man, did you?" Luke waved his finger at the officer. "Those southern boys aren't afraid to fight."

"Are you insinuating that West Point officers *are*?" The lieutenant colonel's face turned beet red.

"No . . . it's just that I haven't seen any who have . . . they seem to have all the nice staff jobs and get command of units *after* all the dirty shit details have been done by *other* officers."

"Damn it! You hold your tongue, young man, or I'll have charges pressed against you!"

"For what, sir? Telling the truth? Bravo Battery

was a snake pit four months ago . . . *you* know that, Jeffers knows that, and I know that . . . Why didn't you assign one of your West Pointers to clean it up then?"

The personnel officer smashed his fist down on the patio table and stood up. "Personally, Captain! I think spending five years in Vietnam has softened your brain!"

Luke's face darkened. "You know, sir, it seems that has been the second time today that someone has said that to me."

"Then there must be some truth in it." The senior officer sneered.

"Aren't *soldiers* supposed to fight? Isn't that the *whole*, mind you, not a secondary reason, but the *whole* purpose of our existence . . . to fight for our country?"

"You are a fucking fool, Arrowood! A fucking fool!" The brigade personnel officer turned to leave and saw all of the soldiers who were sitting at the other tables staring at him. He hadn't realized that their conversation had gotten so loud and that everyone on the patio had stopped talking and was listening to his conversation with Luke. He took a couple of steps away from the table and then remembered his reason for flying all of the way from Camp Red Devil to Da Nang. He opened his briefcase and removed a manila envelope. "Here!" He threw the packet down on the table. "Your new orders!"

"Colonel?" Luke's soft voice stopped the officer. "I'm probably a *fucking fool* for staying here in Vietnam for five years . . . but this war isn't going to be lost because of us *fucking fools*!"

The personnel officer started to answer and was cut off when the watching troops started clapping and cheering Luke. One of the soldiers near the exit pushed his wheelchair up to the screen door so that the lieutenant colonel couldn't open it. The young soldier had both legs missing. "Sir?"

"Yes, soldier?"

"Am I a *fucking fool*, too?"

The deck became quiet waiting for the officer's answer.

"I mean, I could have ran off to Canada to escape the draft . . . or I could have burned my draft card and joined a hippie commune . . . but I came here instead and lost my legs . . ." The soldier's voice became filled with emotion, ". . . please . . . answer me . . . am I a *fucking fool*, too?"

The lieutenant colonel shook his head.

"I can't hear you, sir."

"No . . ." The officer whispered the word.

"Pardon me, sir?"

"I said, no!" He turned away from the blocked doorway and hurried down the wooden steps to the sand and raced across the beach to another exit.

Luke watched the officer struggle through the loose sand and felt the tears rolling down his cheeks. There wasn't any reason why he should be crying, but he was and he couldn't stop. A hand touched his. Luke turned his head, but the tears coating his eyes prevented him from seeing who it was.

"*He's* the fucking fool, sir." The soldier in the wheelchair had joined Luke.

Luke nodded his head and turned to look out over the sand. He couldn't see into the future, but if he could have, he would have seen the chubby lieutenant colonel who had waddled away from the deck wearing three stars on his collar and in charge of all the administration for the Army.

It was a good thing that Luke couldn't see into the future, especially into the office that was next to the three-star general's.

Luke waited until after supper to open the manila envelope the brigade personnel officer had hand delivered to him. He read the orders, signed by the brigade commander himself, that made him the new commander of the brigade's Recon Company. Luke closed his eyes and leaned his head back against his pillow.

He felt mixed emotions over losing his battery, but at the same time he liked the idea of commanding the recon unit. He smiled with his eyes closed and thought good thoughts. Bravo Battery was capable of taking care of itself now, and he was sure that they wouldn't let anyone screw it up again. The men had been taught some good lessons, and the Sapper attack had cemented them all together.

"Sir?"

Luke opened his eyes and saw Sergeant Cole and Talbot's friend standing at the sides of his bed. "Hello." He closed his eyes again.

"We heard what happened out on the patio. It's all over the hospital."

"I figured it would be."

"You don't sound too happy about it, sir." Talbot's friend sat down on the edge of the bed. "Everyone, and I mean everyone, is on your side. Man, what a fucking asshole!" He punched the sheet with his fist. "To come in here and call you a fucking fool!"

"That's the problem."

"What is, sir?"

"*He* screwed up, but I've got to go back to the brigade." Luke showed Sergeant Cole his new orders.

"They've taken you out of Bravo Battery!"

"Yep . . . you're looking at the new commander of the Recon Company . . . thanks to the *brigade commander*." Luke rolled his eyes. "I'd hate to think where I would have ended up if Jeffers and our friend the personnel officer would have selected my next assignment."

"I would say the place would be very *hot*, sir."

"*Very!*"

"With your luck, sir, you would find a way of getting an ice-making machine down there." Cole patted Arrowood's leg. "Seriously, sir, we sure are going to miss you back at Bravo Battery."

"Thanks, Sergeant . . ." Luke inhaled a deep breath, "but I think the NCOs in the battery can handle it now, don't you?"

"Without all of the bullshit!" Cole flashed a look over at Talbot's friend.

"He's right there, sir, without all the bullshit!" Talbot's *ex*-friend passed a look back at the sergeant. It was time to soldier.

CHAPTER NINE

✪✪✪✪✪✪✪✪✪✪✪✪✪✪✪

REST AND RECUPERATION

The chartered United Airlines jet left from the Da Nang airfield for Sydney, Australia, at two o'clock in the morning for the R&R flight Luke was on. He had boarded the aircraft with mixed emotions with the rest of the laughing and joking men. His wife's letter kept popping up in his mind, especially the line about his being in Vietnam for five years.

Luke put the headphones on and rotated the selector wheel to a channel he liked. Peter, Paul and Mary's hit tune, "Leaving on a Jet Plane," was just starting to play, and struck Luke as very ironic.

The first hour in the air was filled with the noise coming from the men on the plane who had just left dangerous field assignments and were excited over the trip away from death, but slowly they calmed down and fell asleep. Luke unbuckled his seat belt and walked slowly down the aisle of sleeping soldiers to the lavatory in the rear of the aircraft. He looked at each one of the faces as he passed and, in their sleep, they looked like high school boys on a field trip. None of them should have been there fighting a war that was becoming increasingly unpopular back in the States.

A soft glow from the night-lights on the plane reflected off the open eyes of the soldier sitting in the aisle seat in the last row by the bathrooms. Luke had been around long enough to recognize fear on a man's face. The fear didn't make any sense. If they had been on their return flight to Vietnam he could have understood it, but going to Sydney shouldn't cause the soldier to be afraid unless he was afraid of flying.

Luke used the latrine and washed his face in cold water before stepping back into the small area where the stewardesses fixed meals for the passengers. He could see that the soldier was still awake and that something was scaring the hell out of the man. Luke poured himself a cup of coffee and sat down in the jump seat across from where the soldier was sitting. "They made a fresh pot of coffee if you want some."

The soldier's eyes focused and he gave Luke an embarrassed look before nodding his head. He fumbled with his seat belt and became even more embarrassed as he struggled to his feet. It took the soldier ten minutes to get his coffee and return to his seat. Luke waited.

"I . . . I've never been to Australia before . . ." The soldier tested his voice with the sentence.

"They've just opened it up for R&R." Luke sipped from his coffee and saw that the young man's hands were shaking. "It had something to do with black American soldiers. I guess the Aussies didn't want blacks using their cities for R&R and our government wouldn't open it up just for whites, so it's been closed until recently."

The soldier pushed himself up in his seat so that he could look over the heads of the men on the flight. "There aren't that many blacks on board."

"Bangkok seems to be the black soldiers' favorite R&R spot . . . They call the women there the Greeks of the Orient."

"Yeah?" The soldier's voice quavered.

"I'm Captain Arrowood."

The soldier looked directly at Luke for the first time. "Specialist Bergman, sir."

"What's your first name?"

"Uwe."

"Ow-ve?"

The soldier smiled showing that behind the fear was

a naturally happy young man. "No, it's pronounced, ū-vee."

"Uwe."

"Right . . ."

"What country is that name from?"

"Germany."

"You first generation American?"

A surprised look covered the soldier's face. "How did you know, sir?"

"Usually people from the old country name their children after relatives and friends back there, so first generation Americans have old country names."

Uwe smiled again. "We're old country all right. I've had an ancestor fight in every European war since someone threw the first rock. My dad says that our family fought against the Romans!"

"A warrior clan?"

"Something like that." He rubbed his specialist fourth class patch on his sleeve. "I've got an appointment to West Point as soon as my tour is over."

"The Army's enlisted recruiting program?"

Uwe nodded his head in agreement.

"You don't look too happy about it."

The fear returned to the young soldier's eyes. Luke waited.

"I don't like it . . . none of it . . . I hate this fucking war." The emotional dam burst. "Kill . . . kill . . . that's all they want from us is *kill*!"

The soldier sitting next to Uwe moaned in his sleep and turned his back toward the light in the aisle.

Uwe lowered his voice and continued. "I'm with the Cav."

Luke didn't have to be told that the soldier was assigned to the 1st Air Cavalry Division. As far as the soldiers serving with the unit were concerned, there was only one cavalry unit in Vietnam and that was *The* Cav.

"You know, Uwe . . . I've been in Vietnam a long time . . . five and a half years. You can talk." Luke addressed the soldier by his Christian name on purpose.

Uwe looked for a long time at Luke and then made a profound statement to the officer. "I'm not going back."

"I can understand."

Uwe was expecting a long lecture on the repercussions for deserting or going AWOL from Vietnam. "*Really*, I'm not going back there!"

"Why?"

Uwe had found what he had been looking for: someone who would listen without trying to judge him. "It just isn't *fair*. I wouldn't mind it if everyone shared the shit, but they don't. You officers . . ." Uwe glanced away from the black window at Luke to see how he was accepting the statement and saw an invitation in the officer's eyes to continue, ". . . you officers come out to the field for a couple of months, get your fucking medals, and leave. Us guys have to go out there and fight and *kill* for our whole tour." He huffed under his breath and his eyes flashed. "Oh yeah, we get our five-day R&Rs to go get reminded what it feels like to love a woman, and then they throw us right back there in the fucking killing!"

Luke sipped from his cold coffee and listened.

"Senior NCOs! Do you know how many forty-year-old sergeants I've seen in the fucking jungle?" Uwe waited for Luke to answer and finished when the officer shrugged his shoulders. "None! Not one fucking sergeant first class! Where are they all assigned? Check out the rear areas! All of them have some good reason why they can't get out there and hump the fucking jungle with us! Well, the NVA don't have that fucking problem, believe me! Do you know how old my *platoon* sergeant is?" Uwe answered the question before Luke could respond. "He's *twenty*; two years older than me! Now answer me, *sir*, how can we win a fucking war like that?"

Luke let the soldier's statement float in the air and went over and poured himself another cup of coffee.

Uwe glanced over at Luke when he returned. "I'm no coward, if that's what you're thinking . . ."

"I can see that." Luke looked at the Silver Star on the soldier's khaki shirt that was accompanied by a Purple Heart.

"What a fucked-up war." Uwe put so much emotion into the sentence that the words could almost be seen leaving his mouth.

"We do our best, Uwe." Luke held up his cup as if he were toasting the soldier.

"Yeah . . ." Uwe looked at his watch, "We'd better get some sleep or we'll be too tired to fuck when we get to Sydney." He lowered the back of his seat and closed his eyes as a signal that the conversation was ended. Nothing was going to change by telling an officer how he felt, but it had made him feel a little better.

He thought that he had stayed awake all night, but when the wheels touched down on the runway Luke's head jerked and he opened his eyes. He was nervous and tried busying himself by checking his handbag. His wife hadn't answered his last letter and he didn't know if she would be waiting for him at the ticket gate alone or with the children. He didn't even know for sure if she would be there. Five and a half years in Vietnam had changed their marriage, and for the first time since he had made the decision to stay in Vietnam until the war was over, he doubted himself.

The soldiers on board the aircraft started talking louder and louder to each other until the sound of the individual voices had blended into a loud background symphonic sympathy of human emotions that framed Luke's thoughts.

"Where are you staying, sir?"

Luke looked up too quick from his handbag. "The Hilton."

"Me too . . ." Uwe tried smiling the conversation away from the night before, "Who knows, I might see you there. That is, if you ever leave your room."

"My wife and kids are meeting me here and, believe me, with a seven- and a five-year-old, you *leave* the room!" Luke smiled. "Maybe you can join us for breakfast or lunch during one of our glorious five days of peace."

"I might take you up on that, but first I have a major problem to take care of and I'm not so lucky to have something waiting for me." Uwe shook his head and looked out at the soldiers milling in the aisle. "I have a lot of competition!"

"Don't worry, there's enough to go around." Luke knew that the local prostitutes worked the R&R flights like clockwork, and the soldier's problem would be selecting the one he wanted to spend five days with.

The men in the aisle started moving out of the door. Luke felt his heart starting to beat faster and started to get angry at himself for acting so foolishly. A staff sergeant took a copy of his orders and wrote across the top the name of the hotel where he was staying. "Be back here by eight AM, Friday, sir."

"For sure, Sergeant."

Uwe handed the sergeant his orders and waited while the NCO scribbled the R&R Detachment's code for the Hilton across the top. "Be back here by eight AM, Friday, Specialist."

Uwe looked over at Luke and then back at the sergeant. "We'll see . . . Sergeant."

"Don't play a smartass with me, soldier, or I'll slap your ass in a jail cell for your R&R!"

The other soldiers standing in line started giving the sergeant catcalls and whistles, and a couple soldiers from the 1st Air Cavalry who were in the back started making sounds like incoming artillery and hand grenades exploding.

The sergeant stood up behind his desk and yelled, "Don't fuck with me! I've spent my year in Vietnam!"

Luke eased through the double swinging doors that led out to the airport lobby. He didn't have to scan the crowd; his wife and kids were standing only a few feet away. The boy slipped under the barrier rope and ran to his father. Luke picked him up, letting his handbag fall to the floor and hugged the seven-year-old. The boy tucked his face against Luke's neck and hugged harder.

Luke returned the embrace and buried his nose in the boy's long, black hair. "You smell good, Alex." He whispered in the youth's ear and hugged him harder. Luke could see his five-year-old daughter push against her mother's leg and look over at him with a frightened look in her eyes. He held out his free arm and she ran to him.

"You smell good too, Dad."

The soldiers who had been behind Luke all started laughing at the boy's comment and then started clapping. The family reunion was something they all were wishing for, but the first sight of the women-of-the-night brought them quickly back to reality and the spell was broken.

"You look good, Luke."

"And you look fabulous in that skirt . . ." Luke couldn't take his eyes off the miniskirt his wife was wearing. "I'm afraid to *touch* you here in front of everyone."

"Why?" She grinned.

"It could get embarrassing."

"I've hired a nanny for the kids so we can have a little privacy until breakfast *tomorrow*."

"You're thinking, girl!" Luke threw his arm over his wife's shoulder and started walking toward the taxi stand holding Kim's hand and looking down at Alex, who was struggling with his handbag. He thought to himself how foolish he had been to worry over his family. They were all together again and he planned on making sure that nothing would ever separate them once he finished his remaining five months in Vietnam.

The four days flew by faster than any of them had expected. Luke sat in the patio chair with his feet propped up on the railing and watched the waves breaking against the beach.

"Luke, do you want a drink?" his wife called from inside of the hotel room. "I'm fixing myself one."

"Sure, Jodi . . . why not." He was feeling a little depressed over having to leave the next day. He looked at his watch and saw that it wasn't even nine o'clock in the morning, but time had blended together for them and the only thing that told them what portion of the day they were in was the kids, who maintained a perfect schedule for their meals.

Jodi stepped out through the sliding glass door carrying two tall martini glasses.

"Martinis? This time of the morning?" Luke felt like gagging.

"*Well*, you don't have to drink it!" She pouted and sat the glass down on the perforated steel table.

"I'll drink it, but it just reminded me of a certain lieutenant colonel whom I have little respect for." Luke sipped from the dry martini.

"What do you want to do today?" Jodi curled one of her legs under the other one on the seat as she sat down.

Luke could see the outline of her crotch through the thin material of the short shorts and felt his best friend getting interested again. "Has anyone ever told you that you have a perfect body . . . beautiful hair . . . sensuous lips . . . and the sweetest cunt in the world?"

"All the time . . . *all* of the time, big boy!" She tried acting like Mae West and flipped her hair over one shoulder.

"I bet the surfer boys back in Malibu have a *hard* time on their surfboards when you're down on the beach."

She wiggled her eyebrows and teased him with her lips. "Would you like to see what they're getting for free?"

"You are dead woman!" Luke tried acting angry but broke out in a laugh.

A knock came from the door.

"It must be the kids coming up from the playroom."

She shook her head and smiled back over her shoulder. "You had your chance, big boy, and blew it."

"Aw hell . . . twenty-seven times is enough!" Luke knew he was exaggerating but it had *felt* like twenty-seven times. He didn't hear the kids, and left the patio to see what was going on at the door and met Jodi and Specialist Bergman halfway.

"Well, Uwe Bergman!" Luke shook hands with the soldier. He could feel the firmness in the man's grip.

"I changed my mind about what we had talked about earlier." Uwe glanced over at Luke's wife and rolled his eyes when he looked back at the captain.

"Don't you get any crazy *suicidal* ideas there, soldier!" Luke pointed at him with the empty martini glass and smiled.

"Martinis for breakfast?"

"Want one?"

"Sure . . . I've been drinking worse stuff since I've been here."

"I thought you were staying here at the Hilton?"

"I am."

"We haven't seen much of you."

Uwe glanced back into the dark hotel room from where they were sitting on the patio trying to locate Luke's wife and then whispered. "My *date* took me to meet her family back in the fucking boonies. We had a great time!"

"I was wondering." Luke referred to what Uwe had said on the airplane.

"I thought about it. I had the perfect place to stay and I know they would never have found me, but I just couldn't be the first one in my family to turn coward."

"I'm glad to hear that."

Jodi joined them with the pitcher of martinis. "Let's get a little nasty here this morning. We can sober up before dinner and dine out in style tonight."

The door to the motel room flew open and the children ran through the room out to the patio. Kim was trying to say something but she was out of breath.

Alex tried waiting patiently but couldn't and blurted out: "Come on, Kim. Tell them!"

"Alex!" she gasped and then burst out, "We saw a kangaroo! A real one!"

"Really?" Luke sipped from his drink. "And where, pray tell, did you see a *real* kangaroo in the city?"

"The doorman brought it on a leash so that we could see a real kangaroo!" Alex helped his sister out.

"Alex! You promised to let me tell Daddy!" Kim started crying and crawled up in her father's lap for comfort.

"There was no danger to the children, sir." The hotel's busboy had been standing in the dark room watching.

"Thank you." Jodi went over to her purse and tipped the young Australian and thanked him for bringing the children back upstairs.

"You have a good-looking family, sir." Uwe had noticed back at the airport that Luke's family was the kind of family you would see in a television commercial.

Luke brushed his hand through Alex's hair. "Except this boy needs a haircut!"

"Don't you dare, Luke!" Jodi took her seat again. "Boys are wearing long hair nowadays."

"My son isn't going to be no damn pinko commie hippie son of a bitch!" Luke was joking and the children could tell from the tone of his voice that he wasn't really mad.

"I don't know . . . the peace movement has some good points." Jodi's whole bearing seemed to have changed almost instantly. She seemed to have slipped from her role as an Army officer's wife to something else. Luke sensed it, and the old fear he had on the airplane returned.

"You know . . . I was wondering . . ." Uwe saw that something was happening between the captain and his wife. "I'm just about burned out from four days of extracurricular activities . . ."

Luke interrupted. "You?"

Uwe shrugged his shoulders and held his hand up,

palms up. "Hey, Captain! You know us teenage soldiers . . . we're only good for short bursts, but at frequent intervals over a rapid *intensive* period of time, and then we need time to recover our . . ." He cut the sentence off.

"You, young man, are going to be a tease when you get back to the States." Jodi winked at Uwe. "If you were a couple of years older . . ."

"Jodi!" Luke flashed a look over at Kim. "The children have ears."

"If he was older, what would you do, Mommy?" Kim figured that was her clue to say something.

"Nothing, dear." Jodi looked at the drinks the men were holding. "Is everyone good?" She waved her empty glass in the air.

"Yes! My God, woman . . . I'll be stone drunk before ten!" Luke laid back in his chair.

"As I was saying, sir . . . I'm free for the rest of the day and was wondering if you would loan me your kids for the afternoon. Sydney has a great zoo and I thought they might enjoy going there."

Alex and Kim burst into a frenzied begging spree.

"Go ask your mother." Luke shooed the excited children back into the hotel room.

They returned almost instantly. "She said to ask you."

"Fine! Then you can . . ." Luke paused to add to the children's excitement.

"Daddy!" Kim started hopping up and down on her toes.

". . . can . . . GO!" Luke looked over at Uwe. "I appreciate this."

Uwe shook his head. "You don't know how much it will mean to *me*."

Luke's mind returned back to the war for the first time since he had been in Sydney. He understood what Uwe was trying to say. Almost all of the soldiers in Vietnam missed their families.

*   *   *

Luke had planned for a special dinner just for Jodi and him. Uwe had made it even better when he had called and asked to extend his time with the children and take them to a movie. He had promised to have them back in the hotel before ten and he would stay until they got back from dinner, if Jodi would leave a pitcher of her famous martinis for him while he baby-sat.

Sydney at night is probably more breathtaking than it is during the daytime and is filled with world-class restaurants and nightclubs. Luke had selected a famous seafood restaurant that was famous for its lobster dishes. They had a fabulous candlelight meal and Luke capped off the night by hiring a taxi to just drive around the city and down the beaches. The cabbie took them to a number of the most romantic spots in the city, where they parked for a couple of minutes to soak in the view. They returned back to the Hilton just as the first rays of sunlight were appearing over the edge of the ocean.

"Uwe is going to kill us!" Jodi fumbled in her purse for the key to the room.

"He's probably sleeping on the couch."

Jodi pushed open the door and saw that the couch and the patio were empty. Luke looked around the room and saw the children's bedroom door was open and looked in. Uwe was sitting in a chair between the foot of the kids' beds, watching them sleep. He turned his head when Luke walked in and smiled. "You've got a pair of great kids, Captain. I only wish mine will be as good."

Luke laid his hand on Uwe's shoulder. "They will be."

"If I make it back this time."

"You *will*. Just keep your powder dry and your shit together and you'll make it home." Luke squeezed his hand and felt the man's body trembling. Anger filled the captain's thoughts. War was pure shit and should only be for *old* men.

Luke went out on the patio after Uwe had left to

go pack his things, and thought about the war and the people he had met there. Uwe would make a great officer and would probably be one of the better West Point generals of the future. The young soldier was strong, yet sensitive to those people around him.

"I like him, too." Jodi joined Luke on the patio.

"He's a mixed-up kid, but he'll make it. He's got guts and drive."

Jodi nodded her head and looked out over the ocean. Luke knew that something was bothering her from the way she stuck out her lower lip and tilted her head to one side. She had been doing that a lot during the whole R&R, but she had never even broached what was bothering her.

"You don't have to hold it in any longer, Jodi. I know something's bothering you."

She kept her eyes on the rising sun and the fishing boats that were heading out to sea.

"I'm making this my last tour in Vietnam. I know that I said I was going to stay until the war was over, but who would have believed it would last over seven years?" Luke felt no guilt in breaking his word. "I'm coming home for good in five months. They tell me that I have to go to a number of career schools to catch up on my training so that I can be a better officer during war—" Luke looked over at his wife to see if she had caught the sarcasm and saw that her eyes were cloudy. "What's wrong, Jodi?" He reached for her but she backed away.

"It's too late, Luke."

"Late for what?"

"I want a divorce."

The shock hit Luke like the blast from a two-thousand-pound bomb. "A what?"

"I can't handle it anymore! Being alone every night with the children. Cooped up in a house without any company! I'm *young* and I need to live my life!" She started sobbing.

"I'll be home in five months . . . for good!" Luke felt the frustration boiling up inside of him. He had been right. His instincts had been correct when he had received the one page letter.

"I can't wait five months! Or five days!" She couldn't look at her husband. "I've thought about it and I want out of this marriage."

"And the kids? What about *our* children?" Luke felt like crying.

"I know you love them and they love you . . . We'll make sure that you have generous visiting privileges. . . ."

"We? What in the hell do you mean by *we*!" Luke's rage erupted. "What is *we*'s name?"

"He's a college professor from Pepperdine University. We met on the beach and became good friends and then we fell in love. . . . Luke, I didn't mean for it to happen . . . it just did!" She started crying.

Luke looked down from the patio and felt like jumping. He had to fight himself so that he wouldn't. "Look, Jodi . . . let's work this out. If you . . . if you, made a *mistake*, I'll forgive you. I know how lonely it has been for you. I've been lonely too! For God's sake, let's try and work this thing out!"

"It's too late, Luke." She wiped her eyes. "I don't love you anymore."

The words cut deeper into Luke's flesh than any NVA bullet could do. "Why did you come here, then? You screwed me . . . *loved* me . . . and now you tell me that you don't love me!"

"I was making sure, Luke. I had to know for *sure*."

"You bitch! You fucking bitch!" Luke left the patio and went into their bedroom. He became even angrier when he saw the bed they had made love in. "Bitch . . ." he whispered the word between clenched teeth. He couldn't believe what was happening to him.

He showered and changed into his khaki uniform for his flight back to Vietnam. The familiar routine kept his mind from exploding. He packed his gear in his handbag and opened the bedroom door. Jodi was still sitting out on the patio with her back to him. Luke went into the children's bedroom and saw that they were still sleeping. They had had a very long day at the zoo with Uwe and had worn themselves out. He watched them for a couple of minutes and then leaned over and kissed Kim. She wiggled and buried her face in the pillow. Alex opened his eyes and lifted up on one elbow. "You leaving now, Dad?"

"Yeah, buddy, I've got to catch my flight."

"Oh?" The seven-year-old was still half asleep.

"Give me a kiss, Slick."

Alex hugged Luke and then kissed his cheek. "Why are you crying, Dad?"

" 'Cause I love you so much, son."

"Oh." Alex thought for a second and added, "I know that."

CHAPTER TEN

✪✪✪✪✪✪✪✪✪✪✪✪✪✪✪

THE BOB HOPE SHOW

The brigade commander laid the report down on the center of his desk and turned in his swivel chair to look out of the screen window that covered two of the walls in his corner office. The building was the typical one-story administrative hootch the engineers could throw up in a single day using precut lumber. It was like building with a Lincoln Log set. The hootch sizes were based on four-by-eight-foot sheets of plywood, which was the basic Lincoln Log. The floors of the hootches were sheets of plywood and the sides were usually upright two-by-fours with screening nailed to the two-by-fours from four-foot-wide rolls all around the sides and ends of the building, and sheets of plywood were nailed to the bottom half so that the plywood would go up four feet from the floor. The screening was usually covered with sheets of plywood hung from hinges so that it worked like a shutter at night and could be hooked from the overhanging rafters of the corrugated steel roof. The troop barracks could have the shutters, if large amounts of plywood was available, but normally their shutters were strips of canvas that could be rolled up during the day and at night when the lights had been turned off.

A flight of Huey slicks was taking off from the brigade helipad filled with infantry troops from the 1st Battalion, 11th Infantry. He was partial to that battalion because they were one of the few *light* infantry battalions left in the United States Army; everything else was becoming mechanized. Light infantry walked, while mechanized infantry rode on top their M113 personnel carriers to battle. The flat-topped tracked vehicles weren't designed to carry the infantry troops on top, but there wasn't a commander in Vietnam who could get the men to ride *inside* the vehicles. The North Vietnamese ten-*dong* note depicted a convoy of American M113s destroyed by RPG-7s and American soldiers walking toward the NVA with their hands held up in surrender; that's what the NVA thought about the *armored* M113 personnel carriers.

A knock on his door brought the colonel's thoughts back to his office and the matter at hand. "Come in."

The door opened, and Lieutenant Colonel Jeffers entered accompanied by the brigade's personnel officer.

"Help yourselves to a cup of coffee if you want one." The colonel waved two fingers at the plugged-in coffeepot in the corner of the large room. Jeffers poured two paper cups of coffee and mixed cream and sugar in both of them before handing the personnel officer one. The colonel didn't miss much and noticed that Jeffers knew how the other officer drank his coffee. "When are you going to give up, Jeffers, and listen to me?"

"About what, sir?"

"About Captain Arrowood. "

"I don't understand, sir."

The colonel sighed and then slammed his fist down on his desk. "Damn you! Don't play any of that dumb shit with me!"

Jeffers looked over at the personnel officer with a phoney confused look on his face and then back at the colonel. "I honestly don't know what you are referring to, sir."

The colonel smiled and leaned back in his chair. "The funny thing about the statement you just made is that those who are *dis*honest, use the word honest the most . . . have you ever noticed that?" He looked over at his personnel officer.

"Sir! Even though I have graduated from West

Point almost twenty years ago, I still adhere to the *Code!* I will not lie, cheat, or steal, or tolerate those who do!"

The colonel leaned forward in his chair and looked Jeffers directly in the eyes. "Then we have a real perception problem, Lieutenant Colonel!" He picked up the paper from the center of his desk. "How in the hell could you rate Captain Arrowood as *average?*"

"Sir, I filled out that efficiency report according to the regulation and it is my honest opinion that he is an average officer."

"Just from what little I have seen, Jeffers . . ." The brigade commander struggled to control his temper, ". . . what *little* I have seen of that man's performance, I would rate him as the best captain in this brigade . . . not second, but the best!"

"Sir!" Jeffers couldn't stand hearing the senior officer talking that way about Arrowood. "You don't know the man!"

The colonel cocked his head to one side and raised his eyebrows. "Really? What more should I know about him? He took command of the worst artillery battery in I Corps and within a *month*, he turned it around! He defeated an elite NVA Sapper Company, eliminated racism, reduced the drug-abuse problem in the unit, and upgraded the troops morale a thousand percent! Now what more could he have done in *two* months?"

"He doesn't have any respect for senior officers or discipline!" Jeffers tried holding his ground.

"That is true, sir." The personnel officer joined sides with Jeffers. "When I went to the hospital to tell him about his new assignment, he was very rude and disrespectful. If he hadn't been wounded, I would have pressed charges against him."

"But you only called him a *fucking fool,* instead?" The brigade commander hooded his eyes as a signal that he was about ready to lope off some heads.

"How . . . how did you . . ." The lieutenant colonel's face turned red.

"Don't be such a dumb shit! I received a call from the hospital commander within an hour after it happened. His exact words were, 'You tell that son-of-a-bitch never to step inside my hospital again!' unquote." The colonel glanced at Jeffers and added, "I didn't like that stunt you pulled replacing Arrowood as the commander of Bravo Battery without informing me first and I like this efficiency report even less. In fact, I am going to ask you very nicely to reconsider this report." He held the document up in the air. "Because if he is just an *average* officer, I can assure the both of you that I consider your levels of performance less than his. Do I make myself perfectly clear?"

Jeffers nodded in unison with his friend, the brigade personnel officer.

"And one more thing before you move your sorry asses out of my office. I want this bullshit to stop!"

"What's that, sir?" The personnel officer's voice was so low that Jeffers who was sitting next to him could barely hear.

"I am very proud to have been a graduate of West Point. Very proud of that accomplishment in my life, but not so damn proud that I screw over other officers who have a different source of commission than mine. OCS and ROTC have produced some excellent officers along with our sister academies." He looked at the personnel officer. "I want assignments made based on the man's *ability* and not his source of commission from now on . . . do you understand me?"

"Yes, sir."

"Jeffers . . . you now have academy graduates commanding all of your batteries . . . good luck and don't fuck up!" The brigade commander waved for them to leave the room and went back to looking out of the window.

Jeffers waited until they were out in the hallway before commenting. "I can't believe he said that to us!"

"Shut the fuck up, Jeffers! You've caused me

enough damn trouble!" The personnel officer left Jeffers standing in the hall alone.

Luke pretended that he was sleeping. He didn't want to talk to anyone and was thankful that the officers sitting in the seats next to him were so exhausted from their R&R leave that they were sleeping soundly.

The captain's voice came over the intercom. "We are descending from thirty-two thousand feet and will be landing in Da Nang shortly." A low, collective groan came from the soldiers who were awake.

Luke squeezed his eyes shut and hoped that a SAM II missile would come up out of the jungle and blow the airplane up. He wanted to die and he didn't care how; slowly, fast—just die. He had tried calling his wife three times from the airport, but she had refused to accept all of them. Luke couldn't control his emotions at all. He fluctuated from extreme self-pity to an anger that felt like it had to burst out of him or he would burn up. He wanted to kill her one minute and the next he wanted to make love to her, and then he just wanted to die and end all of the pain he was feeling inside.

The aircraft touched down and the engines roared as the captain braked hard. Luke leaned forward against his seat belt still wishing that the NVA would blow the plane up.

"Fuck!" The lieutenant sitting next to Luke mumbled the single word that summed up the feelings of all of the men who were returning to Vietnam from their R&R.

Luke stumbled through the processing line not paying attention to anything. He left the air terminal and felt the heat coming up off the tarmac where all of the vehicles were parked that were dropping off or picking up the soldiers.

"Sir!"

Luke ignored the voice and kept walking until he felt someone grab ahold of his arm.

"Sir, you were sleeping all the way back and I didn't

want to wake you up." Specialist Bergman held out his hand to shake with Luke. "I just wanted to thank you for everything. I'm glad that I came back here and thanks for sharing your family with me. I really needed that. We're close back home and your kids reminded me what it's all about."

Luke stared at the soldier for a long time before taking his hand. 'You're welcome, Uwe."

"There's rumors that my brigade might be transferred up to I Corps . . . maybe we'll meet again?"

"I'm commanding the Recon Company for the 1st Brigade, 5th Division, out of Quang Tri . . . Camp Red Devil. You're welcome to stop by anytime and bring your buddies. We're based in a rear area; hot showers, A-ration meals . . . the works!"

Bergman chuckled. "I will take you up on that for sure!"

"Later." Luke made like he was shooting Berman with his thumb and forefinger and left to catch a ride on a departing 5th Mech helicopter that was starting to warm up.

The platoon leaders from the Recon Company all sat together around a table in their club. The Recon Club was the most popular club at Camp Red Devil and was always packed with troops coming in from the field and on occasion by one of the Special Forces SOG Teams that launched out of a special site near Quang Tri.

"Red, I don't know if we should prejudge him. I say give the guy a fair chance!"

"Fuck it, Lu! The guy killed a fucking American soldier out at LZ Sandy! I say the motherfucker is crazy!"

"The guy was on fucking *drugs* and he opened fire on the captain. What in the fuck should he have done?"

Lieutenant Doak shook his head and sipped from the Shasta soda he was drinking. Beer and liquor weren't served in the club until 5 PM, but sodas and snacks were served all day long. The club was used as a meeting place during the day for off-duty soldiers. "I don't like it at all!"

"What are we going to do about it? He's been assigned to the Recon Company by the brigade commander." Lieutenant Wong leaned back in his chair. "I've heard the guy has been in Vietnam for five years! I don't know about you guys, but I *like* that!" Lu scanned the lieutenants sitting at the table and looked up at the man sitting at a table all by himself in the shadow near the corner of the club. "He had to learn something about recon being here that long."

"You learn recon by reconing . . . sir." The voice came from behind the lieutenant.

"Are you back already, Sergeant Forbes?" Lieutenant Wong turned around on his seat to face the sergeant.

"We came in at first light." Forbes took a seat at the table next to the company officers. "You talking about the new CO?"

"Officer talk." Red Doak didn't like Forbes at all.

"In Vietnam, there ain't any officer talk that doesn't concern us EM." Forbes glared at the lieutenant, forcing the young officer to break his eyes away first.

"I buy that . . . sometimes." The man sitting in the shadows spoke up from his seat.

"Buy what, friend?" Forbes leaned to one side, trying to see who was speaking. The stream of bright light coming from the screened windows made it even more difficult to see the man.

"Officers should share information with their men." The voice remained low-pitched. "But by being a recon man doesn't give a person the right to all information . . . what would happen if the recon man was captured?"

Forbes had heard enough. "Get the fuck out of here! What are you, a fucking *staff* puke?" Forbes touched the cloth headband he was wearing and then rubbed the three-day growth of beard on his chin. He had come over to the club directly from his hootch, where he had dropped off his gear after returning from his mission.

"Nope . . ." The shadow left its seat and walked over in the light to the table where the officers were sitting. They all could see the captain bars on the man's collar.

Forbes shrugged his shoulders. He wasn't worried about telling a staff captain to get out of his club.

Lieutenant Wong read the name tag on the officer's jacket and brought his hand up to his mouth to hide the smile. He was the only one who could see the tag at the table.

"If you're not assigned to the Recon Company, you don't have any fucking business in our club." Forbes nodded at the door with his head.

The captain remained standing next to the table. "Lieutenant Doak, are you the executive officer here?"

"Yes, sir." Doak glanced over at Forbes, who was telling him with his eyes to shut up.

"How about giving me a tour of the place?"

Doak frowned and shifted his position so that he could read the captain's name tag. "Yes, sir! Shit, sir, I didn't see you sitting over there!"

"No problem. We've all got our own opinions and I respect a man who isn't afraid to state his."

Forbes still hadn't figured out what was going on and was about to make another comment when the captain looked directly at him. "You could use some lessons on how *real* recon men dress."

Lieutenant Wong couldn't control the laugh that was struggling to break free and tried muffling it but failed. Forbes fired a hate-filled look at him and then returned his attention to the captain. "Who's going to teach me? I've pulled more recon missions than anyone else in this company!"

"This company is only a small part of the war reconnaissance effort."

"Who in the fuck are you to tell me about recon!" Forbes stood up to face off with the officer.

"Your new company commander for starts."

The whole club became quiet as the recon men all turned to see the man that so many rumors had been floating around about.

"Let's go, Lieutenant Doak, we've got a lot of stuff to cover today."

"Yes, sir!" Doak loved the way that Arrowood had handled Forbes. The sergeant thought that he commanded the company and gave all of the officers a very hard time. Forbes was good in the field as far as reputation went, but there were a lot of unanswered questions when he returned from his patrols. Forbes's men were extremely loyal to him, which was good and bad. It was good because it formed a well-organized recon team, but it was bad because they *never* disagreed with anything Sergeant Forbes said or did. The team acted like the prima donnas of the Recon Company and had their own table reserved for them in the club, which again wasn't bad if it was handled in the right way. The best should be recognized and rewarded for their accomplishments.

Lieutenant Doak stopped out behind the four Recon Company hootches and pointed to the perimeter bunkers. "We don't pull perimeter guard, but that is always a threat to the men. Every time a new brigade headquarters commandant is assigned, we go through a long routine to justify our exemption. I think the brigade NCOs are jealous." Doak shrugged his shoulders. "Anyway, that's the sector of the perimeter we are assigned to reinforce during a ground attack, but our prime mission is to act as a brigade reaction force to defend the headquarters command bunker. Rarely are there more than fifty recon men back here in the company area at any given time."

"What's the assigned strength?"

"Right now, it's a hundred and twenty-three with four men in the hospital for wounds and two for illnesses. We have fifteen men on R&R and one on emergency leave back in the States. That leaves a hundred and one for duty, including the officers."

"Do the officers go out in the field?"

"Yes, sir, regularly with all of the teams except RT Jackson. All of our teams are named after famous people."

"Why not RT Jackson?"

"Sergeant Forbes doesn't like officers in the field with him and he normally has had his way." Doak made sure to phase that in the past tense.

Luke looked at his watch. "I have to attend the brigade commander's staff meeting at four."

"Yes, sir. We rotate that duty so that you don't have to waste so much time sitting on staff calls, unless you want to change that policy."

"No, I like that idea. It gives all of the officers a chance to *develop* their careers."

Doak smiled. He was already beginning to see why the officers out in Bravo Battery liked Arrowood.

"I would like to see all of the team leaders and officers after supper. You pick the location." Luke winked and left the lieutenant. He could see Jeffers walking fast down the road toward the command bunker where the evening staff meeting was conducted to update all of the brigade staff and commanders in Camp Red Devil on the units' and Corps' activities.

He wasn't looking forward to his first brigade staff call, but it was going to be a part of his job and he figured that he might as well get used to it and start off on the right foot. The only reason why he was invited to the senior officer meeting was because he reported directly to the brigade commander.

The huge bunker complex smelled of stale cigar and cigarette smoke. Luke saw Jeffers glance over at him when he had entered the bunker, but Jeffers would never recognize a captain in a gathering of senior officers, which was all right with Luke. He found himself a place to stand in the back of the bunker and waited for the brigade operations officer to start the briefing.

Locations of the troop night lager sites were posted

and briefed along with the activity for the day of the combat battalions. There had been no enemy contact for over a week in the brigade's area of operations, and the brigade commander was feeling the pressure from higher headquarters to find the enemy. Luke looked over at an acetate-covered sign that seemed macabre, but reflected the whole war effort in Vietnam. The left side of the three-by-four-foot sign had colored flags: red, white, and blue for the United States, red with a gold star in the center representing North Vietnam; and a half red-and-blue flag with a large gold flag in the center that represented the Vietcong forces. There were two more columns of numbers; a monthly total for killed in action and a brigade total. The columns read:

	KIA MONTH	KIA TOTAL BDE
NVA	134	697
VC	54	234
USA	11	143

Luke looked over and read another chart on the opposite side of the main battle map that showed the number of enemy POWs taken and suspected VC interned for questioning. The figures were impressive. Luke's eyes went back to the killed-in-action chart and wondered how many of those numbers had families and how many of the KIA Americans had been married and how many of their wives had dumped them.

"Captain Arrowood?"

Luke looked over and saw that everyone was looking at him. Jeffers was smirking.

"Captain Arrowood, would you mind sharing with the rest of the staff what seems to be so interesting?" The brigade operations officer locked his hands behind his back and waited for Luke to try answering. "I've been calling you for the past couple of minutes, so whatever your mind was on, must be something worth sharing with all of us."

"Yes, sir. I was thinking how many of the KIAs on that chart had families." Luke didn't hesitate in answering the lieutenant colonel.

The brigade commander grinned and took a long sip from his coffee mug. The operations officer couldn't think of a comeback for Luke's answer and coughed before he changed the subject. "Anyway, Captain Arrowood is our new Recon Company commander and comes to us from the artillery battalion, where he did a superb job as you all can recall defending his base against a very large NVA Sapper attack."

Jeffers felt his face getting red. He hated it when someone praised Arrowood.

The brigade commander stood and turned to face the assembled officers. "I just wanted to alert all of you that we have been allocated five-hundred seats for the Bob Hope Show in Da Nang."

A low groan came from the infantry battalion commander, who had been in there and had sat in on the briefing.

"I know!" The brigade commander's voice was sympathetic. "But we have to send that many, plus we have been detailed to send our Recon Company out to screen for rockets and mortars."

"Sir, can we go back and ask . . ." The infantry battalion commander tried finishing his question but was cut off by the brigade commander.

"Sorry! The numbers are firm and written in stone. Bob Hope will not perform for less than ten thousand troops and what old Bobby wants . . . he gets!" The colonel looked over at Luke and added, "Going to the show won't be a problem, protecting ten thousand troops all bunched up like that will be! You've got your work cut out for you, Captain Arrowood, and I know I don't need to tell you what'll happen if a Bob Hope Show gets incoming rockets."

One of the senior officers piped in. "God help us if Bob Hope gets killed!"

"Fuck Hope!" The colonel bit down on his cigar.

"He's lived a damn good life! I'm concerned about the troops. It would be a fucking slaughter!"

Luke was beginning to like the old warrior more and more. The man had his heart in the right place.

"You'll have only one day to do whatever you have to do before you're deployed. I'm sorry, Luke, I wish I could give you more time." There wasn't an officer in the bunker who didn't catch the colonel's referral to Luke by his Christian name. That was the old man's way of letting the staff know that Arrowood was off-limits to any political bullshit.

"We can handle it, sir. I'll get the operations order from your operations officer as soon as this meeting is over."

"Good; and now, gentlemen, let's go to supper." The colonel left the bunker followed by his senior staff.

Jeffers waited until the bunker was almost empty before calling over to Arrowood to come to where he was standing. Luke took his time getting there and nodded his head without daring to speak.

"I just wanted you to know that I maxed you out on your efficiency report." Jeffers sneered. "I don't think that you deserve such a high rating, but the system is inflated and I don't want to hurt your career."

Luke kept looking into the lieutenant colonel's eyes.

"Well! Aren't you going to thank me?"

"Can I see a copy."

"Don't you trust me?"

"No . . ." Luke whispered the word.

"You God damn ungrateful son-of-a-bitch!"

Luke ignored the comment. "Why did you give my battery to someone else? You knew that I refused to go to a Stateside hospital so I could keep it."

"I make the assignments in my battalion, Captain! Besides, Charlie and Bravo batteries are switching locations. Charlie Battery has been living in knee-deep mud now for six months and needs to dry out."

Luke couldn't believe what he was hearing after all

of the hard work the men in Bravo Battery had done to make LZ Sandy a liveable place. "Isn't the Charlie Battery commander one of your West Point pets?"

Jeffers tightened his jaws. "Are you insinuating that I play favorites?"

"Yes . . . very much so."

"You know you've just made an enemy, don't you? And I can be very tough!"

"Sir, you declared yourself my enemy the day you read my 201 file and saw that I had a direct commission." Luke turned and walked away.

"Come back here!" Jeffers screamed so loud that the enlisted staff inside of the bunker stopped working and looked over to see what was going on.

Luke kept walking.

The Recon Company cadre were waiting for Luke when he arrived back in the company area. Lieutenant Doak had used the time to brief the team leaders on a number of policy changes in the brigade while they waited for the staff meeting to end.

Luke didn't waste any time going through unnecessary details. "By now all of you have heard rumors about me." He took his time looking at each one of their faces and continued talking. "I would have liked a little more time to get to know each of you before I made any major policy changes, but I'm afraid we don't have any time. There is going to be a Bob Hope Show in Da Nang . . ."

"What in the hell has that got to do with policy changes in the Recon Company . . . *sir*." Sergeant Forbes shifted the toothpick in his mouth from side to side.

Luke stopped talking and stared at the NCO for over a minute before answering him. "I think you all know by now that when Bob Hope plays for the troops . . ."

"Is the whole company going to the show . . . *sir*?" Forbes ended the sentence again with a sarcastic pitch in his voice.

"None of us are going to the show, Sergeant Forbes. We've been detailed to screen against a possible rocket attack." Luke fought to maintain his patience. Lieutenant Wong snuck a quick glance over at Doak and smiled. Both of them knew that Arrowood wouldn't take much more crap from Forbes; he couldn't, if he was going to win the respect of the company cadre.

"That sounds like easy duty to me! We can catch up on our sleep." Forbes coughed out a phony laugh and looked around to see if any of the other NCOs were enjoying his baiting the new captain. "What do you think, Mulhouse? Can we catch up on our sleep?"

The baby-faced buck sergeant didn't answer.

"Well, Mulhouse!" Forbes spit a brown streak of tobacco juice on the plywood floor of the company office and used the sole of his jungle boot to spread it out with. The black stain was almost worn off the leather of the boot from heavy wear, which was a sign to everyone that the owner of the boots had been around and wasn't a rookie. It took at least six months of constant wear to get the leather down to its basic color.

"Like I was saying, there are going to be a number of policy changes in the company that will be effective as soon as possible." Luke used the index finger on his right hand to beckon to Sergeant Forbes with. "Would you please come up here by me, Sergeant?"

"What for?" Forbes grinned.

"I want to show the rest of the cadre what a *good* recon team leader looks like."

Wong glanced over at Doak and then over at the other company officers. He was shocked that Arrowood would recognize the troublemaker in front of the whole cadre.

Forbes spit again on the floor and missed seeing the expression on Luke's face. It was a major mistake on the sergeant's part. Doak had caught it and watched with a renewed interest.

"There are a few bad habits that have slipped into

the recon profession in the past couple of years and I think that I should point them out to the rest of you." Luke pointed at Forbes's boots. "Let's start down at the bottom and work our way up. Those jungle boots were designed with a number of important factors in mind. The vents built into the arches of the boot were put there to allow air to flow through the leather portion of the boot and, most importantly, to allow water to drain out quickly and for the boot to dry. If you notice, Sergeant Forbes has allowed clay to clog the holes . . . that's bad." Luke pointed to the rolled up jungle fatigue trousers. "The ties at the bottom of each pant leg were put there for a reason; to close off the bottoms so that insects and mosquitos can't get to your legs. I will accept the pants tucked into the tops of the boots or the ties used over the *top edge* of the boot. Now let's get to the jacket . . ."

Forbes had figured out that Arrowood was making a fool out of him and was so angry that he swallowed some of his tobacco juice and choked.

"That brings up another point. I don't like spitting on my office floor. Be civil enough to use a butt can or spit outside." Luke pointed at Forbes's cutoff sleeves. "I don't mind sleeves being rolled up when we are in a base camp, but out in the field we'll travel with our sleeves rolled down at *all* times."

"You're crazy, Captain! Maybe you don't know it, but it gets *hot* out there in the jungle! We wear T-shirts on my team."

"Really?" Luke looked over at Lieutenant Doak, who shrugged his shoulders. No one knew what went on out in the field with Forbes's team because no officer or NCO had ever accompanied him on a mission. "That's *changed* as of now, Sergeant." Luke pointed at Forbes's three-day beard. "When you return from a mission, the first thing that will be done are the de-briefings and then *everyone* showers, shaves, and puts on a clean uniform *before* appearing to the rest of the rear-area personnel. There won't be

any more of this cheap rookie profiling going on."
Luke knew exactly what Forbes had been up to.

"Captain, I've had just about enough!" Forbes was
trying desperately to regain his position back as the
bad ass of the company.

"Not yet, Sergeant. We've got to cover that drive-
on rag you're wearing on your head." Luke looked
over at the smiling cadre, who were enjoying the show
more than a strip tease and that placed it high on their
lists. "I will allow drive-on rags in the field, but only if
they're made from camouflaged triangular bandages.
None of this purple and orange shit your girls send
you from home. We aren't knights from the round
table . . . we're *recon* men." Luke flipped the tails
from Forbes's Confederate flag designed drive-on rag.

"Sir?" Sergeant Mulhouse raised his hand.

"Yes, Sergeant?"

"How about Ranger hats? Can we wear them?"

"I would prefer you wearing them. They were
designed by men who knew what they were doing and
they're practical for the field with their small bills to
keep the rain out of your eyes." Luke pointed at the
shotgun leaning against the wall. "I don't know who
that weapon belongs to . . ."

Everyone in the room looked at Forbes.

". . . but each team will carry identical weapons so
that we can interchange ammunition with each other.
I'm playing with the idea of shotguns with each team
to be used at night for close infighting, but we'll have
to modify the barrels and handles a little. We can talk
about that later on . . ."

"What in the fuck do you know about recon . . .
sir!" Forbes was out of control.

"Some . . . I spent two years with MAC-SOG,
working up north." Luke nodded his head in the right
direction and didn't need to say how far up north he
was talking about, everyone in the room had heard
stories about the super-elite Green Beret SOG Teams.
A year with the unit was almost suicidal but having
spent *two* years with them was legendary. Luke con-

tinued with his briefing. "We'll wear our gear in a similar fashion also, so that during the night we can locate equipment on our wounded or dead. Flashlights, ammunition, knives, strob lights, and especially medical supplies will be located in the same places on each recon man's gear. One team will be a *team*, and when we link two teams together, we'll have one larger team and so on . . ." Luke looked at Doak, ". . . any questions?"

"Lots, sir!" Doak couldn't help but smile. "But later, when we have more time."

Luke nodded his head. "Now all of you know basically what I expect from you. Go back to your teams and spread the word."

The cadre stood to leave and Luke raised his hand. "Oh . . . one more thing! All of the officers will be assigned to teams for this screening mission. I will be going with RT Jackson."

Forbes's eyes widened. That was the final insult. "Sorry, sir. I don't allow anybody to travel with my team. I find them to be excess baggage."

"I'm not going to travel *with* your team, Sergeant Forbes, I'm going to command it."

"Bullshit!"

"What did you say?"

"I said bullshit, sir! There isn't an authorized slot on a recon team for an officer. I'll take this to the brigade inspector general if I have to!"

"You'll have to, then, because I'm *commanding* RT Jackson for this mission."

"You'll do it without me, then!"

"Are you refusing to go on an assigned mission?"

The cadre watched both of the adversaries closely. Forbes knew that he could afford to push the captain as far as he wanted to because the brigade operations officer thought he was the *best* noncommissioned officer in the brigade and would back him if he had to.

"If you are going to take over my RT, then you'll have to do it alone. Recon is a voluntary assignment and I don't feel like volunteering for this mission."

"Who told you that shit, Sergeant?" Luke was losing his patience.

"Our old CO."

"All right, until I can find the time to sort that out, you can stay back here and help the cooks in the mess hall until we get back."

"Whaa . . . what!"

"You heard me." Luke left the office with Forbes standing openmouthed in the center of the room.

Sergeant Mulhouse was in his glory. Forbes had made his life miserable because he had a baby face and because he never cut corners on a mission. "Hey, Forbes, do you think they'll make you peel potatoes?"

"God damn you!" Forbes tried kicking the buck sergeant in the rear, but Mulhouse easily dodged out of range laughing.

The Recon Company cadre left the office with Forbes standing in the center of the room in shock. He was the best recon man in the company and had proven it a dozen times with his after-action reports, and this captain had made a complete fool out of him. He couldn't let that go without some kind of revenge.

Luke hadn't fully realized how much of a reputation he had made for himself in the brigade. The incident with Talbot in the battery had shocked the whole command and then when some of the blacks had tried killing him in the artillery battalion area his reputation had really grown, but it was what had happened out at Bravo Battery during the Sapper attack that had made him a legend. When Luke had saved Sergeant Cole and Talbot's friend from burning to death, even the black militants had started liking him. Luke really didn't have to do another thing to prove himself. He could stay back in the company's rear area and live forever off his well documented reputation. But there was one problem: Luke wanted to die.

The company officers waited outside of the orderly room for Captain Arrowood to join them. He was on the land-line to brigade headquarters getting some last minute instructions from the commander himself. Luke left the office smiling.

"It must have been a good conversation with the old man." Doak wiggled his mouth. The heavy layer of camouflage grease paint always made his face itch when he first put it on.

Luke chuckled. "Nothing earth-shattering. He told me that if anything occurred in our sector that I had better not return to Camp Red Devil alive, *but* he said it in a nice way!"

"That's nice!" Lieutenant Wong chimed in. The morale in the Recon Company had gone up for almost no apparent reason, except that Sergeant Forbes had been knocked down a notch and Luke had assigned each one of the recon teams a private table in the club and had told the men that he wanted their team insignia painted on each one of the tabletops when they returned from securing the area around the Bob Hope Show. The men were already getting excited over what motto they should choose for their team slogans and how they should design their tabletops. Wong gave Luke credit for knowing how to really motivate men.

"We've got an hour before we have to load up on the choppers." Luke pulled his sleeve down to cover his watch. "Lieutenant Doak . . ."

"Yes, sir?"

"I want you to go over to the brigade's mess hall and ask Sergeant Forbes if he would like to join us as my second-in-command . . ." Luke saw the look in the officer's eyes and quickly added, ". . . of RT Jackson, of course."

"Whew! I thought for a minute there . . . sir." Wong wiped the sweat off his face. He wasn't wearing any camouflage paint.

"Did you bring what I asked you to?" Luke hefted his rucksack and slipped one of the straps over his shoulder.

"Yes, sir, it's all in my pack."

"Good."

Doak glanced over at his friend and asked with his eyes what Arrowood was talking about, but Wong only shrugged his shoulders and gave the XO a dumb look.

Lieutenant Wong and Luke took their time checking the gear each one of the recon men was carrying and noticed that there were a lot of brand-new boots being worn by the men, along with new Special Forces camouflage tiger fatigues and matching hats that had been modified. The wide brims on the hats had been cut back so that the three-inch-wide brim was removed except for a small bill in front that kept the rain and sun out of the wearer's eyes and a half-inch border was left all the way around the sides and back to deflect water. Another elastic band was sewn to the top edge of the cap so that camouflage material would be anchored better. The caps were the hardest part for Luke to pull off with only one day to prepare. The five years he had spent in Vietnam had given him a very large scrounging base from which to work. He had contacts with supply people who had left Vietnam and had returned for their second, and in some cases, their third tours.

Luke removed the shotgun from the side of Sergeant Mulhouse's pack and hefted it. "What do you think, Sergeant?"

Mulhouse shrugged his shoulders. "I don't know yet, sir. It feels funny not having my pistol."

"We all have to give up something."

"I'm not against the idea, sir. It makes good sense, but I just need some time to get used to it."

"I could only get seven of these, but by the time we return from this mission, I've been promised one for every team member."

Wong waited until they were between recon teams on the large perforated-steel-planking helipad. "That was one of the smartest things you've done so far, sir. I don't think there were two pistols alike in the whole company!"

Luke nodded his head. "I can understand why

they're a little nervous. A pistol gets a certain reputation after having been handed down a couple of times and the owner starts to feel that the weapon is good luck."

"Yes, sir, but it's impossible to resupply ammunition for them and a couple of the handguns weigh more than those modified shotguns! One of the guys actually carries a long barrel .44 magnum to the field!"

Luke smiled. "I believe that!"

"No, really, sir! It's true." Lieutenant Wong stopped next to the team he was going to insert with and dropped his rucksack down on the hot PSP. "Well, I'll be a mainland Chinese!"

Luke looked over to where Wong was staring and saw Sergeant Forbes hurrying to get to the pad before they started loading up.

The cold air rushing in the open doors of the chopper felt good. Luke rested the back of his head against the panel and felt the vibration from the chopper's engine. He wondered how many of the men riding inside of the Huey knew that the jet engine weighed less than some of them did. He had always thought the engine of a helicopter had to be huge. Luke kept his eyes resting on the Vietnamese landscape below the chopper and fought to keep his mind from thinking about his family. He had received a certified letter from a stateside law firm the night before but hadn't opened it. He knew what it was.

Sergeant Forbes sat across from Luke studying a small map of their area of operations. The terrain looked good and was composed mostly of open elephant grass and abandoned rice paddies with strips of thick jungle. The Corps commander had selected a site near the South China Sea for the Bob Hope Show, which made it a little easier to secure the area. Half of the possible sites for rockets and mortars were eliminated unless the NVA had ships in the area, and that was very unlikely with the Navy destroyers working the coastline protecting the recommissioned battleship *New Jersey* that was working the coast.

The chopper blades changed pitch and the aircraft banked slightly to the left and started decending. Luke felt his stomach turn sour. This was the part that he hated the most during a helicopter insertion. If the landing zone was hot and the NVA were waiting for them, it would be extremely difficult to orient himself and fight back effectively. An hour on the ground was all the time he needed to assemble his team and orient everyone.

The doorgunner removed his hand from his headset and tapped Luke's shoulder before pointing to the ground. The chopper hovered five feet above the blowing sea of elephant grass. Luke slid over the floor of the chopper and rested one foot on the strut just long enough to make the jump to the ground. He had made enough helicopter inserts to know that elephant grass could be very deceptive and what looked like five feet could very easily end up being a ten-foot jump to the actual ground. Luke had misjudged by two feet, but the weight of his heavy rucksack still made him land hard. He cursed the pilot under his breath and took off running away from the aircraft until he reached a narrow strip of jungle that bordered the old rice paddy they had landed in. More than one soldier met his Maker lingering around a chopper during an insertion when the NVA decided on putting an RPG round up the aircraft's exhaust.

Forbes used hand signals to bring the team together. He kept glancing over at Luke for his approval. Forbes knew that the captain had won over the whole company and that, if he didn't want to end up as the permanent laughingstock of the whole brigade, he was going to have to win the officer's respect on this mission.

Luke shot an azimuth with his lensatic compass and held his arm out, signaling the direction he wanted the team to take. RT Jackson's objective was a low hill that commanded the other terrain in the ten-square-kilometer area they were responsible for patrolling. The Bob Hope Show was going to take place at three o'clock in the afternoon the next day, which would give them plenty of time to check out the area. Luke's thoughts wandered for a couple of seconds, and he thought about the power that the actor had over the military. He didn't think that even the President of the United States could gather ten thousand soldiers together in one place during a war where no place was *safe* from an attack by the enemy. It was all just a matter of if the VC or NVA *wanted* to attack or not. That wasn't saying a hell of a lot for the American war-effort. The three o'clock show time wasn't selected for the benefit of the troops, even though they did benefit indirectly from the late afternoon show. The men had to fly and ride in from all of the units in the Corps area and, if the show had been in the morning, they would have had to start arriving before daylight, which was a major pain in the ass to those who had to get them there. During World War II, where there were large numbers of soldiers in secure areas, a Bob Hope Show made sense, but in Vietnam it played with death. Someone always died protecting those watching the show. Luke wondered if Bob Hope knew that.

Forbes led the team to the observation site, pointed out the position he wanted each one of the men to set up in, and looked back over at Luke for his approval. Luke nodded his head and dropped his rucksack down next to a large rock before removing his personal pair of German binoculars that had been given to him by a Navy SEAL he had worked with when he was with MAC-SOG. He adjusted the setting on the binos and swept the area out in front of him before handing the glasses to Forbes so that he could take a look at what they had to search. Eighty percent of their AO was nine-to-twelve-foot-high elephant grass and overgrown banana trees. The area looked like it might have been a part of a French plantation at one time.

Forbes handed the glasses back to Luke and pointed

over at a V-shaped strip of jungle that seemed to point directly at Da Nang like the point of an arrow. Luke smiled and nodded his head; he had seen the terrain feature, too. Forbes pointed at himself and then over to another member of the team and then back to the V. He wanted to take one man and check the area out. It was less than a thousand meters from where they were located.

Luke leaned forward and whispered in the sergeant's ear. "In the morning. Right now, let's just get settled in for the night."

Forbes nodded his head in agreement and left to set up his night-watch position on the back side of the hill.

Night brought a full moon that made the teams feel a lot better. They could see clearly as far as the elephant grass would let them. A herd of deer passed Luke's position a little after midnight and right before dawn it sounded like the whole area was coming apart when a large herd of pigs moved through the area going northwest.

Forbes slipped next to Luke and opened the map. He looked around the area before whispering. "Do you want to break up and check out different sites?"

Luke thought for a couple of seconds and nodded his head. There were six of them, and three men could easily recon an area. "Roger—we can hit four of the areas on the map apiece and be back here before three when the show starts." Luke made sure that the piece of terrain that was shaped like a V was one of his objectives. Of all the areas in his AO, the V was where *he* would set up 122mm rockets.

RT Jackson left their rucksacks stashed at their night lager sites and took with them only what they would need in case they got in a firefight. The PRC-25 radio was the heaviest piece of equipment they carried, and the two men that went with Luke were shocked when he had insisted on taking his turn carrying it.

Luke spent a lot of extra time searching the V area and found nothing. He was sure that the location was perfect for rockets and his suspicions were confirmed when they located a bunker that had been used recently, but there was no sign of a large force having ever been there. Luke suspected that the site was used for observation. He started to leave and stopped the men while he shot an azimuth from the point of the V toward Da Nang. The deflection mated up perfectly with the site the Bob Hope Show was going to take place at. Luke wrote down the grid coordinates, just in case he might need to call in some artillery on it in a hurry. He still felt that the NVA would use the area if they decided on shelling the show.

Forbes was waiting on the hill when Luke's portion of the team returned. All of their uniforms were saturated from sweating and water was becoming a real problem. "Sir, did you find any water back there?"

Luke nodded. A small stream meandered through the V site that was clear and drinkable.

"We're hurting, and this sun . . ." Forbes looked up at the red orb . . . "is going to kick our asses before we're extracted."

"Do you have any water left at all?"

Forbes shook his head. "None—I thought we would find some down below, but it's as dry as a month-old bone."

Luke handed Forbes his canteen. "Finish it." He looked at his watch. "It's two, and the show starts at three. I should be able to make it to the V and back in an hour if I hussle."

"You going alone?" Forbes's voice rose above a whisper.

"Sure."

Forbes beckoned for one of his experienced men to come over and join them. "Take him with you to help carry the canteens."

Luke locked eyes with the NCO and saw that the man was concerned over his welfare. He didn't know that Luke *wanted* to die and any fear he might have had was gone.

"Please, sir?" Forbes's whole attitude had changed since the humiliating incident back in the company area. Luke knew that the NCO would either join him or hate him afterwards, and he was glad that Forbes had decided to join him.

Luke gave a curt nod and reached out for the canteens. He emptied his rucksack and filled it with the plastic water jugs. The walk back would be a hell of a lot tougher than going there once the canteens were filled.

The two of them followed the trail Luke had made earlier but didn't move so fast that they became careless. They had seen but little sign of the NVA, but that didn't mean the enemy wasn't there. A single NVA soldier could easily kill both of them from an ambush. A monkey's warning howl stopped Luke in his tracks. He beckoned for his teammate to slip off the path and followed suit. They waited ten minutes before Luke stepped back out on the fresh trail, but this time Luke started moving with extreme caution. Monkeys did not give fake warnings. Something had bothered the sentinel. It could have only been a snake or a small predator, or it could have been NVA soldiers. Luke almost fell into the stream. He had been moving so cautiously that he wasn't looking down, but up in the trees and at man-high levels. He slipped the rucksack off his back and signaled for his teammate to fill them up while he searched the immediate area.

The sound reached Luke seconds after he was out of sight from the man filling the canteens. He wasn't more than ten feet away from the stream. He listened and kept changing the direction his ears were in to home in on the sound. He heard it again, and this time he identified it; men whispering in Vietnamese.

Luke backtracked until he reached his teammate. The look on his face was all the man needed to see. He stopped filling the canteen in his hand and took the time to screw the cap back on before picking up his weapon. Luke signaled with his hand in the direction the sounds had come from and started going back in that direction. The man with him touched his arm and pointed back to where the rest of the team was located. Luke understood what he wanted to do but they didn't have time. He pulled his sleeve up and pointed at his watch dial. It was two thirty-five. He had to know for sure if the NVA soldiers he had heard talking were just scouts or a part of a larger party. The V was too far away from the show site for mortars to hit, so it would have to be a rocket detachment or scouts.

Luke could see the soldier wasn't very happy over the idea of trying to take on some NVA with just the two of them and understood why. He beckoned for the man to get closer and touched his ear with his lips before whispering so low that he could barely hear himself speaking. "Go get Forbes."

The soldiers shook his head violently. He wasn't enthused over taking on the NVA with just the two of them, but he wasn't about to leave the captain all by himself.

Luke smiled and shrugged before starting back toward the place he had heard the voices. The NVA had gone, but they had left evidence that they had been there. Luke saw the olive-drab, painted rocket leaning against a bamboo launcher that was propped up to the right angle with crossed bamboo struts. A wire ran from the 122mm rocket back into the elephant grass. The NVA had picked the V site for their rockets. Luke had been just a little bit too early the first time around to catch them setting the rockets up. Luke followed the wire back toward the tree line and saw that there were other wires coming out of the elephant grass and joined up with the one he was following. Before he had gone a hundred feet, there were nine more wires with his. Ten 122mm rockets hitting ten thousand troops all bunched together would kill hundreds of soldiers.

The NVA officer behind the electrical hand detonator saw him the same time that Luke saw the North Vietnamese. Luke had the advantage because the NVA officer had to drop the detonator and wires before he could pick up his weapon. The sound of his CAR-15 submachine gun sent monkeys screaming through the treetops.

Sergeant Forbes heard the shots and reacted instantly. He formed the remainder of the team and went down the hill at a jog in the direction of the V.

Luke tore the detonator out of the dead NVA officer's hands while his teammate kept turning around in a combat crouch waiting for the elephant grass to explode with NVA soldiers. He didn't have to wait long. AK-47s started raking the area, firing wildly into the grass. The recon man returned fire and dropped down near Luke with his eyes wide open. He had a good reason to be afraid.

Forbes moved faster than it was safe to move through the elephant grass, but figured the NVA would open fire when they got in range. He was right. Forbes's men opened fire not knowing where Luke and his teammate were. It wasn't a matter of choice, but of survival. Actually, without knowing it, they had forced the NVA squad closing in on Luke to stop and turn and fight.

The fighting in the high grass turned quickly into mini-wars, with one or two men fighting the same number from the other side. The NVA had moved the 122mm rockets forward over a week earlier when their intelligence reports had told them about the upcoming Bob Hope Show in Da Nang. The only thing that they had to wait for was the exact location of the show and that wasn't very hard to figure out once the American engineers had started building the huge stage near the sea. They had hidden two flights of ten rockets each in the jungle and had sent a small detail forward to assemble the rockets for launching. The NVA soldiers were artillerymen and not trained infantry; otherwise, Luke would not have been able to sneak up on them so easily. The infantry would have posted guards.

Luke kept the ten wires in one hand as he moved back down the wires toward the rockets. His teammate played rear guard for him, keeping the NVA firing wild. When Luke reached the first rocket site, he kicked the long missile over on its side and then cut through the grass and repeated the process. Bullets cut through the thick green leaves all around Luke but he knew that he couldn't afford to stop, just in case he had missed one of the wires. He didn't know that there was another ten-rocket battery only a few meters away that was being wired to a detonator by another NVA officer.

Forbes heard an AK-47 firing and threw a hand grenade in the direction the sound had come from. The AK-47 stopped barking its death song. Luke used the barrel of his hot CAR-15 to part the grass and came face-to-face with Forbes. Both of them almost shot each other. Forbes had already started pulling the trigger on his M-16 and only had time to instinctively jerk the barrel to one side, sending the rounds cutting through the grass. "Fucking close call, Captain!" Forbes spoke in a normal voice.

"They were setting up rockets. We've found ten of them." Luke scanned the area around them.

"Let's get the hell out of here and call in an air strike!" Forbes was making good sense.

"Not enough time!" Luke and Forbes had backed up and found themselves on a slight rise in the ground where they could see over the tops of the bamboo. "Look!"

Forbes could see the tips of a half-dozen rockets sticking above the grass. "Fuck!" He knew that it was too late to stop them from being fired.

Luke looked around in frustration and felt the breeze blowing against his sweaty face. "Fire!"

"Fire at what, Captain?" Forbes swung his weapon around searching for a target.

"Fire! Do you have a lighter?"

"Fuck, yes!" Forbes understood what Luke was talking about and started lighting the dry grass on fire all around him. The wind was blowing in the direction of the rockets and would spread very fast once enough of it was burning.

The team smelled the smoke and figured out what was going on and started lighting the grass on fire from their locations, and within a couple of minutes red flames and black smoke were leaping up for a hundred meters.

The NVA officer smelled the smoke and knew that the Americans had started the grass on fire. He struggled to attach the wires to his detonator before the flames reached the rockets. It took him a couple of minutes to attach the wires and he rotated the handle.

Nothing happened.

He panicked and turned the crank again, and this time one of the rocket motors started and a red streak shot up off the ground. The flames had burned through the wires and had short-circuited the system for all but one of the rockets, and the flames had burned through the dry bamboo supports for the launcher of that one and changed its flight angle.

Luke saw the rocket leaving the ground and groaned.

Automatic weapons fire increased from the jungle, where a detachment of NVA were coming to support the artillery crew. A pair of Cobra gunships appeared above the black smoke from the fire. Lieutenant Doak had called for them when he had first heard the automatic weapons fire in the distance and no one had come up on the command frequency to call for support. He had figured Captain Arrowood's team was in deep trouble and couldn't stop fighting to call for help. He was right.

The gunships saw the rocket lift off the ground and watched it streak through the sky toward Da Nang. The rocket flew perfectly through the air, rotating slightly in a slow spin to maintain its trajectory.

Bob Hope stood in the middle of the new-smelling plywood stage, holding a golf club. He looked out into the roaring crowd of military men from all of the branches of the service and gave his famous grin. The crowd went wild. He took a slow swing with his golf club and the noise grew to an earsplitting roar. He bowed to the crowd and the men stood up, yelling at the tops of their lungs. Hope walked over to the mike and spoke into it. "Thank you for your warm welcome!"

The troops started laughing even harder.

Bob Hope turned around slowly and acted shocked and surprised when he saw the four beautiful scantly clad movie and rock starlets. The act had been timed perfectly and each time that Bob Hope had made a move during the introduction, one of the girls had snuck up on the stage behind him causing the troops to roar.

"Well, at least it's a sunny day for our show that I know you're going to enjoy!" Hope knew that the troops had been sitting under the tropical sun for hours waiting for the show to start and was trying to make a joke out of it. "We have a few more of these kinds of treats for you . . ." Hope pointed with the handle of his golf club at the dancing girls and the men went wild. "You like *round-eyed* women?"

A small group of the soldiers at the foot of the stage tried climbing up to where Hope and the girls were and a detail of MPs pulled them back down on the ground.

A dull thud rolled over the stage from an area behind the troops. Only the men who were sitting on top of a huge pile of empty fifty-five-gallon drums could see where the single 122mm rocket had landed next to an airfield. When the dust settled, eleven airmen from the maintenance area were lying dead.

"Is someone trying to shoot at me?" Hope reached up and pulled the visor of the Marine helmet he was wearing down lower over his eyes and puffed out his chest. He strutted over to the edge of the stage with his golf club held under his arm like a swagger stick.

"Well, I'm not afraid because the United States Marine Corps is here with us today!"

The large group of Marines from the 1st Marine Division stood up and cheered. Hope knew how to work a crowd of military men. He had been doing it since World War II; surround yourself with nearly naked women, crack a few jokes, work the pride the men have in their units and you've got yourself a sure thing.

The camera crews made sure they got a lot of film of the troops and constantly panned the crowd between Hope's jokes. People back home in the States would sit in front of their TV sets hoping to get just a glimpse of one of their loved ones and Hope knew that. He *donated* his time entertaining the troops and the United States government *donated*: the *extras*, the security, the props, the transportation and time taken away from their wartime missions. The only people who didn't *donate* willingly were the sponsors of the prime-time Stateside showing of the Bob Hope Show at Da Nang.

The soldiers donated their lives.

CHAPTER ELEVEN

✪✪✪✪✪✪✪✪✪✪✪✪✪✪✪✪✪✪✪

PROJECT DEATHWATCH

The medical teams waited until the chopper blades had stopped moving before unloading the two dead soldiers and the wounded man. Luke stood to one side and watched them pull the soldier out of the helicopter and place him on a stretcher.

"What's his name?" Luke whispered.

"Sir?" Lieutenant Doak leaned over so that he could hear what his captain was saying.

Lieutenant Wong had heard the question and answered for the XO. "PFC Rowdy Williams, sir. He was a real cowboy from Wyoming."

"I didn't even know his name."

"Sir, I wouldn't hold that against yourself . . . you've only been in the company a couple of days." Doak watched the medics zip up the rubberized bodybag.

"Rowdy Williams . . ." Luke rolled the name off his tongue. "Sounds like a name someone would place on a kid they knew was going to be filled with a lot of spunk."

"He was fun to be around." Sergeant Forbes joined the conversation. "And he was a damn good soldier. That's why I sent him with you to get the water. You couldn't ask for a better man to watch your ass for you."

Luke swallowed. "Doak, I'll need both of their home addresses so that I can write their parents a letter. They should know how they died."

"Sir, there's a brigade policy that states the brigade personnel section will be the ones to insure the next-of-kin is informed of the death." Wong was trying to keep Luke out of trouble.

"Thanks, but in this company, that's *my* job." Luke tried smiling at the lieutenant to let him know that he wasn't angry with him. "I'll wait a couple of days so the people back in the States can do their notification first."

"You've got to look at the good side, sir." Doak left the helipad with Luke and walked next to him. "If those rockets would have reached their target a lot more than two men would have died, that's for sure!"

"I wonder where that one rocket ended up landing?" Luke kept staring at the sandy soil in front of him as he walked. "Check that out for me, will you, Doak?"

"Sure. I'm curious about that to, now that you've mentioned it. Someone should have reported seeing a rocket hit along the beach. Maybe with a little luck it landed in the sea."

"Maybe . . . with a little luck." Luke didn't like having to rely on luck. He stopped in front of the brigade TOC. "I've got to debrief the staff. Will you make sure the men are debriefed and taken care off?"

"Roger, sir." Doak paused and looked back over his shoulder at his new captain. "The men think that you're all right, sir."

Luke nodded his head and pressed his lips together tightly before entering the sandbag archway into the stale smelling bunker.

"Luke Arrowood!" The brigade commander stopped talking to a group of his staff officers and beckoned for Luke to join them. "I heard a little about your mission! Well done!"

"One rocket got away, sir."

A grim expression crossed the older man's face. "It landed at an airstrip and killed eleven men. Another hundred meters and it wouldn't have done any damage. The airmen were on a work detail at the far end of the strip."

Luke recalled watching the rocket leave the ground and the feeling of helplessness he had when he saw it streaking toward Da Nang.

One of the staff officers saw the pained look on Luke's face and spoke up. "It could have been worse. The rocket could have landed in the massed troops for the show."

Luke's mind's eye saw the bamboo support for the 122mm rocket burning and break just as the rocket left the makeshift launcher. If it hadn't been for that slight adjustment, the rocket would have probably landed in the mass of soldiers and other lives would have been lost and the eleven airmen would still be alive. War chose its victims by a method only it knew.

"Sir, I have an idea that I think might be a real asset to the brigade." Luke glanced at the staff officers but decided on continuing anyway. It wasn't smart to present an idea in front of so many people because it might only take a single murmured dissenting voice to kill it. Luke had learned that lesson when he had first gotten his commission. The accepted way of presenting an idea in the military was to first present it to people you knew would support it and, once you had your solid supporters, then you presented it to an open forum. He was breaking the rule because it was a perfect opportunity to get the brigade commander's support and once he had that, he didn't have to worry about opponents.

"I'm waiting . . . shoot!" The colonel smiled a friendly grin.

"Lately we've been having a difficult time finding the enemy and when we do, especially with our five-man recon teams, the enemy is a vastly superior force and the recon men are forced to let them pass."

"Why?" The officer who asked the question was a recently assigned major from the States. "Aren't your recon teams armed?"

"Yes, they're armed, but their mission is reconniassance and not infantry."

"I would think that once a soldier located his enemy that he would kill him." The major stared at Luke, waiting for an answer.

"Five men, sir, aren't a match for a hundred or more NVA; even my recon men would have a hard time with odds like that . . . unless . . ."

"What, Captain?" The major tried acting suave.

"Unless we had a trained artillery forward observer with us." Luke held his hand out in front of him to empathize the core of his idea. "We've tried training infantrymen to call in artillery and it works, but not very well—and when you add an hour or longer for a fire mission to get cleared, the NVA are long gone before the first round lands."

"Wait a minute, Arrowood! You know the procedure better than anyone else in this room!" The brigade artillery liaison officer had joined the gathering around the commander. "All fire missions have to be properly cleared."

Luke saw the look in the brigade commander's eyes and knew that he was starting to side with the artillery. No commander wanted an incident where artillery rounds landed on their own troops. "Sir, that's exactly the reason why I want *artillerymen* trained as recon men. That way, the artillery will be confident of their observer and the infantry will be able to play the part that they're trained for. If the artillerymen are trained in the skills of artillery adjustment *and* recon, they'll be a valuable functioning part of the team and not excess baggage."

"Where do you plan on finding these extra officers?" The artillery liaison officer was playing his trump card to kill the idea. "And please explain to me, Arrowood, just how your men are going to take it when artillery lieutenants take over their recon teams."

"I won't have to explain that."

"Do you think artillery lieutenants are going to serve *under* NCOs?"

"No . . . the forward observers will be enlisted men."

"What!"

"Enlisted men, trained to adjust artillery and mortar fire. Preferably, enlisted men who have worked on the guns before so they aren't afraid of them."

"Colonel, he's gone too far this time! Arrowood knows better than to even suggest such a foolish idea!"

Luke looked at the senior officer. "Sir, think about it from an infantryman's point of view. A large NVA force is moving through the jungle and out of the clear blue sky artillery hits them. The commander reacts and moves his troops out of the area, but the artillery keeps falling on his men and he can't break contact. His losses are high and he hasn't been able to kill a single American, because he can't locate the hidden recon team and the FO with them."

The brigade commander pressed his right index finger against his lips and finally shook his head. "I like the concept."

"Sir! I'm advising you that it can't be done! Enlisted men aren't capable of adjusting artillery fires!" The artillery liaison officer was trying desperately to nip the idea in the bud.

"You say that it can't be done . . ." The colonel looked over at Luke and then at the faces of his staff, ". . . and Captain Arrowood says that it can be. Let's give it a try on a test basis. How many men do you think you'll need?"

"I'd like to start with eight or ten, sir. We should have some dropouts and I'd like to field at least three or four."

"Fine! Have the artillery battalion give you the men and my personnel section should be able to get them into the Marine Recon School for a short course." The colonel flashed a look at his staff officer responsible.

"Thanks, sir. I appreciate the chance to work on this."

"Anything else?" The colonel grinned. "Now that you have my attention?"

"One thing, sir. I'm going to need a special clearance for my FOs from the artillery. When we call for a mission in the field, I want a five-minute-or-*less* reaction time from the time the fire mission is called to having the first round on the ground."

"That's impossible!" The artillery liaison officer almost choked on his own words.

"I can't see why." Luke didn't back off a single verbal step. "All of the other units in Vietnam can do it . . . why not the mighty 4th Battalion, 5th Artillery?"

'You are way out of line, Captain!"

"Enough! Gentlemen!!" The colonel shook his head. "Captain Arrowood is assuming the responsibility and that is all I need to hear."

"Even if rounds fall on a recon team?" The major was trying to shift everything on Luke.

"Sure . . . I'm not afraid of responibility, sir." Luke glared back at the major. "I'll pick up my volunteers in, let's say, two days?"

"I have to talk to the artillery battalion commander first."

"I think the brigade commander has already agreed to the idea, Major."

"All right, two days, but don't expect the best men in the battalion. I don't think any of them will volunteer for such a harebrained idea."

Luke smiled and winked at the major. "Let's let them decide, sir."

The evening staff briefing had been very successful for the Recon Company and, after most of the staff had seen earlier that the colonel backed Arrowood, it was only a matter of what Luke wanted and how much and they busted their asses to get it for him—all except Jeffers. Luke had seen the artillery battalion commander talking heatedly to the brigade commander before the meeting. It was obvious that, whatever Jeffers was saying, it wasn't liked by the colonel. After a couple of minutes, the colonel wagged his finger at Jeffers and the lieutenant colonel took his customary seat for the staff call.

Luke left the brigade TOC exhausted after the long night out on patrol and having spent the whole afternoon in the bunker with the brigade staff. He stepped outside and the night air seemed pure and fresh after the cigar smoke in the bunker, even though there was always shit being burned somewhere on the large base and it depended on which way the wind was blowing from on how bad the smell was. Mornings were the worst because that's when most of the shit-burning details were pulled, and it was very wise to get to breakfast early before the smell ruined your appetite.

The night breeze felt good against Luke's bare skin. He had gone back to his hootch and slipped into a cutoff pair of tiger pants and had strapped on his pistol before walking out to a bunker with a third full bottle of Wild Turkey in one hand and the unopened certified letter in his other hand. He took a seat in the bright moonlight and tore open the envelope. He didn't hesitate anymore and read the divorce decree that had been signed by a California judge. She hadn't wasted any time. Luke was sure that the paperwork was already in progress when she had gone on R&R with him. She had kept her word and had given him unlimited visitation privileges with the children. He refolded the letter and shoved it in his back pocket. It was over.

The booze went right to his head. He hadn't eaten much during the day and had sweated a lot. The bourbon went through his system like a dry sponge sucking up water.

"You're a cheap drunk, old boy." Luke talked to himself on his bunker seat. The alcohol had broken down his defenses and he felt the tears welling up inside. From out of nowhere, he could smell his son Alex's hair.

"You's a brave motherfucker, I mus' say." The voice came from behind him toward the perimeter bunkers.

Luke instantly tucked away his self-pity and even the alcohol knew better than to try and muddle his thoughts now. Luke came to a full alert.

"Du yu 'member me?" The voice hissed. "I was thu one who gave yu thu *warning*, over by thu artillery hootches."

Luke remembered the shooting incident very well. He started to turn around slowly.

"I wouldn't try that, Captain." The second voice was much more refined and educated, and told Luke there were at least two black soldiers behind him in the dark.

"What do you want from me?" Luke used the time to check out anything in the area that he could use.

"Du yu 'member my man, Talbot?"

"Yes."

"Yu killed a bruder an we's jus' can't allow for tha' kind of honkie shit tu go on."

"Talbot was on drugs . . . you know that."

"Hit doant matter!" The uneducated black's voice rose.

Luke wanted to just jump up and get it over with. It was all getting to be too much for him. "What do you want?"

"You know we were going to kill you, but after you saved Sergeant Cole and our brother's life in that bunker, the brothers have decided on just teaching you a *lesson*."

"A lesson?" Luke felt the weight of his pistol against his side. He didn't think they could see it in the shadows on the opposite side of the bunker from the direction the two voices were coming from.

"Some of the brothers wanted to cut your nuts off, but the more reasonable brothers won and were going to just cut *one* of your ears off as a warning to any other white motherfuckers who might be thinking about zapping a black brother of ours!"

"Why don't you guys get off this black-white shit! We're all fighting a common enemy: the North Vietnamese!"

"You honkies talk that shit to us black people when you want us to fight your wars for you but when the wars are over you shit in our faces again! That ain't going to happen anymore! We want our piece of the pie!"

"It sounds like you want the *whole* pie." Luke couldn't help being sarcastic.

"Why not! For three hundred years, white people have been shitting on black folk . . . now it's our turn!" The educated black voice rose slightly, but still was low enough not to draw attention from the fighting bunkers around the perimeter.

"All I have to do is yell and the guards will come." Luke tried bluffing his way out.

"Du hit an' youse one dead honkie!"

"Our people are burning down your fucking cities. Do you know that? We're scaring the fuck out of you white motherfuckers back in Detroit!"

"Are you from Detroit?"

There was a pause. The educated voice realized it had said too much. "Yeah! A lot of brothers are from Detroit."

"I've been there."

"Then you know how bad our people are treated."

"Maybe, but what I saw was a black man and a white man working side by side in an auto plant, drawing *exactly* the same pay."

"Yeah! Those who have jobs, but a lot of brothers can't find good work."

"I think that isn't a racial problem . . . everyone is having problems finding auto factory jobs right now."

"We aint here tu talk tu thu motherfucker!" The uneducated voice cut in. "I'll du it!"

Luke prepared himself to leap forward and roll on the ground until he could get his pistol out of its holster. But he hadn't realized how fast the pair of adversaries could move or how much the alcohol still controlled his motor movements. A strong hand grasped his lower arm from behind.

"It won't hurt much. You're lucky that there's a doctor over in that hootch."

The next minute seemed like a timeless void to Luke as he struggled to clear his mind and find a way out.

"Evening, Captain." Lieutenant Doak appeared between two of the hootches in the moonlight holding one of the modified shotguns Luke had scrounged up for the recon teams.

The hand released Luke.

"Ain't nowhere for you boys to go . . . look around."

Recon men appeared from behind the buildings and stood up from where they had crawled out near the perimeter while the pair of blacks were talking to Luke.

"Do you have a problem, Captain?" Doak approached the bunker. "Well . . . well . . . well. What do we have here?"

Luke turned around and looked for the first time at the faces of the men who had tried to kill him earlier with the M-16 back at the artillery battalion, and who were about to cut off his ear. He had never seen the heavyset uneducated one before but the educated black was the chaplain's assistant and had been out at LZ Sandy for the services after the Sapper attack. The moonlight reflected the hate in both of the black soldiers' eyes.

"What should we do with them, Captain?" Lieutenant Doak kept the barrel of his shotgun pointed at nut level.

"Run them over to the provost's office. Major Redmond will know how to handle it."

"Sergeant Forbes . . . tie their hands behind their backs and frisk them before taking them over there." Doak sat down next to Luke on the sandbags and waited until the detail had left before continuing. "I hope you don't mind, but I've had guards watching you twenty-four hours a day since you've been here . . . even when you took a shit."

"Thanks, I didn't think that I needed that kind of protection, but I guess that I did." Luke felt drained.

"There were rumors floating around Red Devil that the blacks were going to frag you ever since that incident back at LZ Sandy." Doak didn't look at Luke but looked up at the bright moon instead. "This shit is getting bad."

"What's that?"

"This racial shit. I don't know where it's going to end."

"A lot of years of bitterness are coming out. It'll all balance out." Luke felt weak, not physical weakness but mental. He was very tired of all the bullshit. Fighting with the staff so that he could do his job and the Jeffers bullshit added to that didn't help. Now the racial shit. Hell, compared to the shit he was getting from his side, the NVA seemed like friends. "I'm tired."

"I would be too, sir." Doak lit a cigarette and offered the pack to Luke.

"No, thanks."

A blue streak of processed lung smoke preceded the words out of Doak's throat. "Don't give up, sir. You're a rare officer and the men need you. I'll tell you right now, there isn't a man, black or white, in the Recon Company that won't die for you on the spot."

"I haven't been here a week." Luke appreciated what the lieutenant was saying, but didn't believe it.

"Your reputation has been here a lot longer, sir." Doak hot-boxed his cigarette and ground it out under his boot. He nodded with his head. "Looks like Major Redmond wants some more information."

Luke could see the black major walking across the clearing toward him with MPs accompanying him. One of his recon men was in the lead.

"Captain Arrowood, it looks like trouble tends to follow you around." The major smiled in the moonlight.

"Seems that way, sir." Luke remained sitting on the bunker.

"We're going to have to ship you out of the brigade." Redmond hefted his pistol belt up over his belt buckle. "I can't guarantee your safety here anymore."

"We can." Lieutenant Doak took a step closer to the major and his captain. "The Recon Company *will* guarantee his safety."

Major Redmond didn't know what to say and kept staring at Luke. The highly confidential file on the black militants was growing in the brigade and, from other military police reports he had been reading, the problem was spreading throughout all of Vietnam. There wasn't a really safe place for Arrowood in-country.

"We'll have guards posted around the clock and, when the captain's not out in the field, we'll insure his safety."

"I don't know if I'm worth all of the trouble, Lieutenant Doak, but I sure appreciate the offer." Luke stood and brushed the dirt off the seat of his pants.

"You're worth it, sir. As far as the men in the company are concerned, you're the best commander to come along in a very long time and we need you to set up this artillery FO program for us. It's a great idea." Doak's white teeth shined in the moonlight.

Luke shook his head in wonder. "How did you know about that idea? I just told the colonel at staff call today."

"Sir, if you only knew how many people *act* like they're working when you're around but are actually listening to every word you say." Doak shifted his shotgun to his other hand. "You're a legend-in-your-own-time."

"Where have I heard that shit before!" Luke tried making light of the high compliment.

"Let's give it a shot for a couple of weeks, but if there's another incident like this one, I'm going to have to ship you out of here, Captain Arrowood. Fair enough?"

"Fair enough." Luke shook hands with the wide-shouldered major.

A strong breeze started blowing in from the highlands sending dust devils between the hootches. A loose sheet of roofing tin started flapping and making noise.

"A storm's coming in from the west." Luke faced the strong breeze and felt the wind pick up his hair and massage his scalp.

Major Redmond's eyes held the worry he felt for the captain but his helmet shadowed them so no one could see. "I'm having that pair shipped to LBJ in the morning." He referred to Long Binh Jail, using the initials of a famous American. "We can't charge them for the shooting incident even though I'm sure that they did it, but the threat to cut off your ear should get them a couple of years in Fort Leavenworth." Redmond scanned the shadows and saw the recon men waiting there. "You have enough witnesses."

The wind suddenly increased to a monsoon force.

"I'll see you later, Major. We have to secure the company area before it blows away." Luke saluted the senior officer and started walking fast toward his company troop billets. Lieutenant Doak followed him, and the men in the shadows hurried to get back to their own hootches.

Luke sat alone in his room that was sectioned off in the back of his orderly room. He opened a fresh bottle of bourbon and felt like getting ripping drunk, but ended up sipping instead of guzzling and sat on his cot with his back against the plywood wall. He had lit a Coleman lantern and had placed the small photograph of his wife and children at an angle next to it so that he could see them from his seat. The storm shook the whole building. Luke could feel the vibrations against his back. He drank straight out of the bottle and used a green towel to hold against his mouth when the sobs started getting louder than the storm.

*   *   *

Lieutenant Colonel Jeffers sat behind his desk and glared at the three soldiers standing at attention in front of him. He reached up and grabbed the edge of his desk and spun his swivel chair around so that his back was to the men and watched a detail painting the stage over at the Artillery Bowl. He made the three men stand at attention for over a half hour while he watched the detail and shuffled through a small stack of papers on his desk. Slowly, he lit a cigar and leaned back in his chair before he spoke. "Are any of you planning on making the Army a career?" He looked at each one of their faces and stopped when he reached the officer. "How about you, Lieutenant Fields?"

"No, sir."

"Are you sure?" Jeffers glanced down at the top of his desk and pulled the lieutenant's green 201 personnel folder out of the stack. "It shows here that you were the honor graduate from your class and that you received a *regular* Army commission. You're throwing a lot away just to crawl around in the jungle for a couple of months. *First* lieutenants don't do those kinds of things!"

"First lieutenants aren't supposed to be forward observers either, sir, and I figure that as long as the battalion wants me to be an FO, I'll do it where it will do the most good."

"Are you getting smart with me, mister?"

Fields looked directly into the battalion commander's red-rimmed eyes and paused before he spoke. "No, sir. I *was* removed from Bravo Battery's fire-direction center to go to the field as an FO, wasn't I, sir?"

Jeffers blinked his eyes very slowly like a crocodile sunning itself would do. "That can be changed very easily."

"Don't bother, sir. I'm voluntering for duty with the Recon Company under Captain Arrowood." Fields could see that just mentioning the captain's name made Jeffers angry.

"That could reflect on you efficiency report, young man." Jeffers rolled the cigar between his fingers and kept the tip in his mouth.

"Is that a threat, sir?"

"Advice." He exhaled the smoke out of his lungs around the cigar in his mouth.

"I thought officer efficiency reports were based on performance that had already occurred?"

"There's a portion for potential and for judgement." Jeffers thought that he had the young lieutenant trapped, and smiled.

Lieutenant Fields shrugged his shoulders. "So then I get a bad OER. Like I said, sir, I'm not making the Army my career, so I can afford to do what's *right*."

Jeffers bit through the end of his cigar and was forced to spit it out in his wastepaper basket. He pointed at the door. "Captain Kreps! Get them out of here!"

Kreps left his seat in the corner of the office and opened the door for the three men to exit. All of their gear had been stacked next to the battalion headquarters door outside of the building. None of them said anything as they picked up their duffel bags and threw them over their shoulders. The trio was a fifty meters down the road before Lieutenant Fields reached over and slapped one of the soldiers on his back. Specialist Pilgrim tried jumping up and clicking his heels, but his duffel bag was too heavy and he ended up landing flat on his back in the dust. Dotson threw his duffel bag on his friend's chest and started laughing.

Jeffers watched the happy soldiers grab ass on the dusty road and puffed from his fresh cigar. He wondered why he couldn't draw that kind of a reaction out of soldiers. He could see that they were excited going to the Recon Company and probably to their damned deaths and it was all because they wanted to be with that damned captain.

Luke heard the knock on his door and looked up from the stack of personnel folders he was going through so that he would get a better idea as to the backgrounds of his men. "Come in." His eyes went back down to the folder in front of him. The door opened and someone walked over to the front of his desk. Luke shaded his eyes with his hand and continued reading.

"Lieutenant Fields, reporting for duty, sir!"

"Specialist Dotson, reporting for duty, sir!"

"Specialist Pilgrim, reporting for duty, sir!"

Luke smiled before looking up. "Lieutenant Colonel Jeffers promised to sent me the *worst* artillerymen in the battalion and I can see from the likes of the three of you that he has kept his word!"

The three artillerymen stood at attention smiling.

"*But*, with a lot of hard work and proper supervision, we might turn the likes of you into basic, *novice*-level recon men . . ."

"Novice-level, my ass." Dotson whispered under his breath.

"Do you have something you would like to say, soldier?" Luke tried frowning but he was so happy seeing the three of them that he could only smile.

"I said that novice-level would be very fine, sir."

Lieutenant Doak stood leaning against the side wall of the office watching with a grin on his face. It was obvious that all four of them were close war buddies.

"You all might as well stand at ease, now that you're here and tell me what's been going on out in Bravo Battery."

All three of them started talking at once and then slowed down to interrupt each other with details while they took turns telling their stories.

Lieutenant Doak left the room and returned an hour later and they were still talking as rapidly as they had started. "Sir, the rest of the FO volunteers are here."

"Good!" Luke pulled his hat out of the side pocket of his tiger fatigues and slapped it against his leg to shape it before slipping it on his head. "Let's go meet the rest of your team."

*   *   *

The ten artillerymen were shipped to the Marine Force Reconnaissance School at Dong-Ha for a two-week course. The Marines weren't too happy having soldiers in their school and made the training for them extremely difficult, especially when the drill instructors found out that they weren't even infantrymen, but artillerymen.

Luke had set up a twenty-hour block of instruction with the brigade surgeon's office for the returning men. Out of the original ten who had started the training, four had dropped out during the Dong-Ha phase and returned to their batteries, much to the delight of Lieutenant Colonel Jeffers. The remaining six men breezed through the medical and NVA weapons portion of the training.

The second phase of the training was completed with courses in artillery adjustment, map reading, the use of the compass, and hands-on training with artillery and mortar crews in the brigade. The reasons Luke wanted to get the men out to the different artillery and mortar units was twofold; he not only wanted them familiar with the artillery pieces they had been trained on but he wanted the artillery and mortar crews to *see* them and be able to identify with them as people and not voices coming over the radio in the middle of the night. Luke had briefed Fields on what he had wanted, and Fields had made sure that they had visited each of the fire-direction centers and had introduced themselves.

The third phase of their training was mainly in qualifying with American and North Vietnamese weapons. Luke was a strong believer that a soldier would never be without a weapon or out of ammunition if he knew how to operate all of the weapons on a battlefield.

Ten men had started the training and two months later four of them finished: Lieutenant Fields, Dotson, Pilgrim and a Japanese-American from San Francisco named Hito, who had been a computer specialist in Charlie Battery's FDC.

CHAPTER TWELVE

✪✪✪✪✪✪✪✪✪✪✪✪✪✪✪✪✪✪✪✪

LZ NANCY

The blue leather box sat open on the center of the desk. The light shining in through the window reflected off the octagon-shaped brass metal lying on the tan velvet lining inside of the box. Luke reached over and touched the eagle embedded on the coveted military award for heroism.

"It's a good-looking meal, isn't it?" Lieutenant Doak entered the office followed by Fields.

Luke rubbed his fingers over the wide blue stripes and tapped the thin red lines on the white background before answering his executive officer. "Next to the Medal of Honor, this is the medal that I admire the most."

"The Soldier's Medal is our highest heroism award, isn't it?" Fields was as proud as Luke was over the medal.

"Bingo! It's our highest military peacetime award, if you call winning it in Vietnam peaceful." Fields took a chair in front of Luke's desk and swung it around so that he could sit down on it cowboy-style.

"What's going on, sir?" Fields leaned up against a two-by-four support post.

"The armor commander has requested some recon teams to work the hills to the west of LZ Nancy. I think it would be a perfect place and time to test our new artillery forward observer concept."

"How many teams, sir?" Lieutenant Fields became more interested in the conversation at the mentioning of the artillery FOs. He had thought that it would be another meeting that dealt only with the regular recon teams.

"Three." Luke reached into the lower drawer of his desk and removed a fatigue jacket and a camouflaged cap. "What do you think of this idea?"

Fields took the cap and jacket and looked at what Luke was showing him. A black shoulder patch with a red border and white letters was sewn on the shoulder and on the center of the cap.

"What do you think?" Luke was waiting for Fields's response.

"Deathwatch?"

"Well?"

"I like it!"

"I made up enough patches so that every one who has qualified as FOs can have five of them."

"Where did you come up with a name like Deathwatch?" Fields liked the sound of it.

"I was trying to think of a name that would tie in with what they were doing. They're *watching* and when they see a target they bring death and destruction on it; thus the name Deathwatch." Luke shuffled through some papers on his desk and pulled a single sheet free from the stack he had just gone through. "You'll like this, Doak."

"Orders?" Doak could tell by just glancing at the paper from the format, that it was some kind of orders from higher headquarters.

"Read them." Luke smiled.

Doak flashed a worried look at Fields. He didn't want a transfer to a line infantry unit now that Arrowood was in command of the company. He had requested a transfer under the old commander, but it had been turned down. Doak read the first couple of lines fast and then slowed down. "Well, I'll be a fucking leg!"

"The Army has finally seen the light and has done something right for a change."

"What's going on?" Fields was in the dark.

"We are now officially, P Company of the 75th Rangers!" Doak could barely contain his excitement. "We're *official* Rangers!"

"I don't know if that's going to make our Ranger tab-wearing friends very happy."

"Fuck them!" Doak let his excitement go. "I have a hard time with people who think *school* training is better than *combat* experience. Staying awake for four days in a Georgia swamp does not compare to staying awake for four days in a Vietnamese jungle where there are things a little more dangerous than a water moccasin."

Luke gave Doak a knowing look and shook his head slowly. "You don't know the power of the paper pushers, my young friend."

"Will we get Ranger patches?" Lieutenant Doak looked up from rereading the orders.

Luke used the toe of his boot to shove the cardboard box out from behind his desk. Lieutenant Doak dropped down on one knee and opened the flaps and whistled between his teeth. "They're beautiful!" He held up a bundle of twenty-five Ranger tabs that were designed along the same patterns as the World War II tabs, but had embroidered on them the new company and unit.

"The quartermaster is going to send over two men with sewing machines this afternoon to have the patches put on our uniforms, and in the morning the brigade commander is going to formally present us our new colors." Luke laced his hand behind his head. "I hear that General Westmoreland might fly in for the ceremony. He likes Rangers and airborne types."

"Westy himself?" Doak was impressed.

"That's the rumor, so make damn sure the men are looking sharp!"

"When are we going out to LZ Nancy?" Fields kept his eyes on the Ranger tabs and laid the fatigue jacket and cap back down on Luke's desk.

"*After* the ceremony." Luke could see what the lieutenant was thinking and added, "Project Deathwatch is *assigned* to Papa Company, Lieutenant Fields, and is authorized to wear the 75th Ranger tab."

Lieutenant Doak slapped Fields on his back. "Big boys now! Let's see how you all perform in the field."

"Don't worry about my Deathwatch men . . . executive officer! You're going to see some fantastic results from them."

"Money talks . . . bullshit walks . . ." Doak teased his peer.

"We've got a lot to do before the ceremony in the morning so lets get moving."

Doak picked up the box of Ranger tabs and started to leave behind Fields and stopped in the doorway. "Have you heard about the chaplain's assistant and his buddy?"

Luke looked up from the papers he was trying to get through before he left the office. "No . . . what?"

"They couldn't find enough evidence to court-marshal either of them. They'll be back here at Camp Red Devil this week." Fields shifted the box under his arm. "The chaplain's assistant played his role to the hilt and the chaplain himself flew down to LBJ and testified that his man wasn't capable of violence." Fields hesitated before saying what was on his mind. "Personally, I think the whole fucking senior officers corps is afraid of the blacks."

"Why do you say that?"

"Look around you at the shit that's going on and nobody sees anything, except the lower-ranking enlisted men and the line officers. I mean you have to be blind not to see the all-black hootches and the gangs of black soldiers roaming around the base camps at night . . . it's getting bad, sir. Racism in reverse."

Luke thought about the all-black hootches over in the artillery battalion area and had to agree with Doak. A white officer walking through any of their barracks got dirty stares and the hootch would become quiet until he left. Something was going on among the black soldiers and it wasn't good. "Let's make damn sure whatever is going on doesn't spread to our company."

Doak nodded his head in agreement. "You can bet your ass on that, sir!"

Luke waited until his executive officer had left before he allowed the worry to show on his face. Why they would let those two men return to Camp Red Devil after what they had tried to pull was almost unbelievable. Even a transfer within the brigade area would have been better than returning them to the base camp. He knew that he would have to be very careful now, especially when he was in the *safe* rear area.

The ceremony went perfectly and General Westmoreland did show up to present the new P Company colors to Luke in person. Luke had been surprised when the general mentioned to him about his being assigned to Vietnam for over five years. His reputation was spreading even to the senior staff. The brigade commander used the ceremony as a chance to present some valor awards to the recon men and, again, General Westmoreland made the presentations. Morale in the recon company was high when the chopper left, and the men were sent back to their hootches to change uniforms. The three recon teams that had been chosen for the LZ Nancy detail had all of their gear ready to go and only needed to switch into sterile uniforms before leaving on the trucks that were waiting to haul them out to the armor base camp. Luke had made it a firm company policy that when the men went out in the field they wore uniforms that didn't have patches or rank sewn on them.

Luke stood watching the men disappear into their hootches and snuck glances over to where the brigade personnel had stood to watch the ceremony. A large group of black soldiers had assembled near the Artillery Bowl, and it was very obvious that there wasn't a white face in the crowd. A gap had appeared between the blacks and the nearest white soldiers watching the ceremony without anyone realizing that it was happening. The whites were shying away from the blacks. Luke wondered why the brigade commander couldn't see it if he could, or for the matter, any of the staff.

"Worried?"

Luke looked over to identify the owner of the voice. "Hello, sir."

"That's going on all over Vietnam. It's worse in the States, but isn't as visible because everyone goes home at night and the white soldiers rent apartments off base." Major Redmond crossed his arms over his chest and stared at the black leader who was staring at him from behind a pair of mirrored sunglasses. "I came over here from Baumholder, Germany, and it's so damn bad over there that the local German civilians have formed vigilante groups to protect their children and property."

"Why?" Luke was puzzled. "This is the best that it has ever been for blacks and minority groups in the military. I mean there are people who are sincerely trying to drive racism out of the military and now this shit!"

"I've been *told* that some blacks want revenge for the way their ancestors were treated." Redmond flashed Luke a stern look. "Don't believe that bullshit! It's a con game. What you see over there are a bunch of street hoods trying to rip off as much as they can get, and they know that the senior officer corps is terrified of being labeled racists and will give in before they have a race riot on their hands."

"You were told about this revenge stuff?"

Major Redmond nodded his head slowly. "I was the military police commander at Baumholder and they actually tried recruiting me!"

Luke didn't realize how serious the situation was becoming until the major had made his last statement. "What are we going to do?"

Redmond shook his head. "Captain . . . I don't know."

"It looks like a very serious conversation that's going on here." The brigade commander joined Luke and Redmond.

"We were just discussing the polarization that seems to be going on between the races, sir." Luke watched the colonel's eyes and saw what he had hoped he wouldn't see.

"Nonsense!" The colonel's eyes darted, revealing his fear, and then the old soldier gained control of himself. "They enjoy each other's company is all. We haven't had any problems from our black soldiers here in the 1st Brigade, and I intend for it to stay that way!" He left Luke and Redmond to join a group of officers in front of the brigade headquarters.

"Well, that ends that friendly discussion on the topic!" Major Redmond touched the brim of his helmet. "If you will excuse me, I have some police matters to tend to." He reached over and touched Luke's shoulder. "Be careful . . . OK?"

"Always, Major . . . always."

Lieutenant Fields felt his stomach roll and a shiver ripple over his skin, sending a cold chill throughout his whole body. It wasn't fear that he was feeling but excitement. He had spent the whole afternoon in the 1st of the 77th Armor Battalion's tactical operations center bunker talking to the armor staff. The armor officers had their own way of doing things, and that usually meant charging aggressively with their tanks. Fields had a hell of a time convincing them that he wanted to infiltrate to his assigned recon sites on foot and not on the decks of tanks. He had won the argument late in the afternoon, and the three recon teams left the base camp on the back of three quarter-ton trucks. Fields had doubled up PFC Hito with Dotson because the Tennessee soldier had had a difficult time during the map-reading course and he wanted Hito to check him out. Pilgrim was assigned to Sergeant Forbes's team, and he had gone with a new buck sergeant and commanded that team.

Arrowood had made it clear to everyone that when an officer went in the field with a team, that officer was in command.

The recon teams acted like they were checking the barbed wire around the perimeter of the base camp, and when they reached their assigned dropoff points, they disappeared. Fields had selected sites around the base camp that were all on the reverse slopes of hills surrounding the camp. He had made those selections for two reasons: first, to protect the team from grazing fire from the perimeter guards and, second, because he figured that if he was an NVA commander, he would use the hills to block being seen by the guards. The armor staff had teased him on his selection of night-observation sites for the teams because none of the locations were more than five hundred meters away from the barbed wire. Arrowood had trained Fields well, and the young officer refused to give in to the ribbing. He had analyzed the terrain surrounding LZ Nancy and figured that the NVA were using the shallow valleys between the hills as main avenues to skirt around the base camp without being detected. LZ Nancy had received a serious rocket attack two days earlier and that was why the armor commander had asked for the recon teams to work his base camp area.

Night dropped her cloak over the rolling hills surrounding LZ Nancy that were crisscrossed with tank trails. All of the perimeter guards had been told that there were American recon teams nearby and to be extremely careful. Sergeant Forbes's team had been assigned a sector that overlooked the main highway and the secondary road the engineers had built to LZ Nancy. Fields was hoping that they would pick up some nighttime activity on the roads with the starlight scope they had brought with them.

Pilgrim had plotted their location before it had gotten dark and had called in a number of defensive concentrations that he could use as reference points to shift from if a target appeared or he could fire in the event the NVA discovered the recon team and attacked. Pilgrim had checked his data four times before calling it in to Charlie Battery's FDC at LZ Sandy. He had hoped that Bravo Battery was still there because he knew everyone in the FDC and they would have been more supportive. The Charlie Battery radio operator took his data, but the fire-direction officer called back worried over how close the DEFCONs were to the main base perimeter. There was a policy that a thousand-meter no-fire zone circled each of the base camps in the brigade area unless the base was under a ground attack. All of Pilgrim's DEFCONs were inside of the zone.

A hand flare lit up the night almost directly above Forbes's team. One of the perimeter guards must have gotten nervous. A second flare appeared in the sky a couple hundred meters away. Followed by a red one. The team pressed their chests down against the ground trying to blend in with the low shrubs that covered the hillside. Pilgrim kept one eye closed so that he could retain his night vision and used the light to scan the terrain out in front of their position. Nothing moved in the bushes. The wide tracks the tanks had made shone up like ribbons on the hillsides and valleys surrounding the base area. Pilgrim felt a little secure being so close to the main base camp, but at the same time it was a false sense of security because, if the NVA did attack, there was no way that they could get back inside before daylight and the perimeter guards would shoot at anything moving. The team would have been safer out in the jungle where they could have gotten a helicopter extraction if things got too bad.

Pilgrim had dozed off a little after one in the morning and was woken when something ran over his hand. A chill went down his back as he tried figuring out what it had been and he settled on a ground lizard over a spider. He raised himself a little off the ground and looked over to where Sergeant Forbes was lying and could see in the dim moonlight that the NCO was resting his chin against his folded hands. He couldn't tell if Forbes was sleeping or awake and lowered himself back down in the bushes. Pilgrim lay there for a second trying to figure out if his imagination had been playing tricks on him, but he had thought he had seen movement out of the corner of his eye when he had lowered himself back down on the ground. He waited and listened.

Twenty minutes slipped by and then a soft thudding sound reached his hiding place. Pilgrim felt his heart start to beat faster. His ears became his primary sensory organs. It was fascinating how the human body worked. When it was light outside it was the eyes that accumulated most of the data, when it got dark the ears took over, and when it really got dark and noisy out like during a storm, then the nose took over and one's sense of smell seemed to increase. Pilgrim thought about the comment his grandmother used to make to him when he was little and had been caught smoking cattails down by the creek. She had told him that God had given him a perfect body in which to live and if he abused it then his body would give up. He had taken her advice and had stayed away from drugs in high school. It was paying off for him now.

The sound of a person walking reached him, and then he heard another, similar sound. Pilgrim wondered if Forbes was awake. He decided on risking taking another look at the sergeant, but slipped the safety off the CAR-15 submachine gun that Captain Arrowood had given him. Sergeant Forbes's head had turned away from him to one side and he couldn't see his face, but from the way the sergeant's shoulders were set, he guessed that Forbes had fallen asleep. Pilgrim turned his head the other way, but couldn't see his teammates to his left side unless he lifted up a little higher so that he could see over a shrub that during the daytime hadn't looked like it would have been in the way. Pilgrim slipped his trigger finger around the trigger guard on his weapon and lifted up until his chest was a foot and a half off the ground.

Once he had cleared the top of the low bush with his eyes, he saw the moving silhouettes. The muscles in Pilgrim's throat closed. He felt a tremendous urge to urinate and fought against it. The lead silhouette stopped, and Pilgrim could see the person's arm lift up from its side and half the column of shadows that almost instantly dropped down and blended in perfectly with the shrubs. He didn't move. The top five inches of his head were sticking up above the shrub, but he was hoping that if he didn't move, the silhouette that was still standing wouldn't see him. Pilgrim wondered if what he was seeing were Americans. Maybe another patrol had been assigned to their sector by mistake. He tried sending brain waves over to where Sergeant Forbes was sleeping, trying to wake him up.

A small group of black silhouettes rose up from the opposite side of the very shallow valley the recon team was hiding in and started walking single file toward the shadow that was waiting for them on the tank trail at the very bottom of the depression. When the three shadows were within a few feet of the single human silhouette, the lead shadow spoke, erasing all doubts in Pilgrim's mind as to whether they were Americans or not.

Pilgrim had to make a number of decisions. He didn't know if he was the only one on the team who was awake or not, and he didn't know if Forbes would want artillery fired or not. He also didn't know how many more of the silhouettes were behind the first one, and that thought made up his mind for him. He lowered himself slowly back down to the ground and picked up the handset to his PRC-25 radio.

"Red Can 14 . . . this is Running Bear 3 . . . fire mission . . . over." Pilgrim pressed his lips against the holes in the black mouthpiece and whispered so low that he wasn't sure himself if he had spoken.

"UNKNOWN STATION . . . repeat your call . . . OVER." The voice coming back over the air sounded like it was being played at a rock concert over loud-speakers into Pilgrim's ear.

Captain Arrowood had been lying on his cot with his arms folded behind his head. He had a portable PRC-25 sitting on an ammunition box next to him so that he could monitor the recon team's frequency during the night. He had heard Pilgrim's fire mission come in over the speaker sitting only inches away from his ear.

"Running Bear 3 . . . fire mission! . . . over."

There was a short pause. "Running Bear 3 . . . send your mission . . . over."

"This is Bear 3 . . . from DEFCON Five . . . Azimuth 130 . . . left 100 . . . drop 50 . . . NVA in the open . . . battery one round . . . fire for effect . . . over."

Luke sat up on his bunk smiling. Pilgrim had done well. He started slipping on his boots and shirt when a loud voice came over the radio.

"Running Bear 3 . . . this is . . . Red Dragon 3 . . . you are requesting a fire mission in a safety zone, request denied . . . out."

Luke stopped tying the lace on his boot in shock. He couldn't believe that Captain Kreps had *canceled* a fire mission from a recon team in the field that had identified the target as being NVA in the open!

Pilgrim felt the fear enter his body. He hadn't expected the battalion FDC to cancel his fire mission. He didn't know what to do next and lifted up again to see if the NVA were still there. The silhouette was still there, but this time his arm was pointing down the tank trail toward the highway, and the first shadow started walking back down the tank trail the way the silhouettes had come.

Pilgrim felt the warmth in his crotch and the fear left him when he realized that he had just urinated in his pants. Anger replaced the fear. He jumped up and leveled his CAR-15 at the group of silhouettes and shadows. Five NVA fell from his first long burst. Pilgrim dropped down on one knee to reload, and the night air was void of any noise and then all hell broke loose. The rest of the recon team opened fire at the same time the NVA did, sending red and green tracers bouncing up in the sky. Some of the perimeter guards got nervous seeing the firefight only a few hundred meters in front of the bunkers and opened fire.

Pilgrim heard someone calling him on the radio and picked up the handset. It was the armor battalion's heavy mortar platoon asking if he needed any 4.2 support. Pilgrim gave the lieutenant the grid coordinance for his DEFCON 5, just in case they had screwed it up like the artillery had, but the armor lieutenant had all of the data plotted and had laid each one of his mortars on one defensive concentration for the recon teams from which they could adjust fire and had kept one of his mortars ready to fire illumination for the base camp. Pilgrim had been lucky because the lieutenant had used his DEFCON 5 to lay on and was ready to fire as soon as the charge had been cut.

The large mortar round whistled over his head and landed less that twenty-five meters down the tank trail from where he had thought it would land. He moved it fifty meters in the direction the other NVA had escaped in and walked it back toward the main road in fifty-meter increments.

The recon team next to Pilgrim's opened fire and by that time the whole perimeter around LZ Nancy was popping hand flares and opening fire on anything that moved.

Luke sat on his bed and listened to the armor heavy-weapons leader supporting his teams, and started getting very angry. He slipped the radio over one of his shoulders by its straps and left his hootch at a fast walk. The artillery battalion FDC was a couple hundred meters away from his company area. Luke didn't notice the two shadows get up and follow him as soon as he had stepped out of his hootch until he was out on the main road.

"Is there a problem, sir?" It was one of his recon

men who had been assigned to pull guard on his hootch at night. Luke had forgotten all about them.

"Our teams are in contact at LZ Nancy."

"Serious, sir?"

"I don't know yet . . . they're still fighting." Luke kept walking fast and the men followed him. Lieutenant Doak had told all of them that they should not let Captain Arrowood out of their sight even if he went to one of the shitters in the middle of the night.

Luke didn't pause at the bunker's entrance and went storming inside. Captain Kreps was sitting by the radios monitoring what little traffic there was between the recon teams and the armor battalion. The fighting had seemed to have died down and Kreps took the handset and called Pilgrim while Luke stood there in total disbelief over what he was hearing.

"Running Bear 3 . . . this is Red Dragon 3 . . . over."

Luke could tell Pilgrim's voice when it came on the air. The young soldier was still angry over something. "This is Running Bear 3 . . . over!"

"Bear 3 this is Dragon 3 . . . what is your situation? over."

"Bear 3 . . . we jumped a large number of NVA and they ran off but I think we hit quite a few of them . . . we're waiting for first light to check out the area . . . over."

"This is Dragon 3 . . . I want you to report to me the first thing in the morning. I'll have a chopper waiting to bring you back here. Do you read me? . . . over."

"Bear 3 . . . read you loud and clear . . . over."

"Dragon 3 . . . out."

Luke stood behind Captain Kreps trying to control his anger but lost. "What in the fuck do you think you're doing, Kreps!"

The artillery battalion operations officer whirled around on his chair with an expression on his face like a fourteen-year-old boy would have after having gotten caught masturbating by his mother. "What in the hell are you doing in here, Arrowood?"

"This is an *operations* bunker, isn't it?"

"Yes!" Kreps face glowed red.

"My question is what in the hell are you doing *ordering my man* to leave the field who's on a combat mission!"

"Lieutenant Colonel Jeffers wants to talk to him about the fire mission he requested. He wants to know who authorized placing them in a *no-fire zone* outside of the perimeter surrounding LZ Nancy where we can't support them."

"You and Jeffers have got to be the dumbest sons of bitches in the whole United States Army!" Luke began to lose focus in his eyes and read the warning sign and backed off before he went wild and killed the stupid ass right there in front of fifteen men. "It is extremely obvious now that the NVA and Vietcong have been using the no-fire zones around the large base areas as their own personal private roads! This is a fucking *war*, asshole, and those recon men are assigned to my company and not to your fucking incompetent, bumbling artillery battalion that has damn near been the cause for three recon teams being whipped out, because you stupid assholes have created the *worst* crime an artillery unit can commit! You have *refused* artillery *support* to the soldiers you have pledged to support!"

The artillerymen working in the FDC lowered their heads in shame. They knew that Captain Arrowood was making sense.

"Would you like to talk to me in that manner, *Captain* Arrowood?" Jeffers's voice came from the dark entrance to the bunker.

Luke spun around, making the antenna on his radio slap against a twelve-by-twelve support post. "We can talk about it in the morning with the brigade commander . . . sir . . . after *I've* released and debriefed my teams. My soldiers will not . . . I repeat . . . *will not* . . . report to this unit in the morning!"

"They're artillerymen . . . correct?" Jeffers sneered.

"*Correct*, sir . . . damn fine artillerymen." Luke looked over at the FDC men watching them and none of them would make eye contact with him. He returned his eyes to Jeffers. "Artillerymen who are *assigned* to Papa Company, 75th Rangers, sir!"

"Oh! How cute! The Department of Defense has given you boys a title!" Jeffers sounded like a fag.

"You know, sir . . . now I know why you kiss ass with the senior officers and whine around your peers, because they would kick your ass if you talked to them that way."

Luke felt a hand grab his shoulder and spin him around. Kreps caught him square on the jaw and Luke saw blinking lights. "I've had enough of your shit, Arrowood. You're not going to talk to my commander like that!" Kreps had been the boxing champion at West Point for his last two years there and was very confident of his ability to use his fists.

Luke blinked his eyes and reacted. He swung the PRC-25 radio hard and caught Kreps in his crotch with the flat side of the radio. The wind left Kreps's lungs and his eyes looked like they were going to bust out of their sockets. A low groan used up the remaining air in his lungs and he couldn't draw in fresh air. He sank to his knees holding his best friends. "Don't fuck with a *combat* soldier, Kreps . . . we fight to win."

"That is a court-marshal offense!" Jeffers screamed at Luke and then took a step backwards when he saw the look in the captain's eyes. "At least ten men saw you strike him with that radio!"

Luke looked at the artillerymen and shook his head in disgust. He reached up and pulled the crossed cannons he wore on his collar off and threw the artillery symbol on one of the charts under an adjustable light. "They can report what they saw any way they want to."

Luke signaled with his hand for his men to follow him out of the bunker.

"Don't you ever set foot in this battalion area again!
DO YOU HEAR ME, YOU BASTARD!"

Luke inhaled the air outside of the bunker and
ignored the smell of burning shit. It always seemed
stronger in the artillery area. He wondered if artillerymen shit more than other soldiers.

Pilgrim swung his CAR-15 slowly from side to side
as his eyes slipped over every single bush and shrub
out in front of him. The sound of tank engines starting
up inside of the base camp flooded the sound waves
surrounding the camp. The armor battalion commander was sending his reserve tank company out to
sweep the whole perimeter area. The M48s had neon
searchlights mounted over their main guns that turned
night into day.

Sergeant Forbes had taken over operating the radio
and signaled for Pilgrim to drop down next to him.
He whispered. "The armor commander wants to
sweep the area before the NVA can haul away their
dead."

Pilgrim nodded and whispered back. "What about
us?"

Forbes nodded his head. Pilgrim had made a good
point. How were they going to warn the tanks not to
fire on them?

"Tell the armor guys that we'll turn on our strobe
lights when they get close and they can skirt around
us. Warn our other teams, too."

"What in the fuck did I do before you came, Pilgrim?" Forbes smiled.

"Stayed awake on patrol, probably." Pilgrim winked
back at the recon sergeant.

"If you tell *anyone*! I swear, I'll de-nut you!"

"The secret is ours, Sergeant." Pilgrim gave the
NCO a grin in the dark that only showed his white
teeth reflecting the moonlight.

CHAPTER THIRTEEN
✪✪✪✪✪✪✪✪✪✪✪✪✪✪✪✪✪✪✪✪✪✪✪

TASK FORCE REMAGEN

First morning light reveal what had happened the night before at LZ Nancy. The whole brigade staff was waiting for a complete after-action report.

Sergeant Forbes had his men spread out to sweep down the slope to the bottom of the depression. The tank company had stayed far enough away from the recon sites to prevent accidentally running into them in the dark. The tank platoon that had come nearest to Forbes's recon team had stayed on the opposite side of the depression and had engaged a small force of the Vietcong trying to escape back to the other side of the highway.

Pilgrim was the first one down to where he had seen the shadows and silhouettes. Sergeant Forbes saw Pilgrim drop his CAR-15 to his side and look over at him.

"You'd better come over here, Sarge." Pilgrim's voice didn't sound very enthusiastic. Forbes ran through the bushes over to where Pilgrim was standing looking down at the ground.

"Oh, shit!" Forbes pulled his camouflaged cap off his head and slapped the side of his leg with it. "Motherfucking shit! We should have been told they would be out here!"

"What are we going to do, Sarge?" Pilgrim sounded scared.

Forbes looked down at the three South Vietnamese soldiers. All of them were wearing berets, which meant that they were assigned to the South Vietnamese Ranger Battalion. The other men that were lying dead along the tank trail wore a mixture of South Vietnamese gear and peasant clothes and were probably South Vietnamese Popular Forces out on a patrol that was being led by the Rangers. Forbes rolled the three bodies over and saw that one of the South Vietnamese wore three gold lotus flowers on the front of his jacket between the buttons. It was the insignia of a captain in the South Vietnamese Army.

"We fucked up, big time." Forbes stood there shaking his head.

"Not *we*, Sergeant . . . I fucked up. It was me who opened fire and it was me who called in the mortars . . . it's my fault." Pilgrim felt very bad, not for himself, but for Project Deathwatch. This incident would totally destroy the project.

"I command this team, soldier!" Forbes's voice growled out of his throat. "*I* assume full responsibility for everything that happens! What in the fuck do you think I am? One of those rear-area *infantry* NCOs running a PX!" Forbes snatched the radio handset. "I've got to call the armor commander and have him come out here. We'd better report this early so that the general can cover his ass with the ARVN up in I Corps."

The recon team was sitting in a small group near the dead men when the armor commander's tank came over a low rise and worked its way slowly over to where the team waited. Three more tanks appeared on the high ground surrounding the site and idled their engines as they guarded the site.

The armor commander hopped off his tank wearing a smile on his face. Forbes could see that the second man off the tank was a South Vietnamese lieutenant colonel because he was wearing two silver lotus leaves in the same location on his uniform where the dead captain wore his.

"What's so important, Sergeant?" The armor commander was still wearing his smile until he saw where

Forbes was pointing with the barrel of his weapon. "Shit! They're South Vietnamese soldiers!"

The ARVN lieutenant colonel ran over to the dead captain and grabbed him by the hair so that he could get a better look at his face. "Nguyen Qut! Nguyen Qut!" The ARVN officer's voice rose even higher and he became more excited when he changed languages and spoke in English. "This is Nguyen Qut!"

"Who's he?" Pilgrim whispered to Forbes, knowing in his heart that this Nguyen Qut had to be the son of some South Vietnamese general.

The armor commander hurried over to the ARVN officer's side. "Are you sure!"

"Yes! He was assigned to my unit when he was a lieutenant! I am very sure! This *is* Nguyen Qut!"

The armor commander broke out in a wide smile. "Who killed him?"

Forbes spoke up for the team. "We don't know . . ." He was trying to protect Pilgrim.

"Then I'm going to recommend your whole team for Bronze Stars for Valor!"

"What's going on, sir?" Forbes was losing his patience. Only a few minutes ago he thought his whole team was going to jail for killing allies and now everyone was smiling and happy.

"Captain Nguyen Qut, was a South Vietnamese Ranger who turned Vietcong terrorist about three years ago. This single South Vietnamese traitor has caused untold harm to the South Vietnamese Army because he knew many of the secret plans for long term projects that couldn't easily be changed and because he always wore the uniform of a South Vietnamese Ranger when he performed his atrocities. He was the most wanted man in South Vietnam and you not only killed him but his two assistants! They were NCOs who decided to join him."

Pilgrim had to sit down on the ground.

Forbes dropped down next to the soldier from Tennessee and draped his arm over his shoulder. "War is some weird shit."

*   *   *

Captain Arrowood was still angry from what had occurred the night before over at the artillery battalion. He sat in a rattan chair outside of the brigade commander's office waiting for the rest of the officers to arrive for the meeting that he had requested.

Major Montgomery took a seat across from Luke. "I want you to know that I am going to tell the old man what I know about all of this and it will be to your benefit."

Luke looked over at the artillery battalion's executive officer. "Why the change of heart all of a sudden?"

"It's simple; you're right."

"Just like that?"

"Just like that. You were right doing what you did out at Bravo Battery and I felt very bad supporting Jeffers, but he was the commander . . . still is." Montgomery rolled his eyes. "He's probably going to end my career because of this, but I have to do what is right."

Luke smiled without showing his teeth and slowly shook his head from side to side. Major Montgomery was making a political change and was trying to get on his good side in front of the brigade commander, and he knew that the colonel would not allow for Jeffers to screw the major once that had happened. Montgomery was maneuvering, and that didn't mean he wouldn't maneuver against Luke if the time came that he didn't need him anymore. "I don't think that I need your help, sir."

Anger flashed in the major's eyes. "It's always good to have an expert give his opinion in your favor. I know a lot about Jeffers that would cement your case against him."

"I don't want to cement a case against Jeffers or anybody else! I want to fight this damned war knowing that people who wear the same damn uniform that I do are *all* on my side!" Luke stood and flexed his jaws as he looked down at the major. "Is that asking too much?"

"Relax, Captain!" Montgomery stood up so he wouldn't have Luke hovering over him. "Like I said, Jeffers is a bad officer and should be relieved."

"Relieved? And who's going to take his place?" Luke was guessing, "you?" He turned his head to one side and looked at Montgomery like he was looking at a little boy who was being lectured. "Major Montgomery! You wouldn't be on the lieutenant colonel's promotion list by some chance, now would you?"

Montgomery's face turned pink and then red. "Yes, yes, I am as a matter of fact, I'm due to receive my orders for promotion . . . soon."

"Like next week?"

Mongtomery shrugged.

"Like today." The brigade commander stood in his office doorway holding a set of orders for Montgomery's promotion to lieutenant colonel. He had heard the whole conversation. "I must agree with Captain Arrowood, Major. It is disgusting that some officers cannot change from peacetime tactics during a war. You can rest assured that you will never command a battalion in my command or for that matter, any other command in Vietnam."

Major Montgomery could not hold back the hate he felt for Arrowood. "We all have our days, Captain!"

"I think you should get back to Jeffers before he notices that you're gone." Luke stared down the major and watched him hurry off down the hall.

"Well, Captain, it's not often a young captain beats out two very well trained military politicians so thoroughly. Come on inside and let's talk about this LZ Nancy affair. Your Project Deathwatch has really started out well!"

Luke took the seat that was offered to him in the colonel's office and waited until the gray-haired soldier had thought through what he wanted to say to him. The colonel tapped his right index finger against his lips for a long time before speaking. "Captain

Arrowood . . ." There was a long pause before the senior officer continued, ". . . we have a very serious problem here at Camp Red Devil. It's like a cancer that is slowly, but surely, eating away at our army and unless something is done *very* soon, we're going to be in serious trouble and personally, we'll lose this war and be forced to withdraw from Vietnam."

Luke didn't say anything even though the colonel paused in his speech. He realized that the old soldier was using him for a sounding board and was really preparing this speech for someone else who had a hell of a lot more rank than captain.

The colonel looked out of his windows and continued talking. "When I was in the Pentagon . . . that was right before I received orders to come to Vietnam . . . I thought that we had the most powerful army on earth and I really believed that with all of my heart! We evaluated our soldiers on how many graduated from high school and on what category they fell into on the IQ tests and we totally *failed* to realize that we were recruiting young punks off the streets and at the same time we took away the NCOs' power to control them. I thought that all of the modern equipment we were pumping into the military would win the war for us and I forgot the lessons that the German Army had learned the hard way during World War II: *men* win wars, not equipment."

The colonel sighed and stared out of the window at something that caught his attention. Luke waited patiently until the officer was ready to continue.

"Christ, Luke! What a damn mess we're in! The black soldiers have just presented me with an ultimatum. They want me to reduce the blacks in the troop units to fifteen percent! Now how in the hell can I do that! They're the ones who took the tests back in the States and qualified for their job specialties. They want to OJT here in Vietnam for staff positions as clerks and they can't even type or read a damn map!"

"What are you going to do?" Luke could see the dilemma the colonel was in.

"The only thing that I can do! Everyone stays in their assigned MOSs! We can't play switchy-poo, just because a bunch of militants threaten us!"

Luke nodded his head. It was a good start. "What about all of the senior NCOs who have medical profiles?"

"What about them?" The brigade commander realized that he was confiding in the captain and that opened the door for honest talk.

"Well, I don't know if you've noticed, but there aren't too many of them in the *field*. They seem to have ended up in the headquarters elements in all of the units and I don't think there are a half dozen in the field with the infantry."

"I can't override a medical profile, you know that! Damn, I'll have the inspector general from MACV-Headquarters in here within an hour if I tried pulling that!"

"Sir . . . we have black soldiers who don't want to fight the NVA, but will gladly fight white soldiers in the rear and frag officers. We have senior NCOs who will fight to the death for a promotion, but pull out their medical profiles the instant you tell them they have to perform those duties they are trained for in combat. We have an officer corps that is very interested in pulling six months in the field, but only if they receive their *fair* amount of valor awards and then they'll serve their remaining six months on a staff somewhere. We have junior enlisted men who are getting deeply involved in drugs and we have an enemy that is *dedicated* and very well trained who wants to kick our asses!" Luke ended his speech. "Sir . . . *someone* had better open their damn eyes and earn those fucking stars they're wearing on their collars!"

The brigade commander leaned back in his chair and stared at Luke. The young captain hadn't missed a single point and he knew that everything Luke had said was true except there wasn't a damn thing he could do about it with out receiving his retirement papers from the Army. "What I plan on doing about it, Captain Arrowood, is to put the whole damn brigade in the field and work their asses off! And that includes my rear-echelon types. They might hide behind medical profiles, but with the infantry units gone, they'll have to pull their own guard!" The colonel smiled over his plan. "Half of the brigade is going out west to the Khe Sanh plateau and the other half is going up on the DMZ. Task Force Remagen is going west and will be composed of: two mechanized infantry companies from the 1st Battalion, 61st Infantry; a tank company from the 1st Battalion, 77th Armor; a 105mm artillery battery, a reinforced armored engineer platoon; a platoon of 40mm *dusters*; and a battalion headquarters element that will have five of your recon teams attached to it. The task force up at the DMZ will be called Montana Mauler and will have the rest of the brigade's combat elements in it."

"That's very interesting, sir, but you mentioned that the artillery battery was 105mm. Don't you mean 155mm?"

"NO! We are borrowing a 105mm self-propelled battery from the Corps reserve because *none* of the 155mm batteries in our 5th Battalion, 4th Artillery have enough howitzers operationally ready to move out of their base areas!"

"What about Bravo Battery, sir? I personally can vouch for their maintenance and combat readiness. When I left there, all six of the howitzers were operationally ready and we tested them daily."

"How long ago was that?"

Luke shook his head. The captain who had replaced him had given in to the battalion maintenance personnel and must have allowed for his howitzers to drop their combat readiness status.

The brigade commander rapped his knuckles on his desk. "I've replaced Jeffers with a new lieutenant colonel who has just arrived from the States. I wanted to relieve the son of a bitch, but he's too powerful back in the Pentagon and I couldn't get general headquarters approval. He's been given an administrative transfer along with Major Montgomery and Captain Kreps."

"This Task Force Remagen sounds interesting, but so does Montana Mauler."

"We should see action at both locations, but I'm not going to use recon teams up north. The Marine Force Recon Battalion is very jealous of other teams entering their area and the whole DMZ is theirs."

"Fine with me, sir. They can have it!" Luke wasn't too happy over going to work the hot Ben Hai River area.

"The Khe Sanh plateau isn't exactly child's play. We're going to have to use old Route 9 to take our tracked vehicles in there and that's why we need the recon teams. The road is extremely dangerous, with cliffs on both sides. Your teams are going to have to secure the flanks of the column." The brigade commander watched Luke's reaction to what he was saying closely. "Intelligence reports have indicated that the North Vietnamese are moving across the Laotian border in the direction of the A Shau Valley. Air reconnaissance has revealed the NVA have built an extension to Route 926 that runs from old Route 92 on the Ho Chi Minh Trail across the lower end of the Khe Sanh plateau in the direction of the A Shau Valley. Long-range patrols have reported hearing trucks and tracked vehicles moving along the new road.

"The 3rd Marine Division has deployed one reinforced regiment to prevent the NVA from using Route 926 or the extension they've built and Task Force Remagen is going to cut both of the routes in half and destroy critical bridges in the area."

"It sounds very interesting, sir. *I* think that I might go with my teams this time." Luke liked the plan. It was also very dangerous.

"I was hoping that you would say that, Luke." The colonel rose from his chair. "I've got a number of briefings concerning both operations that I have to attend to right now." He held out his hand for Luke to shake. "Thank God that we still have a few officers like you left in the military!"

"You should tell my wife that, sir." The statement slipped out before Luke could stop it.

The colonel stopped walking. "Are you having some marital problems, Luke?"

"She's divorcing me because I've spent too much time in Vietnam."

"I'm terribly sorry to hear that, Luke. Is there anything that I can do? Write her a letter? Call? Anything?"

"No, sir. It's already over with." Luke saluted and left the room.

The brigade commander watched Luke leave his office and shook his head. He was secretly glad that his military career was ending. He figured they might give him a mercy star after commanding the brigade, but not much more.

Luke had a very difficult time selecting the five teams to go with him to Khe Sanh. All of the team leaders wanted to go. There wasn't a soldier in Vietnam who hadn't heard about the big battle that had taken place on the plateau that occupied the most northwestern corner of South Vietnam. The Marines at the Khe Sanh Combat Base had been surrounded by a multiple division-size force and were trapped. The 1st Cavalry Division and large elements of Marines had attacked along Highway 9 and opened up the trap so that the Marines at Khe Sanh could escape. It was a near-disaster, with General Westmoreland pledging that Khe Sanh would not fall to the North Vietnamese, while the NVA commander swore that the Marine base would be the Americans Dien Bien Phu.

The Special Forces camp at Lang Vei had been overrun in mid-February of that year by an NVA force using PT-76 light-amphibious tanks—the first time that the enemy had used tanks against a fortified position inside of South Vietnam. The tankers from the 1st

Battalion, 77th Armor were excited about a possible tank battle on the plateau and had spent days preparing their tanks for battle. The rounds they had normally fired through their weapons were canister because of the lack of hard targets and the grape shot-type pellets had caused havoc to their gun tubes and had knocked almost all of their weapons out of bore sight.

Luke decided on his five teams and assigned an officer to each team except Forbes's. There were only four officers assigned to Papa Company, including Lieutenant Fields. Luke decided on going with Sergeant Mulhouse and RT Marshall. There would be two Project Deathwatch men with most of the teams, but Luke figured that would make them even stronger in the field, where targets for the FOs would be larger and more varied than around Camp Red Devil. The teams that were remaining behind would be pulling night ambushes to protect the perimeter of the base camp. The whole company would be active in the field until the major operations were over.

The five recon teams traveled with the task force headquarters element and acted as guards for the vehicles as they convoyed west along Highway 9 that went from the coast of South Vietnam west into Laos and ran parallel below the DMZ that separated the two Vietnams. Navy Seabees were resurfacing the two-lane highway with asphalt to reduce the mining incidents along that very important stretch of roadway. Luke had counted five vehicles that had been destroyed by mines, cluttering up the sides of the highway. The Marines had closed the Khe Sanh Combat Base on the plateau after the big battle, and the most westerly Marine base was now Vandergrift near the old Vietnamese town of Ca Lu, which was the assembly site for Task Force Remagen.

Luke rode in an open jeep behind a platoon of M48A5 tanks. Only a very foolish NVA commander would attack a column of tanks and infantry M113s the size of the task force in the open rolling hills that bordered Highway 9 for the first fifty miles of their trip. Once they reached the mountains and the highland jungle, the situation changed and the whole convoy was very vulnerable to harassing attacks from the NVA, where they would knock out a single vehicle in a convoy and disappear into the jungle just to pull the same tactic a couple of miles down the road. The tactic was extremely nerve-wracking to the armor crews. Task Force Remagen was lucky and made the trip all of the way to Ca Lu without incident. The armored vehicles skirted around the large Marine base at Vandergrift and assembled at their jump-off site in a huge circle, like the pioneers did when they circled their wagons for the night. The Marines at the base were happy to see the large task force because the NVA had been rocketing the base every single day for over a month and there had been a lot of casualties.

Luke spent the rest of the afternoon checking his teams to make sure they were properly equipped for their insertions along the unprotected strip of Highway 9 from Ca Lu to the old French Fort, which had been the last stronghold of the NVA during the attack against Khe Sanh. Once the task force reached that location, they could pretty much maneuver on their own in the rolling hills of the plateau.

Lieutenant Wong and the rest of the recon officers studied the large-scale map of the terrain between Ca Lu and the plateau. The recon teams used 1:50,000-scale maps and the headquarters map was on a scale of 1:25,000 and showed much more detail. From Ca Lu the road wound upward through a long valley for about thirty-five miles until it reached the high plateau of Khe Sanh. There were several very narrow and dangerous defiles and one unfordable mountain stream along the road that required an armored vehicle-launched bridge to span it. The task force was not going to waste any forces to secure the bridge, so when the last vehicle crossed over it, the engineers would retrieve the span and follow the task force. In effect, the whole armored task force would be trapped on the plateau and were relying on a *single* piece of equipment for their escape if needed.

"I don't like that site." Lieutenant Wong tapped the water obstacle with his retractable grease pen.

"You're lucky, my man. It's yours." Doak looked around at the terrain from where he was sitting at the beautiful green hills surrounding their campsite. "I hear they used to tiger hunt around here when the French still operated their plantations on the plateau."

"Oh great! I needed to hear that shit right about now!" Fields folded the top of his C-ration can back to make a handle for the can before he sat it over a burning piece of a heat tablet. He glanced over at Doak. "Are you bullshitting us?"

" 'Fraid not. Some of the biggest tigers in Southeast Asia were taken on that plateau."

Lieutenant Wong looked away from the map over at the ruins of the old city of Ca Lu. "Have you guys ever noticed that every country the French colonized has either gone communist or turned into a country with a brutal dictator?"

Lieutenant Fields wiggled his eyebrows and looked over at Wong as if the man had gone nuts. "What in the hell has that got to do with what we're doing out here?"

"It's interesting. The French must have been really shitty administrators. With the English, it's almost one hundred percent the other way; the countries they colonized have gone either democratic or socialist."

"Real interesting conversation." Luke squatted down next to the map inside of the M577 command tracked vehicle where the lieutenants had gathered. Wong and Fields were sitting on the lowered rear ramp eating and Doak was studying the map. "We leave at first light in the morning, so have your teams ready and waiting at the helipad by four-thirty. I think I've covered everything else in the briefing earlier. If they need me, I'll be catching some Zs in my hootch."

*   *   *

There was very little conversation out at the helipad. The teams sat in tight little groups waiting for the sky to lighten enough for them to insert. A cold chill covered the ground along with the thick ground fog. Luke inhaled the fresh air. He smiled to himself and wondered how long it had been since he had smelled air that wasn't tainted with the smell of burning shit. He felt his folded up map against his leg inside of his pocket and wondered if he should have added anything else to the data he had marked on it. He had all of his team leaders mark their maps with the locations of all of the old landing zones the 1st Cavalry had used during their rescue mission the year before because they could still be used for emergency extraction sites if the teams needed them. All of the helicopter pilots flying the northern sector knew where each of the LZs were by memory and the names—LZ Mike, Cates, Thor, Tom, Wharton, and Snapper—were famous.

The crews for the five choppers arrived and the teams loaded up. Luke made sure that he went over to each of the teams and said something encouraging to each man. He knew that the men were extremely uptight over inserting in the traditionally NVA-held territory, where you could run into an NVA company much easier than running into a squad. Luke slid onto the steel deck of the chopper and signaled with his thumb to the crew chief that they were ready to go. The choppers took off in a single flight and flew over the Marine 105mm battery that would be supporting them. Luke had gone over the night before and briefed the battery commander personally on what his Project Deathwatch was all about so that the officer wouldn't hesitate to respond to artillery fire missions from enlisted men, even though there were officers with most of the teams.

The choppers dropped their noses when they reached the edge of the mountain slope and caught a strong wind coming from the west. A pair of Cobra gunships had been waiting for them and broke their figure-eight patterns and wove back and forth over the treetops in parallel flight with the slicks. The first chopper in line dropped down, followed by the second one a couple of miles later. Each one of the chopper pilots followed suit when they had reached the insertion sites for the teams. Luke's team was the last one down and the most westerly of the five teams.

The elephant grass and shrubs were still waving from the prop blast when Luke heard the minigun from one of the Cobras fire, followed by a volley of rockets. A hot shiver burst down his spine as he crouched waiting to hear NVA weapons open fire. The highland jungle became quiet when the sound of the choppers departed. Luke used hand signals to get his team moving away from the insertion site as fast as they could move. If the NVA were nearby, the last place he wanted to be was where the chopper had touched down. A single chopper landing gave away the size of his team, and the NVA weren't dumb, even though the choppers made a number of false insertions by acting like they were dropping down at sites and taking off again before they returned to Vandergrift.

It took Luke's team an hour to get over to their first observation site on the escarpment that overlooked Highway 9 below them. Sergeant Mulhouse released a soft whistle when he looked over the edge of the fifty-foot cliff down at the highway and then out over the sloping terrain down to the river and then out over the rolling hills until his eyes rested on a red laterite slash on the earth's surface that had to be LZ Thor.

Luke touched Mulhouse's shoulder and then pointed down at the destroyed bridge site that crossed over a gorge and the white-water river running below it. The site was even more of a bottleneck than the map had reflected. Two NVA with RPG-7 launchers could hold that terrain against an armor column forever. Luke realized his team had their work cut out for them. They had less than twenty-four hours to reconnoiter the area before the lead vehicles in the task force reached the bridge site.

A flight of noisy parrots nearly caused Luke to wet his pants. The jungle had been quiet until they had arrived, but that was good. The parrots signaled that there weren't any NVA nearby or they wouldn't have landed in the trees so close to the camouflaged recon team.

Sergeant Mulhouse raised his hand and stopped the team. He had spotted something in the rocky crevices that overlooked the crossing site. Luke slipped up next to the buck sergeant and followed with his eyes to where he was pointing. A tiny flicker of something shiny flashed against his eyes. Luke started moving forward. Mulhouse covered his advance while the rest of the team took up defensive positions with their backs to the cliff in a semicircle. Luke stopped and picked up the empty cigarette package that had been crammed in the crack. It was folded up neatly. Luke opened it and looked at the brand before showing Mulhouse the Marlboro pack. A corner of the silver foil had caught the sunlight and had drawn Mulhouse's attention, or they would have passed it by. Luke looked around the area from where he was standing in the rock crevice and realized that he had a commanding view of the highway and all of the terrain surrounding him. It was as if he were hovering in the sky in a transparent box. The rocky crevice was like a pulpit on the cliff's face, and they would have passed it by if it hadn't been for the light flashing off the foil.

Mulhouse leaned over and whispered in Luke's ear. "Marine outpost?"

Luke didn't answer and dropped down on one knee to search the area down at ground-level. He found a couple dozen cigarette butts in a slight depression that the person who had been there had used for an ashtray. The area could have been used by a Marine, except the cigarette package wasn't weathered and had to of been shoved in the crevice within a couple of days. It could have been a Marine Force Recon

Team working the area, but they were smarter than that. Luke picked up a burned match off the ground and held it up. It was wooden and had had a sulfur head.

Mulhouse used the barrel of his weapon to point at a small name that had been carved on the stone surface; Cao Van Vien 6.4.69 Haiphong. Luke smiled at the graffiti; even the North Vietnamese had their Kilroys, and then the smile slipped off his face. He glanced over at Mulhouse and saw the same thing in the sergeant's eyes. If the NVA used the same day, month, year system Americans did, the graffiti had been put there the same day!

Luke quickly put the team on alert and then drew as close to the scratched graffiti as he could so that he could see the scratch marks. Tiny particles of stone were still in the grooves. The author of the graffiti was nearby!

Sergeant Mulhouse read his captain's facial expression and found himself a hiding place in the rocks. Luke followed suit and the team waited.

The sound of someone walking on a trail reached the hidden recon team. Pebbles clicked together as they rolled downhill. Luke pressed his back against the rocks and waited. A tan pith helmet with a red-and-gold star appeared from behind the rocks followed by the upper torso of an NVA soldier who was carrying his AK-47 slung over his shoulder and a tin bucket of rice. He was mumbling something under his breath that Luke didn't understand, but from the soldier's facial expression, Luke figured out the man didn't like having to eat his breakfast at the observation post. Luke reached back and removed his Randall survival knife from its sheath. He would have to take the soldier out quietly or the rest of the man's unit would be alerted by the gunfire. Sweat broke out on Luke's forehead and his palms became sweaty. He started worrying about being able to hold onto the knife when he stabbed the soldier. The NVA paused a couple of feet out of range and looked back the way he had come and spat down on the ground before mumbling something that had to of been cussing in Vietnamese.

Luke left his hiding place and grabbed the surprised soldier in a classical hold from the rear and shoved the sharp blade through the NVA's heart. There was a strong tug against Luke's arm as the soldier's muscles tightened for their last time, and then the man relaxed in Luke's arms and slipped down on the ground. Luke removed his knife and cleaned the blade on the NVA's shirt before putting it back in its sheath and picking up his rifle.

Mulhouse stared at Luke, not believing how cool the captain acted after knifing the NVA. Luke signaled for the team to search the trail in the direction the soldier had appeared from and then took up the rear-guard position. Luke struggled to keep from throwing up. It was the first time that he had killed a man in hand-to-hand combat with a knife. He had been in some very close calls in his years in Vietnam, but he had always gotten out of them by using small arms.

The team smelled the fire before they saw the thin column of smoke curling up from a thick stand of jungle that filled a small horseshoe canyon. Luke could see immediately that the site was protected by the canyon walls from artillery because the opening was facing north and the artillery rounds would have an extremely small area in which to hit the NVA down below. A short or a long round would just land on the top of the rocks or go over the cliff and land down on the highway. The site was a perfect one for a small base area.

Luke marked the location and had his team back off until they were far enough away so that he could use the radio. He called in a high-angle fire mission and the Marine FDC informed him that he would be receiving support from an 8-inch battery out of Vandergrift. Luke was glad that they hadn't assigned him one of the 105mm batteries because the 8-inch howitzers were the most accurate artillery pieces in the world and he was going to need some great gunnery in order to hit the canyon. All he needed was one round to land inside of the horseshoe, and the NVA strong point would be wiped out.

The first round whistled directly over their heads and landed seventy-five meters over the gap of the canyon. Luke dropped a hundred meters, and the second round hit the near lip of the steep-sided NVA hideout. He asked for another round at the same data and it landed down in the canyon. Four out of the next five rounds landed inside of the horseshoe shaped canyon.

The recon team slipped down the side of the hill and cautiously approached the wreckage of small trees and jungle shrubs that covered the canyon floor. All of the trees had scars on them from the shrapnel and most of the smaller trees and plants had been mowed down from the exploding artillery rounds.

The light RPD machine gun opened fire from the entrance of the cave that had been hidden from view until the artillery had destroyed the natural camouflage. Two of the recon team members fell dead.

Mulhouse reacted instinctively. He pulled a hand grenade off his webgear as he fell down to the ground. Luke had been caught next to the canyon wall and rock chips from the impacting rounds cut his hands and face.

The explosion from the hand grenade stopped the machine gun from firing, but the recon team wasn't about to make the same mistake twice. Luke got angry with himself. He had assumed that the heavy artillery rounds had killed all of the NVA in the canyon and he *knew better* than to make an assumption about anything when it came to the NVA! Luke bit his lip and looked around at the walls of the canyon that were pockmarked with shallow caves. It was obvious that the NVA were holed up in a large cave; if he just had looked, two Americans would still be alive.

Luke didn't have to be told that the remainder of

his team was trapped in the canyon. The NVA in the cave kept them from advancing any farther into the canyon and any NVA out in the jungle could easily close the exit. Luke wasn't going to *assume* that the NVA didn't have radio contact with their headquarters. He knew that he was going to have to react quickly or the whole team was going to die. He felt the blood running down his face from the rock fragment cuts and ignored the stinging sensation. He was hunting.

Mulhouse jumped up and fired a full magazine into the dark opening of the cave and a heavy volley of AK-47 fire answered him. Very few of the NVA in the canyon had been caught by the artillery fire. Mulhouse popped a white phosphorus grenade safety pin and tossed it underhand into the cave. "Good-bye, bitch!" He was glad to get rid of the explosive because white phosphorus grenades had been known to go off on a soldier's webgear if they got hit by stray rounds, especially a tracer round. He didn't like carrying them, but Captain Arrowood had made it mandatory for each recon man to carry one WP grenade on his gear.

The grenade worked.

A dozen NVA broke out of the dark entrance of the cave screaming as the hot particles burnt through their living flesh. White phosphorus didn't need oxygen to burn and it would not stop until it had burned a hole through the human flesh. It was a hell of a way to die.

The recon team's bullets mercifully ended the horrible screams coming from the NVA soldiers. Luke almost felt sorry for them, but his mind reminded him of what the NVA had done to the Marines they had captured during the Battle for Khe Sanh, and all of the pity left him.

Luke whispered under his breath. "A tit for a tat . . . motherfuckers!"

Mulhouse called over to Arrowood after the screams had stopped. "Sir! Do you think we should call back to Vandergrift for some help?"

"I think so!" Luke smiled at the sergeant. The young NCO had performed superbly under pressure, and he was proud of the man.

"Gold Stripe 3, this is Banjo Player 6 . . . over." All of the radio call signs had changed for Task Force Remagen and would change about once a week until the operation was over. Gold Stripe referred to the armor commander who was the senior headquarters for the task force. Banjo Player was the code name for the recon teams, and each person had their own number so that, if you knew the codes, you could tell exactly who you were talking to. The number six always referred to a commander, three was the operations officer, five was the executive officer, four was the logistics officer, one was the personnel officer, and then it went to individuals out in the field. One-three or thirteen was normally the operations center.

"This is Gold Stripe 3 . . . send your traffic over . . ." The call told Luke that the armor operations officer was personally on the line; if it had been one of his people, they would have answered as one-three.

"This is Banjo Player 6 . . . we've encountered an unknown sized NVA force in caves at grid coordinates . . . 3 . . . 2 . . . 2 . . . 1 . . . 4 . . . 6 . . . I repeat coordinates . . . 322146. We need a special engineer team to work the caves . . . over."

There was a long pause, and then the armor S-3 came back on the air. "Player 6 . . . roger . . . we will send out a reinforced team to provide you support. Expect them in . . . three zero mikes . . . over." The operations officer told Luke that a special team would arrive at his location in thirty minutes.

"Roger, Gold Stripe 3 . . . much obliged for your help . . . out."

RT Pellam had been inserted two thousand meters to the east of Captain Arrowood and RT Marshall. Lieutenant Wong and Specialist Hito both sat out in the open on the rocks that overhung the cliffs and watched the road. They heard the small arms fire to their west and knew that Arrowood had made contact with the NVA. Lieutenant Wong felt his stomach growl and reached into his shirt pocket for a package of Rolaids. Hito watched the lieutenant out of the corner of his eyes, but his main concern was watching out for helicopters that had been patrolling the hills south of Highway 9. He didn't need some trigger happy door gunner to open fire on him.

"Aie!"

Lieutenant Wong was startled overhearing the loud voice so close to where he was setting.

"Aie! Lai dai!" The North Vietnamese soldier was asking Wong to come over to where he was.

Lieutenant Wong waved his hand from side to side and then beckoned for the NVA soldier to join him on the rocks.

Hito pushed the safety switch off his AK-47 and casually moved the barrel until it was pointing in the direction the NVA soldier had called from in the thick underbrush.

Wong stood on the rocks and stretched before sitting down again.

A scolding voice came from the jungle telling Wong to get off the rocks and find a position from where he wouldn't be seen by an American helicopter.

Lieutenant Wong picked up his gear and slid down the side of the rock to the shadows. A minute later, a platoon of NVA soldiers appeared from the edge of the jungle and started walking in single file toward Wong. The NVA lieutenant screamed over at Wong asking if he was crazy for doing something so stupid after hearing the firefight to their west where an American reconnaissance team had inserted.

Lieutenant Wong remained silent.

The NVA officer stopped walking and screamed for Wong and his comrade to come down immediately from the rocks and report to him. The NVA platoon relaxed with their weapons held over their shoulders by the barrels, and some of the NVA soldiers found themselves comfortable seats on the rocks from where they could watch their lieutenant chew out the stupid scouts for being so foolish as to sit in the open on the rocks.

The four members left in hiding from RT Pellam opened fire with two out of five of their Claymore mines and then followed up with hand grenades and small-arms fire. The NVA platoon was taken totally by surprise and died without knowing that the two dressed like their comrades and sitting out in the open were really American decoys drawing them into a trap.

Lieutenant Wong wiped the sweat off his forehead with the back of his hand. "Fuck me!"

"I ain't doing that fucking shit again!" Hito pointed at the lieutenant. "I don't give a fuck what the results are! That scared the hair off my dick!"

"Good work, Lieutenant. You sucked those suckers right up to you." The soldier spoke with a midwestern accent. "They would have smoked our asses."

Wong nodded and reached over and squeezed Hito's shoulder. He could feel the Japanese-American shaking under his hand. "Good work."

Hito nodded his head and reached up to pull his NVA pith helmet down lower over his eyes. "You know they can shoot us on the spot as spies if we get captured."

"True . . ." Wong pointed with his AK-47 at the dead NVA soldiers. "But they have to catch us first, partner."

"You've got to give the captain credit. Dressing up like NVA is working." Hito wiped his open hand over the front of his NVA shirt.

Lieutenant Doak and RT Rogers listened to all of the action going on to their west. They had been the first team that was inserted along the highway and, if they had to, they could walk back to Ca Lu. Doak wondered if the NVA had been waiting for them to insert. The large armored column moving west along Highway 9 from the coast would have been sure to tell the NVA that something was going on, and when the column didn't stop at any of the DMZ outposts but went into the highland jungle past the Marine base at The Rockpile, the NVA knew that the objective of the armored column had to be Vandergrift or Khe Sanh.

Small-arms fire came from Forbes's location and, shortly after that, the soft popping sounds came from where Lieutenant Fields had inserted. The NVA had made contact with everyone of the recon teams except Lieutenant Doak's.

"What in the fuck is going on, sir?" Dotson whispered in Doak's ear.

The lieutenant shook his head, puzzled. The only thing that he could figure out was that the NVA had been waiting for them. He was close in his guess. The NVA battalion commander who had been responsible for harassing the large Marine base at Vandergrift had been alerted about the large armor column heading west on Highway 9 and had been given orders to ambush the Americans if they tried negotiating the highway from Ca Lu out to Khe Sanh. The North Vietnamese general who had commanded the forces that had surrounded the Marines on the plateau in 1968 had been relieved of his command by General Vo Nguyen Giap himself and sent to live out the remainder of his life near an American POW Camp outside of Hanoi. The new commander of the northwestern sector had sworn that the Americans would never occupy the Khe Sanh plateau again, and so far he had kept his promise. The Special Forces camp at Lang Vei had been closed, and the huge Marine base at Khe Sanh had been deserted in a hurry. The NVA were still looting the American sites. They had gotten enough equipment from Lang Vei to support one of their Laotian sanctuaries. The 100KW generators alone were worth the losses they took capturing them. They had electric lights in their bunkers for the first time since the war had started.

Captain Arrowood called all of his teams on his

radio at the same time and had a short conference call. He realized that the NVA had a general idea where all of the teams were located on the cliffs and it looked like they had pulled back into the jungle just far enough to let the Americans pass and then they could return to their fortified positions and ambush or harass the main column. Luke had been right. The NVA commander wanted the small recon teams to report back that everything was clear, but the first contact had made one of the NVA platoon leaders jumpy, and he had moved out of his hiding place to support his friend and had been ambushed.

Luke informed all of his team leaders to call in artillery and walk it back and forth from as close as a hundred meters to the cliff and back a thousand meters into the jungle. He warned them that he was going to request napalm strikes all along their line of recon teams. The highway was a perfect reference line for the incoming fighters, and using it increased the accuracy of their napalm drops.

The NVA battalion commander ordered the remainder of his unit to pull back into the jungle after he suffered over two hundred casualties. He reported back to his headquarters that he had engaged a Marine regiment and had inflicted severe damage to the unit. The recon teams had suffered five dead and three wounded.

The armor commander of Task Force Remagen decided on asking the Marine brigadier general commanding Vandergrift for Marine support in securing the cliffs overlooking the road. They had originally thought that the recon teams could hold the high ground against the small units of NVA that had been reported west of the large base area, but it was obvious now that the NVA were there in force. The Marine brigadier agreed to reinforce each of the recon teams with a Marine platoon to secure the cliffs.

Project Deathwatch was earning its keep. When the brigade tallied up the project's results, the operations people were impressed. Papa Company of the 75th

Rangers was wracking up a very high kill ratio, and everyone knew it was because of the extremely accurate artillery and air support. Arrowood had proven that artillery enlisted forward observers working with a recon team were a cheap and extremely deadly weapon.

CHAPTER FOURTEEN

✪✪✪✪✪✪✪✪✪✪✪✪✪✪✪✪✪✪✪✪✪✪

SWIMMING IN THE YE PON

The Marine platoon had brought body bags with them for the Papa Company dead. Luke was very upset over losing two of his team because of such a foolish act on his part. He had stayed in Vietnam to save lives, and assuming that all of the NVA had been killed because the artillery had hit its target had been a fatal mistake. He had seen Arc-Light bombing attacks against NVA positions where an observer would have bet anything that no human could have survived such a horrible carnage; yet, after all of the two-thousand-pound bombs had exploded, NVA soldiers would appear from their bunkers.

Luke kept his eyes averted from the body bags when he slipped over the Huey's floor and sat cross-legged in the open doorway. Sergeant Mulhouse checked to make sure the body bags were zipped up and had the information on the ID cards filled in properly.

The chopper lifted off the ground and flew over the edge of the cliff and made a huge circle over the area so that they could approach the armor assembly area at Ca Lu. Luke kept his eyes on the jungle below them and saw the sharp spine of rock sticking up by itself in the distance. A column of smoke curled lazily up into the Robin's egg blue sky from the very top of the rocks. Mulhouse nudged Arrowood and pointed at the outpost. He had to yell over the loud noise coming from the chopper. "Who in the hell is way out here?"

Luke had heard about the site when he was in Special Forces, and even then it had been kept secret and hadn't been posted on any of the Corps battle maps. "It's a forward radio-relay site."

"For whom?" Mulhouse was confused as to why they would need a radio relay site all by itself in the middle of some of the most hostile jungle in Vietnam.

"CIA and SOG teams." Luke kept his eyes on the strip of ground on top of the ridgeline that couldn't have been more than twenty meters wide and fifty meters long. He could see the alpine trail winding its way up to the top of the rocky cliff. There was only one way up or down from the site. All resupply and extraction would have to be done by helicopter. One corner of the small site was studded with a half-dozen radio antennas and an olive drab communications van that was the whole purpose for the site. One of the guards sitting on a small bunker waved up at the passing chopper, but most of the men ignored the aircraft.

"What's its name?" Mulhouse twisted his head to get another view at the disappearing site. The area the Americans were occupying was so narrow that an NVA artillery or mortar team would have to hit the top of the ridge perfectly or their rounds would fall six hundred feet to the jungle floor and cause absolutely no damage to the site. The inaccessibility of the site made it priceless to the allies and a constant thorn in the side of the NVA. Lights from NVA trucks could be spotted from the relay site as far away as the western side of the Khe Sanh plateau. NVA gunners had even tried hitting the radio facility with recoilless rifles and had only succeeded in having their weapons destroyed from extremely accurate air strikes.

"What's the name of that place?" Mulhouse was impressed with the location of the site.

"Hickory . . . it's top secret." Luke watched the helipad approaching and braced himself for the soft landing. He didn't know why, but he always thought the chopper was going to land harder than it did and held onto anything that was bolted down in the aircraft.

Luke's team was the last one to return to Ca Lu and the armor task force headquarters. He had stayed at the canyon until the engineers and Marines had secured the cave. They had trapped nine North Vietnamese regulars in the cave who had refused to surrender. When the engineers had used tear gas to drive them out of the caves, the NVA came out screaming and cursing the Americans and were easily shot. Luke couldn't figure out why they had been so fanatical until the cave had been searched and the engineers had found an NVA heavy-machine-gun ammunition box filled with personal items that had been taken from dead Marines. In the back of the cave was a macabre shrine the NVA occupants had made using Marine skulls to circle a large, bleached-white tiger's skull. Evil and Satanism was everywhere, it just operated under different names. Luke had the engineers carefully remove the skulls and tag them for shipment back to the States. Nine names would be removed from the MIA list for the Marine Corps. The back of the cave was a storehouse that looked like an American supply sergeant's private reserve: C-rations, clothes, sandbags, cases of American ammunition for small-arms and even a case of Claymore mines complete with hand detonators. Everything in the cave was American except for the dead NVA and their weapons. The defenders of Lang Vei and Khe Sanh had departed in a hurry and had left tons of equipment and supplies behind in their bunkers.

"It looks like your recon men earned their pay today, Captain." The armor task force commander reached up and patted Luke's shoulder. "Good job!"

"Thanks, sir. We took some casualties and I'd like to consolidate a couple of my teams. It will mean less coverage in the field, but my men will have a better chance to survive. The NVA out here don't move around in small groups."

"That's why we've come out here, Captain." The armor officer winked. "We're planning on kicking a lot of ass!"

"First you have to get out there, sir, and then you'll have to make it back. That highway is a gauntlet." Luke hoped the armor commander wasn't going to underestimate the NVA's capability.

"I've been promised a Marine battalion to secure that ridgeline until we return back down Highway 9." The lieutenant colonel's voice changed and was filled with respect. "Thanks to your recon teams. We didn't think the NVA would dare pull an ambush from up there with our air-strike capabilities."

"Why not, sir? They ambushed a French convoy from exactly the same sites."

"Where did you hear that?" The armor commander looked surprised.

"I wrote to the military historian's office at St. Cyr in France and asked for their support in sending me copies of all of the French battles during the Indo-China War. They were so surprised that I would ask for their help that they sent me much more than I asked for." Luke smiled and winked back at the armor officer. "In fact, they were shocked that West Point or one of the branch career courses hadn't asked them for the information. We're basically making the same mistakes that the French did against the *same* NVA commanders who had conducted the original battles."

"Captain Arrowood, you are amazing. Has anyone told you that before?" The senior officer was genuinely impressed.

"The NVA think that our general officers are arrogant schoolboys, and I tend to agree with them." Luke tested the statement against the armor commander.

"That was a decent fight you people started up there!" The Marine brigadier general joined the small group of officers.

"Thank you, sir." Luke stood at attention and the general nodded for him to be at ease.

"Captain Arrowood was telling me that he'd read

about all of the French battles in this area. It seems that we're making basically the same errors as the French . . ."

"Fuck the French!" The brigadier rolled his cigar to the other side of his mouth. "They got their asses kicked fighting these gooks. I don't plan on that happening to me."

"Captain Arrowood mentioned that the French were ambushed from above by the Viet Minh, which makes sense to me. The tanks couldn't raise their main guns high enough to engage the enemy and could only use the machine guns mounted on the commander's cupola and were easy targets for NVA snipers. It was only a matter then of dropping satchel charges down from the cliffs to wipe out the column."

"Like I said, I don't plan on taking lessons from the French in fighting battles! They've got their asses kicked since Napoleon!"

"I'm not French, General . . . but I would try and knock out the first and last vehicles in the convoy to block the highway and then I'd take my time destroying the rest of the vehicles one at a time working from both ends." Luke looked the gruff Marine general directly in the eyes as he spoke.

"There are Marines securing that area now. It would be impossible for that to happen without removing them." The general grabbed the bill of his starched fatigue cap and lifted it off his head to scratch an itch and then replaced it.

Luke wanted to add something else to the conversation, but realized the Marine brigadier's thinking had locked in somewhere between Iwo Jima and Pusan. The man had no business fighting a guerrilla war. He was like an iron rod sticking out in a field of bamboo.

"I think you're making a lot of sense, Captain Arrowood, and I'll brief my commanders before we depart in the morning."

"One more thing, sir . . ." Luke could see the armor commander was becoming impatient, ". . . the river-crossing site has changed a great deal since those aerial photographs were taken."

"Shit!" The armor commander had been working hard for the past three weeks getting ready for the operation and the last thing he needed was a major change in plans the night before they jumped off. "What's the problem?"

"There's been a rock slide and there's no room for a vehicle to turn around at the site. I recommend that the AVLB lead the column so that it can lay its bridge over the gorge and cross over where there's a place for it to pull off the road and let the tanks pass."

"You mean let an armored vehicle-launched *bridge* lead an armor task force into battle!" The lieutenant colonel shook his head. The cadre back at Fort Knox would never forgive him if he did that.

"I know it sounds bad, but that's the only way you're going to cross that gorge with your tanks. There's a spot in the highway that's wide enough for the AVLB to switch places with a lead vehicle about ten thousand meters from the river-crossing site." Luke went over to the map and pointed out the location he had spotted from the air. "I'd have a couple of engineer mine-detector teams check that site out very well before I used it, though. It's a perfect place for a mine."

"You know everything, don't you, Captain?" The Marine general flexed his jaws.

"I try to be thorough when I debrief a mission, sir." Luke tapped the site for the vehicle switch with his forefinger. "*I* would mine that site, if I were the NVA, and I'd do it in such a way that you would find one maybe two mines with no problem, but I'd have a killer mine well-concealed to knock out the AVLB."

"*You* know that we're bringing an AVLB, Captain, but the NVA don't know that . . . do they?" The brigadier shook his head. "You're giving them too much credit!"

The armor commander kept looking at the place

Luke had marked on the map. It made very good sense.

The general looked at his watch. "They'll be serving dinner in a half hour in my mess, Colonel. I expect you there for cocktails."

"Yes, sir! I'll be right with you." The armor commander showed the spot on the map to his operations officer. "You heard Arrowood. Check it out and see if we can change the column line-up, and have the AVLB second in line and make the switch here . . ." He tapped the map.

"Thanks, sir." Luke wiped his forehead with the back of his hand.

"Don't thank me, Captain. It's me who owes you. I would have looked like a fool having a hundred armored vehicles lined up on that road that couldn't move forward!"

Sergeant Mulhouse waited until the officers had left the battle map and then went over to locate where he had seen the radio-relay site on their way back from their mission. It took him a couple of minutes to find the small pinnacle sticking out of the jungle. The contour lines were so close together that they appeared as one fat brown line on the map.

"Find something interesting?" Luke had poured himself a cup of coffee from the staff's pot.

"That radio-relay site." Mulhouse looked up from the map at Luke. "It's like a fort in the middle of a green sea. We're the closest American base to it."

"They won't rely on us to help them if they get in trouble. There are only two ways to the top of Hickory; by air and up that trail. The NVA would suffer tremendous casualties trying to take the site."

"How about a traitor?"

Luke smiled and nodded his head. "Make that *three* ways to the top." He looked down in the paper cup he was holding and thought about what Mulhouse had just said. If Hickory was over overrun, it would probably be because of a traitor up on the site. "Let's go get some Cs!"

"Aren't you eating with the general tonight?" Mulhouse had eavesdropped on the conversation.

"Smart ass! I wasn't invited." Luke tried cuffing the back of the buck sergeant's head, but Mulhouse ducked.

The recon team leaders were all waiting for Luke to come back from the debriefing. Forbes had made a huge pot of C-ration stew, using a half-dozen boxes of C-rations and a full bottle of Tabasco sauce. Luke ate and briefed the team leaders on their mission in the morning. They had been assigned to secure the area at the mouth of the highway when it broke free of the valley onto the plateau. An old French fort used to command the site but the NVA had used that position during their siege at Khe Sanh and it had been leveled from numerous air strikes. Luke consolidated his recon teams and put Mulhouse under Forbes, making one team out of two, and then he shuffled a couple of people around to make up for the wounded. A month earlier, he wouldn't have been able to have accomplished such an easy task because of the team rivalry.

Luke found himself a comfortable spot next to one of the tracked vehicles and sat down with his poncho liner wrapped around his shoulders. The evening brought a chill in the air in the highland jungles. He leaned back against the track and thought about the horseshoe canyon and the nine fanatical NVA soldiers. There was something about the shrine they had made with the human skulls that still bothered him. Luke had seen enough atrocites during the war so that skulls shouldn't have bothered him, but they *had* bothered him and that was making him worry. He drew the shrine again and again in his mind as he sat in the dark thinking and then it struck him.

"Mulhouse?" Luke called over to the sergeant in the dark.

There was a short pause and the team leader appeared next to him. "Yes, sir?"

"Did you bring one of the NVA pith helmets back with you?"

"Yes, sir . . . we brought back a couple of them for souvenirs. You don't mind do you, sir?"

"No . . . it's legal. I just want to see one, if you have them close by."

"Sure, sir. We put them in the command track. It'll take only a minute."

Mulhouse was gone for a couple of minutes and then returned carrying three NVA tan pith helmets and a flashlight.

Luke glanced at the first one and was sure when he saw the second one. The red stars on the front of the pith helmets were turned upside down. "Look at this." Luke pointed out his observation.

Mulhouse shrugged his shoulders. He didn't understand, but Lieutenant Doak did as soon as he saw the second NVA helmet.

"Do you think that they were some kind of a special team and wore their commie stars upside down as a code?" Doak didn't want to come right out and say what he was thinking because it would sound crazy.

"We found a shrine inside of the cave. The skulls we brought back were a part of it with a tiger's skull in the center."

"I saw the tiger's skull. One of the men brought it back for a souvenir. The teeth alone will sell for a small fortune back in Da Nang. They make them into necklaces."

"The nine American skulls formed a pentagram with the tiger's skull in the center of the pentagon."

Doak swallowed hard. "I thought the Vietnamese were all Buddhists and stuff like that."

"I think the French tried making a lot of converts and, usually, when you hate your masters, you'll hate their religion."

"So they took all of the evil they could from the Catholic Church?"

"It looks that way. I can't see an NVA commander

allowing his men to wear their helmet stars upside down unless it benefited him in some way."

Mulhouse was lost in the conversation between the two officers and excused himself to go get some sleep.

Luke waited until the sergeant had gone. "There's no need in scaring the men," he whispered. "Let's keep this to ourselves."

"No problem with that, sir! This is some really sick shit though!"

"What better place for a Satanic cult than a war?" Luke pulled his poncho liner tighter around his neck. He felt a chill. He was worried and hoped that the cult was a small one and that they had killed all of them in the cave.

Luke had decided to stay behind and go with the armor command section for the ride down the valley. The Marines securing the high ground and the recon teams covering the plateau entrance to the valley had made the trip almost enjoyable. The tanks had a difficult time negotiating a number of places on the road where the cliffs dropped down from above and landslides had eroded away huge portions of the shoulder, causing the end connectors on the tank tracks to grade against the cliff and the track on the other side to hang over the drop-off on the left side of the vehicles. The smaller M113s and command tracks negotiated the sites easily. The AVLB had barely fit into the exchange area and Luke had been proven almost one hundred percent correct. The engineers had found two antitank mines at the turnaround and searched the area thoroughly for a third and found a Chinese anti-personnel Claymore mine rigged to be set off two different ways: by a trip wire or by a hand detonator that was attached to a wire running up the cliff to a site from above.

The ravine river crossing was executed perfectly and the AVLB picked up the bridge when the last vehicle had crossed over. For all intents and purposes, the task force had trapped themselves on the Khe Sanh plateau.

A consolidated sigh seemed to leave all of the soldiers once they broke free of the valley out onto the plateau. It was as if everyone had been holding their breaths during the whole trip. The armor company broke out of the line formation into a classical tank attack formation and went racing off over the rolling terrain like a bunch of schoolboys leaving a stuffy school building on the last day of school. The tanks had been assigned to reconnoiter the old Khe Sanh Marine Base while the mechanized infantry companies were assigned objectives to the west and southwest of the valley entrance for the first night. A small team was left behind to secure the task force headquarters along with the recon teams that had been pulled back inside of the headquarters perimeter for a day's rest.

Task Force Remagen raced all over the plateau performing classical tank maneuvers with mechanized infantry. The armor commanders were spoiling for a battle in terrain in which their tanks were designed to fight. Secretly, the tankers prayed for an encounter with the armored force that overran the Special Forces camp at Lang Vei.

The next ten days on the plateau revealed very little and only the recon teams found any sign of the enemy. It was obvious that the NVA used Highway 9 on the plateau as their own private road and rarely used the jungle or the elephant grass to hide in. The tenth day brought the main force of the task force to the banks of the Ye Pon River that separated South Vietnam from Laos.

The task force commander lifted his goggles from around his eyes and looked out over the river from his seat in the cupola of his tank. The Ye Pon was about a hundred meters wide and ran about three feet deep with a number of deep holes along the banks. The armor officer pushed the switch on his radio and spoke to his operations officer. "We'll make camp here for tonight."

Luke hopped down from his track and looked over the site. The security platoon had set up in a fan shape against the river bank, and a pair of tanks had taken overwatch positions on the river.

"Well, are you going down to the river and take a bath or not, Captain?" The armor commander called over to Luke from his tank.

Luke shook his head nervously. "Have you forgotten where we are, sir?"

"Don't look so damn worried, Captain. I've got a tank company and a mechanized infantry company with us. Anybody who wants to mess with that kind of firepower would be a fool and, besides, we haven't even seen an NVA soldier since the valley."

Luke pointed across the river. "That's where they are, sir . . . lots of them."

"Maybe they'll come over and join us!" The colonel picked up his towel and a bar of soap. "It's been ten days since I've washed and I'm not going to let you rattle your sword and screw up this opportunity!"

Luke signaled Dotson and Pilgrim to come with him and the lieutenant colonel down to the water. The site was perfect for a large number of men to bathe at with large rocks bordering the riverbanks and gravel on the bottom of the river. The water ran swift, but not dangerously swift, and would massage your skin as you sat down in it. After ten days of eating dust and being baked in the sun, the water looked very inviting. A platoon of tankers had already beaten the task force commander down to the river and were about to change over with another platoon when Luke arrived.

"Captain! Does that look good!" Dotson wanted to join the laughing tankers.

Luke scanned the opposite riverbank. One NVA with a machine gun could kill a dozen men before the tanks could open fire and be gone back into Laos without worrying about being chased. "I don't like it at all!"

Dotson sighed. He knew the captain wasn't going to let the recon teams use the river.

All of the tankers who had been in the water got out bitching because they had to leave and started dressing on the rocks, when the other platoon arrived and started undressing. Fifty men were on the rocks in different stages of undress and Luke noticed that only a few of them had brought their weapons with them.

"Just a second, sir." Luke stepped out on the rocks until he was a couple of meters out in the river.

"What's going on?" There was a tinge of anger in the lieutenant colonel's voice. He wanted to get in the water.

"Did anyone *clear* the river?"

"How in the hell do you clear a river?"

Luke removed one of his M26 fragmentation hand grenades and pulled the pin. "We call this a *DuPont Spinner*, they're great for fishing." He threw the hand grenade out into the river and the troops watched the water spray up. Within a matter of seconds a dozen medium- and small-sized fish floated to the surface. Luke saw a deep hole in the river and threw another DuPont Spinner in the hole.

"All right! Enough screwing around, Captain. We want to get cleaned up." The armor commander stepped out in the river just as the grenade exploded and four very large gar fish floated up to the surface. The smallest one was seven feet long.

"Holy shit!" One of the tankers who had just finished bathing reached down unconsciously and placed his hand over his crotch. "I was swimming there!"

The grenade had killed one of the gar fish, but had only stunned the other three. Within seconds, the gars had recovered from the shock and erratically began swimming back into their water hole.

"I'd stay close to the bank if I were you, sir." Luke beckoned with his head for his men to follow him and he led the way back to the command track.

"We could use a bath, sir." Dotson risked asking the captain.

Luke flashed a look at Dotson that almost caught the soldier's hair on fire. "We're going to find a place to wash, Dotson . . . but not in the river. You might get your sorry ass shot over here, but *not* under my supervision . . . not because I've done something stupid!"

"Yes, sir." Dotson felt like a fool.

"I saw a stream flowing into the river a few meters over in that direction. We should be able to find a spot where we can clean up at without exposing our asses to every NVA within a dozen miles of here!"

Luke led the way to the stream and they found a perfect spot about a foot deep and four feet across where they could take turns bathing. The water was even cooler than the river because it was flowing through thick jungle and bamboo thickets. The team checked the area for snakes and scorpions before undressing. Luke kept two men on watch with M-60 machine guns while his men took their time in the luxury of the water.

The recon teams were met by the infantry commander on their way back to the tracks. "Where did you guys wash up?"

"There's a stream a couple meters in that direction." Luke pointed with the barrel of his weapon. "A nice site and close to the perimeter."

"Good! My men are about ready to frag me because I won't let them get in the river."

Task Force Remagen lagered for the night near the river with the headquarters element protected in the perimeter of one of the infantry companies from the 1st Battalion, 61st Infantry. The Duster Platoon and the engineers also stayed with the infantry company. Two of the 40mm twin-barreled antiaircraft guns had been positioned along the river, and the other two tracked vehicles had been placed in the infantry perimeter that overlooked the plateau. Luke had one of his teams go with each of the Dusters to provide a little security for the vehicles so that the crews could man the guns and get a little sleep during the night. The Duster Platoon hadn't seen much action since coming to Vietnam because they had been used for perimeter defense in the main base areas and rarely had the chance to get out in the jungle or on patrol. They had been assigned to the task force to provide heavy grazing fire with their armor piercing rounds if the mechanized infantry were attacked by Russian-made PT-76 armored vehicles the NVA were using in that sector. When the NVA had attacked the Lang Vei Special Forces camp with PT-76s, no one knew that the skin of the light amphibious vehicles could be penetrated by a .50-caliber round. At night, the sound of a tank is enough to scare almost anyone, especially if you're not expecting an armored attack. The Special Forces men at Lang Vei engaged the PT-76s with their 57mm recoilless rifle and destroyed one of them before the camp was overrun. The task force had really gotten their use out of the Dusters when they traversed the valley. The twin guns on each one of the tracked vehicles could traverse 360° and fire straight up if it had to.

The evening briefing had last longer than usual, mostly because all of the officers and senior NCOs were feeling good after their baths and swim in the river. The armor task force commander looked over at Luke and grinned. "Our recon company commander is a little pissed at us for going swimming in the river today. I don't think he respects the power in an armor company."

All of the armor officers chuckled in response to their battalion commander's joke.

Luke skirted around the ribbing. "We found a decent stream about twenty-five meters outside of the infantry perimeter in that direction." Luke pointed to the northwest. "It runs into the river."

"Are you afraid of gar fish, Captain?" The operations officer tried making light of Luke's overconcern. "We were down there for most of the day and nothing happened; besides we've got two tanks and a pair of dusters watching over the men."

"Sir . . ." Luke tried keeping the tone of his voice light and smiled when he spoke to the armor major, ". . . the NVA might get caught by surprise *once*, but don't think for a minute that they don't know by now that you did spend most of the day swimming in the river. If you try it again tomorrow . . ."

The task force commander cut Luke short. "Enough doom-and-gloom talk!"

"I've put the river off-limits to my men, sir. They're going to use the stream until we leave here." The infantry company commander supported Luke's position.

"You grunts are a bunch of chickenshits!" The armor lieutenant colonel wasn't trying to be catty. He was still in a good mood from his swim and was trying to joke. The infantry officer didn't take the comment as a joke.

"When you're riding inside one of your tanks, sir, your skin might be protected from AK-47 rounds, but bare-assed in a river is a different story."

"How damn many times do I have to tell you that no NVA in his right mind is going to attack an armored force of this size!" The lieutenant colonel was beginning to get angry. "Unless they're in regimental or larger strength!"

"They've been known to travel in groups that large on this plateau, sir."

"All right! Damn!" He looked over at the operations officer. "Put the river off-limits for any more swimming and bathing. Use it only for drinking and water for the vehicles." He looked over at Luke and smiled. "Do you feel better now?"

"Yes, sir."

The lieutenant colonel shook his head. "You grunts! Go get some sleep, we've got a big day ahead of us tomorrow."

The infantry captain left the briefing with Luke. "I'm glad he changed his mind. It was too risky down there. I don't even like spending the night so close to that damn river! Half of my maneuver capability is gone with the river in the way."

Luke nodded his head in the fading light in agreement with the captain. "Some food and a couple of hours sleep and I'll be good for another fifty miles."

"What's that M88 doing down by the river?" The captain pointed to the huge tank retriever.

"Looks like their stocking up on their water supply." Luke could see one of the crew handing up a five-gallon water can to the man standing next to the open cupola. "That's a weird vehicle. I hear it can pull five tanks at one time-dead weight."

"They've had problems with them lately. They run on gasoline, and the M48s change back and forth from gas to diesel engines, making a resupply for them very difficult. I think they're carrying a reserve of gasoline with them inside."

"Inside the hull?"

"Yeah, that thing burns like three gallons of gas per mile!"

"I don't think that I would want to ride inside of a vehicle that is carrying gasoline out here."

"Me, neither."

"Are you moving out in the morning?" Luke asked the infantry captain.

"Probably around noon. We've got a three-day patrol to the northern corner of the plateau—an area that I would just as soon stay away from."

"My recon teams spotted a lot of old signs up there. Be careful." Luke liked the infantry captain.

"Yeah . . . keep your powder dry, too." He left to go brief his lieutenants on the upcoming operation for his company.

Luke went over to the Duster where Lieutenant Fields had set up his poncho hootch. "Need some company for supper?"

"Hello, sir! Come on over. We were just about to eat some of this Duster crews' ham-and-eggs pie."

"Pie?"

The Duster lieutenant turned away from the dutch oven he had set up behind his track. "Yes, sir. We use C-ration crackers for the crust and then mix the eggs with ham and a little secret ingredients . . ."

"Turkey loaf and boned chicken." Dotson had been transferred to Fields's team to replace the wounded men.

"*You*, soldier, can be shot for giving away secrets during wartime!" The Duster officer smiled and then frowned at Dotson. "How did you know?"

"It ain't hard when the empty cans are right over there." Dotson pointed at the pile of C-ration cans behind the track.

One of the Duster crew members sat against the sprocket near the back of the track bouncing a small antipersonnel hand grenade in his right hand. It was one of the new type that had picked up the nickname of cherry grenade because the shape was different from the M26 and it could be thrown like a baseball. Also, it was a little smaller than the regular M26.

"That could be dangerous, soldier." Luke nodded at the grenade. The Duster lieutenant looked over and saw his man playing with the device.

"I've got the pin in it, sir." The soldier acted like he was testing the recon captain.

"Put the damn grenade away!" The Duster lieutenant spoke as if he was about ready to give up on the man. He was obviously a troublemaker in the platoon.

The soldier bounced the grenade one more time and then reached up to hook it back on his webgear. He missed the D-ring, but the pin caught on it and slid out. The safety handle flipped through the air and landed on the ground in front of the soldier who froze with the live grenade still in his hand. The lieutenant reacted instantly and grabbed the grenade out of the man's hand and in a powerful underhand throw lobbed it halfway across the river before it went off.

"Shit! That was close!" Dotson was the first one to recover his voice.

The soldier looked out over the rippling water

where the fragments had landed. "You saved my life, Lieutenant."

"Not on purpose, soldier."

Luke could see that the officer was still angry at the private.

The Duster lieutenant picked the private up off the ground by the front of his jacket. The grenade incident had been the last straw. "You've caused me all the trouble that I'm going to take from you, soldier!"

The private tried leaning back away from the lieutenant's threatening fist.

"You've smoked so damn much of that dope that your fucking mind has turned to weed! This is your last fucking chance; either you clean up you act or I'm going to start kicking your fucking ass *every single day* until one of us is too fucking tired to continue!"

The NVA sergeant and his squad had just gotten into position on the western side of the Ye Pon River when the hand grenade had gone off. The water had magnified the sound and the rookie sergeant thought that the Americans had seen his team and were firing their tanks at him. The RPG-7 gunner had taken part in a dozen attacks against Marine positions and knew that the explosion was probably one of the American guards goofing off or nervous and wasn't nothing to worry about. He laid five rocket-propelled grenades down in a row on the piece of cloth that he had brought with him for that purpose and adjusted his sights.

The driver of the huge M88 tank retriever lifted the heavy five-gallon can of water up to his shoulder and then jerked it up to the man on the track's deck.

"That's enough! Let's get her back inside of the perimeter before it gets any darker!" The armor motor sergeant stuck his head out of the commander's cupola next to the .50-caliber machine gun he had mounted on the track. The M88 was designed to tow disabled tanks and wasn't designed as a fighting vehicle.

The first RPG-7 round hit the front of the sloping retriever's crew compartment and penetrated inside.

The NVA gunner felt the hand tap his shoulder and knew that he was loaded again. He fired, and the second round penetrated four inches lower and detonated the gas cans.

"My God!" The words tore out of the Duster lieutenant's throat and he dropped the private down on the ground. A column of fire roared out of the commander's cupola on the M88 that was parked down next to the riverbank with the crew sergeant bouncing up in the air from the force of the explosion that was taking place inside of the armored vehicle.

Luke turned and saw the hellfire, and with his mind's eye he heard the screams. It was just dark enough for the column of red and orange fire to look even more sinister.

The Duster lieutenant reacted instinctively and climbed up on his vehicle screaming for the crew to take their battle stations, while Luke and the recon team found their foxholes along the riverbank. The twin barrels of the 40mm weapon lowered until the lieutenant had the far bank in his sights. The loader on the weapon threw in a magazine of HE rounds and the loader on the other side followed suit. The gunner for the Duster had been over at one of the other positions trying to scrounge up five gallons of oil and came running back when he heard the RPG-7. The lieutenant saw the flash from the edge of the jungle and swung the guns around until the spot was in his sights. The sound of the twin guns going off sounded almost comforting to the soldiers on the perimeter. The guards along the river watched the far jungle erupt from the impact of the 40mm shells. Trees toppled over and hunks of earth flew up in the air. You couldn't hide behind a riverbank to escape from a Duster, as the NVA sergeant found out.

The M88 burned for the rest of the night with the small arms rounds inside going off like popcorn popping. Periodically throughout the night, one of the tanks would fire a canister round across the river or one of the infantry tracks would open up in a mini-mad minute. The whole western perimeter was nervous after having watched the horrible death of their buddies.

Luke leaned against the back of his foxhole and felt the cool earth through his jacket. There was no moon out and everything was pitch black. His thoughts went down the full spectrum of human emotion and tried stopping on his pending divorce, but rather than feel that pain again he thought about the burning M88.

CHAPTER FIFTEEN

✪✪✪✪✪✪✪✪✪✪✪✪✪✪✪✪✪✪

MARINE PLATOON

The armor commander couldn't look Captain Arrowood in the eyes the next morning during the briefing. The smell coming from the M88 hung over the whole area. Luke had stopped on his way over to the command track and surveyed the destruction. The paint and rubber track pads had burned off the vehicle. The flames had been so hot that all of the crew's bodies had been cremated. A couple of the men from the armor company were scooping cans of water out of the river and throwing them on the hull to cool it off enough so that they could go inside and try and find some remains from the men. Luke could see that they wouldn't find much.

"Gentlemen . . . because of the RPG attack last night against our position, I've decided to pull back away from the river and establish a semipermanent fire-support base on the plateau from where the artillery battery can support all of our units. We will conduct raids against these objectives on the plateau." The lieutenant colonel tapped each one of the numbered goose eggs drawn on the battle map. "The recon company will be responsible for conducting patrols along the Ye Pon River and alert us to any attempts at a river crossing by a large NVA force." The armor officer did not look over at Luke as he briefed the commanders and staff for the task force. He knew that Luke had given him some very good advice the day before, and every time he thought

291

about the naked men bathing in the river like a bunch of high school kids, a shudder tore down his spine that made his hands shake. What *could* have happened occupied his mind. One brave NVA machine gunner could have butchered half a company before they could have even returned fire. Letting the armor company bathe in the river was one of the stupidest things he had ever done in his military carrer, and it would haunt him the rest of his life, even though the worst hadn't happened.

The armor commander looked up from his map smiling. He was thinking about an old saying that God protected children, drunks, and *fools*.

Luke briefed his teams and emphasized the importance of knowing where they were at on the map so that they could call in accurate artillery fire. None of the men needed to be told that the NVA out on the Khe Sanh plateau moved in large groups and *knew* that they owned the land. Luke decided that he would keep Lieutenant Doak behind with the task force headquarters and go out with RT Rogers and Dotson. Everyone was getting tired after almost three weeks in the field, and Luke knew that he would have to start rotating teams, with one standing down to rest. This would be the last time that all three of the teams were out at the same time. Luke went over and personally briefed the artillery battery commander of the 105mm self-propelled battery on the exact AOs the recon teams were working. He established two artillery high burst reference points for each team, just in case they got lost and needed to orient themselves.

The teams were dropped off in their AOs by the mechanized infantry companies when they passed near the areas in their tracks. It was an excellent stay-behind tactic and was almost impossible for the NVA to pinpoint the exact location of the recon team, unlike when they were inserted by helicopter.

RT Rogers was broken down to two men per M113, and when they had reached the area they were going to patrol the men slipped down off the slow-moving tracks and disappeared into the thick jungle that bordered the meandering river. Luke assembled his men and waited until the sound of the tracks faded away. His ears rang for hours from the loud noise the tracks had made. Luke wondered how the infantrymen riding on them could even hear it when the NVA fired at them.

Slowly, the jungle sounds returned, and Luke tuned into his environment along with the rest of his recon team. Luke was very proud of the way they were turning out. He didn't think there were better recon men in Vietnam. They moved like shadows through the jungle and had turned hand signals into another language.

Luke could tell from the shadows that it was getting to be late afternoon, and signaled for the team to form into a night-star lager position, with him occupying the center of the star with the radio. As long as it was daylight, each one of the recon men at the points in the star stayed out about twenty meters in the jungle, but as it grew darker they came back in closer until they were almost touching and, with the absence of any moonlight, they would close in until they could touch each other's boots as they lay spread-eagled on the ground.

Luke waited until each one of the men was in position and had had time to check out his area before making a radio call back to the task force headquarters and telling Lieutenant Doak that they were in their night lager site.

"Running Deer 5, this is Running Deer 6 . . . over."

Static filled the airwaves.

"Deer 6 . . . 5, over."

"Deer 6 . . . Yellow . . . Prime . . . DEFCONs, XXYTGB, PPDEES, JHFLZT, PPSATE . . . read back, over."

Lieutenant Doak read back the coded defensive concentrations to Arrowood.

"Deer 6 . . . do you have any traffic for me? Over."

The task force commander had been standing behind Doak and tapped his shoulder signaling for the lieutenant to hand him the handset. "Deer 6, this is Buckshot 6 . . . I want you to be on the lookout for a Marine platoon in your AO . . . It seems that there's been a mix-up and your AOs overlap . . . Do you read me? . . . Over."

Luke felt his face starting to burn from the blood rushing to his cheeks. "Buckshot 6 . . . roger . . . send me their last known position in code . . . over."

Luke waited for over a half hour for the task force staff to call back to Vandergrift and get the information for him. He couldn't believe that they would fuck up and put two friendly units in the same AO without telling them. A thought crossed Luke's mind as he sat next to the radio; did the Marines know that his team was in their AO?

"Running Deer 6 . . . this is Buckshot 3 . . . over."

The task force commander let his operations officer call Luke.

"Buckshot 3 . . . Deer 6 . . . over."

"Buckshot 3 . . . in reference to your last question . . . I send . . . XXYTFS . . . over." The S-3 held his breath, knowing that Luke was going to go berserk when he broke the code. The last known position for the Marine platoon was less than a thousand meters to his south.

"Deer 6 . . . Does the friendly unit know that I'm here? . . . Over."

"Buckshot 3 . . . No . . . There hasn't been any contact with them for quite a while . . . over."

"Deer 6 . . . out." Luke hooked the handset on the backpack strap and closed his eyes before he shook his head slowly. It was unbelievable, totally unbelievable! He had to reach each one of his men and warn them before it was too late and they accidentally opened fire on the Marines.

Luke had pulled his team back into a nighttime position while it was still daylight so that he could

control them better. All of them were extremely
jumpy, knowing that a Marine platoon was wandering
around their AO without the Marines knowing that
they were there.

The shadows were lengthening and night was starting to fall in the jungle. The process was very fast
once the sun slipped over the mountains. Luke had
picked a site for the night near the river that gave
them some cover. A large tree had been knocked
down from a B-52 bombing run and gave protection to
one of the team members while a number of boulders
protected some of the team. Luke had set up his one-
man command post between the huge roots of a giant
mahogany tree.

The sound of a rolling rock reached Dotson on his
position on the ground. He listened and tried seeing
through the ground cover for the creature that made
the rock move. A minute passed. Dotson knew that
the sound was so minor that the rest of the team
hadn't heard it. He shifted slightly on the ground and
was about ready to look in another direction when the
torn cover on a helmet rose above the green foliage
and a very tired looking black face cleared the under-
growth below it.

Dotson felt the sweat running down his face. He
didn't know what to do next. He knew that he had to
do *something*. He whispered loud enough for the black
face to hear him. "If you shoot me, motherfucker, I'm
going to bleed all over your black ass!"

The Marine point man raised his hand and halted
the platoon. "What in the fuck are you doing out
here!" He whispered, but the surprise in his voice
made the transmission louder than he would have
liked.

"Recon team . . ." Dotson signaled with his hand
for the Marine to follow him back to where Captain
Arrowood was waiting.

Luke sighed in relief when he saw the Marines. It
would have been a disaster if they would have made
a chance encounter. The Marine lieutenant dropped

down exhausted next to Luke's radio. "Lieutenant Morgan, sir."

"How many men do you have with you, Lieutenant?"

"Thirteen, sir."

Luke was expecting a much larger number. "Marines must have small platoons."

The lieutenant's eyes narrowed trying to smile. "It's supposed to be over forty, but I haven't had a replacement in five months."

Luke looked nervously around the surrounding jungle. He hated talking, but he needed to get some more information. "Your men look like shit. How long have you been out here?

Lieutenant Morgan used the radio to rest his arm against and leaned his head back against the tree root. "Twenty-seven fucking days!" Morgan glanced up at Luke. "I don't want to bother you, but do you have some food?"

"Sure . . . LRRP rations . . ."

"We haven't eaten in three days . . ." Morgan felt embarrassed, ". . . our last resupply was fifteen days ago."

"Fifteen days!" Luke couldn't believe his ears.

"Yeah, ever since this Army task force got here, our choppers have been resupplying them."

"Damn!" Luke's anger gained control. He could see that two of the Marines sitting close to them were wearing rags for uniforms and one of them had an olive drab towel tied around his waist instead of trousers. "Where's his pants?"

Morgan glanced over at the Marine. "Would you believe they fell apart?"

Luke opened his rucksack and gave the lieutenant all of his LRRP rations and signaled for the rest of his team members to do the same. "Why haven't you made contact with your base camp?"

Morgan kept his eyes on the food and answered. "Our radio batteries went dead after the first fifteen days. We haven't been able to make contact with Vandergrift since then. We had asked for new batteries during our last resupply, but they must have forgotten them."

"Do you mean that they just *left* you out here without sending a rescue party?" Luke was having a very difficult time understanding Marine philosophy.

"No one *left* us out here sir, we're Marines on patrol!" Morgan opened a package of rehydrated LRRP rations and then handed it over to one of his men who was worse off than himself.

Luke left the lieutenant and called back to the task force headquarters to let them know that the missing Marine patrol had been found. The Marine liaison officer with the task force informed Luke that there would be a resupply for the platoon at first light in the morning, and he gave Luke the landing zone's location in code.

Luke informed the lieutenant, who didn't seem all that excited over the information. Morgan was hoping that his *platoon* would be extracted. "Lieutenant Morgan, my men can pull guard tonight. Let your men sleep and rest up."

Morgan didn't look up from the LRRP ration that he was devouring. "Thanks."

First light brought a different scene for Captain Arrowood's eyes. The dim light from the night before had hidden the true condition of the Marine platoon. The men looked pathetic, and none of them, including the lieutenant, had a decent set of clothes covering their bodies. Jungle ulcers covered their arms and bare skin on their faces where their beards didn't cover.

"Lieutenant Morgan, I'm going to recommend that your team be extracted back to Vandergrift. You're in no condition to continue patrolling along this river."

"I appreciate your concern, sir, but don't waste your time making the call. My captain will bring us in when he's ready."

"What in the fuck is the man's problem?" Luke swept his hand out over the platoon. "These men are in horrible shape."

"We're being punished."

"Punished? For what!"

"He caught one of my squads smoking dope and he figured if he keeps us on patrol we can't get any stuff to smoke."

"We?" Luke took a closer look at the Marine officer.

"I was with them." The lieutenant played with the strap on his rifle. "Personally, I think he wants us to run into a large NVA force . . ."

Luke had heard of officers smoking dope with their troops, but this was the first time he ever had one admit doing it to his face.

Lieutenant Morgan wouldn't look at Luke and watched a couple of his men trying to clean their weapons with dirty rags. "Don't hold it against him, sir. I wouldn't let me come back to Vandergrift either if I was the captain."

Luke saw the look in the lieutenant's eyes and knew what the junior officer was thinking. "We should get moving toward the LZ."

Lieutenant Morgan nodded his head and struggled to get up on his feet.

A pair of darting gunships arrived before the Marine CH-46 helicopter and circled around the landing zone. Luke had one of his men throw a purple smoke grenade to bring down the larger chopper. The CH-46 pilot dropped down until the belly of the aircraft was hovering five feet off the ground, and his crew threw off the bundles of clothes and boxes and crates of resupply for the Marines. Before the last package hit the ground, the huge chopper lifted directly up in the air and flew away.

RT Rogers secured the area while the Marines hurried to break down the bundles and change into new uniforms right there on the LZ. The resupply chopper had dropped off so much ammunition and supplies that it would be impossible for the thirteen men to haul away a quarter of the pile.

"What are you going to do with all of this?" Luke shook his head.

"Take what we can carry and destroy the rest." Morgan kept sorting through the boxes as he talked.

"Why did you order all of this?"

Morgan stopped shoving items in his rucksack and gave Luke a look like he was talking to a little boy. "I didn't order all of this. I guess they figure I've got a forty-man platoon out here."

"Even if you had forty men, you still couldn't haul all of this away on your backs!"

Morgan forced a smile. "This way they can show the battalion commander back at Vandergrift that they've resupplied my platoon with enough C-rations and ammo to last us a month . . . and no one is going to even think that we can't carry five hundred pounds of bullets and rations apiece."

"This is bullshit! I'm the senior officer out here and I'm giving you a direct order, Lieutenant! Your platoon is coming out with my recon team!"

Morgan's smile widened. "We would be very happy to obey that order." He handed Luke the handset from Luke's radio. "I don't know our new call signs. My SOI and SSI are outdated."

Luke snatched the black, telephone-looking handset out of the lieutenant's hand and pushed the transmission switch using the palm of his hand as he squeezed it. "Buckshot 3 . . . this is Running Deer 6 . . . over."

"Deer 6 . . . Buckshot 3, over."

"Deer 6 . . . request immediate extraction for my unit plus thirteen . . . over."

There was a pause over the airways and the operations officer came back in the air. "Deer 6, Buckshot 3 . . . have you taken prisoners? . . . Over."

Luke looked at the pathetic faces of the Marine platoon and answered. "Deer 6 . . . of sorts, Buckshot 3 . . . of sorts . . . out."

The task-force operations officer looked at the radio and rubbed his chin. He was trying to figure out what Captain Arrowood was meaning, but he wasn't about to deny the captain's request for an extraction and hurried to assemble a large extraction flight.

The task-force commander and half of the staff were waiting at the helipad inside of the base camp for the choppers to land. The flight from RT Rogers' AO to the base area had taken only a few minutes by air, but would have taken a half-day of hard walking.

The Marine liaison officer watched the Marine platoon unload off the choppers. He was embarrassed because he hadn't known the Marines were out there until a message had come into the task force from Vandergrift.

Luke waited until the chopper had lifted off before attempting to speak. "Sir, I've ordered these Marines to come back here with me. I don't feel that they're capable of continuing their mission in the field until they've had proper medical treatment and rest."

The armor commander only nodded his head. He had never seen a more ragged bunch of Americans in his life, and that was looking at them after they had gotten new uniforms.

The Marine liaison officer spoke to Lieutenant Morgan. "Did you have a problem shaving in the field, Lieutenant?"

Morgan came to attention and answered the senior Marine. "Yes, sir! We didn't have anything to shave with, sir!"

"Let's get your men cleaned up and then we can talk." The senior Marine beckoned for the platoon to follow him. He wanted to get the Marines away from the Army types so that they wouldn't show their dirty linen to a sister service.

"What in the hell is that!" The armor commander shook his head as he watched the Marines walk away.

"Sir, I don't think you would believe me if I told you." Luke patted his weapon. "We'll be ready to go back out as soon as we can get some more rations."

The armor officer sensed that something was very

wrong and reached up and laid his hand on Luke's shoulder.

Luke looked at the lieutenant colonel and tried smiling. "I've been in-country too long, sir . . . *way* too long."

CHAPTER SIXTEEN

✪✪✪✪✪✪✪✪✪✪✪✪✪✪✪✪✪✪✪✪

A SMOKING GUN

Project Deathwatch men engaged the NVA three times with artillery ambushes during the forty-seven days they spent on the Khe Sanh plateau with Task Force Remagen. The NVA had attacked twice from their sanctuaries in Laos and had been defeated by the mechanized infantry. Captain Arrowood had noticed that the armor and mechanized infantry companies had never found the NVA during the whole operation; it was always the NVA attacking the maneuver units that told Luke that they were doing something wrong.

The whole task force had pulled back away from the Ye Pon River and tried twice to draw the NVA out onto the plateau, but the NVA commander ignored them. He would only attack from his hiding place in Laos when one of the maneuver units came close enough for his men to cross over the river and attack during the night, and he stopped doing that when it had become evident that the artillery fire wasn't random harassment and interdiction fires.

Luke was very proud of his artillerymen, and knew that the rest of the large units in Vietnam would pick up the idea and then it would make a major difference in the way the NVA and Vietcong maneuvered and traveled.

All of the recon teams had been pulled in and were riding on the headquarters element tracks for the trip back to Ca Lu where the task force was going to spend a couple of days cleaning up their equipment and pulling maintenance on their vehicles before going back to Camp Red Devil. Luke had already made arrangements to fly his teams back to his company area as soon as they arrived at Ca Lu and the large Vandergrift Marine base camp.

The Marine platoon had been attached to one of the companies from the 1st Battalion, 61st Infantry, by the task force commander for the remainder of the operation and were returning to Vandergrift against the Marine company commander's orders, but the armor lieutenant colonel had refused to leave such a small group on the plateau. Luke figured that there would be a good show when the task force reached the Marine base.

Going back down Highway 9 was a lot easier than the first trip had been. The track drivers were much more confident and everyone was anxious to get off the Khe Sanh plateau and back to where there were more American units. Luke kept looking back the way they had come on the road. He felt like he was leaving something behind.

Pilgrim reached over and grabbed Luke's arm. He had been sitting next to him on the top of the tracked M113. "Look! Over there!" Pilgrim pointed down the side of the steep slope at the pair of tigers running through a shallow portion of the river that paralleled Highway 9 through the valley.

The larger male tiger stopped at the edge of a large bamboo patch and growled back at the convoy of noisy vehicles. Most of the infantrymen riding on the tracks had seen the tigers and were standing up on the slow-moving vehicles to get a better look.

"It's not often you can catch a tiger like that." Luke remained sitting with his back resting against his rucksack.

"If you were as big as that sucker is, I think you wouldn't be in a hurry to run, either!" Pilgrim sat down again when the tiger followed his mate into the bamboo. "Do you think we'll be back by noon?"

"Depends if we have any breakdowns or not." Luke

looked at his watch and for some reason, the time caused him to think about the date. "Damn!"

"What's wrong, sir?"

"I've got less than a month left . . ."

Pilgrim frowned. He didn't think Captain Arrowood would ever be a short-timer.

Luke's whole attitude became gloomy. There was nothing for him back in the States but a lot of very bad memories. The war had kept his mind off the reality of what was waiting for him when he returned. He knew that he would have to go to the artillery career course at Fort Sill, Oklahoma, for nine months. His career branch back in Washington, D.C., had told him that was coming, and there was no way that he could avoid it.

"You don't look very happy about going back to the States, sir." Pilgrim unscrewed the cap on his canteen and took a sip of the warm water.

"I'm not." Luke looked up the side of the cliff and saw a Marine sitting on an outcrop of rock with a well-worn M60 machine gun across his legs.

Pilgrim looked at his captain over the top of his canteen and decided that he had not better push the issue. Arrowood had been in Vietnam for a long time and the captain must have had his reasons for staying. All he knew was that the officer had saved his ass a couple of times and if it hadn't of been for the tremendous amount of combat experience the man had, Pilgrim knew that he would have been killed or seriously wounded by now.

The track made a sharp turn around a finger of rock and Luke could see the circled tanks at Ca Lu. It had been a long time in the boonies and he was looking forward to a couple days of rest under a tin roof. Lieutenant Doak had the rest of the recon teams already assembled by the helipad when Luke arrived at the temporary base camp. He could see that his men were in high spirits and anxious to get back to the Quang Tri area where they could get a little drunk and maybe have their ashes hauled a couple of times in the local steambaths.

Luke sat his gear down and looked across the clearing to where the Marine platoon was unloading their equipment from the M113s. A jeep moved slowly across the matted-down elephant grass the tracks had leveled and stopped when it had reached the Marines. Luke couldn't hear what was being said, but he could see that the person who had been riding in the passenger seat was waving his arms and pointing back down the highway toward Khe Sanh. Lieutenant Morgan was shaking his head and then he pointed over at the task force commander's track. Luke watched the pair walk toward the vehicle and shook his head. The Marine company commander was not happy over his lieutenant's return, and Luke figured the captain had better sleep with one eye open for the next couple of nights.

Luke had expected Hueys for the flight back to Camp Red Devil and was mildly surprised when a CH47 landed. The large double-rotored helicopter could carry over thirty men and their gear. The tailgate lowered and the crew chief ran out of the aircraft beckoning for the recon teams to load up. The heat from the rear jet engines made loading a little difficult, but once they were up the ramp it was comfortable inside the cargo compartment. Luke looked out of the window and saw the task force commander talking to the Marine captain. He wondered if he should have stayed behind and then shrugged his shoulders. The armor lieutenant colonel could handle the problem, but Luke was positive that, after what had happened, either the lieutenant or the captain wasn't going to make it alive back to the States.

The smell of burning shit was the first welcome-back sign for the recon teams when they reached Camp Red Devil. It seemed like the place had changed since they had gone to the field. Luke could see that the Artillery Bowl had been painted red and yellow.

Dotson inhaled a deep lungful of air and bellowed

out. "Burning shit! How I love that smell! It's going to feel good to sit down to shit instead of having to squat over a fucking cathole."

"The luxuries of civilization." Pilgrim elbowed his buddy. "Maybe the captain will let us make a *laundry* run into town?" He glanced at Luke out of the corner of his eye and smiled.

"Check with the first sergeant . . ."

"It's an emergency, sir. My glands are about ready to burst! I mean, it's been over a month!"

"Don't plead with me, Pilgrim . . . go see the first sergeant and see if he has any off-base details."

"Yeah, I think I need to get a haircut, myself." Lieutenant Doak rubbed his hand over the back of his neck and looked over at Fields and Wong.

"Me, too!" Wong chuckled.

"Git!" Luke waved the lieutenants off and increased his pace. He knew that there would be a ton of paperwork waiting for him in the orderly room, and avoided the entrance. He wanted to take a hot shower and change clothes before having to face that task and write letters home to the families of the recon men that had been killed at Khe Sanh.

Luke took his time in the shower and scrubbed the accumulated baked-on clay off his body. Washing in cold stream water hadn't really cleaned his skin, and the suntan that he thought he had gotten on the plateau came off with the hot water.

"Captain Arrowood? Are you in there?"

"Yeah, First Sergeant. I'll be out shortly!" Luke called through the stream to the recon company's first sergeant, who was standing in the drying area.

"No rush, sir. The brigade commander wants to talk to you as soon as you're finished cleaning up. He said if you can make it, he'd like for you to join him for supper."

"Shit!" Luke stepped out of the shower room and reached for his towel. "I really wanted to get a little drunk tonight."

"Duty calls, sir."

Luke shook his head. "Always!"

"He sounded really happy when he called for you on the land-line. I think he has some good news for you."

"That would be nice for a change." Luke wrapped the towel around his waist and walked over to his hootch and changed into one of his best uniforms before going over to the brigade headquarters' mess hall.

The long hootch was packed with staff personnel but the serving line was almost empty. They had been serving for over an hour and almost everyone had eaten. Luke picked up a paper plate and plastic silverware and started to go through the serving line when the mess sergeant stopped him. "The colonel wants you to join him at his table, sir. I'll have someone bring you a tray."

Luke looked over to the corner table where the brigade commander and a number of his senior staff were still sitting, drinking coffee. "Thanks, Sergeant."

The colonel looked up and smiled when he saw Luke approaching. "So! How's our recon company commander?"

"Tired, sir." Luke smiled at the staff officers and took the seat the colonel offered to him.

"You should be after spending a month and a half in the field." The colonel leaned back in his chair. "Remagen and Montana Mauler were both very successful!" He placed his hands on the edge of the table when he spoke. "*Very* successful, and I think we're on our way to solving some of our more serious problems." He gave Luke a knowing glance.

"That's good, sir." Luke leaned back and let the KP slide the tray down on the table in front of him.

"I have something for you." The colonel reached into his jacket pocket and removed a yellow Red Cross telegram.

Luke felt a chill on the back of his neck. Rarely did good news come through the Red Cross, unless your wife was pregnant and had a baby. He took the

offered message and held his breath when he opened
the envelope. Everyone at the table was watching him.
Luke's eyes slipped down over the address heading
and locked on the single sentence:

WILL YOU FORGIVE ME
          JODI

He read it again quickly and then read it again
before looking up.

"It's good news, I hope?" The brigade commander
knew what was in the message. The Red Cross director had brought it to him a week earlier and wanted
to know if he should have it forwarded out to Khe
Sanh. The colonel decided that he would personally
deliver the message on his trip out there and then
he had been called over to the 3rd Marine Division
Headquarters and his trip to Khe Sanh had been
canceled.

Luke didn't trust himself to answer and only nodded
his head. He shoved the paper into his pants pocket
and concentrated on cutting the steak on the tray in
front of him. A billion emotions and thoughts flashed
through his mind. He wanted to run out of the mess
hall and find an aircraft that would fly him back to
California. He wanted to hold his wife and kids.

"I'm going back to my office, Captain Arrowood . . ."

Luke looked up and saw the Red Cross director
standing across the table from him.

"Would you like me to send a return message?"

"If you could . . ." Luke's voice fluctuated.

"It wouldn't be a problem at all." The old gray-
haired man smiled.

"I think you have the address?" Luke kept cutting
the steak into smaller pieces as he talked.

"Yes, we do in our files."

"Just send back this . . ." Luke wrote something on
a piece of napkin and handed it to the man.

The Red Cross director waited until he was outside

of the mess hall before he opened the folded napkin and read:

YES . . . LUKE.

The bourbon burned his throat, but the way he was feeling he could have swallowed hot coals and it wouldn't have bothered him. He felt so good that he had to do something or he would burst. Luke sat the bottle down and strapped on his pistol belt. There was still a good hour of daylight left and he figured that he could walk off the excitement he was feeling by checking the recon company's section of the perimeter. Starting in the morning, the recon company would be off the perimeter again and start pulling their normal missions in the field.

Luke stepped out of the door and removed the Red Cross message from his pocket and read the words again to make sure that he hadn't read them wrong the first hundred times. He inhaled a lungful of burning shit-smelling air and smiled. In less than a month he would be back with his family again, and this time he wouldn't let anything separate them.

Forbes and his recon team were sitting behind their hootch getting very drunk along with a dozen of the men from one of the line companies. Luke squinted his eyes in the fading light and thought that he recognized one of the men.

Sergeant Forbes tapped the soldier on his shoulder and pointed over at Luke. The man turned around and stood up. Luke could see that the soldier wore a large 1st-Cavalry patch on his left shoulder and at the same time recognized him.

"Bergman!" Luke went over to where the party was going on. Forbes was too drunk to stand up.

"These Cav guys said that you gave them permission to use our facilities, sir!" Forbes slurred his words.

"I sure did!" Luke shook hands with the specialist. "It's good seeing you again, soldier!"

"We were in the area and I told you that I'd stop by if I could. My squad's been given the night off. My company is over on the other side of Red Devil." Uwe nodded his head in the direction.

"I see that you've found Sergeant Forbes's private stock."

"As soon as he said that he was a friend of yours, sir . . ." Forbes closed his eyes. The talking was making him feel like throwing up. "I could only offer him my best booze!"

Pilgrim had spent the whole field problem at Khe Sanh with Forbes's team and was sitting on the ground with his back against the sandbags of the hootch. Luke looked over at him. "Can you walk?"

"Of course I can walk, Captain!" Pilgrim's feelings were hurt. "You're forgetting that I'm from Georgia, sir!"

"Just asking . . . I don't want you falling down in front of these Cav guys when you show them where they can stay for the night."

"There's room in my hootch, sir." Pilgrim patted the side of the sandbagged hootch he was leaning against.

"Fine." Luke looked out at the perimeter. "It's getting dark and I want to check on the guards before I call it a night and have a few drinks myself."

"I hear you just came back from Khe Sanh, sir." One of the Cav soldiers asked the question from where he was sitting in the shadows.

Bergman nodded at the man. "He was with the Cav last year when they broke the Marines out of there."

"You've extended?" Luke tried looked at the man's face but the shadow from the building hid him.

"Yes, sir. There ain't nothing waiting for me back home." The soldier's voice deepened. "I hear that you've been over here for five years."

"It'll be six years in a couple of weeks, but I'm going home. I've had enough."

"I'm going to stay over here until this fucking war is over."

The soldier sounded like Luke had only a couple of days earlier.

"Pilgrim, show these men where the showers and the club are located so they can clean up and get something to eat." Luke started walking away. "We serve a fairly decent hamburger at the club."

"Later, sir!" Bergman nudged the man sitting next to him. "Let's clean up and then we can do some *serious* drinking!"

Pilgrim walked next to the soldier who had told Arrowood that he had been at Khe Sanh during the big battle that had taken place there. "So you bailed the Marines out of that mess?"

The soldier nodded his head. "It was some bad shit."

"Yeah, I don't think that I would have wanted to stay out there much longer."

Uwe kept his eyes on his squad member. The soldier had a habit of losing it. He had been a specialist fourth class, but had been busted twice and was now a buck private again. Something had happened at Khe Sanh that had fucked with the man's mind.

"We found Marines who were abandoned up on the hills surrounding the main base camp at Khe Sanh." The soldier started walking a little faster.

"What do you mean, abandoned?" Pilgrim glanced over at the Cav soldier out of the corner of his eye and then he looked at Bergman for an answer.

"Fucking abandoned, man! I mean, when the NVA closed the circle around Khe Sanh, the Marines trapped in the base camp couldn't get out and the Marines who were occupying the outposts couldn't get back in. They were chalked off by the headquarters as dead or missing in action. We found those poor suckers half-starved and scared to fucking death." The Cav soldier stopped walking under the shower room lights and Pilgrim saw his eyes for the first time. He looked like a trapped wild animal.

Luke paused at each one of the bunkers and chatted with the recon men who had remained behind to help secure the base camp. He climbed up on the last bunker the recon company occupied that bordered the 5th Battalion, 4th Artillery's portion of Camp Red Devil.

"Careful, sir. Don't make a silhouette."

Luke bent over and scooted sideways to the sound of the familiar voice. "What in the hell are you doing up here, Dotson?"

"Bullshitting with my buddy." Dotson held up the bottle of Seagram's Seven. "Don't worry, sir, he's on guard duty and I'm doing *all* of the drinking."

Luke saw a silhouette sitting on the sandbag ledge on the roof of the bunker. "Soldier . . . that isn't a smart idea sitting like that."

Dotson started laughing. "He can't answer you, sir. He's a dummy. We've been taking sniper fire from that tree line over there." Dotson pointed with the bottle in his hand. "So my buddy here made up Victor Charlie to see if he can draw the sniper's fire, and then we're going to blow his ass away with the 4.2 mortars that I've got laid on that area."

"You're going to call in a fire mission, drunk?"

"Everything has already been coordinated. That's all my buddy has to do is call the mortar platoon and tell them to fire."

"I'm impressed. Your dummy there has fooled me."

"Victor Charlie, sir. He *does* have a name!" Dotson took another sip from the bottle in his hand.

"Don't get so fucked up that you can't find your way back home and end up in the barbed wire, Dotson." Luke chuckled under his breath.

"I'll point him in the right direction, sir." The guard on duty answered for Dotson but kept his eyes on the tree line.

Luke was turning to leave when the sharp crack of a Russian sniper rifle echoed over the cleared ground between the tree line and the bunker. Victor Charlie fell over on his side.

"Mother fuck me! I thought you were bullshitting when you said a sniper was out there!" Dotson spilled his bottle of whiskey as he scrambled on all-fours down behind the bunker.

The guard pushed the talk switch on his land-line and in a calm voice called for the mortar fire mission.

Luke watched the tree line for any muzzle flashes so that they could pinpoint the sniper's location.

The first volley of 4.2 rounds impacted exactly where Dotson had plotted them and the guard requested a battery of five rounds. The tree line erupted with bright flashes as the volleys of heavy mortar rounds started landing.

Luke reached over and took the binoculars off the guard's rucksack and focused them before putting them up to his eyes. There was just enough light left to see by, but it was fading fast.

"Sir . . . you'd better stay down . . ." Dotson sat with his back against the bunker.

The rifle cracked just as Dotson started reaching for Captain Arrowood's sleeve.

Luke dropped the binoculars and reached for the edge of the bunker. He tasted the blood in his mouth and knew that he had been hit in the chest before he felt the pain.

"Fuck! The captain's hit!" Dotson panicked. "MEDIC! MEDIC!"

Sergeant Forbes tried standing but couldn't get up on his feet and fell backwards. He struggled to clear his head. He was sure that he was hearing someone calling for a medic.

Specialist Bergman stepped out of the shower room wearing only his boots and a pair of olive-drab shorts. He stopped and looked over at his buddy. "Is someone calling for a medic?"

Dotson's voice became louder. "MEDIC! DAMNIT, WE NEED A MEDIC!"

Bergam dropped his shaving kit and started running as hard as he could toward the voice and the perimeter bunker. The soldier who had been with him turned and ran over to the recon club to find help. The music was playing so loud in the club that it would have been impossible for anyone to hear the call for help.

Lieutenant Doak looked up from the table and saw the soldier from the 1st Cav standing in the entrance wearing only his camouflage underwear with his hair still wet from the shower. He could see from the look on the soldier's face that something was wrong, and left Fields and Wong at the table to go and find out what the soldier wanted.

"Sir, someone is calling for a medic out on the perimeter!"

Doak didn't look back inside of the club and left the doorway at a full run. Once outside, he could hear the man calling for the medic and adjusted his course back to the bunker. He found Dotson holding Captain Arrowood in the dark that had now covered the whole base area.

"What happened?" Doak dropped down on one knee.

"A sniper!" Dotson nodded out at the tree line with his head.

"We've got to stop the bleeding." Doak had Dotson hold the flashlight as he tore open the captain's fatigue jacket. The hole in Luke's chest was ghastly, and bright pink bubbles bordered the wound. The hole was too big to patch with anything they had with them. Doak looked over at the guard. "Do you have your poncho with you?"

The guard fumbled through his rucksack and pulled out the rubberized rain gear and handed it to the lieutenant.

Luke moaned when Doak rolled him over on his side and wrapped the poncho around his chest. Doak could see the small hole where the bullet had entered the captain's back.

A three-quarter-ton ambulance bounced over the ground back to the bunker from the main camp road. Four medics and one of the brigade doctors who had been on-call jumped out of the vehicle.

Luke fought to focus his eyes in the dim light in the

back of the ambulance. He saw the worried faces of Doak and Dotson when they started closing the doors, and tried speaking—but only bloody bubbles came out between his lips.

Doak watched the ambulance pull slowly away from the bunker and then turned around to see what had happened. Dotson was near tears and couldn't think straight. The guard on duty briefed the lieutenant on what had happened. He told him about the dummy being hit and the mortar fire mission, and showed him where Luke had been standing with the binoculars.

Doak frowned to himself in the dark and shook his head. "Are you *sure* the captain was standing against the bunker with his chest right there?" Doak stood in the exact spot Luke had been standing when he had been hit.

"Yes, sir! I'm positive because I looked back to ask him if he could see anything with the binos and he fell backwards and I heard the sniper's shot."

Doak's voice thickened. "I want you to think hard now, because this is very important. I know that a lot has gone on out here in the past couple of minutes, but I need for you to think straight!"

"Yes, sir." The guard was a sharp young recon man and had just finished his in-country training.

Doak heard someone coming and looked over to see the shadows approaching the bunker. Fields, Wong and Major Redmond, the brigade provost marshal appeared behind the bunker.

"Doak?" Fields's voice was about ready to break.

"Yeah?"

"The captain's dead."

Doak controlled the anger that was busting to break loose inside of him and looked back at the guard. "Soldier . . . this is important. You said that you heard the shot, right?"

"Yes, sir."

"Think now before you answer me. What *direction* did the shot come from?" Doak waited for the soldier to answer.

The guard turned so that he was standing exactly as he had when Captain Arrowood was hit. "Oh shit, sir . . ."

"What direction!"

The guard pointed over toward the artillery hootches inside of the perimeter. All of the officers could see the soldier's arm in the dim light.

Lieutenant Doak had already assumed the guard would point in that direction because of the entry and exit wounds on Luke's body. If he had been standing where the guard said he was, then Captain Arrowood had to have been shot by someone from *inside* the perimeter.

Major Redmond felt the fear well up within him. It had started, and he didn't know where it would end. "I think I can locate a couple of suspects. They've just returned from Long Binh Jail yesterday."

-THE END-

There's an epidemic with 27 million victims. And no visible symptoms.

It's an epidemic of people who can't read.

Believe it or not, 27 million Americans are functionally illiterate, about one adult in five.

The solution to this problem is you... when you join the fight against illiteracy. So call the Coalition for Literacy at toll-free **1-800-228-8813** and volunteer.

Volunteer Against Illiteracy. The only degree you need is a degree of caring.